Blue Vision

Jimelle Suzanne

Rainbow Blessings Press

ISBN: 978-0-9888274-1-7

Copyright 2013 Jimelle Suzanne

DEDICATION

This book is dedicated to Phyllis Whitney. My stunning visit to her home and subsequent meeting with her was nothing short of serendipity and worthy of a short story in and of itself! Perhaps at another time, I will share that with you.

ACKNOWLEDGEMENTS

The person responsible for finally getting BLUE VISION put together as an eBook is my treasured friend Cheri Grimm (www.VirtualAsset.biz) . She has traveled with me through many lives and I am so grateful for her editing and computer expertise. Her daughter Christy (www.ProactivePerformanceInstitute.com) created my beautiful website with sensitivity and creativity. Bless you!

This is a work of fiction but there are elements that are real, the BLUE VISION being one and the Hilton Head Group is another. I wish you blessings and my heartfelt thanks to all of those beautiful souls who have supported me with their wisdom and friendship.

Author and friend Sam Horn (www.IntrigueAgency.com) has graciously offered her expertise on countless occasions and I am forever grateful! Theresa Waltermeyer has generously given her guidance and friendship during the entire process along with Betsy Matthews, Bonnie and Colette Kuki, Cheryl Ludwig, Anna Baker, Blanca Sarmiento, Lynn Spencer and Bill Black. Wade Broadwell, who is an amazing teacher, helped me to understand my first experiences with the BLUE VISION.

Thanks also to Marti Rivers, who always gives me her straight-forward feedback, more jokes than I can remember and boundless friendship. A standing ovation goes to all of the ballet students who listened eagerly as I read portions of my writings aloud. I'll never forget the day that my beloved musician, Michael Brett read the manuscript for the first time. I was stunned to see tears streaming from his eyes. I know he watches and helps me still from *the other side.* I have many loved ones who have left their earthly home and have chosen to stay close and whisper their encouragement into my consciousness, thank you and may you be forever blessed.

To all of the people who have contributed to the journey of this book you will always be in my heart surrounded by rainbows and gratitude.

AUTHOR FORWARD

It is my hope that BLUE VISION will whisk you away to another time and place where visions materialize amidst mundane daily activities and that you enjoy reading about Courtney's journey as much as I have enjoyed writing about it! Perhaps you will find something in the story that lifts you up and makes your heart smile and if that is accomplished then I feel satisfied.

Though the characters in BLUE VISION are fictional, the mental health care system in flux is all too real. Raleigh, North Carolina's daily paper the *News and Observer* quoted Governor Pat McCrory in the January 12, 2013 issue "We have a broken mental health system in our nation and our state."

I have the belief and hope that "we the people" can work within our communities to create a consciousness of compassion and an environment of balanced care for all those precious people who require treatment and daily care in a mental health facility or group home. Blessings and thanks to all of those dedicated people who work selflessly in underpaid positions to help those who are unable help themselves.

Rainbow Blessings.

AUTHOR'S NOTE ABOUT THE PROLOGUE

I have pursued my quest for knowledge and spiritual information for the majority of my adult life. In 1987 I studied under the direction of Marian Starnes. She recommended that I read an amazing book entitled CHALLENGE FOR DISCIPLESHIP by Torkom Saraydarian. I found an ancient parable about the age-old search for the secrets of life. When I told my son James Beaird about it he began to see and describe a beautiful vision, which I then adapted for the prologue of BLUE VISION.

PROLOGUE

THE DAWN OF humanity rises like a fiery orb that dispels the night. Lasers of light silently pierce the veil of darkness draped over the ancient mountain crags. Before there was time, there was only consciousness. Something stirred in the Great Void and a decision was made. New beings were to be created in physical forms. It was decided they were to be given the name Hu-mans, God-man. The newly created planet called Earth will be their home. Man is to be given dominion over the new planet and all of the other life forms that might develop there. The ultimate test for these new beings would be their power of free will. It would be the destiny of each person to bear the responsibility of the choices that they make within the boundaries of earthly life. The subsequent rewards and/or the need for further spiritual development would then be decided by the wisest aspect of the individual who created an event or situation and, when help was needed, otherwise souls from a place beyond Earth agreed to be of assistance in determining the best solution.

In a gesture of loving cooperation, the Sacred Source of the Universal Mind issued an invitation to the wise beings that live in a dimension beyond earthly comprehension. Three holy advisors were asked to travel to the Mountain of Wisdom. The new planet was ready for its evolutionary process and it was time for the most important decision to be made. The Creator wanted input from the living Beings who had been working with their own gifts of self-realization. It would be most pleasing for all of them to make the final decision together.

In three distant cities, preparations were begun for the long trek. Each holy man gathered his supporters together and relayed the message he had received from the Sacred Source. Excitement rippled through the listeners and they rejoiced at the prospect of being part of the magnificent unfolding of what would help to define the Hu-man race, which had been chosen to live on the beautiful new blue planet.

All those making the long journey would need special clothing. Young males were chosen to enter the fields and harvest the necessary plants that would be prepared and woven into a soft sturdy cloth. Young girls stood at the edge of the fields, chanting and dancing, holding the energy of joy and gratitude at the highest level possible. These beings knew how important it was to maintain an uplifted energy when attempting to accomplish any challenging task - especially one that required the holy seers to receive a message from the Sacred Source. They knew that any negativity surrounding their food preparation, clothing and even the sandals they wore on their feet would interfere with the purity of communication with the Sacred Source.

The weavers worked their looms while others chanted sacred texts. Expert tailors sewed the blessed fabrics while listening to music performed by accomplished musicians. Vessels of water were purified with crystals. Food for the journey was blessed by those who performed the ancient ceremonies of preservation and nourishment.

Each chosen seer remained in quiet meditation until all of the preparations were completed. They were not required to participate in the activities because their work was performed on the inner levels of their consciousness. At last all was in readiness. Without verbal communication from city to city and person to person, they knew as one that it was time for the journey to begin.

The holy seers cleansed their bodies and anointed their skin with sacred oils. They dressed in the robes that had been lovingly created. Each of them carried pouches of food and water.

There would be many supporters making the trek with each of the seers and everyone was equipped with the same beautifully created robes and food supply.

At precisely the same moment in each distant city, the holy men and their protectors began their journey. It was the task of each seer to lead their group to the Mountain of Wisdom while maintaining a deep meditative state of mind, as their eyes remained shut. It would be their task to use the vision of their inner knowing in order to find the hidden path to the mountain top.

Powerful women traveled just behind the seers. It was their responsibility to birth the energy through their singing and chanting of the holy music throughout the journey. Perfectly conditioned men followed on the outer perimeter. They focused on protection and the endurance that would be needed for a successful outcome.

It was decided that those who remained in the cities would add their strength and encouragement by gathering in groups to meditate and send energy for the safety of those making the long journey.

The travelers walked steadily over difficult terrain until their sandals fell from their feet in tatters. They were not discouraged by this development and simply rejoiced that now their feet could feel the vibration of the ground beneath them, and this enhanced their ability to find the hidden paths.

The Mountain of Wisdom appeared in the distance - its summit hidden by billowing white clouds. They rejoiced that they were nearing their destination. All of the traveling groups approached from a different direction, but their distances were identical. They found clear pools of water and refilled their water pouches. Shady trees provided cool places to rest. They discovered vegetation that produced wild berries, fruits and nuts in abundance. They lacked nothing during their entire journey and at every opportunity all rejoiced and sang with gratitude for each precious gift they found.

The holy seers did not require the use of their eyes in order to hold the perfect vision that showed them the way and at every turn they found a safe and smooth path. No matter how steep the climb no one felt endangered.

Each group moved as one and found their way to the clearing at the summit. They waited in silence for direction from the Sacred Source. As one, the three seers moved to the center of the clearing and seated themselves around an enormous faceted blue stone.

The women aligned themselves with the other groups and created an inner circle. It would be their task to hold the energy in the vortex that would be created as the Source and the seers brought forth the wisdom. The men took the outer positions to maintain a protective presence.

A great stillness settled over the group as each worked to maintain clarity. Everyone closed their eyes and joined the seers in meditation. Had an observer been present to see the circles, they would marvel at the glow emanating from them as they focused more deeply upon the Sacred Source.

As though a switch were thrown, light radiated from the center of the stone and moved throughout until a blue spotlight shot out from each facet. The women began a soprano OM, while the men chanted in alto tones.

Great masses of white-gold energy streaked across the sky and gathered high above the stone, increasing in brilliance as the OMs intensified. A column of the pure light poured down into the blue stone and spilled across the seers, holy women and protectors.

The Sacred Source began to speak:

"I AM PLEASED THAT YOU HAVE HEARD MY CALL AND THAT YOU SUCCESSFULLY COMPLETED THIS

JOURNEY." The light from the Source glowed brighter with every spoken word.

"MAY ALL OF YOU BE FOREVER BLESSED BY THE WORK YOU DO HERE." The light continually threw starbursts filled with rainbows over the group as the words of the Source echoed melodically across the mountain peaks and valleys.

"WE GIVE THE NAME HU-MANS TO THE NEW BEINGS AND THEY WILL HAVE DOMINION OVER THE EARTH PLANET AND OTHER LIFE FORMS. THEY WILL HAVE THE FREEDOM TO CHOOSE THE COURSE OF THEIR LIVES. THEY WILL BE ALLOWED TO SEEK WISDOM OR CHOOSE TO TURN AWAY. THIS WILL BE THE MOST RIGOROUS TRAINING GROUND IN OUR UNIVERSE!" Electricity crackled around the mountain top, lifting their hair until it floated around their heads like a halo.

"HU-MANS WILL BE ENCASED IN THE DENSITY OF FLESH THAT WILL HAVE LIMITED DURATION AND WILL WALK BLINDLY WITH THEIR EYES OPEN UNTIL THEY PROGRESS ENOUGH TO SEEK OUT AND FIND THE WINDOW FOR THE SECRET WISDOM OF LIFE.

I POSE A QUESTION TO YOU, AND I WILL CONSIDER YOUR ANSWERS. TOGETHER WE WILL CREATE A SOLUTION. WHERE IS THIS WINDOW TO THE SECRET WISDOM OF LIFE TO BE HIDDEN?" The light had now become so bright that the seated figures were only vague shapes within the circles.

The first seer formed his suggestion based on the journey that all of them had just endured. He gathered all of the available energy from the city he had left behind as well as the energy created in their holy circle. He knew that the powerful red energy from the first spinning wheel of light within his body had helped him climb the mountain and he pushed his mind toward the Source for his idea to be considered.

"The secret could be placed upon the highest mountain peak," he spoke through thought transference as was the habit of highly evolved beings.

The Source received the thoughts of the wise man and reached out to him with deep love and gratitude.

"THAT IS INDEED A WISE ANSWER AND I THANK YOU FOR YOUR INSPIRATION. THE HU-MANS, HOWEVER, WILL REVEL IN THEIR PHYSICAL STRENGTH AND TOO SOON WILL CLIMB TO THE MOUNTAIN'S APEX."

Another seer gathered his energy from the orange creative center as he thought about the clear beautiful pools of water that they drank from on their journey.

"The secret wisdom should be placed in the deepest part of the sea!"

The Source was pleased with the amazing ingenuity of this being and a great light went out to encircle him. The seer sighed with joy as he felt the infinite love of the Source.

"HU-MANS WILL BE INTELLIGENT. THEY WILL USE THEIR BRAINS TO CREATE ARTIFICIAL WAYS TO BREATHE UNDER THE WATER. THE GREAT SECRET WOULD BE FOUND LONG BEFORE THEY ARE READY TO UNDERSTAND IT."

The third seer had already begun to gather the yellow-gold light from his solar plexus, and the emerald green from his heart. He did not stop there and continued to gather energy from his throat chakra as well as from the crown of his head.

"The secret wisdom of life should be hidden INSIDE of the Hu-mans. They will be so entertained by their physical form and what it can do, that it will keep them busy for eons as time is established. It will be many millennia before any of them will think to look there."

"IT IS SO!"

The Source caused a brilliant rainbow to curl around the third seer and then expanded the light over the circles of glowing beings. It moved slowly at first, then intensified dramatically in speed and color. The women held the vortex in place as the men worked to increase the power.

The enormous blue stone vibrated and rose into the air above their heads. It began to rotate slowly and pictures formed on each of the facets. There appeared Hu-mans in their early development and village leaders and huge beasts. Villages became towns that grew into cities. Leaders arose, some ruled justly, while others dominated with cruelty and violence. Some Hu-mans evolved and communicated great truths to those around them. The violent ones, drunk with the need for power, destroyed anyone who opposed them.

The circle gazed in awe as the facets displayed other life forms being created from all plant and animal life to winged beings of a lighter density that were referred to as elementals entrusted with the guardianship of nature.

They gasped with dismay when they saw the ages of darkness that may be brought to the earth by a strange mind-set of something called *greed*. During these times, there were only a few who demonstrated a propensity for seeking greater wisdoms beyond their own base needs. Sadly, the levels of violence increased, causing the gradual decline of the lush natural purity of the earth, and the elemental helpers were forced to move under the veil of invisibility for their safety. It was only then that they could work safely with those beings attempting to live in a higher vibration. Some beings glowed with light while others became gray and dark as their activities produced pain and suffering in their fellow man and environment.

When every facet of the stone was filled with a vision, the vibrations grew more intense until the entire mountain shook. The chanting grew louder causing the sitters to levitate several feet above the ground.

The Source directed a powerful surge of light into the stone and it exploded. Billions upon billions of glittering fragments filled the air and became spinning blue orbs. The sound frequency changed to the decibels beyond hearing and silence followed. The mighty will of the Source scattered the orbs through what would become time, space and dimension until they landed between the physical eyes of every Hu-man that would ever inhabit the earth planet. The other colors followed from red to purple forming a rainbow on each form. The colors slowly sank into the density of the Hu-mans and became invisible to all except the Source and those who chose to see with their higher mind.

When the first Hu-mans began their spiritual evolution there were some who immediately found each energy center and its identifying color. Those who discovered the blue light between their eyes were reminded of the Blue Pearls formed by the crustaceans that fishermen found in the sea. They were astounded to discover that as they focused on the blue light they experienced visions. Imagine their delight when they realized that what they saw became future events, or something from the past or even events in their current life. Still others used their Blue Vision to communicate with the highly evolved beings that appeared there from time to time.

People who experienced these amazing visions tried to tell others about what they had discovered, but it was too soon. Many Hu-mans were not ready to accept the new information and became fearful and angered by what they could not yet understand.

When enlightened Hu-mans were violently attacked by

the fearful ones, it was determined that the Blue Pearl or as it was sometimes called, the Blue Vision, should be kept secret until mankind *was* ready.

If you are one of those who are seeking the window that will reveal the secrets of life as shown by the Blue Vision, then simply close your eyes and look within.

BLUE VISION

CHAPTER ONE

California - 1986

Courtney stretched luxuriously in the warm spring sunshine. "I love my ocean lullaby," she whispered to the sea gull that was boldly working his way toward her beach bag. "Getting hungry?" she asked him. She opened her favorite tattered carryall and rummaged through the contents. Her brief search produced a plastic kitchen bag full of stale bread and crackers. "Well what have we here," she smiled as she held the bag up for the sea gull to inspect. "It seems that I just happen to have something that might be of interest to you." The gull flapped his wings and hopped back a few feet as the young woman slowly stood up. "Shall we dine by the water?" she asked the bold gull who eyed her intently.

She stepped off of her beach blanket and walked across the loose sand to the water. The cool Pacific was exhilarating as the restless waves splashed around her bare feet. She reached into the plastic bag and tossed some of the contents high above her head. As soon as the first crusts of bread floated in the air, hungry screeching gulls materialized from every direction. Their dazzling white wings were a stark contrast to the bright blue California sky. Courtney was entranced as the sea birds soared effortlessly, then without warning changed their flight pattern and dove at break-neck speed only to pull up just in time to pluck a tasty morsel from her outstretched fingers. "One day I will choreograph a ballet in your honor!" she called out to them, but the greedy gulls took no notice as they continued their spontaneous flight patterns, which were inspired by their instinct to find nourishment. Their natural grace always inspired her imagination. She rose high on her toes and threw her head back. Her long auburn hair floated on the wind as she stretched her arms wide as if to embrace all that she saw, then with arms moving like wings she danced mirroring the grace of her high flying friends. She needed no other music than the calling gulls and the breaking waves.

"What I would like is a little peace and quiet! You are making those goddamned gulls screech until I can't hear myself think!" The rough male voice jolted Courtney from her musings and she whirled mid-step to find its source.

A man she judged to be in his mid-sixties stood just beyond the splashing waves. He wore a soft-brimmed white beach hat and dark glasses. His broad chest hinted that he might have worked with weights in his younger days. His stomach protruding over the waist band of his baggy blue swim trunks testified to his more relaxed lifestyle in recent years. His fists were jammed against his sides and his thin legs were set wide apart, a veritable study in indignation. He opened his mouth wide and his face reddened as his paunch heaved with the effort of attempting to make his voice heard above the wind, waves and birds.

It struck Courtney that the irate gentleman very much resembled a sea gull with his skinny legs and round belly. She tried to stifle the giggle that rose up in her throat. Just then an exceptionally plump gull guided by curiosity waddled closer to the angry man. As he straightened his arms and smacked them down against his sides in a gesture of exasperation, the gull too flapped its wings and squawked as it ruffled its feathers. This was too much! Courtney could no longer restrain herself and her hearty laughter spilled freely into the wind. The playful sea breeze, wanting to join in on the joke, lifted the old man's floppy hat and carried it down the beach, causing him to momentarily forget his anger and concentrate on pursuit.

Courtney loved the feel of the warm sand under her feet as she slowly made her way back to the beach blanket. She glanced up once and noticed that the old man had managed to retrieve his flyaway hat and was huffing toward an empty beach chair. He sat down heavily next to an attractive older woman who was wearing a wide-brimmed straw hat and dark glasses. She looked up from her knitting and smiled warmly at the man who sat next to her.

A quick glance at her watch reassured Courtney that she had enough time to indulge herself in a little nap under the warm sun. Her parents were having some important people over for dinner and were insistent that she join them. She guessed that her mother had probably found some nice, eligible man for her to meet. Mrs. Hammond was an incurable matchmaker. Courtney groaned at the memory of some of the mismatching episodes she had endured.

The ocean lullaby worked its magic and Courtney's thoughts drifted lazily on the sound of the waves as the breeze played with the long silky strands of her hair. The afternoon sun wrapped her in its warmth as her body relaxed and her mind quieted. Final exams, dinner parties, angry old men all seemed far away. The cries of the gulls wavered and echoed as they faded from her consciousness and she drifted deeper...deeper...into the timeless, altered reality of sleep.

Courtney found herself floating in dark silence. The ocean and the sun were gone; a fact that she did not question but simply noted, with an odd detachment. She no longer heard the gulls nor felt the sea breeze, but somehow it didn't seem to matter. She simply wondered where she was going. A pinpoint of light appeared in front of her and she felt herself moving toward it. The light grew brighter and larger until she could discern vague shapes. Then in one powerful burst she was hurled through the light and found herself in the center of a sparsely furnished room. She saw three beds, three night stands and three lamps. It did not have quite the feel of a home and yet she knew that she lived there. That thought surprised her and she gasped as she tried to sort through her brief confusion. Something was wrong but she could not make her mind focus on what it was. She had to get some air. If she could open a window she would feel better. She spotted two tall windows at the end of the room and they were both propped open, but she could see heavy bars covering the opening! A ceiling fan hummed overhead and the sound of it soothed her until she gradually felt calmer.

    She noticed stiffness in her left arm, and as she moved to find a more comfortable position, she realized that she was sitting on the floor. A child's coloring book lay open in front of her. She stared in wonderment as her arm, moving of its own accord, reached for one of the crayons that lay scattered on the floor nearby and began scribbling on the book. She felt so alone. With a gasp she realized that was someone else's thought. How odd it was to have two sets of thoughts. She sensed that the other thoughts were angry because someone had left her alone. Courtney did not know who was responsible for that but more importantly where was this place and why was she here? A mixture of fear and anger swelled in her throat. The other thoughts began chanting, "This is not fair!" Courtney's thoughts responded, "This is not my life and I don't belong here!" She hurled her crayon across the room then awkwardly grabbed up several more and threw them. They made sharp clattering noises as they broke against the wall.

Panic threatened to overtake her and she struggled to stand up. What was wrong with her usually lithe body? It felt so awkward and unruly. Tears of frustration stung her eyes. She had to talk to someone but only strange babbling noises came from her throat. Why wouldn't the words form? She shivered as the chilling truth dawned in her mind...she was trapped. She fought the terror that threatened her sanity. She must somehow tell someone about this mistake. She knew that she did not belong in this place.

There must be a telephone here somewhere. As she stumbled toward one of the nightstands her left foot struck the leg of the iron bed nearest her and she fell forward. She clutched at the bed linens but succeeded only in dragging them with her as she lost her balance and slid from the edge of the bed to the hard tile floor.

She tried to scream "Let me out of here!" But the words would not form. She heard her hoarse sobs and unintelligible babbling.

There was no telephone beside the lamp. Even if there had been one how could she use it? No one could understand those noises that substituted as words. But someone had to understand. Someone had to hear her cries for help. Someone had to get her out of here! One set of thoughts whimpered like a puppy. The other thoughts began to snarl like some wild creature clamoring to be set free. Her eyes were wild and dark as she threw her head back and opened that place of primal need. The awful tortured screams startled her. Oh my God, she realized they were her own screams! The power of them had pushed her out of her body and she hovered near the ceiling as she watched her screaming animal self writhing in the crumpled bed linens. The two selves merged again as she was pulled into her body by an unknown force. She felt the other thoughts as their angry power surged. They wanted to hit and destroy! From the dark center of that rage she drew upon all of the energy that had gathered and directed it at the lamp sitting just above her on the night stand. With one burst of power the lamp exploded in a shower of sparks and shards of glass.

At almost the same instant the door banged open and two men wearing white jackets rushed into the room. They dodged flying glass and grabbed at the hysterical girl thinking that she had flung the lamp against the wall. A short stocky gray haired woman carrying a syringe hurried in behind them.

Courtney felt her hands being forced into coarse bonds. No! The jacket! She clawed wildly, kicking and biting anything she could reach.

"What set her off again?" growled the tall man with bushy eyebrows.

"Who knows with her? Oomph!" grunted the shorter one cursing under his breath as Courtney's flailing free arm caught him in his midsection. "Hurry it up with that needle!"

"She's tryin' to bite me!" the tall man bellowed as he fought to avoid her teeth and vicious kicks.

After the sharp prick it was only moments before the strength left her body. Strong arms lifted her limp form and she was flung roughly over someone's shoulder. Her head bobbed crazily as the man turned and strode briskly from the room making her feel nauseated. He carried her down a long corridor lined with closed doors. She was aware of the distasteful smells of urine, sweat and disinfectant. Her eyelids grew heavy and she fought to keep them open. Then she was tossed roughly onto a bed and the jacket was removed. Her hospital gown was soaked through and strands of sweat-soaked hair stuck to her cheeks and neck. How she longed for a cool cloth to wipe her face. The room spun and she turned her head back and forth on the pillow trying to make it stop! Hot tears of defeat slipped from the corners of her eyes as she was buckled into the *restraints. She was too weak to put up much of a struggle now.*

"After a little nap she might be calmer. What does the Doc say about upping the dosage?" The voices echoed around her and faded as she floated up to the ceiling and beyond. The terror vanished as she floated out of the building and a sense of peace washed over her as she looked down upon a large expanse of green lawns dotted with gnarled trees and occasional flower beds. Suddenly she was in darkness and without warning, she crashed into some sort of ice-cold container. She shivered and opened her eyes.

"Bernie, Bernie, come to shore right now! The fog is coming in!"

Courtney snapped to an upright position at the sound of the woman's shrill cries. Momentarily disoriented, she wondered where she was as she tried to move her stiff, chilled body. The sun's warmth had been cut off by a thick bank of fog that was rapidly moving toward the shore. The air was chilly and the sunbathers were either packing up or had already left the beach.

"Bernie! Get back here! Bernie! Somebody help him! He's in trouble! Help! Help!"

The woman's frantic screams penetrated Courtney's stupor. Despite the dull ache in her left foot, she quickly jumped to her feet and scanned the water. The tide was coming in. The friendly lapping waves had given way to crashing, pounding surf. The angry swells reflected the gray fog that moved with insidious stealth transforming the bright spring seascape to a cold foreboding place.

A bright spot of color bobbed on the waves. A red vinyl raft and its heavy cargo were tossed crazily amongst gray swells that appeared to rise out of the fog itself. She recognized him as the same gentleman who had been so irate about the noise of the sea gulls earlier that afternoon.

He was still wearing his hat as he straddled his flimsy craft and was waving his arms wildly in an attempt to signal someone on shore. The raft was bent sharply in the middle and looked as if it was deflating. A large wave rose behind him. As the wave continued to gain in strength, Bernie turned to look at it.

Courtney watched helplessly as the mighty wave crested and curled over the top of its hapless victim. His mouth opened wide as if in a scream, and his long arms were outstretched.

Her heart pounded furiously and precious seconds ticked away while she made her decision. At this time of year there were no lifeguards on the beach. A few elderly people were packing up their beach chairs. Others had heard the woman's screams and were hurrying toward the water. None of them looked as though they would be able to attempt a rescue under these difficult circumstances. She knew she was an exceptionally strong swimmer and had passed her Red Cross Lifesaving Test while in high school, but could she handle a frightened two hundred pound man in this dangerous surf?

The woman had stopped screaming. Her face was ashen. She stood with her hands clapped over her mouth as her wide frightened eyes searched the churning water for some sign of her husband.

"God please help me!" she prayed. "I have to try to rescue this man!" She sprang forward and her legs stretched beneath her as her long strides carried her effortlessly across the soft sand. Adrenaline pumped through her and her mind focused on the perilous task ahead.

The shock of the cold water on her feet and legs caused Courtney to suck in her breath sharply, but there was no thought of stopping, or turning back. She ran as far into the waves as she could and then dove headfirst. She swam hard under water for a few yards and then surfaced to fill her lungs and get her bearings. Salt water burned her eyes as she strained to see some sign of the old man and his raft. She saw the raft floating just to her right. One white hand clutched the edge of the raft. He had been thrown into the water by that last wave but he was still holding on. She swam with all of her strength and will toward him. She looked up once but he had disappeared in the swells. Her arms pounded through the water and her legs pushed and churned despite the fatigue that already threatened her. The battle with the powerful tide and the cold water would soon take its toll. She stopped swimming and gulped for air. Bernie and his red raft bobbed up about three or four yards away. Apparently that last surge had actually carried him closer to Courtney.

He had somehow managed to maintain his grip and was now striving to pull his upper body onto the rapidly deflating raft. Courtney knew she must reach him quickly.

"Hold on to the raft! I'm coming to help you!" she screamed above the roar of the waves. The man turned to look at her. His eyes bulged with fear and his mouth was open as he tried to gulp in air and spit out salt water at the same time.

With renewed effort Courtney stroked as hard as she could and with one final lunge her hand grabbed the cold wet material of the raft's edge. "Hold the raft with both hands!" she commanded.

"My...my heart!" he choked as he grabbed his chest with one hand. His pale face was contorted in pain.

"Oh God, give me strength," she prayed fervently. "Bernie you hold on, no matter what! We are going to try to ride this wave in to the shore! We are going to make it!" She yelled with more conviction than she felt.

Courtney could feel the power of another swell building beneath her. Their only chance would be to allow its superior power to carry them closer to shallow water. She knew the dangers of the undertow. If they were caught in it they could be carried far out to sea. Even if they surfaced before they drowned, how could they ever find the shore in this fog? Already her view of the beach faded as the gray veil grew thicker.

She kicked her legs as hard as she could and pulled forward with her free arm. The wave rose like a great gray dragon lifting them high in the air. Courtney held Bernie in the classic rescue hold with her arm encircling his head as the wave crested and began to thrust them downward into the cold gray depths.

Courtney kicked and swam with her remaining strength willing herself forward; she pulled Bernie toward shore using the power of the wave and suddenly they were hurtling toward the beach. The raft was ripped from Bernie's grasp. Her body was slammed against Bernie's in the turbulence and Courtney lost her grip on him. She was tossed about like so much seaweed. Her lungs ached to breathe as salt water poured into her mouth and nose. Again Bernie's body was slammed against her and she grabbed his limp arm while she kicked with every ounce of energy she could produce. Once again Bernie was wrenched from her grasp as she tried to swim with the force of the wave. She was nearing exhaustion and her lungs screamed for air. As her body began to succumb to fatigue, darkness crept into her brain and she wondered if she was dying. Suddenly her face was out of the water and she tried to gulp in air, but she gagged and choked as she expelled water from her lungs. Her shoulder scraped painfully against sand. She was in shallow water! As she scrambled and splashed to an upright position, she saw Bernie floating face down nearby.

People were running out into the water and strong hands helped Courtney to her feet. She was vaguely aware of the crowd of people who had gathered to watch the drama unfold. Several men surrounded Bernie and together they hoisted him up and carried him well beyond the fury of the incoming tide. Bernie's wife sobbed hysterically as she knelt beside his unmoving body.

A plump red-haired woman rushed forward with some towels. She covered Bernie with one and gave one to Courtney, chattering nervously as she went. "Marge honey, Don went to call an ambulance and they will be here any minute. My Roy knows CPR so you just move back here with me and let him do it! Everything is going to be all right." As she spoke the woman pulled Marge firmly to her feet and led her a short distance away. The woman continued to croon soothing words as a lanky suntanned man knelt beside Bernie's lifeless form and began to administer CPR.

Precious moments passed. Bernie did not respond. Courtney dropped to her knees beside them and watched Roy's valiant attempts to coax Bernie back to life.

Such a strong looking man, thought Courtney, *and yet like all of us, so fragile*. Mankind swaggers and proclaims its dominion over all that it sees. In truth we are so very delicate that even the strongest cannot survive if the balance is disturbed for just a moment too long. In a matter of seconds after the body's need for a small thing like one breath of air becomes too great, the life essence simply disengages and moves on.

Once as a child, Courtney saw that essence lift from Grandma Hattie's husband. He had slumped forward in his wheelchair. Then Courtney saw a light rise from the top of his head. The light had tiny sparkles in it like a cluster of fireflies. The sparkles rose higher until they merged with the sunbeams that streamed through the living room window. The sparkling essence followed the beams of light and floated outside, disappearing into the brilliant sun. Though she watched carefully, she saw no such light leaving Bernie's head.

Courtney's left hand tingled oddly and it felt hot despite the chilly mist. She no longer shivered even though the temperature continued to drop as the fog silently wrapped its gray shroud around the little group of anxious people.

Memories crowded into Courtney's mind, tumbling one upon another. Perky, her little dog, the wounded bird, Grandma Hattie's real granddaughter sick with the fever and most vivid of all, her own beloved little brother Shane. Her hand had felt the same way during those extraordinary events.

Shane had been only five years old when he fell out of the row boat. Old Frank had managed to pull him out of the river and get him to shore. But no one could make him breathe until ten year old Courtney put her hands on him.

Roy was obviously too fatigued to continue as he sat back on his heels. The strain of his efforts and the shock of what had happened to his friend showed plainly on his pale face. Marge sobbed loudly and the small crowd stirred as they anxiously waited to hear the wail of the ambulance sirens.

Courtney's hands were both throbbing unbearably now. They seemed to reach out to the lifeless body of their own accord. She slipped her right hand under his neck and rested her left hand on his massive chest. Hot needles stabbed her palms as wave after wave of electric energy shot through her body. The crown of her head numbed as the energy entered. The current rocked her body as it traveled down her neck and through her arms and it synchronized with her heartbeat. She closed her eyes and peered within her inner darkness watching the brilliant flashes of energy. As she concentrated, the sounds of the ocean faded. There was only the heartbeat and the energy.

She allowed her mind to follow the energy into Bernie's

chest and beyond the ribs until she could see the motionless heart. A sparkling flash of energy shot from her hands and into the organ causing the heart to jump. She made the energy pulses travel faster, striking the dormant heart in an almost continuous series of jolts. At last the heart responded and literally came to life with its own beat.

A gurgle issued from Bernie's throat. Sea water trickled from his blue lips. His body convulsed as his lungs purged themselves of the unwelcome liquid. The onlookers collectively held their breath as Bernie took his first ragged gulp of life-giving oxygen.

Roy quickly put his long thin arm around the larger man's shoulders and attempted to turn him on his side. Bernie coughed violently spewing water everywhere. Courtney bent to help Roy hold Bernie on his side. Bernie's powerful arms flailed wildly as he continued to cough and gasp greedily for air. In a few moments the coughing subsided and Bernie's eyelids opened wide. He reached up and clutched Courtney's arm. He was surprisingly strong for a man who had just been very near death. He pulled her down close to his face and his lips moved awkwardly as he tried to form words.

"They told me to give you a message!" he rasped urgently as he struggled to make himself heard.

"Me? Now don't try to talk. You had a close call but you are going to be just fine. The ambulance will be here any minute," Courtney soothed, thinking that his mind was not fully alert yet.

"Listen to me! I have to tell you something." His plea sounded so urgent that Courtney simply nodded her head and let him speak.

"They said…the people I was talking to when I was dead…they said I had to give you a message." His bloodshot eyes bulged in unblinking intensity. "They said you have work to do, and you must begin it now! You must find her before it's too late!" Another spasm of coughing cut the raspy words off as his body jackknifed.

An involuntary shudder shook Courtney as she listened to his strange message. Surely they were just the ravings of someone who had just been through an incredible trauma. In a flash of remembrance, Grandma Hattie's words echoed across time, *"You are special, Child. The good Lord has something in mind for you to do!"*

The stunned onlookers had crowded in close and were suddenly all talking at once. Marge's hysterical grief had transformed into relieved laughter and she babbled incoherently as she buried her face against her husband's neck. Hardly anyone heard the wail of the sirens as the rescue truck screamed into the nearby parking lot. In fact no one acknowledged the presence of the EMT men. They literally had to push their way through the small knot of people to get to Bernie.

Courtney watched dazedly as the professionals efficiently took charge. They checked their patient's vital signs and soon were helping him onto a stretcher. Slowly and unnoticed Courtney moved away from all of the activity. She was shivering uncontrollably and there was a loud ringing in her ears. She broke into a stumbling run as she made her way to her beach blanket. With trembling hands she dug down into her beach bag and found an old sweat shirt and gratefully pulled it on over her long wet hair and her now thoroughly chilled body.

"Please wait!" It was Marge's voice. "Wait please!" She ran heavily kicking up the soft sand in an effort to reach Courtney. "You saved my husband's life and I don't even know your name!" She was panting from her exertion. "Please give me your phone number or address. I want to find a way to thank you for what you did."

"Thhere is no need to thththank me!" stammered Courtney through chattering teeth.

The woman would not be deterred. She became increasingly insistent. To appease her, Courtney finally fumbled in her bag and found one of her father's business cards.

"This is my father's business card. My name is Courtney."

"Thank you! Thank you!" The woman's eyes already reddened from crying, filled with fresh tears. She impulsively embraced Courtney as she tried to choke back the sobs that rose in her throat. The two women looked into each other's eyes for a long moment. In that brief time Courtney felt as though she knew the woman intimately. She felt her pain, her joy, her gratitude and the great depth of her love. Without another word, Marge turned and hurried across the sand toward her beloved husband who had been given the most sacred of all gifts, life, and a second chance to live it in one lifetime.

CHAPTER TWO

Courtney's cozy studio apartment was only a few blocks from the beach. She longed for a hot shower and some hot tea. The little white VW maneuvered easily through the Santa Monica traffic. At last she was pulling into her parking space. She could almost feel the hot water already.

The key slid easily into the lock despite the trembling of her hands. Just as the door swung open the telephone began to ring. Courtney shoved the door shut with her foot, dropped her beach bag and hurried into the tiny kitchen. In her haste to lift the receiver she knocked it to the kitchen counter. It bumped the coffee cup she had used that morning. Though she grabbed wildly for the delicate china cup, it eluded her fumbling hands and smashed on the tile floor. Close to tears, Courtney clutched the dangling receiver and breathed a shaky hello into the mouth piece.

"Twinkle toes, is that you? What's wrong? I heard something crash. You don't sound quite right."

"Oh, Daddy, it's nice to hear your voice. I...I just dropped a cup while I was trying to reach the phone."

"Oh. But something *is* wrong, Luv. I can hear it in your voice."

"S..something happened at the beach...A...A man nearly drowned...I swam out..." Courtney could no longer hold back the sobs. Tears streamed down her cheeks and the rest of her words were lost in a garble of snuffles and sobs.

Clyde Hammond rarely heard his competent, self-assured daughter dissolve into tears. His heart jumped as it always did when something was wrong with one of his children.

"Listen, Twink, I'm calling from my car phone. I was coming to collect you for the dinner party and I'm about twenty minutes away. You can tell me all about it when I get there, OK?"

"OK...I...love you...Daddy," she stammered between sobs.

The hot water splashed over her chilled body. Steam filled the shower stall and fogged the mirrored door of the medicine cabinet. The sobs were gone now. She felt her nerves ease and her body relax as she gave herself completely to the soothing spray of water. Salt, sand and tension streamed in rivulets down the drain. The fragrance of soap and shampoo filled the steamy air. Wonderful normal things like a hot shower and sweet-smelling shampoo should never be taken for granted. Courtney reluctantly turned the water off. She knew her father would arrive shortly and she wanted to greet him with a calm face and a cup of hot tea.

Wrapped in her warm robe, Courtney padded into the kitchen on bare feet. She stopped short at the sight of the shattered china cup. *Broken crayons in her dream.* It had not been the first time that she had dreamed of that place. The memory of the loneliness she had felt in that bare room loomed up like the cold gray fog that had rolled in on the beach.

"No!" she firmly told herself and resolutely shook her head. She reached for her whisk broom and dust pan, determined to focus on cleaning up the tiny slivers of glass before her father's arrival.

Just as the kettle shrilled its signal of boiling water, the doorbell rang. Courtney jumped nervously as both sounds cut through her whirling thoughts.

Mr. Hammond filled the doorway with his six-foot one-inch frame. He held out his arms and Courtney felt herself melt into his strong embrace like a small child.

"Everything is all right now, Twink. I'm here, Luv," he crooned in his deep gentle voice as he stroked her damp hair. Everything was always right with the world when her father held her in his arms.

Courtney sat cross-legged on one end of her small comfortable sofa. Mr. Hammond sat in the wingback chair near her. Between sips of steaming tea, Courtney relayed the startling events of the afternoon to her father.

Clyde Hammond's British upbringing was the perfect background for his career in corporate law. His unperturbed demeanor gave his clients a sense of comfort. His quiet confidence calmed even the most agitated executives. He never pushed anyone to rush their initial consultation because of an overflowing calendar. He rarely even made any notes, preferring instead to listen to his client's problem from start to finish. When the session reached its conclusion, the executive who began red-faced and tense left calm and often smiling. Today Clyde used his placid expression for a different reason. As his daughter's story unfolded, he felt an uneasiness settle into his gut. It was the same feeling he always got just before a seemingly simple case became very complex.

As he watched her face Mr. Hammond marveled, as he had on so many previous occasions, how Courtney so resembled the family. This was a remarkable coincidence considering the fact that she was adopted.

"So, Dad if you get a phone call from a lady named Marge who has a New York accent, you'll know the reason why. I don't even know their last name." Courtney sighed as she finished her account of the incident on the beach.

"Hmmm. Well, when you are feeling up to it you must tell me what you want me to say to those people if they do call." Her father leaned forward and took Courtney's slender hands and held them silently. Gently then he turned her hands so that her palms were up. "Luv, I don't understand the power that came through your hands. I only know that without it your little brother wouldn't be alive today. Now someone else is alive because of it."

Courtney squirmed uncomfortably and attempted to pull her hands from her father's firm grasp. "But, can you believe that it was anything but a quirk of fate?"

"Courtney, do you remember Perky? He was hit by a car and thrown to the side of the road. Killed instantly I suspect, that is until you touched him with your chubby little hands."

Courtney was silent. How could she refute what she knew to be the truth?

"You are extraordinarily gifted, Courtney. Perhaps a higher power has chosen you for something special." Mr. Hammond noted the flicker of fear that crossed his beloved daughter's face and decided to end the uncomfortable conversation. "At any rate, Luv, you are special to your mother and me. Speaking of your mother, she is expecting us for dinner. Run along and get dressed. There's a good girl. Why don't you pack a few things and plan to spend the rest of your holiday with us. We'll have a good long talk tomorrow."

Happy to put aside the memory of the strange afternoon, Courtney quickly packed a small travel bag. She slipped into a light blue silk dress and began to coil her thick auburn hair into the typically severe ballerina bun. "Who will be there tonight?" she asked as she looked into the mirror.

"The firm has taken on two new partners so your mother decided that a dinner party would be the best way for everyone to get acquainted. But of course your mother doesn't need any excuse to have a dinner party." They both laughed at those words. Clarisa Hammond's genteel southern rearing had indeed prepared her to play the ideal hostess, a role she took seriously and one that she loved.

In a short time Courtney emerged from the small dressing area looking lovely and refreshed. The blue silk seemed to reflect the blue of her eyes. Her long dark lashes needed no enhancement. Though he knew she would soon be twenty-five, Mr. Hammond couldn't help thinking how innocent and childlike she looked at that moment.

"Elegant. Perfectly elegant," he beamed as he strode toward his beautiful daughter. In a gallant gesture he lifted her small hand to his lips and then formally offered her his arm. "It's off to the grand ball, M'lady. Your carriage awaits."

Courtney giggled as she grandly took his arm. Inwardly she thanked the fates for bringing her into this loving family. She seldom thought about the fact that she was adopted. She knew that her mother had only been fifteen years old at the time and had died shortly after giving birth. The girl had not even been in a hospital. Apparently, Courtney would have died too if Grandma Hattie had not found her in time.

The white Mercedes carried father and daughter smoothly through the constantly snarled Los Angeles traffic. Courtney leaned back comfortably in the leather seats and allowed her mind to drift. She asked herself the same question she had asked so many times before. Why, out of hundreds of orphans, had she been chosen? Why had she been lifted out of what should have been death or a life of poverty? She could just as easily have met the same fate as the poor girl who bore her. *I don't even know her name,* Courtney lamented. *I should try to find out her name and where she is buried. I would like to put some flowers on her grave. Maybe her spirit would like that. She died so alone. I wonder if she had anyone who...*

"Almost home, Luv. Time to open those baby blues..."

The wrought-iron gates parted revealing the well-lighted private drive. The Mercedes moved along the gently winding road that led to the Hammond's elegant Palos Verdes home. As they neared the house, Courtney could see two young men wearing red jackets helping guests out of their cars.

"Mother thinks of everything doesn't she," Courtney commented in admiration.

"Don't worry, Luv. You have met most of these people. Despite their ostentatious appearance some of them are quite interesting." Mr. Hammond was well aware of his daughter's dislike of people who chose their friends according to the size of their bank accounts.

Clyde guided the car into the large garage next to Clarisa's Jaguar. Once again father and daughter linked arms and made their way into the house.

Even though Courtney and her family had lived in this house since 1973, she had never gotten over the feeling of awe at the beauty and richness of it. It was especially true on evenings such as this when expensively dressed men and women sipped iced drinks and spoke in carefully modulated voices. Classical music played softly in the background and meticulously groomed maids and waiters catered to the needs of the guests. Carefully arranged flowers, candles and indirect lighting, created the perfect mood for an elegant gathering such as this. A well known designer had created the lighting effect to blend with the soft lights of the patio area which could be seen through the great expanse of windows in the living room and formal dining room. Courtney smiled as she remembered her father's wry comments about paying a fortune for lights that no one was supposed to notice.

"Happy to be home, Luv?" inquired Mr. Hammond noticing his daughter's smile.

"Yes. It is beautiful isn't it?"

"Hmph. Perhaps…if you like bloody designer lights that no one will notice." His displeasure was feigned and the two broke into hearty laughter.

"Courtney, darlin'! I am so glad you are here. I was beginnin' to worry." Clarisa Hammond embraced her tall daughter gently and lifted her face for a tender kiss from her husband.

"Hi Mom. I uh… Dad and I…"

"The traffic was rather heavy. Didn't mean to worry you darling," cut in Mr. Hammond.

Courtney knew that this was not the time to discuss her disturbing afternoon and she was grateful for her father's quick thinking.

Clarisa gazed intently at her daughter for a long moment. She could see the slight redness of her eyes and a tension in her manner. She clung to her father's arm as though for support rather than just a casual posture. Something had happened today. She could see it in her husband's eyes as well. She knew that they did not want to spoil her evening and that they would reveal their thoughts at a later time.

"Courtney dear, you look stunning in that blue silk. I have the perfect necklace for you to wear with it tonight. Come and try it on!"

Clyde studied his beautiful wife. To a stranger, Clarisa might appear shallow. She often presented herself as the personification of a southern belle. In truth, she did love beautiful clothes and nothing excited her more than planning an elegant dinner party, except perhaps playing

Chopin on the white Steinway he had given her for Christmas five years ago. Despite the fluff and frill, Clyde knew that his wife was a brilliant woman. He knew she was a shrewd judge of character and he had learned early on to trust her assessments implicitly. Before accepting the offer the new partners had made, he had listened carefully to Clarisa's evaluation of the candidates which included her view of how their abilities and personalities would blend with current members of the firm. She was always right.

Clyde knew instinctively that his wife had seen through the ruse that he and his daughter had created. He knew that Clarisa had accepted the delay in finding out what happened that day and that she would patiently wait for one of them to give her the details at a more appropriate time.

Mother and daughter quickly made their way toward the master bedroom suite. "I have been planning to give this to you on your birthday, but it will be so beautiful with the dress you are wearing that you must have it tonight. Anyway, your birthday is only two weeks away. Sit here honey." Clarisa motioned for Courtney to sit in front of the mirrors positioned above the long elegant dressing table.

Courtney watched curiously as her mother pulled open a drawer and took out a small antique jewelry box.

"There is a little family history that goes with this stone. It has been passed down from mother to daughter for more generations than anyone can count. Some people think that it had its origin in Scotland around the thirteenth century. There are all kinds of tales about magic and the Little People. No one knows where it came from really. I do know that it always gave me a sense of peace and joy to wear it. When I married your father I dreamed of having a daughter to pass it on to." Clarisa opened the box and turned it so that Courtney could see the magnificent gem.

"Oh, mother, the blue topaz," breathed Courtney. "But I thought... I mean since I'm not really..."

"My daughter?" Clarisa cut in. "You are my child just as surely as if you were conceived in my womb. No, I didn't feel the birthin' pains, but when I looked at your tiny pink face, my heart opened and received you as my daughter." Tears had gathered in her eyes as she spoke. Both women plucked tissues from the silver dispenser on the dressing table and dabbed at their eyes.

"What about Shane, Mom, shouldn't he..."

"Now don't you think that big hulk of a brother would look a little silly wearin' this delicate jewel?" At that both women giggled. Clarisa opened her arms to her daughter and enfolded her in a long warm embrace.

"Darlin', it was a happy day when I learned that I was pregnant after all those years and I love your brother. No one can ever take his place. You, my love, are every bit as important to me as he is and you are my only daughter. The blue topaz is to be given to a daughter, not a son." She said it with a finality which precluded any further protests from Courtney.

"Now hurry and put it on; we have guests waiting." Clarisa lifted the large emerald cut blue stone from its box. "This is the original setting but the gold chain is new. The clasp on the original was broken..." Both women jumped as someone knocked loudly on the large doors of the master bedroom suite.

"Senora Hammond!"

"Oh, that's Maria. I told her to let me know when supper was ready to be served. Can you manage dear?" Clarisa stood up as she spoke, already focusing her thoughts on her duties as a proper hostess.

Courtney smiled as she watched her mother hurry from the room. Then, she turned her attention to the necklace.

The clasp was stiff and she struggled to open it. The distant sounds of laughter from the guests, mingled with a Chopin Nocturne, were pleasant in the background. She felt relaxed and detached as if everything were very far away. Her hands felt heavy and her fingers grew clumsy as she worked with the necklace. "Maybe I just need something to eat," she whispered to herself. At last the stubborn clasp opened and she raised her arms to put the chain around her neck. She glanced at her reflection in the mirror but everything was out of focus. Her eyelids felt heavy and she fought to keep them open. Her thoughts seemed to separate and then reform. She was aware that something had gone wrong with the background sounds. Doors slammed and the noise echoed eerily. Her stomach churned as the unpleasant smell of disinfectant assailed her senses. She couldn't understand why that odor would suddenly be so strong.

The blue topaz now dangled directly in her line of vision. She thought it odd that she held the chain in place around her neck and yet the glittering stone appeared to be floating in front of her face. She felt pulled into the blue depths of the gem. The passage of her breath became a roar as her lungs filled with oxygen and released it with each breath. Her reflection stared back at her from the center of the blue topaz. A deep silence engulfed her as she moved closer to the unblinking image of herself. Courtney was appalled at the tangled disarray of her hair. Something about her reflection just didn't seem right.

"Beau...ti...ful." The word was carefully enunciated by Courtney's reflection. At that moment the volume of her heartbeat became a thunderous audible pounding. The beat accelerated and surrounded her threatening to suffocate all thought and breath.

"Hey, Cort! Are you in there?" The pounding heart subsided as the sharp rap of knuckles on the bedroom door broke the spell. "Cort, come on. Mom says 'dinnah' is served. Sheesh! What's the matter with you? You look spaced." A tall young man with sun streaked blond hair and mischievous hazel eyes, strode into the room. He playfully grabbed Courtney's shoulders and gave her a shake. "Earth to Courtney. Looks like the lights are on but nobody's home," he teased. "Come on, Mom won't let me eat if I go back without you."

"Is that all you think about, Shane? Every time I come here I end up talking to the back of your head as you stand in front of the refrigerator looking for something to eat. Here, would you help me with this necklace please?"

"I'm a growin' boy. I have to eat to keep up my strength. Wow! Cool rock, where'd you get it?" Courtney loved their playful banter. She could not remember ever having a serious argument with her brother. As it happens with all siblings, childish squabbles would erupt from time to time. Whatever the problem, it was always quickly resolved because they could not bear to feel anger toward each other. As Shane fastened the gold chain around her neck, Courtney told him the story of the blue topaz.

"That's quite a history. I think I remember Mom talking about it years ago. Actually I don't remember seeing her wear it for quite a long time. Anyway I'm glad she gave it to you. It looks great!" Just then a loud plaintive growl came from Shane's stomach. "I'm weak, I'm starving! Get me some food before I pass out," wailed Shane as he grabbed his midsection with both hands and comically staggered toward the door. Courtney giggled and hurried to aide the starving young man.

Nearly all of the guests were seated by the time brother and sister made their way to the slate covered patio. A smartly clad waiter beckoned to the pair and they followed him to a table with two unoccupied chairs.

"I wonder who Mom has us sitting with?" whispered Shane apprehensively. In spite of his youthful bravado, he could be quite shy when faced with a room full of strangers. Courtney sympathized with his angst knowing that her mother would also attempt a bit of matchmaking for Shane. Courtney followed her brother's stare and found the source of his nerves. Nothing could be quite as intimidating as a beautiful young woman and this blond vision was positively breathtaking. Just then the young woman looked up and flashed a dimpled smile at Shane who promptly flushed a deep red.

"Shane!" Courtney exclaimed in a hoarse whisper, "That's Michele Whitfield."

"Michele?" breathed Shane.

"She certainly has grown up hasn't she," said Courtney with a sly grin. "Look, there is an empty chair next to her." Shane nodded dumbly as she gently pulled her awestruck brother toward the table.

The waiter pulled out an empty chair and Courtney sat down. She watched with some amusement as Shane stiffly seated himself in the vacant chair next to the stunning Michele. The two young people sat silently smiling into each other's eyes after their initial greeting. As she observed them, Courtney felt a tingle ripple through her body as her senses expanded with realizations. She saw Shane and Michele wandering at opposite ends of an elaborate labyrinth through time. Some paths were too overgrown to follow. Other paths seemed clear but only led to a dead end. Both knew of the other's existence but neither could find the path that would lead to their reunion, until now. They each stepped from their dark path at precisely the same moment and both were struck dumb in the dazzling light of recognition. At that moment Shane slowly reached out his hand and Michele delicately placed her hand in his. Shane drew her hand upward and pressed it gently against his lips. *How unlike Shane to do such a thing,* Courtney thought, but the movement was executed with such natural courtly grace he could have been one of Arthur's gallant knights.

"Has someone upset you? May I be of assistance?"

Courtney jumped at the sound of the deep masculine voice near her right ear. She had been so captivated by the charming tableau of the knight and his lady that she was completely unaware of anyone else.

"I did not mean to startle you, please forgive me."

Courtney looked up into the dark brown eyes of the most handsome man she had ever seen. He was frowning in concern. "Oh, of course. It's perfectly all right really," she mumbled in embarrassed surprise as she realized that tears had trickled down her cheeks. How could she ever explain that her overactive imagination could move her to such an emotional display among strangers?

"It's just, uh, allergies," she said with what she hoped was a convincing sniff. Quickly she reached for the white linen napkin which lay near her. The heavy sterling napkin ring seemed to catch on something as she tried to slide the fabric through it. She tugged nervously at the ring and suddenly it slipped free. Her hand shot forward upsetting the brimming water goblet. She moaned inwardly as she heard the young man's sharp intake of breath as the ice cubes and cold water soaked the table cloth and splashed onto his lap. He hastily pushed back his chair and jumped to his feet very nearly knocking over the wine steward who had just bent forward to begin filling the wine glasses.

Mercifully, few people noticed Courtney's mishap as all eyes were drawn to the grand entrance of white-gloved waiters bearing huge silver trays laden with delectable delicacies. At once the air was filled with mouthwatering aromas and the guests focused their attention on the sumptuous feast that was soon to follow.

CHAPTER THREE

Dozens of shrimp cocktails, crisp green salads and delicate creamed soups were hungrily devoured. Happy conversation swelled and ebbed as each course of the meal flowed from the kitchen in perfectly orchestrated harmony. Anyone who might have noticed Courtney's awkward moment had immediately forgotten it, except that is, Courtney herself. She had apologized profusely to the dampened young man next to her. She was grateful for his genuine good humor. He had assured her that his silk trousers had not been damaged by the water. The fact remained however, that she had behaved like an awkward child at her first dress-up dinner. *Unforgivable,* she chastised herself, *I've been all over the world and dined in fine restaurants all of my life and I chose my own backyard to make a fool out of myself in front of the most gorgeous man I have ever met.* With that she felt the heat of embarrassment once again rise in her cheeks.

"You have not touched your wine."

Without really wanting to, Courtney looked up into those disturbing dark eyes. Her heart leaped as his gaze lowered and boldly appraised the soft folds of the low neckline of her dress. Her throat immediately constricted making it impossible to speak and she coughed hoarsely.

"Here, do try the wine. It is quite delicious," he said as he picked up the delicate stemware and placed it firmly in her hand. She lifted the glass to her lips and carefully swallowed. It was a white wine with a slightly floral bouquet. To her surprise her throat instantly cleared and the constriction relaxed.

"Thank you..."

"Antonio." He smiled and watched her expectantly.

"Oh, uh, my name is Courtney."

"Salute Courtney," he said lowering his voice as he lifted his own wine glass in a toast to her. The thick black lashes closed in a display of supreme pleasure as Antonio savored his wine. "Ah, vino, surely a gift from the Gods. No, no, no," he corrected himself quickly. "Why would the Gods have bestowed such a magnificent nectar upon barbaric beings such as humanity? No I think it is more likely that a clever and daring mortal appropriated the secret formula by deceitful means." One dark eyebrow arched and the unfathomable brown eyes squinted, denoting the sinister nature of the ...thief.

Courtney smiled broadly at his dignified but comedic rhetoric.

"A toast to brave souls," he said grandly, sitting up very straight in his chair, "and to the smile of a goddess," he added as he leaned closer to a pink-cheeked Courtney. Their glasses met and the fine crystal rang with a clear high pitched sound. She daintily sipped her wine and felt herself relax. Antonio had made her forget her previous discomfiture and he had succeeded in awakening some long dormant desires.

"Your wrist!" Antonio exclaimed, frowning with sudden concern.

Courtney jerked the wine glass away from her mouth and looked down at her slender wrist. A dark blue bruise wound its way around her right wrist. She frowned as she realized that an identical mark had materialized around her left wrist. How could it have happened? She carefully set her glass on the table and held her wrists together as she compared the two bruises. Both were about two inches wide and created a perfect circle just below the hand. *The dream on the beach. The dream self, secured with restraints to a bed. A heavy sedative.* Images flashed through her mind as she tried to think of an explanation for Antonio...for herself.

"I was on the beach today and a man nearly drowned. I had to swim out to him. He was a little panicky...I must have gotten bruised when he...when I...while we struggled against the tide," gulped Courtney. She heard herself telling Antonio about Bernie's near drowning incident but it was the dream that occupied her thoughts. This dream was only one of many just like it that had come to her throughout her life. Each dream seemed to precede an extraordinary event, and perhaps most extraordinary of all, the dreams always occurred just prior to her birthday.

"Ah...Courtney, I think you are far too modest. It would seem you saved a man's life today," remarked Antonio with unabashed admiration.

"Well, it was just our good fortune that the tide brought us to shore before we both drowned," retorted Courtney, wishing she could gracefully change the subject.

"Perhaps," he said somberly, "but I believe that our toast to brave souls was most appropriate, and now I salute *you*, beautiful brave soul." Antonio's eyes never left her face as he lifted his glass in her direction, then reverently sipped its contents.

A gloved hand appeared in front of Courtney and with it a steaming entree. It was a Cornish hen delicately glazed with an orange sauce and accompanied by a generous helping of wild rice. The conversation was comfortably directed toward the meal and other pleasant generalities, a fact for which Courtney was profoundly grateful.

"Your friend seems to have found an amiable dinner companion." Antonio glanced in Shane's direction.

Courtney had completely forgotten about Shane, but when she glanced across the table she saw the two former childhood playmates deeply engrossed in conversation. It was apparent that they were oblivious to everything and everyone except each other.

"So, this causes you pain?" Disappointment rang clearly in Antonio's voice.

"Oh, not at all. My brother and Michele played together as children. Michele's family moved to Europe, so this is the first time they have seen each other in years." Courtney sensed that Antonio wondered if she was involved with anyone. It pleased her that he had made such an undisguised effort to find out about her romantic attachments.

"Your brother. Yes, I do see the resemblance." Antonio's relief was obvious and he smiled broadly.

Comfortable warmth began to work its way through Courtney's body. She realized that since the incident on the beach she had been functioning in a strange detached manner almost as if some part of her consciousness was outside of her body watching her actions as though it were a separate entity. Now she felt her customary self assurance returning and the Aries fire of her birth sign burned brightly in her personality.

The wine and the conversation flowed with congenial ease. By the time the waiters were clearing away the dishes, Courtney had learned a great deal about Antonio. His family owned the largest winery in Italy for generations. At the turn of the century his grandfather purchased some land in the Napa valley. The new land acquisition allowed the Scolari family to expand their business and eventually become the largest Italian wine distributors in the world.

Courtney studied his face as he spoke with great pride about his family's accomplishments. When he spoke of his mother, his voice softened in unmistakable loving respect. She found it curious, however, that when he referred to his father he often used his first name, Mario. She sensed that

Antonio respected his father and desired his approval but there was no denying the fact that their relationship was strained. Courtney had often listened to her friends as they told her of their problems with their biological parents. She wondered now as she had then why it was so difficult for people to maintain a loving relationship with their family. Courtney had never known her biological parents. They had both died long ago. Perhaps families take each other for granted, secure in their belief that nothing will ever happen to separate them. Even in her earliest memories Courtney had always held a deep sense of gratitude for the loving environment that she was given by her adoptive parents.

"Bananas Foster or Cherries Jubilee, Miss Hammond?" A somber young waiter interrupted the flow of conversation.

"Bananas Foster, please, Richard," Courtney smiled.

"Miss Hammond?" Antonio's right eyebrow shot up. "You are related to Clyde Hammond?"

"He is my father," she responded with obvious pride.

"Ah! I should have noticed the family resemblance. Your father has advised the Scolari family for many years. My father mightily values the words of Clyde Hammond."

"Dessert sir?" the young waiter asked.

"No thank you. I would like a brandy."

"Yes sir. Miss Hammond, would you like something?"

"I would like an espresso, thank you Richard."

"You seem to know this young man rather well," frowned Antonio as Richard turned to leave. "Is he a regular member of your family's household staff?"

"No, not exactly. Richard's father owns the catering business. He was one of my father's first clients after we moved to this area. My parents use his company to cater all of their dinner parties."

"The meal was superb. Perhaps I shall call upon them also."

####

Clarisa Hammond's smile reflected the pride and satisfaction she felt as she watched her guests enjoying their meal. Her party was truly a success. The caterers were flawless in their planning and presentation. Not a single incident had occurred to mar the smooth flow of the evening. Her eyes moved evenly from table to table expertly evaluating the degree of comfort the various groupings may or may not be feeling. Her mother, the grand matriarch of the Camden estate, had prepared her well for occasions such as these. How well she remembered looking into that austere countenance while trying to remember the rules of the complex social graces of the wealthy South.

The warm smile faded and a frown of concern appeared as Clarisa's gaze found her daughter Courtney. It had not occurred to her that Courtney would find the Scolari boy so interesting. They seemed to lean toward each other in their conversation. She had harbored the fervent hope that her daughter would one day fall in love with Michael Stanley. He was advantageously seated to Courtney's left but it was obvious to Clarisa that Courtney had not noticed him. Clarisa knew Mario Scolari and his wife. She had liked and respected both of them for many years. She and Clyde had been disappointed when the Scolari's had declined their dinner invitation due to a prior engagement. At first she had been only too glad to accept Mario's suggestion to allow his son Antonio to attend in his place. Clarisa had never met any of his children and since

Mario had indicated that Antonio was going to be taking an active part in the family business this meeting seemed appropriate. The moment she met Antonio however, she knew there was something about him that disturbed her. She should never have seated that boy near Courtney, she silently chastised herself. It had seemed like the best solution to the already perfect seating arrangement.

"Would you all please excuse me, I just want to have a word with my daughter." Clarisa walked between the tables slowly, often stopping to exchange pleasantries with her guests as she made her way to Courtney's table.

"Shane, I see that you and Michele have renewed your acquaintance." Clarisa smiled warmly at her son and the young lady she would love to welcome into the family some day.

"Mom this is great, but I wish you had told me she was in town."

"Oh, don't blame your mother, Shane. It was I who wanted to surprise you. I made Mrs. Hammond promise not to tell you I was planning to be here." Michele's eyes had not left Shane's face as she spoke. "I wanted to show him that I am not that plain little girl with braces anymore." Clarisa smiled to herself as she remembered their childhood friendship. She had thought even then that Shane and Michele would be a perfect couple.

"Wonderful meal, Mrs. Hammond," commented the young man seated on Courtney's left.

"I'm so happy you are enjoin' yourself, Michael. Have you met everyone here? My daughter Courtney...Mr. Scolari..." Clarisa introduced several other guests and briefly mentioned a business or interest of each.

"...and you know, Michael and his father, Arthur Stanley raise the most beautiful thoroughbreds," Clarisa finished.

Courtney knew her mother very well. She understood immediately that Michael Stanley was the intended match. Dutifully, Courtney turned to acknowledge Michael. He was a pleasant looking young man with sun-bronzed skin, but he seemed pale and uninteresting in comparison to Antonio's dramatic dark features and slight Italian accent.

"Attention everyone!" It was Clyde Hammond's voice coming through the microphone. Clarisa abruptly excused herself and hurried back to the table where she had been sitting in order to be on hand for her introduction.

The guests listened with interest as Clyde introduced the new partners and their wives. They applauded with enthusiasm as Clyde introduced and thanked his lovely wife for planning such an impressive meal. The first partner was then asked to say a few words, which he accomplished eloquently. He was rewarded with smiles, nods of approval and finally hearty applause. The second new partner to speak was a rotund man of fifty who sported a receding hairline and thick glasses. The unfortunate gentleman was clearly uncomfortable in the role of public speaker. His face became shiny with sweat as he stumbled over his words. The guests mirroring his discomfort began to fidget and murmur.

A small dance band had set up their instruments and the musicians sat impatiently waiting for the agonizing speechmaking to come to a close. The drummer leaned far to one side and held his empty champagne glass aloft for a passing waiter to fill. The flimsy stool tipped and the man lost his balance. He was horrified to think of the noise that the shattering champagne glass would make as it hit the flagstones but he need not have worried. The sound of crystal breaking was completely lost in the reverberating crash of foot meeting cymbal. Much to the amusement of the guests and the chagrin of the hostess the cymbals toppled from their perch and clattered to the flagstones, rolling and clanging just out of reach of the fumbling hands of the keyboard man and the vocalist. The speaker gave up any further attempts to finish what he had planned to say and simply sat down and dabbed nervously at his damp forehead with a white handkerchief. A chuckling Clyde Hammond announced that as soon as the drummer regained his composure there would be music for dancing until midnight. The grateful audience applauded briefly and almost immediately began to rise from their seats and move about as the uniformed staff worked quickly to clear away the remaining dishes and rearrange some of the tables to accommodate those who wished to dance.

    Antonio rose and offered his arm to Courtney. "Will you walk with me over here by the pool?"

    "I'd love to." Courtney took his arm and they walked slowly to the natural swimming pool. "There is a secluded bench over there by the waterfall. Would you like to go there and talk?" Courtney asked after they had toured the grounds.

    "I'd love to," Antonio responded with a flash of his even white teeth as he smiled.

    That unsettling tingle had begun again as Courtney, the romantic, wondered how it would feel to be kissed by that full sensual mouth. Her fantasy grew as they walked silently. She imagined being held in a tender embrace followed by long searching looks into each others' eyes and then finally...she imagined him lifting her into his arms and then...

    "How positively charming! Beautiful surroundings, beautiful woman, life is perfect," Antonio spoke in Italian and then quickly translated, not realizing that Courtney had spent a great deal of time in Italy with her parents and had learned much of the language.

    The two young people seated themselves on the little bench. The small waterfall served as a soothing background for their conversation. The night was clear and cool. The stars quietly sparkled overhead with a brilliance that Courtney had never noticed before. She felt a warm soft stir deep within. Her heart was opening to the possibilities of love.

Courtney had always dedicated her time to dance classes and her academics but she was not completely unfamiliar with the delightful intimacies that can occur between a man and woman. She knew instinctively that her feelings for Antonio were much more intense than anything she had felt with her first two loves. She remembered Gene Larson, her first intimate partner. She had loved their friendship and when he had left for New York to try out his acting skills she had been desperately lonely. His letters had become shorter and farther apart and finally stopped completely. It took her nearly two years to forget him. Then she met Jason Debrough who was a music major at UCLA. Jason was handsome and popular, too popular she discovered. She learned that in the year they were together he had also chased everyone in the dance department, several girls in the music department and had been methodically working his way through the psychology department. But the greatest humiliation had been his attempts to seduce several of her friends. Thank goodness one of them had finally worked up enough nerve to tell her about it. Courtney shivered with revulsion at the memory.

"Ah! You are cold," frowned Antonio as he quickly began to remove his jacket.

"Oh, no really, I'm fine." If the truth be known she actually felt rather warm as her thoughts once again turned to Antonio.

"If you are sure..." he hesitated as the male vocalist from the orchestra spoke into the microphone inviting the guests to begin dancing.

"Come, perhaps if you dance with me it will warm us

both." Antonio's dark eyes gazed into Courtney's with an intensity that made her heartbeat quicken. She could hardly breathe in anticipation of the moment that he would take her in his arms and their bodies would touch as they began dancing.

Several other couples moved gracefully to the slow romantic music as they approached the area which had been cleared for the dancing. Some of the older guests were already preparing to leave. The Hammonds were not in the habit of hosting parties that continued into the wee hours of the morning. A society columnist, Lea Brown, always referred to their social functions as 'dignified, sumptuous and short'.

Courtney was mostly unaware of the time or the other guests. She knew only that with Antonio's hand pressed firmly against her back, their bodies moved in perfect accord. She felt his warm breath as he spoke softly near her ear. Delightful tingles danced down her spine as his cheek lightly touched hers as he pulled her even closer. Their faces drew closer and his dark eyes revealed his desire. He placed one hand under her chin and gently tilted her face upward as he lowered his head to kiss her. His lips were exquisitely soft as he pressed them to her mouth. The kiss deepened for a moment and then gently, he pulled away. Courtney swallowed as she struggled to maintain her composure. As she opened her eyes she wondered if anyone had ever died of unfulfilled desire.

"Bellissima Signorina. I regret that I must leave. I have an early morning flight." Courtney frowned her disappointment. "No, no. You must not spoil your lovely face with a frown. I will return from Italy in two weeks. May I call you when I return?" He gently smoothed her frown wrinkles with another soft kiss on her forehead. Then he lightly ran his fingers across her lips. Courtney swallowed but, unable to find her voice, she simply smiled and nodded her consent. Antonio smiled with pleasure.

He lifted her hand to his lips but his eyes never left hers. "Until then, ciao," he said as he kissed her hand. He stood looking into her eyes for a moment longer then turned without another word and strode away.

Exhaustion suddenly engulfed Courtney. She was glad that she had planned to spend the weekend with her parents. She caught sight of her mother speaking with the Whitfields. Shane and Michele stood a little apart from each other. Obviously saying good-bye was difficult. As Courtney walked toward the group she noticed the soreness again in her left foot. She decided that soaking in a hot bath would be just the therapy she needed.

"Darling, the Whitfields are going to be in town for another week. They have invited us to join them for dinner tomorrow. Wouldn't you like to join us dear?"

"Thank you, that sounds wonderful, but I don't..."

"Splendid!" Randle Whitfield broke in before Courtney could finish her polite refusal. His face was slightly wine flushed, and Courtney knew that it would be quite impossible to try to refuse his generous offer at the moment. Randle was anxious to show off his young wife. His first wife, Michele's mother had died in a traffic accident shortly after their move to England. Randle had only recently remarried.

"Mother, would you please excuse me. I'm really exhausted."

"Of course Darling, and sleep as late as you like in the morning!" Mrs. Hammond kissed her daughter lightly on the cheek and then turned back to her guests.

It really was wonderful to be at home Courtney thought as she sighed deeply. She filled the large round tub with steaming water and watched as mounds of frothy white bubbles rose quickly on the surface. She sighed again as she eased herself into the hot water and completely submerged her body. Her head lay against the cushioned head rest and she began to release the tension that had held her captive for the past several hours. Absently she started to brush aside a wisp of hair and caught sight of the bruise around her wrist. She held up her other hand and inspected its identical mark. The bruises had turned a dark blue. This was not the first time she had found marks on her body that she could not explain. For as far back as she could remember that phenomena had occurred on a regular basis. Once when she had found bruises on her stomach and thighs her parents had become very upset. They thought that someone had tried to molest her. She had endured thorough medical exams and hours of questions with well-meaning therapists. Even after all of that, little Courtney had not wavered from her story that the bruise-man did it in her sleep. Bruises were not the only injuries that she had found on her body throughout her life. On several occasions she awoke to find a large painful bump on the back of her head. Once there was even blood on her pillow. Her family had again become very concerned and again she had undergone medical and psychological tests. Her parents hired a specially trained nanny to sit with her through the night and another to be with her all day to insure that no one could harm her nor could she harm herself. Courtney squeezed her eyes shut and shook her head vigorously in an effort to remove the unpleasant memories.

    She reached forward to turn on the hot water and she felt the blue topaz move on its chain around her neck. She lifted the sparkling gem in her fingers and held its smooth hard surface against her cheek. She turned off the hot water and lay back against her cushion. Her eyes grew heavy and her thoughts played with fantasies. Perhaps it held the stories of all of the women who had worn it. Could it have traveled to India as an adornment for a queen? Courtney lifted the stone to her forehead as she imagined a dark-skinned woman riding an elephant. In the same moment blue white lightening shot from the stone and into her brain. She gasped in shock. Her body was immobilized as the light intensified. An invisible force held her a virtual prisoner. Images flashed in the strobe light. Her mind struggled to comprehend what she saw. She could feel her physical eyes as they squeezed shut in an effort to blot out the blinding light. The light could not be deterred and seemed to come from inside her head. She stopped fighting and relaxed as she watched the people in the light. It was as if she could see through a porthole of time. She observed people dressed in the garb of the ancients. She saw piercing eyes, gnarled dwarfs, peasants and royalty, wars and peaceful landscapes. She saw men in ships and on horses. Women sitting in covered wagons and children in British sweatshops quickly changed to railroad trains and automobiles. A single masculine face appeared before her. His dark blue eyes were framed by glasses and white teeth flashed as he smiled from under his neatly trimmed brown beard.

"Cort! Cort! Hey! You'll never guess what's on the news!"

In an instant, like the closing of a camera lens, the light narrowed to a pinpoint and then disappeared.

The sound of Shane's voice through the bedroom door was startling. Released from her trance she bolted upright. The blue topaz fell from her forehead and thumped against her chest. The bath water had become cool and most of the bubbles had disappeared. She wondered how long she had been sitting there. It felt as though only a few moments had passed, but she judged from the shriveled white skin of her fingers she had been submerged for quite some time.

"Hey! Cort!" Shane rapped loudly on her door again. "Are you asleep or what? Your light is still on. Wake up! You're on the news. Some guy says you saved his life!"

CHAPTER FOUR

Esther Camden lounged on her mountain of pillows in the antique four-poster Charleston Rice bed. Stacks of photo albums lay near her small slender body. Her eyes closed slowly as she sighed the sigh of one greatly fatigued. Her thin arms hugged a picture frame to her chest. Two large tears escaped from the thinning lashes and made their silent journey down the still beautiful high cheek bones and finally disappeared as they reached her jaw line.

Without opening her eyes Esther groped for the box of tissues which teetered precariously on the edge of the bed. Her long slender fingers found the tissues and deftly plucked one from the box. She dabbed at her neck and cheeks then absently flung the tissue over the side of the bed. The tissue floated down and joined the growing pile on the floor, all obstinately missing the dainty waste basket which remained empty.

Esther's hand groped again for the tissue box. This time as her fingers pulled on the fragile tissue it ripped. The blue eyes opened and the small woman frowned.

"When I was a girl I wouldn't dream of usin' anything but a dainty silk hanky. Oh these horrid little tishoosh." Esther propped herself unsteadily on her right arm. She still hugged the framed picture with her left.

"Here Charles, you just wait here, that's my beautiful boy." Esther tenderly placed the picture of a handsome young man near her on the rumpled lace coverlet as she struggled to pull one whole tissue from the box. After ripping several and tossing many small pieces over the edge of the bed, she managed to pull one out that didn't tear. She blew her nose and the newly soiled tissue joined the others.

"Charles, how could you!" she muttered in an angry whine. "How dare you go off and die like that. It just isn't right for a mother to bury her only son."

Esther edged herself closer to the night stand and reached awkwardly for the empty glass with her left hand. Her right hand disappeared under the mound of pillows. She found what she was searching for and when her hand reappeared it held the neck of a vodka bottle. Her body swayed slightly as she fumbled with the stubborn cap. Suddenly the cap came off and flew out of her grasp. She listened as it rattled its way to the bottom of the wastebasket and landed with a thunk against the hard plastic.

Esther poured the clear liquid into her glass. When the glass was full she held the bottle up and squinted her eyes. Then she put the bottle to her lips and thirstily gulped at the small trickle of vodka that slowly made its way into her mouth.

Satisfied that the bottle was empty she carefully slid it back under her pillows.

"Oh Sharles, if your father had been alive he never would have allowed you to shoshilize with those awful people. Harold would have known what to do." She twisted around to look at the picture.

"How dreffdul...dreadful," she corrected herself, "of you to sully the Camden name." Esther carefully balanced her full glass in one hand and used the other hand for support as she scooted back to her pillows. Her long satin dressing gown got in her way as she struggled to find a comfortable sitting position. Finally she leaned back against the pillows with another long sigh.

"Things would have been so different if you were still alive" she said wistfully as she picked up the picture again.

"Oh Harold," she wailed as her head dropped back heavily on her pillows, "what have I done to this family?" Tears began to stream from her eyes again as she addressed the ceiling. "I tried to be a good mother but I needed your help," she sobbed at the ceiling.

"Clarisha's gone off to that bahbaric place in California. A daughter should be close to her motah to comfort her in her old age." Esther lifted her heavy head and brought the glass to her lips. She took several large swallows.

"Miz Camden!? You awright?" Hattie was knocking loudly on the bedroom door.

"Hattie? Thisis your day off. What are you doin' here?" Esther struggled to enunciate her words clearly as she tried in vain to straighten her disheveled appearance.

"Running after those granchilren made me hungry. I just thought you might like some of my homemade soup." The sturdy black woman pushed open the bedroom door. Her bright brown eyes seemed to assess the disarray of the room and its occupant in one smooth sweep. Without the slightest hesitation she bustled through the door and began to put things in order. In a few moments the picture albums were removed from the bed, the pile of damp tissues disappeared and the covers were straightened. Hattie chattered about her family as if Esther was listening with rapt attention. Hattie knew perfectly well that Esther had probably consumed enough vodka to fell a two hundred-fifty pound man. She knew too that Esther was a great southern lady with impeccable manners. Her good breeding, if nothing else, would prevent her from passing out until Hattie could get some food into her.

The tray of hot food was just outside the door. Hattie had known what to expect on that particular day. After all it happened every year. Esther's husband had died on that day forty-six years ago. Then her son, her favorite child, died under mysterious circumstances...on the same day, eleven years later.

    Hattie settled herself on the edge of the bed and began to feed the steaming soup to Esther."Guess I didn't fool you giving you the day off!?" mumbled Esther between swallows."No ma'am, Miz Camden. I've worked for you for most of my adult life."

    "Hattie, do you think there is truly a...a place called Hell!?" After a few more swallows Esther had looked straight into Hattie's eyes to ask this sincere question.

    Hattie was visibly surprised and sat with the spoon in midair while she considered her answer. In the years following the deaths of the Camden men Hattie had learned what to expect from her employer. Esther rarely consumed alcohol and absolutely never in excess, except on this one day each year.

    Hattie was always given the day off and Esther always spent the day in her room with her vodka bottle. On the first anniversary of the two deaths Hattie, though enjoying her day off, had felt uneasy about Mrs. Camden and had returned in the early evening. She had discovered Esther's limp body on the Aubusson rug. It seems that, unaccustomed to such a large amount of alcohol on an empty stomach, Esther's system had rebelled. She became violently ill. If Hattie hadn't been there to call an ambulance...well she hated to think of what might have happened.

    In the years that followed, Hattie had always returned to the old plantation house early enough to prepare a pot of hearty homemade soup and fried cornbread. Each time she would find Esther in a pitiful besotted state. Each time she would straighten things up and hand-feed the grief-stricken woman and listen to her ramblings until she dropped off to sleep. But never had Esther asked her a question like this one.

Mrs. Camden had attended her church each Sunday for as long as Hattie had known her. But it always seemed that she would treat the Sunday service no differently than her garden club meeting. In fact, as Hattie reached back in her memory, she didn't recall ever hearing a discussion of a religious nature in the Camden household, nor any mention of the hereafter. Hattie suspected that, while the family members had a healthy respect for the minister's words, they felt religious matters should be kept within the structure of the church. At home everyone seemed preoccupied with their busy and diversified here and now. "Well Miz Camden. The preacher says there is."

"I don't give a damn about what that popeyed penguin says, all he knows is how to count the money in the collection plates and quote bible verses. He doesn't know anymore about heaven or hell than I do!" she raged. "Hattie, I know you...see things...and I want to know right now - have you...seen a hell place on the other side?"

In her vehemence Esther sat forward and grabbed Hattie's suspended hand sloshing warm soup out of the spoon. Hattie made no move to wipe up the spill. Instead she looked steadily into Esther's eyes as she spoke slowly and carefully.

"It's true, Miz Camden, the good Lord give me the sight. In all my years I never once saw hell on the other side. I see it only here. Hell is on earth, Miz Camden."

"You may be right Hattie," sighed Esther as she released her grip on Hattie's arm and leaned back against her pillows.

"I'm so tired Hattie." Esther's words sent a chill rippling down the black woman's spine as she dabbed at the spilled soup with a linen napkin from the tray.

"Yes ma'am, you just lay back and close your eyes.

You just get some sleep. You're going to feel better in the morning." Hattie moved with her usual crisp efficiency fluffing pillows and straightening the bed covers until she saw Esther's eyes close. She picked up the tray of empty dishes and whispered good night as she turned off the light.

"Poor woman," Hattie muttered to herself as she made her way down the elegant winding staircase. "She's got money and a mansion but only a broken heart to keep her company.

"I declare, some folks think family honor is such a big Holy thing. They get all mixed up with honor, honor, honor and pride, pride, pride. What they should be thinkin' about is loving and learning to respect each other; love, love, love!" Hattie pushed her way through the swinging door into the large kitchen and sat the tray on the counter near the sink with a resounding thunk.

At the sharp noise, the lump of gray fur that had blended with the shadows on the kitchen counter suddenly sprouted legs as Storm Cat leaped guiltily to his feet and then to the floor."You old cat!" she scolded. "Sneakin' a nap on the counter. You think you own this here kitchen!?" Hattie crossed to the refrigerator and pulled out a can of evaporated milk and poured some in a saucer.

"There, Mr. Storm Cat, who thinks he's king, drink your milk and leave me be. I got some thinkin' and workin' to do." Storm Cat allowed his servant to stroke his fur as he lapped up his saucer of milk.

Hattie straightened the kitchen and made a few preparations for the meals she would cook the following day. Then she fixed a cup of hot pungent tea and settled herself on a stool at the butcher block island in the middle of the kitchen. Storm Cat carefully cleaned his saucer. When every trace of milk had been licked up he sat down and began cleaning his paws with occasional swipes over his head and ears.

"Lordy, April 14th, this is Miss Courtney's birfday, and I just know Miz Camden has let it slip." Hattie shook her head and made clicking noises with her tongue.

"Just once if she could stop wallowin' in her pain, she could have some happiness with her granchilren and her daughter. But no, she's just grievin' and takin' on and feeling guilty. It's the guilt that does it, Storm Cat. It's her guilt that near eat her up, um mm." Hattie shook her head again and took another sip of tea.

Storm Cat finished his bath and walked over to another kitchen stool. After a moment's hesitation he leaped nimbly onto the stool's cushioned seat and settled himself comfortably as if he wanted to listen more closely to Hattie's conversation.

"Course I got the guilts too, Storm Cat. Miz Camden made me promise to say nothin' to nooobody, and a promise is...well it's a big thing with me. I never break a promise to nobody." Storm Cat blinked and yawned. Hattie fidgeted on her stool as the memories of the tragic deaths crowded into her mind. First Harold Camden, once tall and strong, was reduced to a frail wisp by the cancer that roared through his body like a forest fire.

"Was his need for power and money that sprouted that seed of cancer in his body. That was before your time Storm Cat. I think you'd a liked him; for all his stubborn ways, he was a good man and he sure loved his family." Hattie pointed her finger at Storm Cat for emphasis.

"Mr. Charles was another matter. Whooeee what a piece of work that boy. He could charm you with his smile while he stabbed you with a knife... and wild...why only the good Lord knows what all that boy musta done. Miz Camden said his heart give out when he was driving that car *like a bat outta hell.* Well I expect it did with all that wild living and whixsy. I expect he was sampling them drugs too. Now ain't that a shameful waste of life, Mr. Storm?" Storm Cat looked away in disgust.

"I know we all have purposeful meanin' in this crazy old world, even worthless old cats." Hattie reached out and scratched Storm under the chin. The yellow eyes closed and he purred contentedly as he lifted his nose so she could reach every little spot.

"I never have seen the like when you come walkin' out of the storm that night right into my kitchen just as if you had always lived here. You was all wet and starved near to death. Just look at you now! You are one fat cat." Hattie affectionately ran her hand over the soft silky gray fur. "I figure you was a gift from the Lord. You been a good friend Mr. Storm Cat. I've been lonely without my George. Don't get me wrong, I am mighty thankful for my good life. My chilren is grown and married and happy. I love my granchilren and Miz Camden is almost like family after all these years. She pays me very well and give me this nice place to live for long as...I live, I guess." Hattie paused to sip her tea. Storm Cat turned on his side and watched her through heavily lidded eyes.

"Yessir, I'm a happy woman," Hattie continued, "Though I've had some mighty lonely days. But you come along, Storm Cat, and change that!" Hattie fell silent then as she sipped her tea and meandered along some of the memorable paths of her life, stopping to relive the happy ones and merely observing the painful moments. She smiled as she thought of her marriage to George and the birth of their five children. Then her face grew serious and she sighed as she remembered George's death. She wondered about her own death, how nice it would be if it could be as peaceful as George's had been.

Hattie rose from the kitchen stool and decided to have one more cup of tea before going to bed. Her ample figure moved with the efficient grace and quickness of a much younger thinner person.

    The steaming tea and a plate of reheated corn bread enticed Storm Cat to investigate more closely. He leaped up onto the butcher block island and stealthily crept closer to the plate of cornbread for a curious sniff. Hattie's back was turned as she searched in the refrigerator for the butter. She closed the refrigerator door noisily and before she could turn around, Storm leaped back to his own kitchen stool. Merely an innocent bystander, Storm Cat stretched and settled himself in a more comfortable position.

    As she buttered her cornbread, Hattie went over George's death again and again. He had suffered a stroke and was confined to a wheelchair. Bless Mrs. Camden for her kindness. Of course it was good business for her too when she remodeled several of the downstairs old maids' quarters. It was certainly more convenient to have Hattie living in the old plantation house, especially since Clarisa and her husband had gone off to California for three weeks. They had left Shane and Courtney in the care of their grandmother. The healthy active youngsters had worn through the thin patience of the sedate matriarch in short order and it then became Grandma Hattie's great pleasure to watch over the precocious children.

    Hattie sliced a generous pat of butter and spread it on a piece of warm cornbread.

    Storm Cat watched her every move and when the cornbread disappeared into Hattie's full mouth he licked his whiskers as if imagining how good it must taste.

    Hattie washed down the cornbread with another sip of tea and indulged again in her delicious memories.

    It had been such a beautiful day, the day her George died. A warm breeze blew through the branches of the huge old willow trees that grew in abundance on the property. Some of Hattie's own grandchildren had come to visit that day and Shane was outside with them. Hattie could still hear their excited shouts and bursts of laughter as they played on the vast green lawns.

Courtney had gone out to play with the others, but on that day she had returned to Hattie's kitchen and announced that she wanted to sit with George for awhile. This was not unusual, for though Courtney enjoyed being around other children, she was a serious, quiet child. She seemed to enjoy spending time with adults and often spent many hours alone wandering through the gardens. Hattie remembered looking into the little girl's wide blue eyes that morning. She had the odd sensation that hidden in that small young body was a soul as wise and ancient as old Mother Earth herself.

"She always was a special child," muttered Hattie through a mouthful of cornbread. "Why you know, Mr. Storm Cat," Hattie paused to swallow, "she was born with the veil on her face just like me!" Storm Cat had heard this story a hundred times and he closed his eyes in boredom.

Hattie ignored Storm's loss of interest and continued her narrative. "I was baking sugar cookies when I heard my George call me. I remember how strong and cheerful his voice sounded. Mighty strange considering he could hardly speak at all after the stroke."

"Well you can bet I stopped fussin' with those cookies. Yeah, I thought sure a miracle had happened." Hattie swung her graying head from side to side as she chuckled somewhat sadly. "What a sight I saw. Someways I expect it was a miracle. My George was settin' in his wheelchair like always. His head was dropped down like he asleep. Little Miss Courtney settin' on a little stool beside of him holding his hand."

"Why, I thought George call me, Missy, is he awright? I asked her. She never said a word that child, she just kept on holding George's hand. Then she looked up and pointed her finger. Then I saw it too. I saw it with my own eyes, Mr. Storm Cat. I saw the precious light of life go out of my George's body. It went out the top of his head. It looked like a hunnert lightning bugs. Then it moved real slow-like 'til it found a sunbeam that was shining through the window. Little Courtney and I watched it as it followed the sunbeam. Then it was gone just like that." Hattie's voice had trailed off. She brushed at the tears that had begun to trickle down her cheeks. Finally she picked up her empty cup and the dish that had held the cornbread and carried them to the sink. She paused with a frown, and then she seemed to make a decision. She rummaged through several drawers and cupboards until she found the items she sought. She carried them back to the butcher block and began placing them in a pattern with slow deliberate movements. She placed a white candle, a book of matches, a clove of garlic, salt and a tiny bottle half-filled with clear oil side by side. First she put the candle in a small hand-fashioned clay bowl that she had partially filled with water. Then she delicately touched a lighted match to the wick. She walked to the wall switch and pressed it down. The large bright kitchen vanished in the darkness. Hattie waited until her eyes adjusted to the gloom and then moved toward the softly glowing candle.

Hattie listened to the sounds of the old house as she prepared her "holy space." First she sprinkled salt around the candle so that it made a perfect circle. She picked up the clove of garlic and removed the dry skin. Then she arranged four of the peeled cloves inside the circle of salt near the base of the candle in such a way that they formed a square inside the circle of salt.

Hattie smiled to herself as she unscrewed the cap on the bottle of oil. "Yes ma'am, I think it's time the truth comes out. It ain't right all these secrets being kept." She touched one finger to the top of the bottle and turned it with a quick flick of her wrist. When she removed her finger a small drop of the oil glistened on its tip. Slowly she touched the oil to the space between her eyes just above the bridge of her nose. Her nostrils flared as she inhaled slowly. When her lungs were filled to capacity she opened her full lips and let the air out.

"I take in the Holy Light of Truth," she whispered huskily, "and I expel the darkness of lies!" The aging black woman visibly changed as she repeated her ritual again and again. She stretched her arms above her head and her dark skin glowed with an inner light. Her severely coifed hair became the regal headdress of an ancient priestess. She grew taller, more youthful. Her body swayed gently from side to side and the humble dress she wore only moments before became a long cape decorated with bright feathers, sparkling beads and painted designs. A low steady drumbeat rumbled like distant thunder.

Hattie reveled in the exhilaration of her rising power. She had nearly reached her desired peak and she breathed deeply again. "Holy Light of Truth, fill my Being!" she commanded. Distant drums drew closer. Shadowed figures danced and chanted. Old Hattie, the humble housekeeper, faded and Aeonkisha, Holy Priestess of the Ancient Ones, took her place. The kitchen was a mountain top. Storm Cat was an enormous lion. The candle was a ceremonial fire shooting flames far into the dark expanse of sky. A fierce wind whipped the feathered cape and the lion's roar rose above it all.

Aeonkisha spoke in a voice that echoed through the surrounding canyons. She spoke in a language so ancient that no written record of it would ever be found, but Hattie understood it. Hattie knew that she had stood beside that holy woman and had assisted with ceremonies in another time, in another body, in that faraway place. Aeonkisha had been her mother then, her mentor. In this lifetime she had appeared many times to Hattie in dreams and visions. The Priestess helped her to remember the ancient ways and taught Hattie of her power with the stipulation that it must never be abused. The Power should only be used to help people she loved and never for personal gain or to harm anyone. Hattie had always kept her sacred promise to Aeonkisha.

Hattie knew that the burden of carrying so many lies was killing Mrs. Camden and she had grown to love the older woman and her family. Hattie believed from the center of her being that it was time to use her power to help heal the festering wound that kept the people she had come to love separate from each other.

"I command the web of lies to be destroyed!" roared Aeonkisha. "I command the darkness to step aside and bow before the Holy Light of Truth!" The lion roared again and again, the sound reverberating continuously. The chanting reached a fevered pitch. Sweat poured from Hattie's face and she felt herself losing consciousness. The fire exploded, showering the dark forms of the chanters, the priestess, the lion and Hattie with burning sparks. The mountain shook and a jagged fissure tore through the earth splitting the fire in half. The two halves met and formed a whirling fiery funnel that dove into the fissure taking with it all sound and vision. Silence.

Hattie found herself slumped forward on her kitchen stool. She slowly lifted her head and blinked her eyes. Her body felt heavy and old as she gingerly straightened her back. The candle burned low. She leaned heavily on the butcher block counter as she touched her feet to the floor and stood up. She stretched, yawned and glanced at Storm Cat. He shook his head vigorously and looked questioningly at Hattie with his wide yellow eyes.

"Whoooeee, if these walls had ears!" chuckled Hattie to the cat as she looked into the dancing shadows on the kitchen walls. Just then it seemed that Hattie could see the smiling face of her husband, George, and just behind him she saw the swirling cape of Aeonkisha.

"Hee, hee, hee, well maybe they do," giggled Hattie. Storm Cat laid his ears back and hissed at the cape as it swirled near his head. His paw darted out as he attempted to catch one of the feathers, but the vision vanished.

"Come on Mr. Cranky Cat, let's go to bed." Hattie turned on the kitchen light and carefully began to clear away the remains of her ceremony.

Storm Cat trotted out of the kitchen and sat waiting in front of Hattie's bedroom door. Within moments Hattie was snuggled into her warm bed with Storm Cat curled up next to her. Hattie felt good. She knew that the higher powers were at work. She knew she wouldn't have to carry the awful burden of secrecy much longer. She had not felt so peaceful in years. This would be a good night for deep dreamless sleep.

CHAPTER FIVE

Hattie awoke with a start. She had been dreaming. What was it that had startled her so? She couldn't quite remember. Maybe it was Mrs. Camden, but what about her? Hattie rubbed her eyes and looked out of the window. The sky had turned pink as the sun prepared to make its entrance.

Storm Cat jumped off the bed and trotted to the bedroom door with his tail straight up. He stopped at the door and looked back at Hattie meowing urgently.

"Well awright, awright. I'm comin'." Hattie swung her legs off of the edge of the bed and shoved her feet into her well-worn slippers. She snatched up her robe and fumbled into it as she shuffled toward the door.

Storm Cat meowed impatiently as he paced in front of the door.

"Now you just gonna have to make some allowances for my old bones, Mr. King of the Roost. I'm hurrying fast as I can!" Hattie opened the bedroom door and Storm Cat raced toward the kitchen. Hattie hurried behind him muttering about how it wasn't civilized for a person to have to move that fast so early in the morning.

After she let Storm Cat out, Hattie quickly set about making the coffee. She put in an extra scoop thinking that Mrs. Camden would have 'the bad head' and might need a stronger brew than usual. She pushed the button and the coffee maker sighed.

"You gettin' old, too?" She frowned at the machine. "Lord have mercy everybody's getting' old, ain't nobody gettin' younger and I don't want anymore of your sniveling." The first stream of coffee began to gurgle into the glass pot.

"That's better! Now you just keep on keepin' on and you'll live to see another day. Ain't this nice kitchen better than some garbage dump?" The coffee maker dutifully complied and quietly, if somewhat slowly, spewed hot black liquid.

Humming with her rich deep voice, Hattie prepared to put her muffins in the oven. Then she opened the refrigerator and removed the fruit, which she had prepared the night before. She was so busy, in fact, that she failed to see the call light flashing from Mrs. Camden's room. Hattie's eyes had dimmed through the years but the real reason she didn't see it was because Mrs. Camden hadn't used it in years. The only time the lights had ever been used were when guests stayed at the Willows. When guests were there, extra help was hired and everyone expected those lights to flash in the morning.

Mrs. Camden was an early riser, but she never came down that staircase until she was bathed and fully dressed. Hattie could count on hearing Mrs. Camden's footsteps and dignified "Good morning, Hattie," at 8:00 a.m. sharp. The only exception was of course the mornings after her encounter with the vodka bottle. Hattie didn't expect to see her employer until at least 9:00 o'clock or even as late as noon.

Hattie set the automatic timer and hurried off to shower and dress. Sunshine poured through the windows like a spotlight. It was shining on the light board as if to beckon, to alert, but as it is when the sun shines on a car reflector, it is often difficult to ascertain whether the car lights are on or if it is simply a trick of the sun. And so it was that in her rush she actually glanced at the call board but all she saw was a trick of the sun.

Steam billowed from behind the shower curtain as Hattie stepped under the invigorating spray. She burst into song as she lathered her body with soap, "Oh what a beautiful morning, oh what a beautiful ..." Something began to nag her mind. She stopped singing to think. "Was it the dream?" she questioned herself. Esther Camden had been in her dream. Hattie saw her reaching out for help. A chill passed through Hattie despite the hot water. Her eyes opened wide as she considered the possibility that the dream could have been a warning.

Quickly Hattie rinsed herself and shut off the water. She was trying to stay calm as she rationalized that the dream didn't *have* to mean anything. But there was something else. Something wasn't right. What was it? Hattie's mind probed relentlessly but she couldn't quite get it. Within a few moments she had pulled on her clothes and turned to open the door when she noticed the sunlight coming through the small bathroom window. The light hit the mirror and its reflection momentarily blinded her. That was the precise moment she knew what was wrong. The light on the call board had been flashing. She had thought it was the sun.

Hattie's slightly arthritic body sprang forward and she flew to the staircase unmindful of her bare feet and unfastened buttons.

"Miz Camden, Miz Camden!" she called as she huffed up the stairs, "Miz Camden!" Hattie froze in horror at the sight of the crumpled figure on the floor. "Oh, Esther, look what you done! Lord have mercy!" Hattie knelt beside the small form. There was blood on Esther's temple where her head must have struck her bedside table and her leg was twisted in an unnatural position. Her skin was pale and her small hands were icy. Her eyes were closed and there was no response to Hattie's urgent voice.

####

Clarisa Hammond slept fitfully next to her husband, Clyde, in the predawn darkness. She had not slept well since the night of the dinner party two weeks ago. The news media had hounded them for information, interviews, and photographs. It had been a nightmare. Worse than the media were the hundreds of phone calls and letters that had begun to pour in from people who were desperately ill and others who were obviously pranksters. Their quiet well-ordered lives had become chaotic. It reminded Clarisa of the tornadoes she had seen as a child. One minute the sky was filled with ordinary clouds, the next minute a funnel would appear. Sometimes the funnels would dissipate quickly. At other times they would grow powerful enough to touch the earth. The young Clarisa had thought of them as wild animals whose voracious appetites caused them to devour everything in their path. She had fervently prayed every night that this tornado would run its course and that their lives would get back to normal soon. But no matter how hard she tried, she was unable to shake the foreboding that somehow their lives would be changed forever.

####

Being the center of attention after performing as a guest artist with the Royal Ballet of London was a pleasant experience for Courtney last year. Nothing, however, had prepared her for the kind of attention she had been getting for the past two weeks.

Courtney was not sorry that she had been on hand to help Bernie Steinbaum keep his life...but why did he have to say all those things to the press? She was not a "healing angel that could change the world." She was only

Courtney Hammond...adopted daughter of the most wonderful parents on earth. She hated what all of this was doing to her mother and father. They had even argued to the point of shouting at each other one evening. Courtney knew that their argument was only a result of the strain they were under, but she hated the fact that her family was stressed because of her!

The worried young woman tossed and turned in her bed. The digital clock leered at her through the darkness. "Three o'clock," she groaned. Why did time drag so when you can't sleep? Her thoughts continued on their rampage as she thought of the gallant attempt her parents had made to have a birthday party for her that evening. Her father had decided that she should move back home temporarily until things quieted down. He had hired a private security firm to patrol the grounds so that the family could enjoy their small party. Even with all of the precautions an audacious tabloid reporter disguised himself as a security guard and was caught taking pictures through the windows in the den. Courtney's skin crawled at the memory. She flung her head to one side in an effort to fling away the memory of the hated invasion, but she came face to face with the glaring red numbers of the clock informing her that only three minutes had passed since she last looked at it. Burying her head under the pillows she tried again to clear her thoughts and relax enough to fall asleep. She tried some deep breathing, but soon her mind began another scenario.

A reclusive life in the mountains far away from the madness of the cities sounded good. Maybe she could move to the Swiss Alps. She might as well she thought morosely, she couldn't seem to find the one thing that she wanted to do for the rest of her life. By the time she had reached the age of eighteen, she had known that she didn't want to spend the next fifteen years fighting for recognition as a Prima Ballerina. Yes, she knew she was talented, but she wasn't driven! Choreography had its rewards and she had thoroughly enjoyed those classes at the University, but that too wasn't quite right. In a short time she would have her master's degree in psychology. But what was she going to do with it? Why couldn't she be more like Shane? He had always wanted to study law. He wanted to become a judge and maybe even get into politics. Maybe he would be President.... A president with a no account sister, she thought derisively, the wacked-out woman who suffers from ghostly delusions.

A slight movement on the bed made Courtney's heart stop. She sighed with relief when she saw Pavlova, the old white Persian picking her way daintily across the rumpled blankets. The cat meowed a soft greeting and rubbed against Courtney's outstretched hand.

"You can't sleep either?" Courtney whispered. Pavlova made a little sound as she crept close to Courtney's body and curled herself into a ball.

Courtney's mood changed instantly as she listened to Pavlova's purr. She could feel herself begin to relax. Then she remembered Antonio. He had sent her flowers every day since he had been in Italy. Two dozen long stemmed red roses had arrived for her birthday with a note asking her to have dinner with him Sunday evening.

"That is TOMORROW!" she realized. The note said he would call her in the morning. How he had known it was her birthday, she couldn't guess. The thought that he would go to the trouble of sending her all those flowers not to mention finding out about her birthday was the most romantic thing that had ever happened to her.

Courtney finally managed to shove aside her other troubling thoughts and engaged in a happy fantasy of romps through the Italian countryside with her dark-haired dream man. At last she slipped into an exhausted sleep.

####

The minutes that had passed in hour-long intervals leaped forward with a mercurial madness. Clarisa could hardly believe it as she turned to look at the clock. Five o'clock. She had actually been asleep since three. She stretched and listened to the silence. Her heart was beating rapidly and she had an uneasy feeling. Her ears could detect nothing out of the ordinary. She couldn't remember any disturbing dreams. She chided herself for being foolishly fearful. Then out of the corner of her eye, she saw it. The telephone light was blinking. A call was coming in. They had turned off the ringing mechanism on all of the telephones in the house due to the number of annoyance calls that had been coming in. The blinking sequence changed indicating that the answering machine had picked up the call. Clarisa waited for a moment then quietly lifted the receiver. She heard Clyde's voice giving the end of the message, the beep...then...

"Oh No! I hate these machines. Miss Clarisa, I know you all are sleeping out there in California, but I've got to speak with you!"

"Hattie, is that you? What's wrong!? Is it Mother?"

"Whaat Luv, who's on the phone?" Clyde sat up, wide awake as he recognized the alarm in his wife's voice.

"It's Hattie!" she explained nervously. "Something's happened to Mother!

"Go ahead Hattie, tell me what happened."

Clarisa listened quietly as Hattie told her that Mrs. Camden had been rushed to the University Hospital. She had apparently slipped on the little set of steps that she used to get in and out of her large bed. The doctors found two fractures and a possible concussion. She was still unconscious.

"Miss Clarisa, your mama will probably be awright, but...."

"But what Hattie?" Clarisa prompted.

"Well, she is grievin' something awful, Miss Clarisa. I believe your mama needs you real bad!" Hattie blurted out.

"She needs me? But of course Hattie, I'll see if I can get a flight today."

"I'll get your room ready."

Clarisa hung up the telephone. "Hattie says Mother fell and she has some broken bones and a possible concussion. She says the doctors think Mother will be all right, but I need to go to Charleston right away."

Clyde opened his arms and pulled his wife close.

"Would you like me to come with you?" he asked softly as he pressed his lips against her hair.

"Oh, you are such a love for asking, but," she sighed, "I'm sure mother will be all right and I will be too. There is so much happening with Courtney right now I would feel better knowing that you will be here for her."

"Quite right Luv. I'd almost forgotten. I am certain that things will begin to quiet down now. In working with well-known people I've discovered that publicity is a fickle entity. With all of the strange things going on today something else will happen to catch the public interest and they'll be off and running after another story."

"Yes, I know you're right. My real concern is Courtney and how all of this will affect her life. Clyde, I just don't know how to help her. I'm just not equipped...I mean...I don't understand. So many unusual things have happened to her since she was a child. I just kept hoping that it would all go away. But now it has happened again. What should we do?"

"I know, Luv. I don't understand it either." He paused and stroked the white skin of her bare arm.

"You know, as a boy in England, I remember listening to my mum and her friends discussing a woman who was thought to have amazing telepathic powers. There were even stories that she could do miraculous healings."

"Clyde, do you think those stories were true?"

"Well, hard to say, Luv. I never met the woman. Some folks were very frightened of her. Thought she worked for the Devil himself. My guess is she lived a lonely life because of the prejudice aimed at her from so many people."

Clarisa shivered, "You don't suppose there is a Devil that would try to...to...do those things?" She remembered with dread some of the hellfire sermons she had heard as a child in the fundamental church she had attended.

"I can't say that I believe in a Devil or for that matter a God who condemns some people to suffer while giving others a life of ease," he said thoughtfully. "I must say though that a miraculous cure that frees someone from a debilitating disease or snatches them from the clutches of death sounds rather suspiciously like the miracles I've read about in the Bible, don't you think?"

"I just wish there was some way I could understand all this better." Clarisa closed her eyes and reveled in the safety of her husband's warm embrace.

"I've been thinking the same thing, Luv. In fact, I've decided to begin...discreetly of course...making some inquiries. Perhaps I can call England and ask my mother about that woman. Ah!" Clyde sat up straight.

"What, Clyde! What's the matter?"

"You can have a chat with Hattie," he said eagerly.

"Why yes, that's a good idea. It would be good for

Hattie to speak with Courtney as well. They have always had such a closeness." It must be the circumstances surrounding Courtney's birth she supposed.

She and Clyde had just returned from Europe and were staying at the Camden's townhouse in Charleston. Willows, the Camden plantation was undergoing some repairs and the annual spring cleaning. Mrs. Camden had hired a young girl to help Hattie with the additional tasks. The girl had worked for the family in the summer and during the holidays, but Clarisa had never actually met her. She traveled with Clyde on his business trips and they always seemed to be out of town when Tessa was working at Willows.

"Why don't I brew us some coffee? I'm sure you will want to begin your packing early. If you start now, you can be finished by this evening," Clyde grinned and rolled his eyes.

"Oh you horrid Englishman," Clarisa retorted in mock anger. Quickly she snatched up a pillow and threw it at her escaping husband. He was too quick. The pillow flew past him and landed with a soft sound on the thick carpet. Clyde grabbed his robe and hastily exited, glancing warily over his shoulder to avoid getting hit with the second pillow that his wife was preparing to hurl at him.

Clarisa smiled to herself at the thought of her sophisticated husband romping around the bedroom while dodging pillows. One of the things she loved about him was his sense of humor and his ability to make her laugh no matter how serious things might be.

All through her shower, the story of her daughter's birth replayed in her memory. Tessa had been polishing silver in the kitchen. Hattie had gone into Charleston with Mrs. Camden to do some shopping. Painters who had been repainting rooms on the lower floor had left the house and were having their noon meal beside the river. George,

Hattie's husband was faithfully trimming his beloved topiary creations. George was frightfully hard of hearing and had he been as close as the kitchen garden he still might not have heard Tessa's screams.

"God bless that poor child," Clarisa mumbled quietly, "imagine being fifteen, pregnant, unmarried, with no family."

When Hattie and Esther had returned from shopping, Mrs. Camden had gone straight upstairs to rest. It was unusually hot for that time of April.

Hattie went to find George before going in. When she found him, he drove the big Lincoln around to the kitchen entrance and the two of them began to carry the many parcels inside. It was then that they discovered the dying Tessa. Her baby had been born prematurely, perhaps because Tessa was so young. No one seemed to know. The young girl had not been able to reach the wall phone. Judging from the trail of blood, she had dragged herself across the kitchen floor and attempted to pull herself up by grasping the handles of some kitchen drawers. It was there on the kitchen floor that baby Courtney was born. Tessa had managed to pull a towel from one of the lower drawers and had wrapped the baby in it. She must have begun to lose consciousness soon after that. Hattie said that by the time she and George found her she was laying in a pool of her own blood. The poor girl took her last breath in Hattie's arms.

Clarisa had been so lost in her thoughts, she didn't hear her husband's knock. He stood near the dressing table holding a silver tray laden with coffee, croissants, fresh fruit, and a single red rose in a slender bud vase.

"Oh, look at this lovely tray. Why, where did you find such a perfect rose?"

"I must confess, I've cribbed it. I'm quite sure that Courtney will never notice it's missing. I say, we'll have to build another room if Antonio sends her any more flowers," he joked dryly.

"Yes, we surely will," sighed Clarisa absently.

"Well, let's not jump to unnecessary and alarming conclusions, Lissa. It may be nothing more than a short infatuation." Clyde had a way of reading her mind. He knew of Clarisa's dislike for the young Scolari.

"I've already put in a call to the airlines. They should be able to have a flight for you soon. You go and look after your mother and try not to worry about anything else right now."

Clarisa sipped her coffee and began to apply her makeup. At fifty-seven she was often mistaken for a much younger woman. She frowned at her reflection and patted another daub of anti-wrinkle cream into the delicate skin around her dark blue eyes. She hated to see an older woman trying to look younger by wearing too much makeup. The effect was usually a ghastly mask of smears and creases filled with powder that only served to accentuate crow's feet. She finished her toilette and studied her reflection with some measure of satisfaction.

The boar bristle brush coaxed tangles from the soft waves of her auburn hair. She had only begun to put a tint in her hair three years ago she remembered with pride. Until that time very little gray had been visible. She thought of how handsome her husband looked with his thick silver hair. How fortunate men are, she thought ruefully, they simply grow more distinguished with age.

"Mama?"

Clarisa jumped at the sound of the soft feminine voice.

"Oh! Lord! Honey, you startled me!" sighed Clarisa.

"I'm so sorry, Mom, but I did knock," said Courtney apologetically.

"Oh Darling! It's perfectly alright. I suppose I'm more nervous than I realized. Why on earth are you up so early?"

"Well, I thought I heard a noise and I found Dad in the kitchen. He told me about Grandmother," said Courtney frowning with worry.

"Can I do anything to help you Mom? Shall I help you pack?"

"That would be lovely, Dear, if you're up to it. I'd love to have your company!" said Clarisa gladdened at the prospect of her daughter's presence.

Mother and daughter busied themselves choosing enough clothes and accessories which would be appropriate for the situations that Clarisa might encounter. Esther Camden, regardless of her condition, would be incensed if a member of her family appeared in public inappropriately attired.

The two women had nearly finished packing when they heard male voices and a tap on the door.

"May we come in, ladies?"

Clyde pushed open the door and entered the room followed by a tousled Shane.

"You didn't tell me you were leaving for a month," exclaimed Clyde in mock horror as he surveyed the clutter of luggage, shoes and clothes.

Courtney emerged from the enormous walk-in with clothes draped over her arms.

"Dad, you know how Grandmother is, if Mom isn't dressed to the nines, she could have another coronary!"

They all managed to laugh at Courtney's comment. Shane hoisted one of the heavy suitcases from the bed to the floor with an exaggerated grunt. He plopped himself onto the bed and yawned.

"So Mom, you gonna be ok? Do you think Grandmother is going to be ok?"

Clarisa smiled at her sleepy son, her husband and her daughter. How she loved these moments that had become so rare. There were no servants, no guests, just she and her family clustered in the master bedroom suite on a Sunday morning. She remembered the childish giggles of long ago as two children filled with mischief tiptoed into the bedroom and pounced on their sleeping parents.

"I believe so, Dear. You know your grandmother is the personification of dogged determination, not to mention the fact that she hates hospitals. As soon as she finds out where she is she will demand to be released. Oh I do pity the medical staff that's assigned to take care of her!" They all chuckled knowing how it felt to be in the presence of the intimidating Esther Camden. Each was secretly relieved that it was the serene Clarisa who would be confronting the formidable Grand Dame of Charleston.

The ride to the airport was filled with pleasant family chatter. All too soon Clarisa found herself facing the unpleasant task of saying good-by to her loved ones.

"Courtney I want you to be extremely careful until this notoriety dies down."

"I will, Mom. I'll be just fine!"

"I want you to have one of the security guards with you whenever you leave the house and I don't believe you should be moving back to your Santa Monica studio for a while!" Clarisa stated firmly.

"Mom, you are beginning to sound like Grandmother Camden. I've just turned twenty-five and I've been living on my own for quite awhile. I can take care of myself. I really think the worst is over now anyway." Courtney's tone was filled with youthful confidence.

"Dad and I will keep her in line, Mom. We won't let her out of our sight, even when she has dinner with Antonio tonight!" Shane's hazel eyes sparkled with mischief.

"Oh really, Mr. Shane, I thought you and Michelle had a date tonight!?" Courtney retorted, always ready to match wits with her brother.

"Really you two, your mother could be right. It wouldn't hurt for both of you to have a security guard on hand when you leave the house for the next week or so. I insist upon it in fact. I think the worst is over but in these unstable times I think it wise to be cautious. It makes no difference how old you are, your mother and I will always be concerned about your safety." There was no mistaking the finality of their father's statement. Shane and Courtney exchanged knowing glances. Their father had seldom ever had to raise his voice in order to issue a command. When he made the decision to override their desires, it was usually with their well-being in mind. When the order was issued it was always well thought out, utterly fair, and undeniably indisputable. Clarisa smiled with relief. She knew that her husband would see to it that her two headstrong charges would be well taken care of.

Swallowing hard, Clarisa fought back a lump that rose in her throat as she kissed each one good-bye. It was true that both of her children had grown into adulthood but saying good-by to them or their father would never be easy.

After boarding the plane, Clarisa leaned her head back against the seat in the comfortable first-class section and closed her eyes, fervently hoping that no one would take the seat next to her. There were so many things to think about and she didn't feel like trying to make socially acceptable small talk.

The jet engines roared and the hostess announced the impending departure. The plane moved slowly away from the terminal and taxied into position for takeoff. She felt herself relax as the plane leveled out and the engines settled into a monotonous hum. She opened her eyes and rolled her head to the left so she could look out of the window. The sky was clear and blue overhead. A layer of thick white clouds obliterated any view of the earth. There was something miraculous about flying between the clouds and the sky. The droning engines, the endless sky, and the solitude that one sometimes finds in the presence of many strangers was peaceful. Gradually she succumbed to the crushing fatigue that she had held at bay by nothing but her own considerable will. She adjusted her seat to the recline position and closed her eyes.

Esther Camden's determined face appeared in Clarisa's drifting thoughts and with it a pang of fear pierced her tranquil cocoon. *Mother is going to be fine*, she told herself. But the fear persisted. Inhaling deeply and exhaling slowly did not release the twisted knot in her stomach. Taking a new approach she decided to pursue the fear and try to find its source. Her thoughts began to spiral down the dark musty tunnel where all people hide their fearsome demons.

She saw herself as a young girl reading a book in her room, playing the piano, walking by the river, at boarding school...alone. Someone else might have thought it was a lonely time, but in fact she had been happy then. No, the lonely times were sadly, when she had been with her mother. She knew her mother loved her but somehow Clarisa always felt she had fallen far short of Esther's expectations. Esther had made sure that she was beautifully clothed and educated. She was introduced into Charleston's society as a proper debutante. She was displayed and put away like an untouchable doll. Crying and displays of temper were simply not tolerated. "A young lady of good breeding is expected to conduct herself with dignity at all times," her mother scolded. "The

Camdens have descended from royal blood and it is our duty to live our lives accordingly." Clarisa remembered the stern expression on her mother's beautiful face and the knot tightened in her stomach. Clarisa had found her demon. She was not really apprehensive about her mother's recovery, she was afraid of her mother's anger or disapproval!

"Chicken or steak ma'am?" The words of the hostess seemed so out of sync, Clarisa was momentarily stunned.

"We will be serving dinner soon, would you like chicken or steak?" the hostess repeated. Clarisa's stomach felt unstable. "I'll just have some coffee please." Imagine, she thought incredulously, fifty-seven years old and still harboring childhood fears. How could so many years have gone by so quickly? "Fifty-seven is dreadfully old," she thought as she reached for her compact. "Mother must be...," she hesitated as she patted her nose with the powder puff. "Why...I don't know how old Mother is," she realized in surprise.

"I have spent my whole life worrying about what Mother thought of me and I really don't know very much about her!"

"I beg your pardon, did you say something?" the hostess held out a tray which bore Clarisa's coffee.

"No, not really." Clarisa felt herself blushing. "Thank you for the coffee." She had not intended to verbalize her thoughts. She resolved to finish her coffee and then read the book she had found in the airport book store.

The airport was crowded as she emerged from the plane. Her legs were stiff and her ears still hummed with the roar of the jet engines. She was more than a little disoriented. She paused briefly and found the baggage claim sign, then turned to follow the other arriving passengers.

The air was stale and her stomach fluttered with nerves as she struggled to remain composed through the interminable wait for her luggage and the process of signing papers for a rental car.

She sighed with relief when the ordeal was finally over and she pulled out of the parking lot and turned the car toward Charleston.

A scarlet sun rested just above the western horizon as Clarisa guided the rental car into the University Hospital parking lot. She felt tired and disoriented from the change of time zones. As she emerged from the car she smelled the fragrance of blossoming dogwoods and honeysuckles in the humid air. She lifted her face and closed her eyes. The soft southern air was like no other. In that moment she realized how much she had missed the South. She knew now that Charleston would always be a part of her. It was good to be home.

The woman at the information desk smiled warmly at Clarisa. She located Mrs. Camden's room number and gave Clarisa directions. It was so refreshing to hear the almost musical intonation of the Charleston accent again.

Once on the elevator, Clarisa took out her compact and checked her makeup and brushed a strand of hair back into place. Her mother would not approve of a disheveled appearance. The elevator doors slid open on the third floor and she quickly found her mother's room. Anxiety welled up in her again as she hesitated in front of the closed door. Her clammy hands trembled as she attempted to smooth the beige linen skirt and straighten her jacket. She took a deep breath and pushed the door open.

Clarisa stood in uncertain silence as she studied the still figure in the hospital bed. Puzzled, she wondered if she had entered the wrong room. The person in the bed looked so old and pale. An IV tube was attached to one arm and other tubes protruded from her nose.

Willing herself forward, Clarisa took a few steps toward the bed. She stared in disbelief at the woman who had always been so dynamic, so impeccably groomed. How could this pale, faded shadow be the iron-willed woman who had ruled her family, cowered congressmen, and entertained foreign royalty?

"Mother?" Clarisa spoke softly as she leaned against the bed rail.

The pale form stirred at the sound of a familiar voice. Blue-veined eyelids fluttered and struggled to open. She could only see a hazy outline of her daughter leaning over her. Esther closed her eyes with a sigh, wondering where she had put her glasses.

"Where is Hattie? Would you tell her to come help me find my glasses?" Esther rasped thickly.

"Mother, it's me, Clarisa."

"Clarisa? What are you doing in my room? You should be dressing for the ball." Esther's voice had grown firmer.

"What? What do you mean, Mother?"

"The ball! Your debut!" Esther snapped with some vigor although her eyes remained closed.

"Oh, of course," said Clarisa quietly as she realized that her mother was reliving the past."I...only wanted to see how you are feeling."

"Perfectly well, thank you. Now go get dressed before...you embarrass me by being...late." Esther's voice lost some of its sharpness and Clarisa knew by the hesitation between her words that she was drifting off.

"Mother, I love you," whispered Clarisa. But there was no response.

"Well, hello. I didn't know Mrs. Camden had a visitor. It will only take a minute for me to check her IV."

Hastily Clarisa wiped away the tears that trickled down her cheeks. "I'm her daughter, I just got in from California."

The blond woman clad in hospital whites smiled in response.

"Your mother's doctor is right outside at the nurse's station if you'd like to speak with him.""Oh yes, thank you."

"Then I think you should get some rest. Mrs. Camden was just given some pain medication and she probably won't wake up until morning. She will feel more like talking then."

By the time Clarisa got to the nurse's station the doctor had left. She was so exhausted that she was relieved she did not have to discuss her mother's condition with him tonight. Tomorrow she would be more rested and alert, that would be soon enough.

"Hattie? I'm calling from the hospital. Mother has been sedated so I'm leaving for Willows right now." She hung up the phone with a sigh but in spite of the circumstances she felt a warm anticipation as she thought of sitting in the kitchen with Hattie sipping tea and munching on some homemade morsel.

The sun disappeared below the horizon and the sky was darkening as Clarisa drove down the Ashley River Road. By the time she arrived at Willows, winking stars were visible above her.

In true family tradition, the old plantation was ablaze with light in honor of the expected guest. The Camden's of the eighteenth century would have sent servants and grooms to take care of the new arrival's needs. In those times people often traveled by boat on the Ashley River. Clarisa marveled at the beauty of the old plantation and for a moment she imagined how impressed visitors must have been as they came into full view of the graceful home with a light in every window. She drove past the front of the house which faced the river and around to the kitchen entrance. She was sure to find Hattie there.

"Lord have mercy, Miss Clarisa, you are beautiful as ever. You found the fountain of youth, I swear you did!" Clarisa reveled in Hattie's warm embrace.

"Josh!" Hattie called, "Come help with these suitcases!" A tall muscular young man appeared in the doorway.

"This is Josh, he plays basketball." Hattie rattled on extolling the virtues of her talented and handsome grandson as she led Clarisa into the kitchen. Josh easily carried Clarisa's luggage up the staircase, after which he politely said his goodbyes. After a long hot shower Clarisa settled herself on a stool at the kitchen island while Hattie ladled her steaming homemade chowder into two bowls. "Oh Hattie, you don't know how often I longed for a bowl of your soup and a plate of your cornbread," sighed Clarisa.

"Go on now! You got those fancy chefs out in California. I just cook plain and simple, and it sticks to your ribs!" Hattie chuckled obviously pleased with all of the glowing praise as she rose from her stool to refill Clarisa's bowl.

"Oh no Hattie, I can't eat another bite, I'll just have a little more tea, thank you."

Hattie poured their tea and sat down. After a few moments she looked at Clarisa and frowned.

"Now Missy," she said using the childhood appellation that signified a time for absolute truth. "I know it is nearly ten years since...since you an' Miz Camden quarreled. I know Miz Camden can be ornery as all get out, but she loves you and her granchilren, she just is too proud to apologize. The Good Book says 'pride goeth before a fall.'

Your mama has fallen and she needs help!"

"I know Hattie, that's why I'm here. I'm tired of being angry. Maybe now that she needs help...maybe she will accept it, from me."

"Good," said Hattie, satisfied that the mending of torn family ties could begin.

"Awright, now tell me what else has caused those circles under your eyes," said Hattie squinting.

"Nothing ever gets by you, does it Hattie?" Clarisa smiled.

Hattie's laughter bubbled through the large kitchen, warm and hearty just like the soup that simmered in the cast iron pot.

"Not when it come to the folks I love." Hattie raised her eyebrow and waited for Clarisa to speak.

"It's Courtney," sighed Clarisa with her eyes downcast.

For the next two hours Hattie listened as Clarisa recounted the many remarkable events of Courtney's childhood, some of which Hattie herself had been witness to. Except for occasionally nodding or interjecting a comment, she remained silent and allowed Clarisa to empty herself of the long restrained fears and unanswered questions that had piled one upon another creating the suffocating frustration that she now bore.

Finally Clarisa described in great detail the rescue of Bernie Steinbaum and the attack of the news media. Hattie's black eyes opened wider as the story unfolded.

"Lordy, don't that beat all!" Hattie always knew that Courtney was a special child, chosen to perform the Lord's work in ways uniquely her own. But this...bringing someone 'back'! Well of course, Courtney had done that before with little Shane and her puppy, but something that got so much attention on the TV even! "Whoooee!" Hattie breathed, "I knew she was special!" Hattie shook her head slowly and made clicking noises with her tongue and she closed her eyes as if in deep thought. *Lord, help me to know what to say...what to do!* The black woman prayed silently and waited for inspiration. She felt the familiar inner calmness spreading through her body. Her shoulders dropped down as she gave herself over to her higher power. The slow dripping of water from the faucet became synonymous with a drum beat. The whir of the ceiling fan became a chant. She felt the hair on the back of her neck rise as she sensed the presence of a swirling cape. "It has begun," she murmured, "the web of lies is being swept away. One day soon the light of truth is going to shine!" Hattie opened her eyes and smiled, "Don't you worry, everything is going to be just fine."

Clarisa's eyes filled with tears and suddenly all restraints were gone. She sobbed loudly as the salty tears cleansed her spirit.

"I feel a little silly, Hattie. I'm sorry, a woman as old as I am ought not to lose control like this.

"A good cry can be very healing for the troubled soul. Age got nothing to do with it. If more people would just sit down and let out their emotions in a good old cry, there would probably be less ulcers and heart attacks," Hattie crooned with her arms around Clarisa. "I think we have done enough talking for one night. It's time to do some sleepin'. We'll talk some more tomorrow." Tired though she was, sleep eluded Clarisa as she lay in the antique canopy bed. This had been her room as a child. It had been redecorated years ago, but the beautiful furniture still sat exactly as it always had. How many nights had she lain awake in this bed fantasizing about a brilliant future and of course the knight in shining armor? She turned on her side so she could look out of the large bay window at the clear starlit sky. She remembered wishing she had a sister to play with instead of Charles. The thought of her late brother never failed to send a shudder through her body. He was so beautiful to look at, no wonder her mother had refused to believe that he was capable of such demented behavior. She remembered seeing him torture small animals at a very early age. When she tried to tell her mother, Mrs. Camden had flown into a rage and had accused Clarisa of lying. She rubbed her eyes in an effort to blot out the memory. She thought of her father, a tall, handsome Southern gentleman. She remembered the warmth of his hugs and the sparkle of pride that lit up his face whenever he listened to her play the piano. She still felt the pain of loss even after he had been gone for so many years. Now she may lose her mother.

Strange that Mother would choose to remember the night of the debutante ball in her delirium, thought Clarisa as she turned on her back and stared at the lace canopy above her. Swirling skirts, crystal chandeliers, music…she remembered the debutante ball as one of the most magical nights of her life. Without warning the image of her brother's face flashed into her mind. His eyes were bloodshot. His hair was rumpled and his stiff collar was pulled open at the neck. Fear gripped her stomach as unbidden images,…*memories?* pushed to the forefront of her mind. In one horrifying flash she remembered every detail of the events that she had so successfully buried for most of her adult life. She had gone straight up to her room after coming home from the ball. She was standing in front of the mirror unzipping her beautiful white gown. Suddenly her bedroom door had been flung open. It was Charles. He held something in his hand. A bottle. He staggered into her bedroom and slammed the door shut behind him. Clarisa remembered the stale smell of alcohol emanating from him and the cruelty that twisted his handsome face into a grotesque mask.

He had lunged forward grabbing her bare shoulder with one hand and tearing at the front of her dress with the other hand. She remembered trying to scream but Charles clamped his mouth over hers. She remembered the sour taste and the horror as the fragile fabric of her bodice gave way leaving her exposed to brutal grasping hands.

    Bile rose in Clarisa's throat and she hurried to the bathroom. Finally the retching eased and she splashed cold water on her face. "Dear God what is happening to me?" Clarisa addressed her reflection. "That can't be true, can it?" But she knew it was true. She had been sent away to a British boarding school after that night. That 'incident' was never mentioned or referred to in any way. She was simply packed up and sent away.

    "Now is not the time to try to figure all of this out," she admonished her reflection firmly. "I have to pull myself together and try to get some rest." Clarisa lay on her side so she could once again look out of the window. She missed her family. Not even twenty-four hours had passed and already she wanted the comfort of their presence. Just then a shooting star streaked across the sky. Clarisa wistfully remembered the wishes that she had made as a young girl. She basically still wished the same thing, that her real life shining knight and their two children would always remain closely bonded in love and that someday she and her mother would find even a small fraction of understanding before...it was too late. At last Clarisa's eyes closed and she was plunged into a deep healing slumber.

CHAPTER SIX

Clyde Hammond knocked lightly on his daughter's bedroom door.

"Yes?" came Courtney's soft voice.

"Antonio just called from the gate, he'll be here at any moment Luv!"

"I'm ready!" Courtney opened her door. "How do I look?"

"Smashing I must say Princess." Clyde smiled his approval and bent forward to kiss his daughter on the forehead.

"The Pinkerton man is here also. I've instructed him to keep a discreet distance, but he is not to let you out of his sight."

"Dad, do you really think that's necessary?"

"Yes, quite, don't forget I did promise your mother that I would look after you!"

"It's so incredibly embarrassing to have to tell my date that a security guard will be accompanying us to dinner," moaned Courtney.

"I'm sure that if you explain the situation, Antonio will quite understand. Once he learns the whole story he will probably be grateful that we have taken these measures to insure your safety and the safety of anyone who is with you."

"Ugh. I know you mean well, Dad, but we haven't had a single harassment call since Mom left this morning; oh, did she call?"

"Yes she called while you were in the shower. She said your grandmother was heavily sedated and was unable to converse coherently, but the nurse said she would be more alert in the morning. Mom said she was going straightaway to Willows. She'll call us again tomorrow night." The door chimes rang out interrupting the father-daughter tete-a-tete. Courtney's heart fluttered as she opened the door and looked into Antonio's dark eyes. "Belissima!" He exclaimed causing desire to shoot through her as Antonio's gaze swept appreciatively over her body.

"Courtney?" Clyde's voice broke the silent spell between the two young people.

"Oh, uh...won't you come in?" Courtney felt the heat in her cheeks and lowered her eyes in an effort to regain her composure.

"Good evening Mr. Hammond." Antonio stepped into the foyer and extended his hand." Good evening. Please come in. I would like to speak with you for just a moment." Clyde motioned for Antonio and Courtney to precede him to the spacious living room. Behind Antonio's back Courtney frowned sternly at her father giving him a look that said he shouldn't reveal the whole reason for their chaperone. Clyde merely smiled and held up his finger to indicate she had nothing to worry about.

As soon as they were all seated comfortably Clyde cordially inquired about Antonio's trip to Italy. They exchanged a few dryly humorous remarks about the rigors of international travel. Courtney fidgeted. She crossed and uncrossed her legs. Then her left hand sought out the blue topaz that hung from around her neck. The stone had absorbed her body heat and was pleasantly warm. Her nervous fingers slid the pendant back and forth along the gold chain. Though he appeared not to notice, Clyde was keenly aware of his daughter's discomfiture. He noticed too Antonio's frequent glances in Courtney's direction. A small twinge of concern wriggled its way into the pit of his stomach. *Rubbish* he thought. *There is probably not a man alive that will be good enough for my daughter.* Aloud he said, "Antonio, I know that you two are anxious to be off, so allow me to explain briefly why we have found it necessary to hire a Pinkerton man to be your escort this evening."

Courtney watched Antonio's tanned face carefully as her father gave a very plausible explanation regarding the need for a security escort. His expression registered no emotion. She felt some relief that he didn't seem shocked and in fact nodded as if in complete agreement with her father's concern. Still her fingers danced nervously over the topaz. Suddenly a blue lightning bolt hit her eyes obliterating her view of the two men. In the center of the light she saw a woman's hand with something around the wrist. The hand tried to reach upward, but it was tightly secured to a brown post. The vision vanished and was gone as quickly as it had come. Courtney dropped the topaz and put her hand on her forehead. It was the same blue light that had shown her the people from the past that night two weeks ago.

"Oh no!" she mumbled. "Not again, not now. What is wrong with me?"

"What, Dear? Are you all right?"

"Oh yes Dad, I'm fine. Just a little twinge of sinus," Courtney responded. "Excuse me for a moment." Courtney rose and hurried off to her room.

Sinus? Clyde had never heard his daughter mention having a sinus problem.

Courtney fumbled with the clasp on the gold chain. She knew now that the strange visions were somehow connected to the blue topaz. Maybe it was cursed. Then she caught sight of herself in the makeup mirror in her frantic effort to remove the necklace. Suddenly she laughed at her reflection and dropped her arms to her sides. She saw the sparkling beauty of the topaz as it rested benignly against the creamy skin of her chest. She picked up her brush and ran it through her long softly curling auburn hair. Her mouth was dry so she poured a glass of water from the tap. Feeling refreshed she smiled again at her own foolishness. Swiftly she scooped up her small purse and walked briskly back down the hall, determined to think about nothing except the glorious evening ahead.

    The security guard, a tall muscular man in his late thirties, was invited to sit in the front seat with the chauffeur. Antonio and Courtney settled themselves in the spacious passenger seats.

    Courtney had ridden in a limousine many times throughout her life. Her parents had often rented both car and driver when attending formal affairs. Even though she had dated young men from wealthy families, this was the first time a man had ever called for her in a limousine, except for the night of her senior prom.

    "So, do you always travel in a limousine?"

    "Only when I want to impress a goddess." Antonio lifted Courtney's hand to his lips. Goose flesh rose on her arm as she felt the warm softness of his kiss.

    "I am very happy to see you again." His accented English was music to Courtney's ears. She felt she could listen to him forever.

    "I was afraid you would forget who I am while I was in Italy."

    "How could I possibly forget? You sent me flowers every day," she said with a smile. "How did you know it was my birthday on Saturday? The roses were a wonderful surprise."

    "Ah, if I tell you all my secrets I will no longer be

mysterious and you will lose interest, no?" Antonio reached forward and pressed a button. A door slid open revealing a well stocked bar. "Champagne?"

Courtney suppressed the urge to squeal with delight and instead managed to answer with a dignified, "Yes, thank you."

She was almost disappointed when the big black limousine came to a stop in front of a small quaint building on the waterfront. She wanted each moment of this evening to last forever. Antonio was witty, well traveled, and intelligent and she loved every moment with him.

The maitre d' seated them formally at the table Antonio had reserved, overlooking the water."I have taken the liberty to order our meal ahead of time, I hope you do not mind. The chef here is a friend of my family and he has promised to prepare a sumptuous meal for us."

"That sounds wonderful," Courtney smiled.

"Good. Will you please excuse me for a moment?"

In his absence Courtney studied her surroundings. There had been neither bold display on the outside of the building nor any indication that a restaurant was inside. This she knew was a trait common to the most exclusive eating establishments. She saw that the security guard had stationed himself at a small table near the entrance. He sat with his back to the wall, which gave him an unobstructed view of every table in the room as well as those using the front door.

Loud voices rose suddenly above the soft classical background music. In a dark corner on the far side of the room, Courtney could just make out the forms of three men. As she strained to see in the dimly lit room she realized with surprise that one of the men was Antonio. She glanced at the security guard. "What was his name," she thought, "Raeford?" Suddenly she was glad to have his protective presence.

The gray-haired maitre d' and another man hurried over to the group and tried to calm the arguing men. The voices had grown so loud that Courtney could hear a few of the Italian words. Though she didn't understand everything she was sure they were discussing a business contract. After making many trips to Italy with her family, she had learned about the passionate discussions that Italians enjoyed. There was always a lot of arm waving and loud talking whenever business was discussed or for that matter when *anything* was discussed. This knowledge gave her a sense of relief.

A heavyset balding man strode by Courtney's table. He approached the heated group and authoritatively put his hand on the shoulder of one of the men. The man agreeably stepped aside as he apparently recognized the other's authority. The argument ceased immediately. The heavy man spoke in a voice too low for Courtney to hear. Within a few moments the group disbursed. The balding man turned his back on them and looking neither right nor left strode back to his table. As he passed, Courtney glanced over her shoulder and noted that he sat down at a table with several other men. She surveyed the other patrons again and realized that there were no other women there. *How odd that so many businessmen would be in a restaurant like this on a Sunday evening.*

"Please accept my apologies for leaving you alone so long. I went to speak with my friend the chef and on my way back I was detained by some former business associates." Antonio had taken a white monogrammed handkerchief from his pocket and touched it to his upper lip and forehead. He was obviously still somewhat shaken by his experience.

Courtney glanced at Raeford who sat nonchalantly studying the menu. He looked as though he was completely unaware of the little scene that had just taken place.

"Is everything all right?" Courtney felt her heart beating a little too fast.

"But of course Cara Mia! There was just a little misunderstanding. Let us order some wine." Antonio smiled engagingly, but Courtney sensed a subtle change in his mannerism. His voice was a little too loud and he spoke a little too fast. It occurred to her that she was with a stranger. *Just how well did her father know the Scolari family?* She glanced at Raeford again. He was talking to a waiter apparently ordering his meal. She wondered just how much help he would actually be in a crisis.

By the time the entree was served Antonio had regained his composure. Courtney too had relaxed and they once again enjoyed casual pleasantries.

"Have you ever been to the Napa Valley? That is where the Scolari Vineyards are."

"No, I hear that it is lovely though." Courtney had been to San Francisco many times to study with the San Francisco Ballet Company, but she had never had the opportunity to see the wine country.

"Ah, then you must come. In fact, my sister will be married there in two weeks. Please come as my guest and meet my family, they will love you!" Antonio gushed enthusiastically.

"Well, I am very busy with school and exams...but oh I'd love to." The cold fingers of doubt released their grip and Courtney allowed herself to be swept along on the tales of Italian weddings, pastas, and wine.

"You enjoyed your meal, no?" The maitre d' stood near their table while a younger waiter cleared away the dishes.

"Excellent, my compliments to the chef," Antonio answered enthusiastically. Courtney nodded and smiled in agreement.

"Dessert this evening?"

"Oh, no thank you," said Courtney. "But I would like an espresso."

"Very good, and you sir?"

"Courvoisier please."

The maitre d' acknowledged their requests with a little bow and then hurried off to fill the order.

Courtney felt light-headed and she leaned back in her chair with a sigh. She had consumed more wine than she was accustomed to, and she had not slept well the previous night.

"It would appear that the late evening diners are arriving." Antonio muttered through clenched teeth. Puzzled Courtney turned to watch as several couples were being seated at a large round table behind her. Her eyes were drawn to one of the women wearing a floor length black sequined evening gown. Her hair was bleached blond and she wore it swept back in a severe French twist. Large glistening earrings adorned her ears and what could have been a diamond necklace sparkled against the flawless skin of her neck. Her strapless gown, though obviously expensive was cut so low that Courtney wondered how she managed to keep it in place. The woman also wore false eyelashes and bright red lipstick. She walked unsteadily and when the waiter pulled out a chair she very nearly missed the seat. Courtney thought she was beautiful, but the overall look was overdone and somewhat tawdry. Antonio's eyes too were riveted on the dazzling blond as indeed were the eyes of every male in the restaurant. She looked down at the simple lines of her own dress and wondered if Antonio found her dull in comparison to the flashy woman behind her.

"Your espresso, Signorina." Courtney smiled and gratefully sipped the strong espresso. She had begun to feel a little tipsy herself and she hoped that the espresso would help clear her head.

"I'm afraid I've exhausted you."

"Well, I am a little tired, but I have had such a wonderful time."

"Yes, and so have I. But two weeks seems such an eternity, may I see you tomorrow?" Courtney too felt as though the wine country trip was much too far away and she quickly searched her sluggish thoughts to sort out her busy schedule for the coming week.

"I'm sorry, but tomorrow is my heaviest day at school and I am scheduled to teach some ballet classes for Madame Dubois. I won't be finished until quite late." Antonio's face showed his disappointment.

"Then perhaps Tuesday you are free?" he asked as hopeful as a school boy.

"Tuesday I will be taking company class with Madame, but we will be finished at seven o'clock."

"That is perfect. I will call for you at Madame Dubois' at seven." Antonio reached across the table for Courtney's hand. They looked quietly into each other's eyes each happily anticipating their next meeting.

Raucous laughter from the table behind them caused them both to turn. The six people seated there had been drinking heavily. The waiter had already served trays laden with more drinks and now bottles of wine were being opened. Their voices had grown so loud that they could no longer be ignored.

The glittering blond rose unsteadily to her feet. She leaned forward and put her hands on the edge of the table for support as she edged her feet away from her chair. She reached for her full wine glass and tried to stand up straight, but her body swayed as though the floor moved beneath her. She lifted the glass and attempted to propose a toast, but her words were unintelligible, and she burst into a fit of drunken giggles. Realizing that she could not make a speech she simply lifted her glass again and blurted out "Sheers!" Everyone at the table laughed uproariously as if she had said something clever. She brought the glass to her lips and drank deeply tilting her head back.

"I'm sorry that these rude people have interrupted our evening. Shall we go?" Antonio rose from his chair glowering at the now rowdy group behind Courtney.

Before she could respond she saw Antonio's eyes widen and he lunged forward. Courtney whirled in her chair to see what was happening.

Black sequins scratched against her face as the blond woman's body fell backward across Courtney's left shoulder. Pain shot through her neck. Cold liquid splashed in her hair, then trickled down her neck and chest.

Antonio had not been able to prevent the woman from falling and Courtney was pinned under the weight of the larger woman.

"The gallant Tonio to the rescue," the blond mumbled thickly as Antonio grabbed her arm roughly and pulled her to her feet.

"You clumsy bitch!" Antonio's face was dark with rage.

"Tonio, how can you talk that way to your favorite lady?" She pressed her body against Antonio and wrapped her arms around his neck.

"You are not a lady!" Antonio spoke in a guttural rasp. "Now get out of here," he commanded obviously using great willpower to restrain his anger.

"You're only mad because I spilled wine on your little girl." Antonio shoved the woman away. One of the men who had been sitting at the same table stepped forward and grabbed the blond by the arm, "Come on Lilia, let's get out of here!" Lilia's tight dress and stiletto heels forced her to stumble-trot behind the big man in order to keep up with him as he pulled her along. They continued to argue loudly until they disappeared through the front door.

The whole episode had lasted only a few seconds and Courtney had been unable to move or speak. She wondered how Antonio, so elegantly charming, could associate with such a woman. She was also shocked and frightened by the darkness that she saw settle over him. She had never seen anyone who exuded such hatred and the thought made her shudder.

"Courtney, cara mia, I am so deeply sorry. Oh, your beautiful dress. I am afraid it is ruined, but I will replace it for you!" Courtney looked down at the front of her white dress. For an instant it looked as though blood dripped from a gaping wound and she gasped.

"I will buy you ten new dresses," Antonio promised, misunderstanding her reaction. The blood faded and Courtney saw that the front of her dress was only stained with red wine.

A chilly breeze lifted tendrils of Courtney's hair as she waited for the chauffeur to open the car door. Her neck was stiff and sore and she tried to massage it with her hand.

"Something is wrong?" Antonio asked solicitously.

"I'm fine, really, just a little soreness in my neck."

Courtney gratefully settled herself in the warm comfortable interior of the limousine. She thought about the evening and the events of the past two weeks. How strange it all seemed. Her life had always been busy and interesting, according to some people's standards, even unusual considering the excessive amount of traveling she had done with her family, but now, it had become bizarre. She wondered if it was just one of those cycles that Jung talked about. Could it be that life was truly predestined; if something was trying to tell her about her destiny...she shuddered. She didn't want anything to do with the bizarre. She wanted normal, comfortable, productive, the way things had always been for her.

Without consciously knowing why, Courtney turned. Antonio was watching her.

"You are angry with me?"

"How do you know that woman...Lilia?"

"We met at a social function two years ago. She threw herself at me then and when I refused to give her the attention she wanted she decided to make a scene, just like she did tonight. She wants to be a movie star, you see, so whenever she sees anyone connected with the movie industries at a party or at a restaurant, she creates an incident to get their attention.

"You mean at the restaurant tonight she saw a producer or director?"

"Si, yes, exactly. Do you remember the older man, rather heavy, balding? He sat with several other men at the corner table."

Courtney certainly did remember. He was the man who had interrupted the disagreement that Antonio was having with the other two men.

"He's a director?"

"A producer. I'm sure that when Lilia came in she saw him right away. She just used me as a...a prop in her little drama."

Courtney instinctively felt that Antonio's explanation contained some truth, but she sensed that he didn't tell her everything.

"I so wanted our evening to be perfect. I am very sorry for that unpleasant disturbance. I hope that you will still allow me to call for you after your class on Tuesday, yes?"

Courtney smiled and nodded. She did not doubt his sincerity.

"Now turn, turn." Antonio gently held her shoulder and coaxed her to turn her back to him.

"Why, what are you doing?" She chuckled as she allowed herself to be repositioned.

"I am quite an expert with pulled muscles. I was once a very good athlete."

As his warm hands touched her neck, Courtney knew that he had indeed worked with sore muscles. She could feel his sensitive fingers probing for the injury and applying exactly the right amount of pressure. She felt him lift her long hair and arrange it over her right shoulder. Then his hands began again, his touch growing firmer as he worked to loosen the taut muscles.

Courtney allowed her defenses to slip away and her body relaxed. She closed her eyes and soon the pain diminished. The strong hands worked intensely for a few moments, then they slowed and the touch lightened. She felt him lean forward. His warm breath on the bare skin of her neck and his lips on her flesh made her shiver with pleasure.

Slowly Antonio turned her shoulders until she faced him. Deliberately he brought his face close to hers. His kiss was so soft she held her breath so as not to disturb the sensation. A powerful desire passed through her as she willingly participated in a long probing kiss that left her skin hot and her body trembling.

She didn't know how long the limousine had been stopped when she pushed gently at Antonio's shoulders.

"Apparently we have reached your home. I will call for you Tuesday evening. Thank you," he said simply and brushed his lips against hers before signaling the chauffeur to open the door. As Courtney hurried into the house to escape the evening chill she glanced around to see where Raeford had gone. He was nowhere in sight. In fact she couldn't remember seeing him when they left the restaurant. She would try to mention his disappearance to her father. She was sure the security man was being well paid and she thought her father should be told that this man was not dependable.

####

Madame Dubois was a tiny woman, no more than five feet tall. Her dyed black hair was always worn in a severe ballerina's bun. Her large dark brown eyes were framed by false eyelashes and her lips were always painted performance red. No one knew how old she was and guessing was hopeless. Often she would launch into a story of some performing experience that took place twenty-five years ago. But the next time the story was told, she often repeated herself, the very same experience happened forty years ago.

"Eet is a wandafool theeng to be a ballerina," she would say pleasantly while her students groaned and sweated during the grueling classes. Most people knew she wasn't French, but no one really minded that her accent wasn't authentic. The story went that she had not married until the end of her performing career. She met Armand Dubois, a handsome French danseur many years her junior. She fell madly in love with him and showered him with gifts. They were married and went to France for a lengthy honeymoon. By the end of that summer Armand had been able to spend nearly all of her money and, if that was not humiliation enough, it was rumored that he left her for a man.

Broken-hearted and nearly penniless she got a job as artistic director of the Paris Opera Ballet. Slowly her heart healed and her finances were restored. She moved back to the United States and finally settled in southern California. She often said it brought back childhood memories of the French Riviera. But there was a rumor that she was really born in the Bronx.

Everyone suspected that a portion of Madame's mind had never really accepted the callous deception of her young husband. Frequently she would speak of him as though they had never parted. She was always expecting him to call on the weekend.

Despite her eccentricities she was well loved and respected by her students and ballet company members. Somehow she always managed to keep her students smiling and wanting more. Courtney had never taken such difficult classes in her life and yet never loved dancing more anywhere than at Madame Dubois' Academy De Ballet.

The pianist played a dramatic adage that he had composed himself and Courtney stretched her arms and legs into a full penche' arabesque. Though drops of sweat rolled down her face and splashed onto the floor, she felt no fatigue. She loved to feel her superbly conditioned body responding to the fiendishly impossible combination of balance, strength, and flexibility.

A loud groan rose above the music. One of the young men in the line of dancers behind Courtney had been unable to contain his discomfort as the dancers moved from an arabesque to a developpe' en efface'. Their legs were expected to rise effortlessly above their shoulders.

"Silence s'il vous plait!" Madame gave her reprimand in French.

"We must suffer for our art and we must suffer in silence." Madame dropped her voice for dramatic affect. "Your suffering must be your own sacred secret. Zee audience must never know. You must present zee most placid face, zee most serene smile, like thees." The dancers had slowly lowered their legs to the floor and stepped into the final pose of the combination while Madame was speaking. Comically she gritted her teeth with open lips while the cords in her neck stood out. "You see, thees ees how zee dancer smiles." Low laughter rippled through the heavy air of the classroom breaking the palpable tension that had built up in the slow grueling adage combination."Now, we go to allegro!" Madame spoke rapidly, firing out the French names of the steps in the order they must be performed. Courtney listened attentively as she silently rejoiced. She loved the fast complicated beats the best.

"Shall we marque first?" The class responded with nods and affirmative murmurs.

"Bon! Five, six, seven, eight, begin!" The dancers counted the steps to the beat of the sprightly tune being played by the pianist. Some of the dancers moved their hands, simulating the moves their feet would make. Others moved their feet to commit the intricate combination to memory.

"Questions?" Madame paused briefly. "No? Bon! Let us begin. Three groups s'il vous plait."

Courtney stepped into the first group. The pianist played a short introduction and the sweating dancers sprang into the air. To the untrained eye all of the dancers moved with effortless grace, their upper bodies seemingly unaware of their flying feet. But Madame's sharp eyes caught the slightest imperfection in each student and she barked counts and commands over the music. "Keep your shoulders down! Leeft your chin! Extend your arms! Land in feefth position not third!"

All three groups performed the combination several times. Finally Madame said "Merci Beaucoup!" That was what she always said when she was sure that everyone had performed up to their potential. It was also the signal that they would move on to another combination of steps. "Across zee floor s'il vous plait!" The dancers obediently moved to the rear of the studio, knowing that Madame wanted them to do a combination of steps which would move from one corner of the room diagonally to the other corner.

The first series of steps were turns. The dancers were instructed to go one at a time until everyone had executed the combination twice and then they were to repeat the whole thing from the other side of the room.

"S'il vous plait." Madame nodded to the pianist. The serious young man with thick glasses bent over the keyboard. His long nimble fingers played the intro to the Chopin Waltz music that Madame favored. Then without warning, he jumped into a frantic rendition of "The Flight of the Bumblebee." Everyone froze in disbelief.

"What ees zees?" Madame demanded. The music stopped and the pianist turned to face the class. He shrugged and held up his hands with a broad grin. "A little joke?"

The room was silent. It was so uncharacteristic of the serious young man to speak - much less make a joke - that they could hardly understand what had happened. Finally one of the male dancers let out a hardy chuckle. The spell was broken. Everyone laughed including Madame. Soon the Chopin Waltz filled the room and the dancers lightened with humor floated and spun in a relaxed proficiency that kept Madame nodding her approval at every student.

Madame walked over to Courtney as she waited for her last turn across the floor.

"Ma cherie, may I speak weeth you after class?"

"I do have some plans Madame, but I can stay for a few minutes," Courtney panted.

Madame looked at her with one eyebrow raised.

"Ahh. A young man no doubt!" she winked knowingly.

Courtney felt her flushed face turn even redder as she nodded in assent.

"Oo la la!" Madame grinned. "I promees not to keep you for more than a moment."

At last Madame announced the last combination. It was to be a series of large jumps across the floor.

Courtney had held her excitement in check all day. But now in just a few moments she would see Antonio again. It was her turn to execute the jumps. She stretched into the beginning arabesque pose then chasse' tour jete'. She soared into the turning jump landing lightly on one foot. Then she began soutenou turn, tombe' pas de bouree' to gather momentum then her body lifted from the floor into a grande jete'. Her legs stretched into a perfect split as her body hung suspended in the air. Then she struck the last pique' arabesque on pointe holding it as if she never had to come back to earth.

Applause momentarily drowned the music or had the music stopped? Courtney glanced at the piano. Joseph was standing up applauding with the dancers. What on earth possessed that boy today? Finally Courtney realized that the class was applauding her!

"Wandafool cherie. Your feet have surely taken weeng!" Madame smiled with pride. Courtney smiled self-consciously and then made an exaggerated bow. As she rose she blew kisses to her adoring public. Everyone smiled. Out of the corner of her eye Courtney noticed someone standing in the doorway. Her heart leaped when she saw Antonio.

Madame saw him too. For a moment her eyes widened with surprise. Then she turned and looked at Courtney's smiling face.

"Finis. I will see you all tomorrow!" Madame made a short bow to the class and fresh applause broke out as the customary sign of respect and gratitude to the teacher.

Courtney bent to pick up her dance bag. Her heart pounded with excitement as well as exertion.

"Cherie, will you introduce me to your handsome preence," Madame whispered near Courtney's ear.

"Of course, Madame." Courtney smiled.

Antonio took Madame's small hand and brought it to his lips as Courtney made the introduction. Madame was charmed instantly.

"I must speak weeth our beautiful ballerina for a moment and then she will be yours."

"But of course, Madame Dubois."

As Courtney followed Madame into the office near the studio entrance, she wiped her face with the towel she had pulled from her dance bag and then draped it around the back of her neck. "Ah, he is so like Armand," Madame muttered dreamily. "But now cherie, here," Madame handed Courtney an envelope. "I have reeceev thees from zee Charleston Ballet Company in South Carolina. You have family in zee south, no?"

"Yes," said Courtney puzzled.

"They are looking for a new artistic director and several other positions are open as well. They have asked me to help them out but alors I am far too busy and of course there is Armand."

"But, Madame, that is so much responsibility...I really don't know if I'm..."

"Ready?" Madame finished for her. "Ah, my dear, I deed not mean that you should make a decision right now. Please only think about it. Read zee letter when you have time and we will talk later. Now go to your young man and have a wandafool evening."

As Courtney left the office she carelessly stuffed the letter into a zippered pocket and then slung her dance bag over her shoulder. How could she possibly go anywhere now that she had met Antonio?

CHAPTER SEVEN

"I'm sorry I am really a mess. I need to shower before I can go with you. I should have told you to meet me at seven-thirty so you wouldn't have to wait," Courtney apologized.

Antonio looked at her flushed skin and damp hair. Fine auburn wisps curled around her face and soggy tendrils hung down her neck. To him she looked more appealing than any woman he had ever met.

"On the contrary, you look ravishing." His eyes told her that he spoke the truth.

"Why don't you just slip on your jacket and shoes? My penthouse is only a short distance from here. I have a wonderful Jacuzzi that will be just the thing for your tired muscles."

Antonio opened the studio door and Courtney stepped outside. The limousine was nowhere in sight.

Antonio seemed to read her thoughts. "Tonight we are slumming!" he grinned and pointed to a red Ferrari parked at the curb.

A delicious sense of freedom swept through Courtney as Antonio climbed in and started the powerful engine. It had been easy to convince her father that Raeford was no longer needed as a security escort. The annoying phone calls and letters had stopped as suddenly as they had begun. She was planning to move back to her cozy little studio in Santa Monica on the weekend, and to top things off, here she was, getting ready to spend the evening with the most exciting man she had ever met.

The penthouse was spacious and avant-garde.

Courtney sniffed the air.

"I hope you don't mind. I have taken the liberty of preparing something to eat."

"Not at all. I haven't eaten a morsel all day."

"Let me show you to the Jacuzzi and I will put the finishing touches on our meal."

The hot swirling water wrapped Courtney in warmth and contentment as she eased herself into the huge round tub. She reached for the slender stemmed glass of wine that Antonio had poured for her and took a sip. She closed her eyes and savored the exquisite moment.

All too soon the timer stopped the Jacuzzi pump. Antonio had warned her that staying in too long could make her dizzy. She stood up slowly and reached for the shower control. The bath water drained away and the shower sprayed into the center of the tub. She had the strangest feeling that there should be white robed attendants holding large towels for her to step into. She knew of course that there were no attendants and when she finished her shower she slipped into the thick robe that Antonio had left for her.

"Have you finished your bath?" Antonio tapped discreetly on the closed door.

"Yes. Come in, it was wonderful."

"Good. Now come with me. Here is the surprise I told you about."

Antonio opened a door which revealed an adjoining guest bedroom. The room was spacious and sparsely furnished. Nothing was out of place and yet there were dozens of boxes stacked on the bed.

"It's a lovely room." Courtney frowned slightly in an effort to see what Antonio was trying to show her.

Antonio laughed at her charming naïveté and took her hand.

"Do you not remember my promise to you?"

"What promise?"

"I said that I would buy you ten new dresses to replace the one that was ruined Sunday evening." Courtney was speechless.

"Come, come open them."

"But I really can't, I mean it wasn't necessary."

"Oh, but it was. I always keep my promise. Here, try this one on. There is lingerie in those boxes and shoes here. Why don't you get dressed and after dinner you can look at the rest." Antonio pulled out a soft apricot silk sheath and draped it over the top of the stack of large boxes. Then he took the lid off of one of the shoe boxes and gestured toward the boxes of lingerie as he talked.

"Don't take too long. Our scampi is almost ready."

To her delight everything fit perfectly and soon Courtney was seated at the dining room table across from Antonio. Candles flickered from their many locations around the room and soft music played in the background.

"How perfect. Everything is just perfect. Thank you." Courtney smiled into Antonio's dark eyes.

"But everything must be perfect when entertaining a goddess." Antonio lifted his wine glass in a silent salute. "Now try your scampi and tell me how you like it."

The candles burned low as the two young people finished their meal and sat in a comfortable silence while they sipped their wine. Finally, Antonio stood up and walked over to Courtney.

"May I have the pleasure of this dance?"

Courtney smiled and extended her hand. He pulled

her gently up. As their bodies touched she trembled slightly. Heat seemed to radiate from their close proximity until Courtney could hardly breathe.

Antonio stopped moving his feet. He freed his left hand from hers and placed it on her smooth cheek. Then he lowered his parted lips to hers. The kiss increased in its intensity as he slid his hand down to her neck and then under her long hair.

Courtney felt a passion unleashed within her body like nothing she had ever experienced before.

"I want you Cara Mia," murmured Antonio as his lips found her ear and then traveled softly down her neck. He drew back slightly and sought her answer with his eyes. Not trusting her voice Courtney merely nodded her head and smiled. He kissed her again and then turned to blow out the candles on the table.

Courtney watched him as he moved round the room extinguishing the candles. Her heart pounded so hard that she felt the fabric of her dress vibrating from its force. Her skin felt hot, but her hands were cold. The blue topaz grew heavy around her neck. She had grown so accustomed to it that she had hardly noticed its presence...until now.

This would not be Courtney's first experience in the arms of a lover, but it was somehow different. Antonio was different. He was not a college student, but a well-traveled experienced man. She sensed a power about him unlike the other young men she had known. It thrilled her and yet was it fear that she felt? She took a deep breath in an effort to relax and slow the pace of her runaway heart.

At last Antonio stood before her with his hand outstretched. She placed her cold nervous hand into his warm firm grasp.

"You are so beautiful," he said with longing. "Do I move too quickly?" perceptively sensing her uneasiness.

"Uh, no. It's just that I've been so busy with school and my dancing for awhile ..." Courtney's voice trailed off. She didn't know how to tell him that she had not dated anyone for a long time. She felt like an awkward child next to him and she was afraid that he would think her too immature. She needn't have worried. It was the combination of her charming innocence and sensual beauty that he found irresistible.

"Come, we will sit by the fireplace and sip some cognac." Antonio led Courtney through the living room and into his spacious bedroom. He motioned for her to sit on the white fur rug in front of the fireplace while he bent to turn up the gas flame.

"I realize a gas fireplace isn't quite as nice as a real one but the building code here forbids anything else."

"Well, I think it's wonderful." Courtney smiled feeling more relaxed.

Antonio poured their cognac then settled himself comfortably near Courtney on the white rug. Skillfully Antonio directed the conversation to Courtney's interests. He asked about her course of study at UCLA, her dancing and her family. They shared their travel experiences in Europe and joked about missed flights, lost luggage, and reservation mishaps. Several times Antonio got up to refill his glass, but Courtney hardly noticed. She was having a wonderful time.

Antonio drained his glass once again, but instead of getting up to refill it he set it on the smooth black and white marble hearth. He took Courtney's glass from her and set it near his. Without a word he drew her close and kissed her gently. His hands moved to her shoulders and easily slipped the soft fabric down revealing the smooth skin of her right shoulder. He bent to kiss her neck softly and she felt his warm tongue brush across her bare skin. Then he lifted his head and kissed her again, his mouth covering hers entirely.

Expertly Antonio's hands found the zipper of her dress and Courtney felt the apricot silk slide off her shoulders as he pulled the zipper down. She freed her arms from her dress and slipped out of it completely, revealing the ivory satin teddy and matching panties that she wore underneath. Antonio watched her movements admiring the provocative curves of her slim young body under the satin fabric. He could restrain his desire no longer. He must have her and explore her splendid body and he must taste its fresh sweetness. She would belong only to him.

Courtney moaned softly as his hands moved over her body, deliberately arousing her desire to a dizzying peak. She was unaware of the process of disrobing, she knew only that their naked bodies lay pressed together and she was lost in his kiss.

"It is for me to give you pleasure. Later will be for me, "he murmured as he pinned both her slender arms against the fur rug. With one hand and his mouth he continued to probe and kiss until Courtney felt she would scream from sheer ecstasy. Just when she was certain she would go mad from the pleasure she felt the convulsive release of her passion. Antonio too sighed and groaned as his body gave in to its terrible wonderful need.

The lovers lay in exhausted satisfied silence. Courtney could tell by Antonio's regular breathing that he had already succumbed to fatigue. Quietly she sat up and looked around for a blanket. She went to the king size bed and pulled at the black and white satin comforter. She dragged it to the white rug and tenderly covered Antonio's sleeping form. Then she lay next to him and pulled the cover over herself. It had been a long day. She closed her eyes and almost immediately fell asleep.

A distant roar startled her. She struggled to see where she was, but it was too dark. A male voice was speaking, but the roar made it impossible to understand the words. She strained her senses, reaching out to clear away the interference. The roar faded and the voice grew more distinct as she heard it call her name. Then the roar blotted out the rest. She took a deep breath and readied herself to fight her way to the voice. Her nostrils flared as she caught the scent of the sea. That was it! The roar was the waves. But why was she at the beach in the darkness? Two eyes opened in front of her in such close proximity to her face that they almost seemed to surround her. She drew back. With surprise she recognized the face of Bernie Steinbaum, the man she had rescued that day on the beach.

"What are you doing here?" She tried to ask the question and although he seemed to understand her she couldn't hear the sound of her own voice.

Bernie's mouth moved as if speaking, but the words were strangely out of sync with the motion of his lips like a foreign film that has been dubbed in English.

"You must accept your destiny. The time of decision is now. Your gift is needed. You must pass the test. Find her. Find her. Find her now, before it's too late." The words echoed over and over. Hair stood up on the back of Courtney's neck. Goose flesh rose on her arms. Why did he demand these things of her? She wanted those disturbing echoing words to stop.

"STOP IT!" she cried out with all of her will, but the words still echoed. She squeezed her eyes shut inviting the darkness to hide her from those piercing eyes.

The echoing voice faded and the roaring softened into

another sound. A soft cool wind blew across Courtney's face and lifted her hair.

"You are a special child." Courtney was relieved to find herself looking into the smiling face of her beloved Hattie.

"Hattie, I'm so glad to see you! Please tell me what is happening!" Courtney's dream lips moved heavily. Her words had a maddening way of coming from inside her head.

"It will be all right baby. It's just that...the good Lord has something in mind for you. He has asked you to do something for Him."

"I don't understand," Courtney's dream self wailed. "Why should he pick me? What am I supposed to do?" She was angry now. Why should she stop her life to pursue a quest that was dictated by a God she couldn't even see?

"Silence!" Hattie's face dissolved and in her place stood a tall lean black woman. Her long cape rippled in the suddenly fierce wind. A huge lion with glowing golden eyes stood calmly nearby.

"It is your destiny. You must rise up to meet it. The time is now. You must assist in destroying the web of lies. When this task is complete, then your true work will begin. There are many who need you and the gifts you possess."

"No! No! This is crazy, it's just a crazy dream...I'm dreaming that's all...this is just nonsense. I want out. Let me out. Wake up! I just need to wake up."

"It is your destiny. You cannot escape it." The woman's voice echoed.

Courtney squeezed her eyes shut. Laboriously she turned and tried to move away. Her leaden limbs responded to her panicky need to flee with agonizingly slow movements. It was as though some unseen force held her captive.

"You must proceed with your eyes open." Courtney's eyes flew open on their own volition. "Now go!" the voice commanded. "Meet your challenge without fear. I, Aeonkisha, stand by your side!" The lion's jaws opened. His mighty roar carried with it an undeniable power and Courtney was catapulted forward into a dark silent void. She rested, floating in the silence. "I must be dreaming," she told herself. "But how do I wake up?"

A glimmering pinpoint of light appeared in the darkness. "That must be it!" Excitedly she moved toward the light and it grew steadily brighter. "If I can just get to the light I'll wake up!" She stepped out of the darkness into a white room. The tile floor felt cold and solid under her bare feet. Relief flooded through her tense body as she blinked in the bright light. "I can feel the floor, I know I'm awake..." she stopped abruptly as she realized she was not at home. She was in that place again. That hospital. No! She must have gone the wrong way. She tried to find the opening that she had just come through, but the wall was solid.

Courtney whirled around looking for an escape. Was this what the vision wanted? Was she to become ill? She could see her own inert body on the hospital bed. Her arms were secured with straps to the metal bars on each side of the bed.

"Is this my great destiny?" she asked the sleeping girl. Courtney moved nearer to the bed in fascinated horror.

"Is this what is going to happen to me?" she whispered. She looked down at the thin body and wild oily hair. She reached out to brush the matted strands away from the pale face, her own face. She was so absorbed she did not hear the footsteps approaching. As Courtney's hand touched the sleeping girl a terrible buzzing stabbed *through her brain. Her body shook uncontrollably. Something lifted her and sucked her downward. Silence.*

Panting heavily, Courtney opened her eyes. A ceiling. She was lying in bed looking at the ceiling. "Oh, thank God, I'm awake in my own bed," she cried, but even as she spoke she knew it wasn't true. Instead of her own soft voice she heard guttural gibberish. She jerked herself forward in an effort to sit up. But she could only raise herself a few inches. She screamed as she realized she was now inside the body that only seconds before she had gazed down upon.

The footsteps stopped. The door banged open. A large man wearing a white jacket leered at her from under heavy black eyebrows.

"Oh, yer awake and waitin' on me, huh? You liked it so much last time you wanna be wide awake this time, huh?"

Courtney struggled furiously to free her hands. She tried to tell him he had no right to come near her but the only sounds she could make were squawking gibberish.

The man closed the door. He turned and peered through the small window, then faced Courtney. She continued to struggle vainly. In two strides he was at her bedside and his pants were already sliding to his knees. He pulled back the rumpled sheet exposing her writhing body. She felt his powerful hands forcing her legs apart.

"No!" her mind shrieked, "Somebody help meeee, Aeonkisha!" She didn't know why she said it, or thought it, but the name of the vision woman rose easily to her consciousness and settled there. It aroused an inner strength. She said it again. Then she chanted it over and over as she kicked and fought against her depraved attacker.

Courtney heard the rip of fabric and she knew that the flimsy hospital gown was gone. "Aeonkisha, Aeonkisha,

Aeonkisha." Her mind held the image of the regal black woman. A burning energy began to surge through Courtney's body. She felt powerful. The big man began to press himself into her. She smelled the sour liquor on his breath as he panted into her face. She stared into his bloodshot eyes. A blue lightning bolt shot through her. Courtney's hands magically lifted out of their restraints. With every ounce of strength she possessed, she shoved hard against the man's shoulders. She saw his eyes open wide in disbelief as he was thrown back.

Courtney sprang up from the bed. Her feet touched the floor as the man's body smashed against the door several feet away. She had no idea how she had summoned the strength to push him that hard.

"You bitch!" the man growled as he began to scramble to his feet, "I'll teach you how to play rough!"

Before Courtney had a chance to react she saw his flushed face grow pale. His mouth dropped open. She turned to look behind her. Her other body lay unmoving on the bed. Her hands were still bound with straps. She saw the torn gown in a heap on the floor. Both of her bodies were nude and bruised.

A familiar roar filled the white room. A flash of amber gold fur... The lion stood menacingly between the man and the two Courtneys. One enormous paw flashed out and the man's white shirt was in shreds. Blood oozed from the scratches. The lion took a step forward.

"Agh, ah, ah, agh!" The man croaked as he fumbled for the door handle. By this time his white trousers were tangled around his feet making a smooth escape impossible.

A swirling cape brushed Courtney's arm. "Face the fruit of your evil works." The black woman pointed at the stumbling retreating man, then she turned to face Courtney. As their eyes met she felt herself pulled *backward and up.*

"You have passed your first trial. Well done."

The black woman looked less stern. The force continued to pull her higher. She looked down at her dream body. The eyes of her other self were open and for a moment their eyes locked. Then the room vanished.

#

Courtney realized that she was looking into the dancing flames of the fireplace. Her head throbbed painfully. Her body felt cold and she reached for the comforter. "I'm sitting up," she whispered with surprise. "How could I have been asleep sitting up?" Bile rose in her throat and she knew she would need to find the bathroom quickly.

She splashed cold water on her face after the violent retching passed. Her temples throbbed painfully and she pressed her fingers hard against them. "There must be some aspirin here somewhere," she moaned. After a brief search she found some. She took a large gulp of cool tap water and finally managed to swallow three of the small white pills.

Antonio was still in a deep sleep when she returned to the bedroom. She eased herself down beside him. He didn't stir. She closed her eyes and prayed that the pounding in her head would stop soon. With a shiver she remembered the dream. "Guess I better be careful about how much I drink in the future," she muttered wryly. Her headache eased and her breathing slowed as she drifted into sleep. The room was quiet except for the faint sound of the gas fire, the rustling of a cape and the swish of a tufted lion's tail.

CHAPTER EIGHT

Courtney's eyes fluttered open as she felt Antonio's soft kiss on her lips.

"Awaken my sleepy goddess," he murmured near her ear. "Would you like some French roast coffee?"

"Mmm. That sounds wonderful," Courtney smiled sleepily. Antonio was already dressed, she noted as she watched him walk briskly from the room. He returned momentarily carrying two steaming mugs.

"I'm sorry but I must dash off for a business meeting. You are welcome to stay as long as you like. I should be finished by noon. Perhaps we could have lunch."

"That would be nice, but I have a class this afternoon."

"Ah, yes of course." Courtney was secretly pleased to see the genuine disappointment on his face. For a split second she toyed with the idea of giving up her classes, her degree, and her dancing. In fact at that moment she didn't care if she ever went out into the world again. It would be so lovely to stay in the penthouse with this beautiful sensual man forever.

"May I see you tonight?"

"Yes," Courtney said simply as she mentally rearranged her busy schedule. "I will be at my parents' house at about seven-thirty."

"Good. I will call for you there. Goodson, my chauffeur will take you to your car when you are ready to leave." Antonio leaned forward and kissed her gently.

"Perhaps you would enjoy the symphony tonight?"

Antonio asked as he stood up.

"Oh, yes. I would love it." Antonio smiled at her delight. He held out his hand and when she placed her hand in his, he pulled her to her feet. The satin comforter slid to the floor and the hot coffee sloshed dangerously near the rim of the cup as she moved. But Courtney hardly noticed as Antonio intimately caressed her warm soft skin. She was breathless when he pulled away from her.

"Until tonight," he whispered against her mouth. Courtney swallowed and smiled her answer.

Antonio straightened and brought one of Courtney's hands to his lips.

"Oh, disaster Cara Mia. What have I done to your tender skin?"

Courtney saw the bruises on her wrist. They were the same as before. *Her dream self strapped to the bed.*

"Oh, I'm sorry, I did not realize I was so rough with you."

"No, no really you weren't." *No not again! Why is this happening?* "I...I think my wrists have...uh, poor circulation. It's nothing really. I'm fine."

"Well then if you are sure, I really must go. I will see you tonight." Antonio kissed her again then strode from the room.

As Courtney showered she tried to sort through the strange events of her dream and the reappearance of the bruises on her wrist. But her many questions remained unanswered.

"I am so glad that I always carry an extra pair of pants in my dance bag," she told herself approvingly. She thought of the faded jeans like an old friend. After slipping an equally aged gray sweatshirt over her head she felt more relaxed. She picked up a fluffy bath towel and began to dry her hair as she walked back into the bedroom.

The telephone was ringing as Courtney entered the room. She heard Antonio's recorded message then a woman's voice.

"Tonio, if you are there pick up the phone. Tonio, answer me!" The exasperated woman finally hung up. Her voice sounded familiar.

Courtney stopped drying her hair. *It was the woman in the restaurant, Lilia. The woman who spilled the drink.* The incident replayed in Courtney's mind and she gasped as she remembered the vision of the gaping chest wound which had been brought on by the spilled wine. She shivered. Suddenly she wanted to get out of the penthouse and into her own world. She grabbed up her dance bag in one hand and her shoes in the other and hurried out the door. She trotted right into the large uniformed chauffeur, startling both of them.

"Miss Hammond? Are you okay?"

"Oh, yes I am fine thank you. I'm sorry, I didn't see you. I need to get to class, I was hurrying," Courtney babbled in embarrassed confusion.

"Mr. Scolari has instructed me to take you where ever you wish to go."

"That is very kind of him. I really just need to get to my car. I left it at the studio." "Very well then, please allow me to drive you there."

In the dim light of the subterranean parking garage Courtney noticed a tall man walking briskly in the opposite direction. The chauffeur opened the door of the limousine and as she stepped inside, she realized that he reminded her of Raeford, the Pinkerton man.

By the time Courtney arrived at her parents' home that evening she had managed to push aside all of the troubling memories about her dream. She was also determined not to feel jealous of the woman who had called Antonio. After all he is an eligible bachelor, and a gorgeous man. "He probably has lots of women calling him," she told herself, "but it is me he wants to be with, at least right now."

"Hello Luv." Clyde Hammond bent to kiss his daughter's forehead. "Spoke with your mum!" he said brightly.

"How is she? How is grandmother Camden?"

"Dame Camden will be released from the hospital in a few days. She is mending nicely. Your mother will have her work cut out for her I expect. She plans to stay on at Willows for another fortnight."

"Yes, I can imagine," Courtney chuckled. "I don't remember Grandmother Camden ever being ill. She is accustomed to being in control at all times. Oh poor Mom!" She rolled her eyes and sighed dramatically.

At the sight of his daughter's antics Clyde threw back his head and laughed heartily."By the by, Maria told me that Mr. Scolari's chauffeur was here early this afternoon. He brought in dozens of parcels for you. Seems the young man must be quite smitten...wouldn't you say?" Clyde gave his daughter a sly sidelong glance.

"Well, uh, when we were having dinner Sunday a woman spilled some wine on me..."

"Yes Luv, I remember, you told me," Clyde broke in, amused at his blushing daughter.

"Well, anyway, he insisted on replacing the dress that was ruined," Courtney finished uncomfortably.

"It would appear that he is bent on replacing your entire wardrobe," smiled Clyde.

"Oh Daddy. Now he is going to pick me up at seven-thirty, please behave yourself." Courtney felt only slightly defensive. Her father had never said anything to embarrass her in the presence of her boyfriends.

"Where will you be off to this evening?"

"We are going to the symphony."

"Mm...lovely. Your mother mentioned that she was disappointed that she would be unable to attend this one. Apparently Yitzhak Pearlman is to be featured tonight."

"Oh, Oh yes. I am really looking forward to the performance." Her cheeks no longer burned and she thought she was behaving in a dignified manner.

"I'll wager you didn't know or care who the featured performer is," retorted Clyde with a knowing twinkle in his eye. "Hungry, Luv? Maria has prepared a delicious crab salad for us."

"Famished." Courtney knew better than to respond to her father's comment. She was no match for his razor sharp wit on this particular subject. After all what could she say? Clyde's observation was absolutely correct. She didn't know or care where she and Antonio were going, as long as they were going somewhere...together.

Father and daughter enjoyed their meal and lighthearted conversation. Inwardly Clyde Hammond was uneasy. He had wisely refrained from verbalizing his growing concern to his wife and daughter. He knew himself to be a peaceful sort, but if Scolari or any other man did anything to harm his daughter...well...he was certain that he would be capable of murder. He watched his daughter's gestures and her beautiful expressive face...the way little wisps of hair curled at her temples. Yes, indeed, if any harm ever came to her or any member of his family he would be capable of murder.

"So, how are things going with the new partners?"

"Extremely well. In fact, so well I've decided to have a

bit of a holiday next week." "You are?" Courtney was incredulous. Her parents had always taken vacations but only after meticulous planning months in advance. Her father always said that handling a busy law practice was like trying to ride a wild horse. You could predict a rough ride but not where you would end up.

"Yes Twink, your old dad is slowing down. I plan to relax more than I have been."

"That is hard to imagine Dad. Are you joking with me? You aren't ill are you?"

"Oh, I didn't mean to alarm you. I've never felt better, but I'm not a spring chicken anymore. I just thought it would be nice to go see your mother and give her some moral support. Maybe I'll have a go at some of those golf courses in Charleston."

Then Courtney understood. Her parents had never been able to remain apart for more than a few days at a time.

"I'm sure Mom would love it. I bet she is just as lonely as you are Dad."

"Blatant, am I?"

"Blatant," nodded Courtney. Her father feigned an expression of defeat and they both chuckled.

"Actually I'm planning a short trip also. Antonio has invited me to his sister's wedding next weekend."

"Mmh," Clyde mumbled with his mouth full of orange sorbet.

"You and Mom have been to the Scolari Vineyards haven't you?"

"Yes, it's a spectacular place. The Scolaris spare no expense to create lavish parties. They are a bit extravagant for my taste but, I'm sure you will enjoy yourself immensely. You are flying into San Francisco and, uh, driving in from there?"

Courtney wondered why her father seemed so uneasy. "Actually, Antonio will be driving us. He wants to go into the city on Friday evening. His family has a townhouse there. Then we will go to the wedding on Saturday. We won't be back until Sunday night.

"Mmmh. You won't be staying at the Scolari estate?"

"No. Antonio said it would be a little frantic there with all of the relatives coming in from Italy, as well as from other states."

"Pity." Clyde frowned.

"Dad, now you know I'm an adult and I'm quite capable of handling myself and besides Antonio is a wonderful person. You have nothing to worry about!"

Clyde managed a smile that he hoped would mask the fear that gripped his heart.

"It's getting late. Antonio will be here in twenty minutes!" Courtney jumped up and hurried from the room. Her father sighed heavily as he sat unmoving in the now silent kitchen. He thought of his beautiful wife, Clarisa. "They both seem to possess a special light that fills every room they walk into," he murmured. "When they leave, the light goes with them. So odd that an adopted child should be so like other members of the family," he mused.

The next few days passed quickly for Courtney. She and Antonio were together every night. He called her several times throughout the day...every day. Courtney had never been happier in her life. She loved the formal evenings and late afternoon picnics. She delighted in their conversation and yet she was comfortable in their silence. The passion she felt during their intimate moments surpassed anything she had ever experienced. Courtney had fallen deeply in love.

"But you must let me help you move your things to the studio. Better yet, I'll send Goodson to do it and you and I will stay here in bed all day." Antonio nibbled at her ear and her neck as he spoke. His hands found every soft sensitive place on her body and soon she was lost in her rising passion. An hour later Courtney swung her feet over the edge of the bed and determinedly stood up. "This has got to stop for awhile. I'm exhausted!" She laughed as Antonio made a playful grab for her firm smooth buttocks.

"No! No!" she shrieked as he leaped from the bed. She scampered around the bed, but Antonio simply bounded across the mattress capturing her easily and smothering her with kisses. "Saved by the bell!" Courtney panted as the telephone rang.

"No, not saved. This is only a slight delay." But as Antonio reached for the telephone Courtney wriggled free and made her escape to the bathroom. Twenty minutes later she emerged drying her hair with a towel. She stopped short at the sound of Antonio's angry voice.

"All right! I'll meet with you. But I warn you, you play a dangerous game..." When Antonio caught sight of Courtney he abruptly ended the heated conversation and hung up the telephone.

"I am sorry to startle you with my angry outburst...but business sometimes requires a firm hand." Antonio had donned a black silk robe with white satin piping around the collar. He walked briskly to Courtney and gathered her in his arms.

"It seems I cannot help you with your moving after all. Something has come up. I must go to a meeting. But I'll call for you this evening at your studio in Santa Monica. Perhaps we can go for a moonlight stroll on the beach." He looked into her eyes meaningfully and then bent his head down and brushed his lips lightly against hers.

Even though Courtney had resisted Antonio's offer to

help her with her things, she still felt some disappointment that they would not be spending the day together. She put the top down on her VW and drove toward her parents' Palos Verdes home. By the time she arrived, her disappointment had flown away with the brisk spring wind that pulled at her shiny auburn hair until many tendrils escaped their severely coiffed captivity.

"Hi Dad!" Courtney popped her head into the study where her father sat hunched over his desk.

"Well, who is this lovely young stranger," Clyde responded dryly as he looked over his glasses at her.

Courtney only giggled as she skipped over to her father and kissed the top of his head. "Where is Shane this morning? I thought he would be here today. I was hoping he might help me take my things to Santa Monica today. I haven't seen much of him for the last three weeks."

"It seems that Shane has the same disease you have, Twink. He and Michele have been spending quite a lot of time together. He *is* here though. I think he's in the kitchen... eating most likely." Clyde raised his eyebrows and rolled his eyes. Shane's voracious appetite was a source of amusement for the entire family.

Shane helped Courtney load her suitcases into her tiny car. He teased her unmercifully about her large wardrobe. She in turn teased Shane about his relationship with the fair Michele. Brother and sister enjoyed their time together as each realized that times like these had grown increasingly rare. Each without consciously knowing the other's thoughts decided to make the most of this opportunity to share the day and enjoy each other's company. Little did they realize that it would be the last time they would be able to do so in just this way.

"You can't possibly squeeze another thing into this pitiful excuse for a car. I'll put the rest of this stuff in my car and follow you to Santa Monica."

The two young people worked together and soon Shane's car was as full as Courtney's. They drove to Santa Monica and pulled up in front of the apartment complex.

"I do love the smell of the ocean." Courtney got out of her VW and stood sniffing the air."Yeah, I guess it's okay, but the only thing I'm really interested in smelling right now is a double bacon cheeseburger. Let's hurry and unload this stuff so we can go eat!"

Brother and sister said goodbye in the late afternoon. Then Courtney hurried off to the market. Tonight would be the first time she would be entertaining Antonio in her home and she was anxious to make a good impression, everything must perfect.

The time passed quickly as she put away her clothes and meticulously prepared the hors d'oeuvres. She started a crackling fire in the fireplace and then took her shower.

"Surely he will be here any minute," she told herself as she brushed her hair. She hurried into the kitchen to open the bottle of wine she had selected that afternoon. She stood by the window in her small but elegant living room and watched the fog begin to descend over the city. Goose flesh rose on her arms and a strange churning began in her stomach. Something was not right.

"I'm sure Antonio is just fine," she told herself, but in spite of the reassurance, her willful mind created pictures of the red Ferrari crumpled against another car with Antonio's lifeless body laying against the steering wheel.

The hours ticked by. All that remained of the cheery fire were glowing embers. She had made several calls to Antonio but each time she was greeted by only the recorded message. She had been worried for his safety at first and had even placed a call to the highway patrol to see if there had been any accidents involving a red Ferrari. At last she only sat quietly in the glow of the red embers in the fireplace. How could she have been so foolish to think that such a sophisticated, exciting man would want to continue to see her?

Slowly Courtney turned to look at the digital clock. The red numbers glared through the dark room. It was midnight. "Well, time to clean up and put everything away," she told herself sternly. "I should have been working on my thesis anyway," she said aloud to the fire. "Antonio obviously needs a flashy woman like Lilia. She found herself replaying the whole evening again. She remembered the romantic atmosphere of the restaurant. She liked the way Antonio had ordered their meal ahead of time. When her mind pictured Lilia, she studied her for a moment. With a sigh she knew she could never be like her. Then she remembered the woman falling, the spilled wine, and the gaping wound.

"Ugh!" Courtney exclaimed and she shook her head in an effort to free herself from the memory of the vision.

Courtney slept fitfully that night. Her dreams were filled with guns and blood. Sometimes she awoke suddenly as though someone had made a loud noise right next to her. Each time she sat up startled, she heard nothing unusual. Finally, at six o'clock she decided to get up and go for a walk on the beach.

The sky was clear and the wind was brisk as she plowed through the cool soft sand. She was glad she had worn her jacket. After walking for about an hour, she realized that she was ravenous. Her mouth watered at the thought of pancakes and eggs. She walked back to her apartment but instead of going in she climbed in her VW and drove straight to her favorite coffee shop. On the way in she bought a newspaper, then settled herself comfortably in a small booth. A perky young waitress brought her some coffee and she sipped gingerly at it as she unfolded the bulky Sunday edition.

Absently she read the headlines at the top of the page and worked her way down. "Former Vegas Show Girl Found Dead." Courtney wasn't really interested in the gory details, but found herself scanning the article. Absently, she sipped her coffee and looked at the picture of the unfortunate woman with her perfectly coiffed blond hair, false eyelashes and sultry expression. *It was Lilia.* Courtney froze. Her heart skipped a beat as she tried to comprehend what she was seeing.

"Excuse me." The waitress stood near the table. She held a plate filled with steaming eggs and pancakes in one hand and a coffee pot in the other. "This plate is a little hot."

"Oh, of course. I'm sorry." Courtney spoke in a monotone. Her movements were slow and automatic as she moved the newspaper aside.

"Personally I don't know how anyone can digest their food properly while they're reading all that bad news," the waitress observed. "More coffee?"

Courtney hardly tasted the delicious breakfast that she had intended to savor. She ate because of the physical need for sustenance. She read, and then reread, the article about Lilia's death. The police stated that her body was brutally beaten and they believed that she had been sexually assaulted. They further stated that her luxurious condo had been ransacked and, due to an empty jewelry box, they surmised that the assailant was possibly in the act of burglarizing her home when she may have arrived unexpectedly and surprised him.

"Why didn't I try to say something to her," Courtney groaned as she put her elbow on the table and rested her head in her hands. "I was actually jealous of that poor woman, now she's dead and that means the vision was real," she mumbled aloud.

"Everything okay?" the waitress was looking at Courtney's pale face.

"You're right, too much bad news," Courtney smiled weakly.

During the short drive home she wrestled with her jumbled thoughts. If this vision was real, then did it mean that her dreams were real too? Did this mean that she would end up in a straight jacket or strapped to a bed like her dream suggested? She shuddered at the thought. "Ridiculous," she told herself, "how could those dreams be real?"

"There has never been any indication that those dreams are connected with reality," she said aloud as she stopped for a red light. "But," she sighed, "the vision was real. Lilia is dead. She died as a result of a gunshot to the chest."

Courtney threw her head back and gazed unseeing at the clear blue sky as she stepped out of her car. Her steps were leaden as she walked to her front door. Antonio might have heard about Lilia's death last night. "Is that why he didn't call?" she mumbled to herself.

The message light was blinking on her answering machine as she walked into her apartment. It looked almost evil in the interior gloom of the studio apartment. Courtney turned on the lamp near the telephone. She sat cross-legged in the wingback chair and picked up a pad and pencil. The machine indicated that there were five messages. Her heart pounded as she pushed the button. Relief flooded through her as she heard Antonio's anxious voice. All five messages were from him. He sounded desperate and pleaded with her to call him. He apologized profusely for not calling last night and explained briefly that something terrible had happened.

Courtney sat quietly for a moment after she had listened to the last message. She had felt elation at first, but now she was close to tears. How could she face Antonio? She had "seen" what would happen to Lilia and she had done nothing to warn the unfortunate woman. At last she made her decision. For now she would say nothing to Antonio about the vision. After all, she reasoned, she had thought it was only her vivid imagination at the time. How could she explain it to Antonio when she herself couldn't understand it?

Just as she reached for the receiver, the telephone rang. Courtney jerked her hand away as if the instrument had burned her skin. It rang again. Courtney smiled at her own foolishness. "Cara Mia! I am so happy to hear your voice! Where have you been? I've been trying to reach you. I am so sorry about last night! I must see you! Can you ever forgive me?" Antonio's Italian accent had become more pronounced as his words tumbled over each other. At times he broke into Italian. She listened intently without interrupting his flow of words.

"So please, may I see you? Today! Now!" Courtney took a deep breath.

"Yes, of course."

"Bona. Grazie! I'll be there right away."

Courtney hung up the receiver and raced into the kitchen. She filled the tea kettle with water and set it on the gas stove. She knew that it would take Antonio at least forty minutes to get there, but she wanted to take a shower after her sandy walk on the beach. Hurriedly she turned the flame on under the kettle and then she raced off to the shower. Soon, steam billowed out of the shower stall and her dark hair was hidden by a thick layer of suds. Then over the sound of the shower spray she caught the faint sound of the doorbell. She stopped her hasty scrubbing and listened. The sound came again and still again until it seemed that whoever was there had refused to release the button. At first she thought she would ignore it. The only person she wanted to see right now was Antonio and it would still be thirty minutes before he got there. The doorbell stopped ringing and now someone was pounding.

"Oh I'm coming! Just a minute!" Courtney was aggravated at the inconvenient interruption. She turned off the water and reached for her robe. Water and suds dripped from her hair and her feet left wet prints on the carpet as she made her way to the front door. On tiptoe she peered through the peephole. It was Antonio!

"Antonio, how did you get here so fast?"

"Was easy. I was only a few blocks away. I called you from my car phone." He looked haggard. His hair was unkempt and his shirt collar was unbuttoned. Courtney could smell alcohol on his breath.

"It looks like I am just in time for a hot shower."

They spent the day wrapped in each other's arms. Antonio told her about the business meeting. He and his associates had been unable to come to an agreement on some investments. The meeting had lasted long into the night. They had all had too much vino and tempers flared. By the time they disbanded it was well into the wee hours.

"I wanted to call you but it was four o'clock in the morning," Antonio shrugged. "Instead I decided to drive to the beach and watch the sunrise. I think I slept for a little while. When I woke up I called you. Am I forgiven, Cara Mia?"

Courtney looked into his dark brown eyes. They were red-rimmed and bloodshot from too little sleep and too much alcohol. She leaned forward and kissed him softly. She could and would most definitely forgive him she thought, but will he forgive me? She raised her eyes to his once again, inwardly hoping that he would not guess her secret.

"You must not look so concerned, frowns do not become you." Antonio touched the worry wrinkles on her forehead. "I am fine and my business associates and I will work things out nicely," he crooned, misinterpreting her expression. "Now there is one more thing I must tell you. While I was trying to call you from the restaurant this morning I bought a newspaper. Do you remember that unfortunate incident with Lilia?"

Courtney nodded silently.

"Much to my shock, she was murdered last night in a burglary. Poor woman, I've known her for some time. I do not like to think about the last words we exchanged that night. But she made a spectacle of herself and I was angry. After all I wanted to impress you." Antonio dropped his voice and paused as his eyes traveled over Courtney's slender body. "As I sat in my car reading that article over and over I felt shame that I was not kinder, more compassionate. But I must confess that I was afraid you would think ill of me for knowing a woman so obviously deprived of cultural education." Antonio knitted his eyebrows together looking apologetic.

"But I..." Courtney started.

"No. No. Let me finish." Antonio put his finger over her lips. "It was my foolish pride that prevented me from conducting myself appropriately that night. That was the last time of course that I was to see her or hear from her and it was so ugly!"

Courtney sat quietly. At first she listened intently to his words and strained her senses to catch even the slightest nuance. As Antonio continued to speak, she found herself analyzing his discourse. At times he truly seemed more interested in telling his story than he was in her reaction to it. In fact, he had been talking continuously for some time. *He must be tired*, she decided, *he is repeating himself now.*

"Would you like something cold to drink?" Courtney asked as Antonio paused to cough.

"Champagne?" He looked hopeful.

"No, lemonade or ice water," she laughed.

"I would prefer champagne." He sounded genuinely disappointed.

Courtney disengaged herself from Antonio's arms and went into the kitchen to prepare their iced drinks. Her hand paused in midair as a thought struck her. Antonio had said he had not heard from Lilia after that night, but she was certain that it had been Lilia's voice on the answering machine that morning. Perhaps the machine had failed to record the call.

Mechanically she released the ice cubes into the glass and then poured the lemonade. She wondered if Antonio was afraid to tell her about Lilia's call. What reason could he have for holding back what she considered to be a trivial incident? Courtney felt a small but unmistakable tremor in her solar plexus. She arranged a few pieces of fruit, cheese, and some crackers on a crystal dish. Then she placed the glasses and the plate on a serving tray. Antonio was still in the bathroom so she set the tray on the coffee table. Carefully she pulled the table closer to the day bed.

The dinner jacket that Antonio had haphazardly tossed across the end of the coffee table earlier now slipped to the floor. She bent to pick it up. Something white fell from the pocket.

"Oh dear, this pocket is torn," Courtney said aloud as she bent again to pick up the white handkerchief. She admired the fine quality of the fabric but she was surprised that it was filled with a gritty substance. "Sand? I can't believe you went walking on the beach in your dinner jacket," Courtney called out laughingly as she gave the fabric a firm shake. A moment later her smile froze as she saw a dark red stain that covered nearly half of the fine white cloth.

"But I did not walk on the beach..." Antonio stopped mid-sentence as he opened the bathroom door. The moment of silence that followed was leaden. "As I said earlier, tempers flared last night. A glass was broken. One of my associates cut his hand. In my effort to help him I got a little blood on my handkerchief," Antonio explained smoothly. He walked over to Courtney and took the jacket and the soiled cloth from her hands.

"The pocket of your jacket is torn."

"Please, is nothing. You worry too much. Come sit down. You have prepared for us such a lovely refreshment." Antonio pulled her close and kissed her lightly. Courtney felt moisture on his face when he kissed her. She could see perspiration on his upper lip and forehead.

"Are you too warm? Shall I turn on the air conditioner or open the windows?"

"No!" he said abruptly, "I am fine. Sit, we will eat something."

They sat in tense silence. Courtney nibbled on a piece of cheese. Antonio took a large swallow of lemonade.

"This is very nice, but I would rather have champagne," he said sourly.

"Well, you haven't eaten all day. I thought you would be hungry by now."

"I'm not hungry, I am only thirsty," he said, growing more agitated.

Courtney was at a loss. She had never encountered a situation quite like this one. She studied Antonio's sudden nervousness. His hands shook as he held the lemonade glass to his lips. "Look, I think you must be extremely tired. Why don't you eat something and then we can sleep."

"No! You look! I am fine." Antonio shouted jumping up. Courtney shrank back in shock at his unexpected behavior.

"Oh no, Cara Mia. I am so sorry; I have frightened you with my ugly outburst. You are right of course. I am too tired and distressed. I must go. I will go home and sleep. Tomorrow I will call you. We will spend the night together." Antonio dropped his voice and spoke in smooth deep tones. Courtney was relieved to hear the calm restored to his voice. She remained wary, however, as she studied his uncharacteristically nervous movements. She noted too that perspiration now ran in streams down his cheeks. The dark stubble of his beard made a deep shadow on his jaw line. There was something hidden...almost sinister about the way he looked.

"I am needing to shave. I will be better tomorrow my lovely goddess. We will have a wonderful evening." He had already put on his shirt and was looking for a missing cuff link.

"Let me help you find it."

"No. I must go home and sleep. You can give it to me tomorrow evening." He kissed her again, and then turned to pick up his crumpled jacket. Courtney reached for her sweat pants and sweat shirt.

"I'll walk you to your car," she said as she discarded her robe and pulled the baggy pants on. They walked out to the street together. Courtney was surprised that Antonio had parked his Ferrari there. But he explained that the alarm system was quite sophisticated so he wasn't worried that anyone would steal it. Her neighborhood was exceptionally quiet and the two stood virtually alone on the street. Finally Antonio got into the sports car. He had tried to make polite conversation, but she could see that he was still nervous, so much so that he seemed barely in control of his movements.

"I promise I will call you tomorrow!" Antonio raised his voice to make himself heard as he revved the powerful motor. Courtney leaned down. She admired the interior. It was spotless and smelled of new leather. He kissed her again and then he was gone.

She stepped up onto the curb and watched the red car as it sped away. A tan car pulled out of a driveway to her left and drove past, disappearing around the corner behind Antonio's Ferrari. The neighborhood was quiet. The sun was setting and the air was cool. Her bare feet were in fact almost cold so she turned and hurried back to her apartment.

Courtney stepped into the now darkened living room and turned on the light. She started forward, and then stopped suddenly as her bare foot hit something hard and sharp. She picked up the object and found it to be Antonio's jeweled cuff link. She examined it under the light. "He really shouldn't be so careless with something so obviously expensive," she shook her head with mild amusement. She noticed something else that lay sparkling on the carpet and she bent to pick it up. "He has lost both of his cuff links," she muttered. The telephone rang, startling her. She put the cuff links on the coffee table and hurried to answer it.

"Darling, how are you?"

"Mom! It is so wonderful to hear your voice." Thirty minutes later Courtney said goodbye. Her mind was filled with amusing and poignant stories about her stately grandmother's slow recovery. She felt better as she walked into the bathroom. She leaned her hands on the edge of the basin and gazed at her reflection. Dark smudges underlined her blue eyes. She touched her face. She noticed something powdery on her fingers. The powder seemed to be all over the sink. "What is this? It's everywhere. Oh well, I'm too tired. I'll clean it up in the morning." Courtney dusted her hands off and then sneezed violently.

"Oh boy, that's all I need. I don't have time to get sick right now," she told her reflection. A few moments later she was snuggled under her comforter. She could still smell a faint trace of Antonio's aftershave on her pillow. She remembered his arms around her and she smiled. She thought about her momentary uneasiness. "Absurd," she told herself. She fell asleep with the memory of his voice in her ear and the feel of his kiss on her lips.

CHAPTER NINE

Clarisa hung up the telephone sighing deeply as she did so. Her shoulders slumped and her head hung forward as she studied her tightly clasped hands.

Hattie hummed a hymn she had sung during the church service that morning. The kitchen was filled with the mouthwatering aromas of cornbread, fried chicken, and sweet potatoes. From time to time she glanced surreptitiously at the pensive woman who sat on the kitchen stool. "How is Miss Courtney doing?" Hattie asked after she finished making her coleslaw in an enormous pottery bowl.

"I don't know, Hattie," Clarisa spoke without looking up. "She said she's wonderful!"

"But you don't think she is?"

"Hattie, I just have this awful feeling. I cannot explain it." Clarisa raised her head and put one hand on her solar plexus. Hattie could see the sparkle of unshed tears in her clear expressive eyes.

"Lord have mercy, our chilren never stops bein' our babies, do they?" The black woman wiped her hands on her white apron and walked over to Clarisa with her arms extended. The two women embraced. Hattie stood rocking her gently from side to side.

"Oh, Hattie," Clarisa snuffled, "does it ever get any easier?"

"No ma'am," Hattie answered solemnly as she drew back from Clarisa and looked her in the eyes.

"Why, thank you Hattie. I feel so much better." Clarisa managed to chuckle through her tears. She was rewarded by Hattie's wide toothy grin.

"Now mama, I'm going to tell you something important, and I want you to listen carefully." Hattie's smile had disappeared. She picked up one of Clarisa's hands and held it firmly with both of hers. "Courtney is a special child. The good Lord has something good for her to do on this old earth. Important jobs mean you need experience...training. Very soon now things are fixing to change. Your daughter is passing the Lord's test."

"Oh dear, what are you saying Hattie?"

"Now don't you fret so," Hattie chuckled. "The Lord knows what He is doing. He has fixed it so special people has special help, like angels watching over them and making sure they will be awright."

"I have known you all my life Hattie. I've come to understand that you know things...and you are always right." Fresh tears trickled down Clarisa's cheeks.

"And don't you foget it Missy!" Hattie pulled a clean white hanky out of her pocket and gave it to the weeping woman and then playfully shook her finger near Clarisa's face.

A noticeable "thunk" on the floor near the kitchen island caused both women to whirl around. A furry gray streak raced toward the screen door.

"You thievin' fur ball," Hattie screeched as she grabbed for the broom. Storm Cat easily dodged her and raced around the island until he could get a clear shot at the door. He knew that even with a huge breast of fried chicken in his mouth he could outmaneuver Hattie.

"Nobody gave you an invite to Sunday buffet you sneakin' Storm Cat." Hattie made a wild swipe at the fleeing animal, but he was already headed for the door.

"Head 'im off Liss." The two women were no match for the crafty cat. Gripping the stolen chicken in his jaws, he threw his weight against the screen door. It opened and Storm Cat and his prize disappeared. The door snapped shut just as Hattie and Clarisa arrived.

"Oh you cat, I'll turn your furry body into a mouse if you ain't careful!" Hattie raged.

Clarisa started laughing. Hattie looked indignant, but before long the corners of her mouth twitched and soon she joined in the uproarious mirth.

"I declare. It is good to see you laughing," Hattie said wiping her eyes. "It proves once again, the Lord works in mysterious ways."

A bell sounded. "Now I know we did the right thing by putting that bell in along with the light for Miz Camden, but I do believe today she is abusing it!" Hattie rolled her eyes.

"I'll go this time, Hattie. I expect Mother is impatient to come downstairs and supervise."

"Oh, I'll bet she is." The two women giggled and then broke into peals of laughter that left them breathless. The insistent bell rang again and again.

"You better hurry on up. I'll be there in a minute to help you put her in that fancy lift."

"Okay Hattie," Clarisa snorted trying to get control of her giggles. "Shall I ring you when I'm ready?"

"Lord girl, don't you touch that bell." The two women shrieked and doubled over laughing uncontrollably.

"Clarisa! Where have you been? I have been ringing for you. Where is Hattie? I want to be downstairs to greet my guests." Esther Camden's voice was filled with indignant agitation. She sat ramrod straight in her wheelchair.

"Mother, you look wonderful." Her white hair was combed smooth and her makeup was flawless. She wore a floral print dress which seemed a little out of character since she usually favored plain tailored clothes.

"Well, it has long sleeves and the skirt is long enough to cover this abominable contraption." Esther had correctly read her daughter's expression.

"It's just a cast mother. But your full skirt does cover it beautifully."

"Thank you," Esther retorted somewhat stiffly, but she was unmistakably pleased by her daughter's compliment. "Now please help me get into the lift, I want to be downstairs before anyone arrives!"

"Just a moment, Mother. You are not wearing the sling on your arm," Clarisa scolded.

"I am wearing the ace bandage and that is all," Esther snapped.

"The only reason the doctor allowed you to come home so soon is because you promised to take good care of yourself and you are to follow his orders to the letter!" Esther lifted her chin like a defiant child as Clarisa spoke.

"I am right-handed Clarisa," Esther said evenly. "I eat, drink, and write with my right hand. My left hand, my injured left hand will be resting quietly in my lap." Esther's voice had risen and become decidedly sarcastic. "It will have nothing to do at all and it will be perfectly fine." As she uttered the last word her eyes opened wide and her eyebrows shot up, as if daring Clarisa ro challenge her decision.

"Miz Camden aren't you a sight to behold. You are going to be queen of the mansion today. Those ladies are going to look at you with the old green monster of envy in their eyes today." Hattie bustled in and with her usual grace transformed the stiff atmosphere into a genial flow.

Within thirty minutes Mrs. Camden was elegantly seated in an antique wingback chair. Her casted left foot was discreetly draped and the first guests began to arrive.

The stately old plantation house seemed to respond to the happily chatting guests. The crystal chandelier glittered in the late afternoon sun that streamed through the windows. The polished hardwood floors seemed to hide their scratches and the tired antiques seemed to glow with life as they were reminded of the glorious parties and cotillions that they had hosted in the past.

"Ugh. The next time I insist that mother should have a party, please remind me that we should hire some extra help." Clarisa leaned wearily against the kitchen counter. "I'm exhausted."

"Yes ma'am. At least we could invite people who eats less. I believe Reverend Fishton must have eat half that fried chicken himself!" Hattie grumbled good-naturedly. "Is Miz Camden asleep yet?" In answer to her question the bell rang. Both women laughed. "I expect she wants you to tuck her in. You go see to your mama and I'll make us some tea." Hattie shooed Clarisa out of the kitchen, then she finished putting away the clean serving trays.

Hattie stood listening for a moment to the creaking sounds of the old house. In the evening shadows she imagined that it looked tired. "You and Miz Camden likes parties, but none of us is young as we used to be," she told the house, "but you and Miz Camden still grand and beautiful...and full o' secrets." The house seemed to sigh. "Don't worry, you'll be free of your secrets soon now, Miz Camden too. Something tells me though you're going to take it better than that stubborn old lady upstairs."

A soft meow came from the screen door. "Well, well, if it isn't the prodigal son come home." Hattie opened the door and Storm Cat answered with another cajoling meow and then he rubbed his furry body against Hattie's leg.

"I suppose you want forgiveness for your thievin' ways." Storm Cat rubbed against her leg again and then walked over to the place on the floor where his bowl usually sat. He sniffed at the empty place and then he turned and looked at Hattie expectantly.

"Not only do you want forgiveness, but you expect to be fed too! Audacious. That's what you are. Audacious." Hattie continued to scold the gray cat as she filled a bowl with food and another with water. "Well, it says in the Good Book to forgive and turn the other cheek. So I expect I'll do just that, but while I'm turning the other cheek I'm going to keep a sharp eye on you next time I make my fried chicken."

####

"Clarisa dear, please fix these pillows for me and hand me that gardening book over there."

"Don't you think it's time for you to go to sleep, Mother?" Clarisa noticed her mother's pallor. "Nonsense. Besides I always read myself to sleep," she said imperially. "I've given dozens, probably hundreds of parties in my life. This was only a Sunday drop-in. There is no reason for me to be tired." Clarisa knew that her mother's fierce pride wore steel armor.

"It was a lovely gathering. I enjoyed seeing everyone, it's been...so long."

"Well, I see no reason why you and Clarence shouldn't bring the children and spend the summer here."

"You mean Clyde," Clarisa looked at her mother sternly.

Esther dismissed her own mistake with a little wave of her right hand.

"The children are grown now, Mother. Shane is in college. He wants to be a lawyer like his daddy and Courtney is getting her master's degree..."

"Yes I know, I know, she has been in Europe with the Ballet Company too."

"So you did read the letters I sent! But why didn't you answer them!" Clarisa demanded.

"I didn't think you would be interested in anything an old fashioned woman in an old fashioned house would have to say," Esther sniffed.

"Mother, you were the one that said..." Clarisa stopped herself. She took a deep breath and allowed hurt and anger to subside before she spoke again. Esther sat staring at her book. She looked at the woman who had once ruled the household with an iron hand. Her hair was slightly disheveled and her reading glasses were perched on the end of her nose. She looked for all the world like a sweet docile grandmother.

"I spoke with Clyde today, Mother, and he is coming to Charleston next Friday." Esther looked up from her book.

"Mmm. You know there are no finer schools in the country than in the south. Why you and your husband thought you should move to a place that has no regard for breeding and manners is beyond me. Your children have probably never heard of a finishing school. They're out there with green hair and chains no doubt!"

"How dare you! My children, your grandchildren, are perfectly wonderful. They are both bright and hardworking and they don't have green hair!" Clarisa was outraged.

"Well, if they are so all-fired wonderful, why in heaven's name don't you bring them to see me?" Esther said mildly, as she peered at Clarisa over the top of her reading glasses.

Clarisa swallowed. This woman was so infuriatingly difficult to understand. She remembered the terrible argument they had. Esther had never really warmed to her husband Clyde and when he decided to join the law firm in California, well...Clarisa was certain that her mother's displeasure had turned to real hatred. As the years passed, Clarisa wrote often to her mother and sent pictures of the children. She called sometimes too, but Hattie was the only one she had spoken to. Her mother was always conveniently indisposed.

Many times over the years Clarisa had fantasized about just showing up at Willows with Shane and Courtney. There would be a moment of silence as her mother opened the door and then there would be tears followed by smiles, hugs, and the family warmth that she longed for. She couldn't bring herself to act on her wishes. She feared her mother's cold rejection. It was better, she thought, to enjoy her fantasy and accept the fact that her mother would probably never change.

More than a decade had passed. Here they were in the very room where they had argued so bitterly. Now after so much lost time her mother sat there amongst her pillows chastising her for not bringing the children for a visit! Clarisa felt almost dizzy.

"Clarisa do sit down, you are as white as a ghost!" Esther's voice was filled with real concern.

"I'm fine, Mother, I guess I forgot to eat anything today." She was glad to lean against the massive old rice bed.

"Well that is absolute nonsense. You go downstairs and tell Hattie to fix you something to eat. You are not ill are you?"

"No, Mother. I am just a little tired." The truth was, she realized, she was exhausted. She hadn't eaten well nor slept soundly in the weeks ever since the media had gotten wind of Courtney's miraculous rescue efforts.

"Actually Mother, I've been thinking that Courtney could use a change of pace. She has been working so hard in school and all...if you feel that you would truly like to see her...well, she will be out of school soon." *How perfect.* She had wondered how she could ever arrange for Courtney and Hattie to spend some time together. Hattie was certainly right. The Lord does work in mysterious ways.

"Of course, I truly want to see her, I thought that is what I just said," Esther snapped.

"Yes, of course you did, Mother. I will speak to her about it right away," Clarisa smiled. It was very clear to her that Esther would never apologize, therefore, admitting she had been wrong. But that no longer mattered. The important thing was that the terrible rift in her family might at long last begin to mend. That thought alone was enough to bring some color back to her cheeks as her feet skipped lightly down the stairs. She was bursting with excitement to relay the good news to Hattie as she hurried into the kitchen.

"Hattie, you will never guess in a million years what Mother wanted!" Clarisa saw a plate of food and steaming tea on the kitchen island. *How had Hattie known she was famished?*

"She wanted you to fluff her pillows and find her reading glasses."

"Almost. She wanted her gardening book. She already had her glasses. But I mean besides that." Clarisa seated herself on the kitchen stool and eagerly bit into a drumstick.

"She wants you to bring her granchilren for a visit."

"Hattie, how did you know?"

"I have been in this house since I came from Daufuski, when I was just a girl. I have come to know that old lady. I know she has a loud bark, but she also had a breaking heart. She had that heart put away in an icebox of foolish pride; now I do believe it's beginning to thaw, praise the Lord. But the good part is, she recognizes what she done. In her own way she is tryin' to make things right." Hattie perched on top of the other kitchen stool while she spoke. She watched as Clarisa stuffed the last bite of cornbread in her mouth.

"Don't you think it is absolutely remarkable that Mother, out of the blue, simply demands that her grandchildren come for a visit? I mean just when we were trying to figure out how to get Courtney here so you and she could...talk! Hattie cleared away Clarisa's empty plate. She put some chicken scraps into Storm Cat's dish and began to fill two bowls with leftover banana pudding. Hattie was chuckling as she listened to Clarisa's incredulous voice.

"Plain remarkable, but then ..." Hattie paused as she turned to look at Clarisa, "The Lord works in mysterious ways!" Before Hattie could finish her sentence Clarisa joined in and they finished the oft-repeated phrase in unison.

####

Courtney awoke Monday morning with the fading remnants of a disturbing dream. All she could remember was the interior of Antonio's car and something sparkling on the carpet. She sat up and struggled to get her thoughts in order.

"Coffee, I just need some coffee," she told herself. She shuffled into the kitchen and soon the small automatic coffee machine gurgled as it sent a fitful stream of dark liquid into the small glass pot. Courtney leaned against the kitchen counter and sniffed the welcome aroma of freshly made coffee. Finally, her mind began to clear. As she thought of Antonio she felt the familiar, powerful chemistry that at times nearly overwhelmed her. Now a new feeling introduced itself. She was unable to completely define it but a vague uneasiness had developed with regard to this beautiful man she loved. But surely everything would work out just fine. He must be the Mr. Right of her dreams or she wouldn't feel such powerful emotions, she reasoned.

"Well, no wonder you're nervous," she scolded herself, "you didn't crack a book all weekend and Professor Wood can be such a beast on Mondays."

Courtney arrived at the door of her first class only to find that the "beast" was not there. The class had been canceled much to her relief.

"Thank God the beast isn't here today. I need some coffee. Want to come?"

"Sounds great!" Courtney smiled at the striking young black girl who had spoken. Latoia was a few years younger and at five feet, eleven inches she towered over her friend. She worked as a model in order to pay for her college tuition. The two girls had noticed each other in school and had often exchanged greetings. Then last Autumn Latoia appeared in the same ballet with Courtney at Madame Dubois' Academy. They felt a kinship that kindled into an almost instant friendship.

The two young women chatted happily over their coffee in the student commons. Each told the other about their busy lives. Without getting into too many details Courtney told Latoia that her life had become much calmer since the beach incident. Latoia listened quietly, occasionally nodding, but she said very little. Courtney appreciated her tactful restraint.

"So, you doin' all right?"

"I'm fine." Courtney was a little surprised by her question and the searching look that accompanied it.

"You just look a little uptight or tired or something."

"Oh, it's nothing big, I'm just a little behind in my studying plus I'm trying to decide what to do with the rest of my life."

"Whew! I'm glad it's just little things, I was afraid it was something important like your love life," Latoia joked shrewdly.

"My love life?" Courtney was taken aback. She had not yet had the opportunity to tell Latoia about Antonio.

"Listen girl, I realize we haven't known each other all that long, but any fool could see from the way you've been acting lately that you've got a man tucked away somewhere. Now give, honey, I want to know all about him!" Courtney gladly shared some of the romantic details of two of their dates.

"The symphony is spectacular and the picnic is the most romantic thing I've ever heard, but let's get serious now. Did you sleep with him?"

Courtney laughed out loud at her friend's blunt question. "Well I guess I wouldn't say we really slept." Both girls laughed.

"Who is this hunk? What's his name?" Latoia probed.

"His name is Antonio Scolari."

"Italian! You got yourself a hot-blooded Latin lover! Oooh, girl! Does he have money, too?"

"His family owns the Scolari Vineyards in the Napa Valley."

"I thought the name sounded familiar. Seems like I just heard or read something about some Scolari's."

"I suppose you could have. Antonio's sister is getting

married this weekend. Antonio is taking me to the wedding. There may have been something about it on the society page."

"That could be it," Latoia said frowning. "Oh, hey! Do you realize how long we've been here? I've got another class!" Latoia jumped up and grabbed her books. "I'll see you at Madam's tomorrow night. The shoot is over so I can finally get back to ballet!"

Courtney still had some time before her next class so she decided to go to the library to do some studying. Enormous as it was, the building seemed stuffy and crowded. She finally found an empty chair at the end of one of the long tables. She put her books and note paper on the table and sat down. She opened the first book and plunged headlong into a complex behavioral comparison using the differing viewpoints of Freud and Jung. She had only worked for a short time when she realized she would need another book. She picked up her bag and automatically draped the strap over her shoulder. She only had to walk down three aisles of books before she found what she was looking for on the top shelf. Standing on tiptoe she maneuvered the heavy book forward until she got a firm grasp. Then she tugged and the book came down. The weight of it caused her to involuntarily step back. The strap attached to her handbag annoyingly slipped from her shoulder to her elbow. She could see that the large decorative buckle on the side of her purse was caught on a book protruding from one of the lower shelves. She reached forward with her left hand to try and untangle the buckle and the book but it was hopeless since the book was already plummeting to the floor. The heavy reference book was also falling. Both books landed noisily, startling most of the people within earshot.

Courtney groaned with embarrassment and pain. Somehow the falling reference book had bent one of her long nails back and it throbbed painfully. As she crouched down to pick up the books she noticed that the smaller book had fallen open. She looked closer and read the word autism.

"Now why didn't I choose an interesting subject like this for my thesis?" she mumbled to herself. She closed the book and started to put it back on the shelf. After a moment of hesitation she reconsidered and stacked it on top of the reference book.

"Ugh!" Courtney grunted as she strained to stand up with her weighty burden. "Shhhhh!" A studious young man with thick glasses glared at her over the pile of books he was working with.

"Well if you had the grace to help me with these I wouldn't be making so much noise," she spoke in a loud whisper as she returned his glare.

Courtney returned to her chair and sat down. The damaged nail on her right hand was very painful. She decided not to start making notes again until the pain had subsided. She looked at her books and wrinkled her nose in distaste. She just couldn't concentrate on Freud and Jung, so she picked up the 'Case Histories of Autism' and began to read.

A loud cough caused Courtney to glance up from her book. She noticed some stiffness in her neck. It must be time to go to her next class, she thought as she rubbed her stiff neck and glanced at her watch. To her astonishment not only had she missed her second class but she had only five minutes to get to her last class of the day. She slammed the book shut and jumped up. Her class was in the building next to the library. She might just make it.

Running hard she bounded up the steps of the next building and threw her weight against the door. She trotted down the hallway dodging other students. She was almost there. She rounded the corner and came to a halt. Several students were gathered around the door that led to her classroom.

"I don't believe this!" she panted. A note was taped to the door. The class had been canceled and the note listed the reading assignments. Courtney scanned the note. She had already read most of the material anyway.

"Do you need some paper to write down the assignment?" Courtney looked down at the short plump Laura who frequently sat near Courtney in this class.

"No thanks Laura, I've read most of it anyway. Can you believe this? This the second class that has been canceled for me today."

"It's my third," Laura rolled her eyes. "I think the whole psych department must have taken the day off.

"You mean to tell me Tallmadge's class was canceled too?" Laura nodded.

"Didn't you see the note on the door?" Laura asked.

Courtney laughed, "No I missed the class. I was in the library and lost track of the time."

"Must be your lucky day. Well, guess I'll go try to do some studying." Laura smiled and started off toward the library.

First things first, Courtney told herself and she hurried to Tallmadge's classroom to write down her assignments.

As she climbed into her little Rabbit, Courtney made a mental note to clean her car and throw away the Sunday newspaper, thereby putting the memory of Lilia's unfortunate demise far away. She pulled the white VW out of the parking space and drove down the endless rows of parked cars toward the exit. Before long her relentless mind was once again replaying the events of the previous day. She wondered if Antonio would call. Lost in her thoughts, it was some time before she realized where she was going. She had automatically been driving to her parents' home.

"I guess it's just as well," Courtney said aloud to herself, "I need to use Dad's computer anyway." When she arrived at the family home, she drove around to the kitchen entrance. She stopped the car and began to gather up the offensive newspaper. All at once she remembered the interior of Antonio's car. It was clean. No newspaper. Something clutched at her stomach. "Now, why should that be strange," she admonished herself. She reached toward the console to clean out the gum wrappers that had accumulated there and another thought struck her. The telephone. He said he called from the restaurant and again from his car. None of the messages he left sounded like he was calling from a pay phone she thought. She remembered the noisy coffee shop where she had eaten breakfast. The telephones were near the entrance. "He must have gone out to his car to make the calls," she reasoned.

"Senorita! Buenos Dias!"

"Hi Maria. I just thought I would use Dad's computer to do some of my work."

"Oh, si, si. Come in. Are you hungry?" Judging from the smells coming from the kitchen, Maria was cooking enchiladas, one of Courtney's favorite Mexican dishes and, yes, she was very hungry. She had eaten almost nothing all day and she was planning to go to ballet class later. She knew Maria's food would give her the energy she would need.

Madame gave a particularly grueling class that evening and Courtney was exhausted as she made her way home. She was pleased though that she had been able to accomplish so much homework. She was completely caught up and she had made a great deal of progress with her thesis. She couldn't help feeling somewhat let down when Antonio didn't meet her at the studio. Of course he had not mentioned that he would be there, but still she had hoped.

It was very dark in the apartment as Courtney entered. She switched on the light. Nothing was out of place and the apartment was empty, but she had the unreasonable notion that someone else was there or had been there. The hair on her arms and legs stood up as she sniffed the air. Cologne? *Antonio's cologne.* He had been there the whole day on Sunday but she thought that it was odd that the fragrance lingered so potently.

Once the tea kettle was placed over the gas flame, Courtney settled down to retrieve her messages. She hoped at least one would be from Antonio. The first voice she heard was her father. She realized with disgust that she had forgotten to turn the volume down and the messages were nearly unintelligible because of the loud squealing feedback. The next voice was her mother's. She sounded happy. Courtney could not understand most of the words but from the tone of Clarisa's voice she knew everything was probably all right. She made a mental note to call South Carolina on Tuesday. It would be fun to speak with everyone including Hattie.

Latoia's voice was the last one on the tape. It was a long message. Courtney could make out only a few words. Something about Madame Dubois' Tuesday class. Courtney guessed that Latoia had gotten another modeling job and would probably not be able to attend class after all.

The last message played, but Courtney could not discern a voice during the squeaks and squawks, so she turned the volume down and allowed the message to finish so that the machine could automatically reset itself. Antonio didn't call.

The tea kettle interrupted her thoughts with a shrill whistle. Mechanically she prepared her tea while she agonized over Antonio's silence. Should she call him?

Would he think her pushy? She sipped her tea for a few moments and then walked determinedly to the telephone.

She nervously punched the numbers and gritted her teeth as she waited for the ring. Almost immediately she heard the recorded message. Courtney took a deep breath and hoped that she could make her voice sound light and cheerful. She spoke clearly and carefully as she left her name and a short warm greeting. Then, after a slight pause she added a rather plaintive "Please call me soon." After hanging up she groaned, "Oh, God, that must have sounded stupid." She sipped at her tea while her mind picked the message apart like a voracious buzzard. Finally, she stood up and stretched. Her muscles were tight and sore from her ballet class. It was time for a hot shower and a good night's sleep. She picked up her dance bag and removed the clothes that needed laundering and tossed them into the wicker hamper. She noticed the corner of an envelope protruding from one of the zipper pockets inside her bag. She realized that it was the letter that Madame had given her to read from the Charleston Ballet Company.

"Oh no." She had completely forgotten to read it. Madame had not mentioned it again. "I really don't see how I can even think about going to Charleston right now." She thought of Antonio's dark eyes and soft kisses. She decided she would read the letter in the morning and then try to think of a good way to tell Madame that she could not accept the position.

After filling her dance bag with fresh clothes she turned to go into the bathroom. The door was closed. She didn't remember closing it when she left that morning. She opened the door and flipped the light switch. It seemed damp in the tiny room just as if she had showered a short time ago instead of early that morning. Then she noticed the open window. She had forgotten to close it; of course, she really didn't remember opening it that morning. The open window would account for the dampness and the sometimes gusty wind could have caused the door to shut. Still she was a little disturbed. Someone could actually have entered her apartment through that window even though it was a little smaller than the other ones; but nothing was out of place that she could determine, so no harm was done. She simply decided to be much more careful about closing windows and locking doors in the future.

After her shower Courtney crawled under the warm comforter, her mind and body too tired to wrestle with her worries any longer. A down pillow cradled her head and she was instantly asleep.

CHAPTER TEN

Courtney was sleeping soundly when the telephone rang at seven o'clock the next morning. She stumbled across the room and groped for the receiver.

"I am so sorry. I have awakened you," came the apologetic voice.

"Antonio? What time is it? I must have forgotten to set my alarm." She glanced at the digital clock across the room. "Where are you?" Judging from the background noise she guessed he was calling from a pay phone.

"Vegas. I had some business to take care of. It, uh, came up at the last minute. There was no time to call you before I left. I tried to call you last evening, but you were not home. I think your answering machine is possibly not working correctly. It was making very strange sounds so I hung up and decided to catch you before you leave for school this morning."

The cloud of doubts and fears that had tormented Courtney for the last twenty-four hours suddenly lifted. She had been acting like a silly teenager she realized.

"I'm so glad you called." Her voice conveyed her intense relief.

"Ah, Cara Mia, I see. You thought I would not call you again, no?"

"Well, I uh, wasn't sure," Courtney faltered.

"You are a rare jewel. A woman so beautiful as you should have twenty men kneeling at your feet," he said with solemn gallantry. Courtney giggled. She was uncomfortable with his lavish praise.

"Now the reason I call is to ask if you still wish to accompany me this weekend."

"Yes. I'm looking forward to meeting your family."

"Good. I will pick you up Friday morning."

"Okay," Courtney was a little disappointed. She had hoped to see him sooner.

"My business is keeping me here for a while. But nothing will keep me from you on Friday," he said firmly in a tone that once again filled Courtney with warm reassurance.

They said their goodbyes and Courtney replaced the receiver. She hugged herself and did a little spin on one foot in the middle of her tiny kitchen. How could she possibly wait until Friday? But on the other hand, she thought, I can probably use the time to find something to wear. She had to pack too. All at once Courtney felt some real concern about her wardrobe. Why hadn't she listened more closely to her mother's advice and updated her surprisingly simple clothing. Well, she had to return her mother's call later. She could ask for her expert fashion advice then.

####

Latoia was awake, but she kept her eyes closed. The luxurious hotel room was quiet and she felt sure that the other girls were still asleep. Her heart pounded in her chest and her stomach was nauseous. She let her eyelids open just enough to see her makeup case. She had put it on top of the vanity the night before. The room was spinning so she quickly shut her eyes again. Over and over she tried to put her thoughts together, but they refused to stay in sequence. As soon as one thought would form it would separate and the fragments would drift away like confetti in the wind. Then the pain hit her. The impact was so great it resembled a physical blow and with it came the roar of a freight train, then darkness.

A noise came from the direction of the door. "What had happened," she asked herself, and then she remembered the pain. She must have lost consciousness. The noise came again and she realized that someone must have come into the room. She didn't move.

"Sleeping like babies, Mr. Scolari."

"They surely are sleeping beauties. They may not feel too well when they wake up. Be sure that they have everything they need."

Latoia heard the door close and, except for the ringing in her ears, the room was once again silent. The young woman clenched her fists willing her mind to clear. With a rush it all came back.

Natalie, one of the models she knew from the agency had called yesterday afternoon. She had accidentally booked two assignments for the same day. She had given Latoia the address and begged her to take the job. Natalie was not normally the generous type and Latoia didn't really trust her. It was common, however, for models to accept several jobs and then just pick the one they liked the best. It was certainly a practice that was frowned upon by agencies and the models themselves would never admit to it. When it did happen it was always described as an accidental overbooking. Latoia went to the appointment in Natalie's place. As luck would have it the woman who conducted the interview was delighted to find out about Latoia's dance background. She said Natalie may not have gotten the job anyway because non-dancers just didn't have the same grace. Latoia was hired on the spot. The money was so good. That should have been her first clue, she thought ruefully. Mama always said if something is too good to be true, it probably isn't. There were only four girls hired for the job. Latoia remembered thinking that it was a little odd that the only girls in the waiting room were the ones that were hired. Most places she had gone to were bustling with activity and a steady stream of girls filed in and out of the interview room from morning to night. Modeling is a competitive business. Latoia had no intention of doing it any longer than she needed to.

The third clue should have been enough to arouse her suspicion when they were told they would be leaving for Las Vegas immediately. Latoia always kept a spare makeup case in her car and a dance bag with a change of clothes. She was told that she wouldn't need it, that everything would be provided and after all they would only be in Vegas for one day, two at the most. But she had insisted on going back to her car for her bag. Thank God for her stubborn ways she thought now, that extra mad money in her dance bag could help her get away from this place, that is, if she could just make the room stop spinning.

Images formed in her sluggish mind, flashes of memory from the previous night. All of the girls had been given lingerie to model first. Each girl was to remove a robe and matching gown to reveal the sheer bra and panty sets underneath, and then they were to dance. Latoia hated it. She knew that she wanted no part of whatever these people had in mind. She had made her feelings known to everyone. They handed her a drink and persuaded her to do the night show and she would be free to leave in the morning. But that's when things got fuzzy.

She remembered dancing before a room full of men in dark suits, buyers they were told. She remembered being zipped into a sequined black gown and being told to mingle with the buyers. Someone put another drink in her hand. She hated alcohol, her father had been an alcoholic, so she never overindulged. Two drinks should not have done this to her. Not ordinary drinks, but these she knew now were far from ordinary. She remembered the music getting louder. She was dancing with a man much shorter and a great deal older than her. He was rude and his hands groped her body. She hated it, but she was so groggy. There were no other clear memories. Everything seemed to simply tumble in semidarkness with occasional strobe-like flashes of light.

Latoia had not moved since well before the two men had entered. She became aware that she had not felt nor heard movement from any of the other girls either. She wondered if they were really asleep or if they were "playing possum" like she was. Just then a soft snore from across the room answered her question.

The nausea was beginning to subside and she was thinking about trying to sit up when she heard voices. The door opened again.

"They're still asleep. You stay here and keep an eye on 'em. They'll probably sleep another hour or so. When they wake up give them some coffee and put this in it. They'll feel better real soon." It was a man's voice.

"You mean I have to take care of them by myself again? What are you going to be doing all this time?" Latoia recognized the voice of the woman who had conducted the interview, Ann Pierce.

"I told you before. I'm going to take Mr. Scolari to the plane. He's got to get back for his sister's wedding tomorrow." The man had raised his voice in agitation.

"What? He's leaving! When do we get our money?" The woman's voice had grown shrill.

"Jesus, be quiet! You want these bimbos to hear you?" The door closed and Latoia could hear their muffled voices arguing; she couldn't understand any more of the conversation, but she didn't need to. She had recognized the name Scolari. It had to be the same one. How many Scolari's could be attending their sister's wedding on the same day? "Courtney has no idea," she thought. "That little white girl is in big trouble. What am I thinking?" she told herself. "This big black girl is in even bigger trouble!"

Opening her eyes carefully, once more, she could tell that the room had slowed it's spinning to a sort of undulating roll. She lifted her head and turned to look at the girl who slept on the other half of her king-sized bed. It was the tiny Asian, Sumai. Latoia rose up on her elbows and looked in the other direction. She saw the other two girls sprawled on a sofa bed. Then she looked back at Sumai. Something wasn't right. She was so pale and still.

"Shit!" Growing up in a rough neighborhood had taught Latoia what dead people look like. Nausea threatened to overwhelm her. She dropped back onto the pillow. Just then the door opened again. Latoia didn't move. She held her breath until she heard it close again. She would have to be quieter. Then another horrifying thought struck her. That man said Scolari had to get back for the wedding tomorrow. Didn't Courtney say they were leaving Friday?

"God help me, I've been here since Monday night!" Her long slim body ached unbearably as she struggled to sit up. "Lord, you have been real good to me in my life and I thank you. I hate to be the whiny type, but I've got this big favor to ask. Get me out of here!" She whispered softly, but she prayed with the intensity that she hoped would move this mountain.

Her terror and a fierce need to survive helped to bring some strength to her lethargic limbs and clarity to her unruly mind. She swung her legs over the side of the bed and tried to stand up. Her head reeled. She bent over and held on to the side of the bed while she forced her feet to move forward. She made her way to the foot of the bed and while holding on with one hand she reached for the closet door with the other. She was completely nude so there was no way to begin an escape attempt until she could find some clothes.

The closet was filled with sparkling gowns and filmy lingerie. Where was her dance bag? She frantically pushed the long gowns aside and peered into the closet's dark corners. She could see nothing. She dropped to her hands and knees and felt along the floor until her hand touched the familiar smooth surface of her bag. She nearly cried with relief. It was like finding an old friend, a tiny island of normalcy amidst these unspeakably bizarre circumstances.

She rolled from her knees to a sitting position and pulled her bag in front of her. She felt inside and found her jeans. She pulled them on and then laid flat to engage the zipper. Another brief search unearthed a sweatshirt and a pair of jazz shoes. It was so good to wear familiar comfortable clothes. Her confidence began to return. She felt inside the bag for the zippered compartment. Relief flooded through her when she found that her money was still there. She crammed the small wad of bills into her pocket. She hoped there would be enough to buy a plane ticket. There was more money in her purse, but she had no idea where it was.

Crawling was the best way to get around she decided, until she could feel steadier on her feet. She didn't want to risk stumbling into something and making a noise that would give her away. She crawled to the door and discovered that it had not closed tightly. She peered through the crack. The woman was watching television with her back to the bedroom door. Latoia silently cheered.

Leaning on the little vanity stool, she pulled herself up to her knees and finally to her feet. She was still wobbly so she sat on the edge of the stool. Now all she had to do was figure out how to get out...alive. She glanced at Sumai and shuddered and then quickly looked away. Her makeup case sat in open disarray on the vanity near her. She was struck with an idea.

Stealthily she reached inside and felt around for the pair of scissors that she knew should be there. Just as her hand found them one of the sleeping girls on the sofa bed groaned and turned over. They could wake up at any moment and she knew her escape would then be more difficult if not impossible. She hated leaving the girls behind, but she felt certain that if she could get away she could get some help for the other two. No, she told herself, she had a better chance to help by going alone.

She reached behind her head and pulled her beaded braids forward. She nipped off several from underneath. Then carefully holding on to the vanity she made her way back to where she had left the dance bag. She grabbed the strap and pulled it up. Then she found her way around the bed to where she had been sleeping. She stuffed the bag under the covers until she was satisfied that at a glance, it might resemble her sleeping form. A wave of dizziness made her sink to her knees and she clutched the edge of the bed. She rested her forehead on the mattress and breathed deeply. After a few moments the dizziness passed, but her body shook with tremors. She wiped perspiration from her face and yet her teeth chattered from the cold. Latoia knew what was happening. She had watched her brother go through it. He suffered the pains of withdrawal and then promptly went back to the drugs that finally killed him.

The young woman's anger at the memory of her twin's untimely death renewed her resolve. She ignored her shaking body and the sweat that now dripped into her eyes. With great effort she pulled her slender form up until her feet were once again beneath her. She punched the pillow a few times and then made an indentation with her hand. Next she arranged her shorn braids on the pillow so that the tips would protrude after she pulled the blanket up. Finally she was finished. She straightened and clenched her chattering teeth. One of the sleeping girls moaned loudly. Latoia knew she had to do something, but what?

Fate made the decision for her. The bedroom door opened and she was momentarily blinded by the wedge of bright light that sliced through the darkness.

"What the hell do you think you're doing?" The sophisticated modulated voice was gone and Ann spoke with a roughness that was probably her normal tone.

As Latoia's eyes adjusted to the bright light she could see that the face she had thought attractive was now twisted into an ugly snarl.

"I was cold and I wanted to get something to eat," Latoia stammered inanely. She simply couldn't think of anything else to say, though the thought of food made her want to retch.

The woman squinted hard at Latoia. It was obvious that the girl was going to be "needing" something very soon. She could see her body trembling and her face glistening with sweat. She had never heard any of them ask for food before. She had heard a lot of them beg, but it wasn't for food. Then the woman glanced down at the bed and she knew this girl had come to her senses and was actually making a pathetic attempt to escape. She grinned. Then she threw back her head and laughed as she thought, "This stupid black bimbo has been seeing too many movies."

"You can't get away with this kind of stuff in real life," Ann Pierce laughed sarcastically expecting to see Latoia's resolve crumble. But instead she saw the girl jump in the air as her legs snapped together and, as she landed, one leg flew up. Ann saw no more.

"Chasse' Grand Battement will forever be my favorite step," Latoia panted. "Guess I don't need to take karate for self defense." Her foot had struck the woman squarely on the chin and she lay unconscious on the carpeted floor.

Latoia stepped over her body and half stumbled as quickly as she could toward the front door. She wanted nothing more than to run headlong into the hall and find the quickest way out of this loathsome place, but the need for caution made her slow down. She forced herself to open the door just enough to peer through the narrow crack. She could see a tall man with red hair standing a few steps away near the elevator.

She had been unable to see the faces of the two men who had entered the bedroom earlier so she had no idea who this tall man might be. He was just standing there looking up at the lighted numbers above the elevator door. Maybe he was just a hotel guest. Suddenly the man turned and looked in her direction. Latoia's heart leaped and she eased the door shut as quickly and silently as possible. She knew that if he was one of them he might come in at any moment. Weak with terror, Latoia leaned against the door awaiting her fate.

Moments passed and she heard nothing except the occasional ding of the elevator bell. Then she heard voices. She strained to hear them as she pressed her ear to the door. Maids, it sounded like maids talking! They exchanged pleasantries and aside from the rattle of a maid's cart there were no other sounds.

"Wouldn't it be funny if I could escape in a laundry cart?" she thought. "That is so corny," she whispered. "But I'll do anything to get out of here." She decided to try another peek through the crack between the door jam and the door. The man was still there! He was smoking a cigarette and looking in her direction! "He didn't look evil," she thought, "but then Ann Pierce hadn't looked evil during the interview either."

The thought of Ann made her turn and look over her shoulder at the woman on the floor. She hadn't moved. Latoia eased the door shut again and hurried over to check on her. She could see the gentle rise and fall of her chest. She wasn't dead, but Latoia could see a little trickle of blood coming from the parted lips. A bruise was beginning to darken her chin. Latoia hated the thought of hurting anyone, but this was a matter of her own survival.

It occurred to her that it might be a good idea to get the unconscious woman out of sight just in case; she didn't know what difference it would make, but still it seemed like a good idea. Gingerly she picked up the woman's arms and began to tug. She was heavier than she looked. After stopping frequently to catch her breath the still wobbly Latoia managed to drag the unconscious Ann across the room to a door which she thought would lead to another bedroom. It was a bathroom. She was too tired to drag the woman any farther, so the bathroom would have to suffice.

A loud knocking on the front door nearly caused Latoia to faint. Panic pushed adrenalin through her system bringing strength to her depleted body. With one great heave she got Ann into the bathroom. Then in a flash of inspiration she managed to lift her under the arms and rolled her into the bathtub. She pulled the curtain shut and turned on the shower.

"Who is it?" Latoia called through the door.

"Room service, Ms. Pierce. I have the food you ordered," a female voice called back. Latoia opened the door for the uniformed maid. "Where's Ms. Pierce?" she asked with a frown.

"Oh, she's in the shower."

"She needs to sign for this."

"I'll sign for it." Latoia was certain that the girl was afraid she wouldn't get her tip. She herself had tipped people well while traveling. Right now though she knew she would need every dollar she had to try and get out of Las Vegas.

"Ms. Pierce forgot to tell me how she usually tips you." The girl said nothing, but silently pointed to the Gucci handbag on the end table near the easy chair where Ann had been sitting only moments ago.

"Of course. I'll go ask her if it's okay if I get it for you." Latoia walked to the bathroom door and opened it. Steam poured out. "Ann is it okay if I get tip money out of your bag?" Then as calmly as possible she walked back to the end table and rummaged through the purse. She opened the wallet and caught her breath at the sight of the fat wad of large bills she saw there. There was nothing smaller than a hundred.

"There you are," she shoved a one hundred dollar bill into the maid's hand. "The food looks great. Have a nice day." Latoia had practically shoved the astonished girl out of the door. As she looked down the corridor she saw that it was empty.

"Say, listen. There was a man out here a while ago standing by the elevator. He sort of looked like a movie star. Do you know who he is?"

"No. I thought he was just another guest. This elevator gets jammed a lot. I saw him go down there. He probably got tired of waiting and took the stairs." The girl pointed to a door at the end of the hall.

Latoia was elated. Freedom was near. She went back to Ann's purse and began to look through it. She found an envelope which contained the driver's license and credit cards belonging to all four girls and another large packet of money.

Latoia weighed her decision in the passing seconds. She was not a thief. She also knew that she probably did not have enough money for a plane ticket back home. The other girls would probably need money too and then there would be Sumai's funeral. She took the money and all of the credit cards; she tried to cram them into the pocket of her tight jeans. When that didn't work, she picked up the Gucci bag.

"Well, they took my purse, not to mention several days of my life." With that she went to the front door, opened it and walked out.

The hallway was empty and silent. She tried to walk nonchalantly, resisting the temptation to break into a wild gallop. She walked past the elevator and headed straight for the doorway marked "Stairs."

As she descended she breathed a prayer of thanks that she was going down, not up. Waves of nausea and dizziness continued to plague her and forced her to stop often and lean against the railing or sit for a few seconds on one of the steps. She lost track of how many flights she had walked. It became an endless journey downward, ever downward. "Maybe I'll find the center of the earth," she grumbled.

Big black letters loomed above her. Latoia fought to clear her vision. "Parking Garage," she panted. She had made it. She was free. She could get a cab. Go to the police station, then home! She pushed against the door and staggered forward.

There was no light immediately above the door. The bulb must have gone out. She stumbled and fell down several steps uttering a muffled shriek as a sharp pain stabbed through her left knee as it hit the concrete. At least she had rolled out of the shadows into the dim glow of one of the safety lights. She looked around for someone to help her. The garage was full of cars and sounds, but she could see no one.

A huge concrete support pillar was only a few feet away and she pulled herself slowly toward it. She hated to be in the shadows again, but it looked like a good place to rest for a few minutes and maybe she could pull herself to a standing position. She was concentrating so hard on her efforts that she failed to notice the black limousine that was just rounding the corner. From behind her a muscular arm clamped down around her ribs and a large powerful hand covered her mouth. Her body was lifted as easily as a child's and she was pulled into the shadows. A harsh whisper in her ear ordered her to be silent.

The black limousine stopped abruptly in the spot where Latoia had fallen only seconds before. The driver got out and opened the passenger door. At nearly the same instant two men banged through the door that Latoia had just used.

"What has kept you, imbecile? The pilot has been waiting for us for thirty minutes already!"

"I'm sorry Mr. Scolari, there was a little trouble. It seems that there was a weakness in the organization. We had to eliminate it...." Doors slammed and the voices were cut off.

Latoia gasped. It was more than she could comprehend. More than she could tolerate. Her rigid body went limp. She hung like a rag doll in the vice-like grip of...God knows who. "Well, God," she prayed silently, "if I'm gonna die, let it be now and let it be quick, but one way or the other get me out of here!"

Tires squealed as the limousine drove away and the vice loosened. "I'm sorry ma'am. Stay calm. I am a friend. Don't scream, please, I am going to put you down now and take my hand away. I'll show you my ID...everything's okay now. I've got this gut feeling that you and me need to have a little talk." He spoke softly as he lowered her to a sitting position on the cold floor. They were well camouflaged in the shadows.

Latoia heard the slight southern drawl and the deep soothing voice. For the moment she could not scream or run or cry or feel anything. She was empty.

"My name is Raeford." Latoia's glazed eyes looked up into the face of the man she had seen at the elevator!

"Here's my ID." She could see something official looking and what she thought was some kind of badge, but she simply could not make her mind focus. The printed words were only black marks.

"Ya see, this fella and I don't see eye to eye on a few things and.." Latoia's mouth started to move though no words came out. Raeford stopped talking so he could hear what she had to say.

"You aren't one of *them*?" He shook his head.

"I'm the good guys. They're the varmints."

"Holy shit!" Latoia laid her head back and shut her eyes. "Have I got a story for you. Are you with the police?"

"Secret Service, and if ya don't mind let that be our little secret." Raeford could see the girl returning from the brink of shock. He desperately wanted to extract any information she might have about Scolari. The Service had been following his activities for some time. His longtime friend and fellow agent, Jim Caulfield had been working undercover as Scolari's chauffer/bodyguard under the name of Jim Goodson. It was Jim's brutal murder which was the little trouble that Scolari's man spoke of.

A small man suddenly burst through the door and half ran half stumbled wildly in one direction, then the other. "They're gone!" his eyes were wide with fear as he turned back to the larger man who had come through the door behind him.

"Whatawedo?" the big man held his hands out imploringly.

"Hell, if I know. The black bitch is gone. The chink is dead. Ann's got a broken jaw. The boss is goin' to kill us, that I know. We got to catch him before he gets on the plane. Maybe we can tell 'im that the FBI is holding us at gun point..." The voices faded as the two men hurried back up the dark stairs and banged the door shut.

Raeford turned to Latoia and pointed his finger at her and mouthed the question "You?" Latoia grimaced and nodded.

"I thought it was just going to be another modeling job. By the way what time is it? What day is it?"

"Thursday, about eight in the morning," came the puzzled reply.

"Those bastards kept us drugged since Monday night! I don't remember much except that I woke up this morning. The other girls were still out and I think Sumai is dead. I kicked Ms. Pierce and got away. Those other girls need help and Courtney, I got to warn her."

"Courtney. Not Courtney Hammond." Raeford looked surprised.

"Yeah. She's a friend of mine from ballet. Do you know her?"

"Yeah. Listen don't worry about her. I'll take care of it. You know you are one tough lady. Ever think about joining the Secret Service?"

"I'll give it some thought but first things first," she groaned as Raeford helped her to stand up, "first, I gotta throw up."

CHAPTER ELEVEN

Courtney opened her eyes. The sun was streaming through the windows of her studio apartment. How she loved this cozy place. She remembered how her parents had resisted the idea of her desire for such a small humble living space. They would have preferred that she live in a secure building with a doorman and valet parking. But Courtney would have no part of it.

Suddenly she remembered what day it was and she sat straight up. Antonio had left a message on her answering machine the previous day. He was to pick her up at ten o'clock this morning. She glanced at the clock. It was already eight o'clock. Thank goodness she had been packed since Wednesday. She bounced off of the day bed and set about preparing to see the man she had fallen in love with.

Her heart beat rapidly in anticipation as she glanced at the clock. It was nine fifty-nine and she was ready. She walked to the front door and opened it. A fresh breeze was blowing straight from the ocean carrying the smell of the sea and she inhaled deeply. She decided to leave the door open so she could hear the approach of the Ferrari. She went into the kitchen to tidy up. Then she returned to the living room to wait. Sirens wailed in the distance and Courtney wondered if Antonio was all right. She looked at the clock, eleven-thirty. She sighed. Once again she had been left to worry, wonder, and wait. She was more angry this time, she realized, than worried. Her stomach rumbled. She had only eaten an English muffin earlier so she decided to fix herself something to eat. She chose a bright red apple from the refrigerator and bit into the sweet cold crispness with gusto. She closed the refrigerator door with a bang and walked back into the living room.

"Well, I'm not going to waste my day worrying this time," she told the framed poster of Baryshnikov. She picked up one of her books, determined to study for the grueling exams that she would face very soon.

At one thirty, Courtney put her book aside. She had absorbed very little of what she read. In fact more than once she had found herself reading the same sentence over and over. She stretched out on the daybed and closed her eyes.

The telephone rang. Startled, Courtney sat up. She looked at the clock. It was four o'clock! She was amazed that she had slept so long. The ring came again and she bolted across the room and grabbed for the receiver.

####

"Damn it all to hell," Raeford swore for the hundredth time. He slammed down the receiver of the pay telephone and lit a cigarette. How could the circuits all be busy for two hours! He was bone tired and his frustration was compounded with grief at the loss of his friend. The normally unflappable tall Texan had nearly reached the breaking point. He took a long drag from his cigarette and blew the smoke out in a white plume much to the disgust of an elderly woman who was talking on the other telephone. She gave him a scathing look and pointed to the "No Smoking" sign on the wall. He dropped the cigarette to the floor and absently crushed it under his boot.

None of the girls could remember enough of what happened to them to be of much help in getting a conviction of Scolari and his boys. According to an informant, Scolari had never boarded his private plane. No one had seen him in LA and he had not been seen in San Francisco. Then there's that Hammond girl. Raeford gritted his teeth. He was convinced that she knew nothing about Scolari although how could she fail to see through his thin veil of respectability...unless...she was using drugs.

"Nah!" he said aloud. No, some wealthy young people were bored thrill seekers. She was not one of them. He had studied her carefully as her security guard and by delving into her background and choice of friends. No, she had no idea who those people were in the restaurant that night. She is just an innocent, a toy that Scolari wanted. The big Texan scowled darkly as he realized how difficult the Hammond girl's presence would make things. She was being used as a cover of sorts. "Or maybe as an alibi," he muttered to himself as his eyebrows drew together in fierce concentration.

Raeford stalked around the hospital waiting room. He knew there was no more time. His supervisors were so damned big on red tape and now with busy circuits, a dead agent, and a live criminal with something big on his mind, it was time for some positive action. He stopped dead still and looked down into the eyes of the little woman who had pointed at the "No Smoking" sign. She stood resolutely in front of him with a scowl on her face. Wordlessly she held up a tissue and pointed at the floor where he had mindlessly crushed out his cigarette. He actually felt himself flush with embarrassment under her gaze. He accepted the tissue and shuffled over to the crushed cigarette butt and scooped it up. He glanced over to the lady and she nodded toward a waste can. He obliged by dropping the soiled tissue into the can. The woman gave a little nod of approval and left the room.

Raeford didn't hear her the first time so she tried again.

"Raeford, that is your name isn't it?"

He whirled around and looked into Latoia's dark

eyes. "Well, you look a sight better than you did two hours ago." *In fact, she is downright beautiful.*

"Listen, I'm grateful that you've helped me and the other girls, but I'm really worried about Courtney. She's...well...she just might not know how to handle herself in a tight spot."

"You mean like you? Nobody would believe you could've handled yourself like you did just by lookin' at you either," Raeford said with respect. "Those guys finished with you?" Raeford nodded to the detectives who had been questioning her. They were talking to the doctor who had examined Latoia.

"Better yet, I'm done with them. I really want to get outta here!" she said vehemently.

Raeford's thunderous expression disappeared and he had to laugh in spite of himself. "I'll just bet you do." He understood her impatience as it was so much like his own." I expect they'll be wantin' you to go downtown with them and fill out some paperwork. They'll want you..."

"Hey my life has been violated here and nobody wants those creeps put away more than I do, but I've been here for hours, I'm tired. My mom's probably freaked out wondering why I don't call and besides that, I got a friend in trouble."

"Whoa! Now hold on tiger." Raeford loved a woman with spunk, but he suddenly realized that this one could start galloping out of control and into trouble. "Look! Don't you go lettin' your recent escape from the jaws of evil give you any notions about becoming an avenging angel!"

Latoia dropped her head down. This was one man she couldn't easily intimidate.

"You have just been through hell and you need to rest." Raeford's tone had softened. "You handled yourself as well as any pro I've ever seen, but you are an amateur.

When you're dealing with scum like Scolari you can't afford to make a mistake. My friend was a pro, one of the best and he's dead. You understand what I'm sayin'?" Raeford put his finger under her chin and gently forced her head up so he could see her eyes.

Latoia gulped. She never thought she could feel this kind of chemistry for a man with blue eyes and red hair. His eyes were so blue that they were almost painful to look into.

"Yeah. I guess you're right, but I'm just scared for Courtney."

The Texan felt something unexpected as he stood looking into the beautiful face of the tall dark-skinned girl. He knew he didn't want to let her out of his life just yet.

"Listen, here's a number you can call to reach me. Just leave your name and I'll call you back as soon as I can. I'll call you anyway in a few days as soon as this mess is cleaned up. In the meantime you finish up here and then go home. Get that knee healed up and get some rest. Deal?"

"Yeah, deal, as long as you promise me that you will help Courtney and let me know when she's safe."

"Done! Hey you got money to fly home on?"

"Uh huh." Latoia's eyes opened wide as she nodded her head. She still clutched the Gucci bag.

Raeford nodded. Then without warning he lifted one large hand and cupped it under her chin and bent down and kissed her full on the mouth.

"Be seein' ya," he murmured as he turned abruptly and disappeared through the door.

####

Courtney sat in tense silence as they sped through the night. The last few hours, in fact the whole day, she thought was indeed a strange experience. When Antonio had finally called he had used terse businesslike tones. She had heard no warmth in his voice, but she had been unable to argue with him, he simply had not given her a chance. He had only explained that due to some unusual problems he would be sending a driver to pick her up and would meet her at a location which he neglected to divulge to her. She had actually gotten into the car with a man that had the coldest eyes she had ever seen and driven with him to a remote roadside rest area in the dead of night! She knew it just wasn't right, but by the time she had come to her senses it was too late, she was too far from home on a dark road with no idea where she was. Antonio met them at the rest area with apologies and a story of car breakdowns, missed planes, and an unbelievable tangle in his business dealings. She wanted to believe him and for a few minutes he displayed some of his former warmth and charm. She relaxed a little, determined to believe that everything was really all right.

The interior of the late model Ford reeked of stale tobacco smoke. The cloth and vinyl seat covers, the medium blue paint, she could swear it was an ordinary rental car, not that she cared really. It was just so uncharacteristic of Antonio. She closed her eyes and leaned her head back against the seat. The truth was, she realized, that she truly could not make an accurate assessment of his character based on what little she knew about him, especially after tonight.

"Oh, you are tired, Cara Mia. I am so sorry that our weekend has started badly. But I will make it up to you. In fact, I was thinking it is time for a vacation, perhaps the Italian Riviera, or maybe Greece. I must get away from these problems of business. It can ruin one's health, this work, all the time, work. Come with me Courtney! We can leave right after my sister's wedding!"

Courtney was stunned. She lifted her head when he started talking. His voice was again warm and gentle. She watched his expression in the darkness. Headlights from passing motorists illuminated his face. She noted the sheen of perspiration on his skin and the dark shadows under his slightly red-rimmed eyes. He did indeed look like a man who needed a vacation. The thought of a spontaneous adventure in Europe was exciting. She had never done such a thing before. Her life had always been so planned, so structured. She had been to Europe many times, but not like this.

"You are so silent, but I see the smile of a woman who would love an adventure. You are tired of your ivory tower, no?"

"It does sound exciting, but I have my classes and my thesis and I don't have very much luggage with me. I would need to let my parents know where I am." Courtney had warmed to Antonio's beguiling charm. He had again succeeded in assuaging her doubts about him, but she had been raised with a strong sense of responsibility. Her family had always taught her that completing tasks and fulfilling obligations should take precedence over frivolous self-indulgence.

"Agh! I will buy you anything you need or want. We'll fly to Paris and I will order the designers to create whatever you wish. As for your parents you can call them if you want to, but my God, you are a woman, not a child who must ask permission to have what you want." His voice was urgent almost pleading.

"Why don't we leave next weekend? I can take my oral and written exams and…"

"Because I want to leave tomorrow!" Courtney could see his hands clenching the steering wheel and his voice was suddenly deep and harsh.

"My passport is at home. I..."

"Your passport is not a problem." He reached inside his jacket and pulled out an envelope and flipped it into her lap.

"But how on earth?" The envelope contained passports and plane tickets to Paris.

"It is a surprise. I have planned this surprise for you. Romantic, no?" He had become increasingly fidgety. He sniffed incessantly as though he had a cold and Courtney noticed that their car was moving very fast.

"A very romantic surprise," Courtney smiled weakly and her voice lacked enthusiasm. Antonio seemed not to notice.

"Si, good. Now you sleep. We will be at the estate by daylight."

"We won't be going into the city?"

"No," he said curtly, "there is not time." He smiled trying to cover his abruptness. "I mean of course I don't want to miss the wedding."

Courtney's heart sank. She knew she dared not question him further. She had hoped they would be going into the city. She could just grab a taxi and maybe leave him a note. She knew now that something was very wrong. She could no longer ignore the anxiety in her stomach and the accompanying voice of doubt. She had doggedly clung to her childish fantasy of this man. He was not the shining knight. He was cunning, perhaps devious. Now in this recklessly speeding car, he was dangerous.

In wide-eyed horror she watched the rapidly approaching headlights of a huge truck. Antonio had chosen that moment to pass two cars on the two lane road. She was certain that death was imminent. She squeezed her eyes shut and clenched her fists. She felt the car accelerate and Antonio cursed its sluggish response. The truck sounded its air horn repeatedly. She was rigidly braced for the impact, but it never came. The car swerved slightly and she heard the deafening roar of the diesel engines as the eighteen-wheeler passed safely. Once again she could hear only the monotonous hum of the motor.

The relieved young woman let her breath out slowly and opened her eyes. There were no red taillights visible in the distance. In fact, she couldn't see lights anywhere across the dark countryside. She had no idea where they were.

"If we come to a service station, I would like to stop and use the restroom."

"But of course, I must also get some gas," Antonio answered solicitously. He sounded so calm, so concerned. She wanted so desperately for him to remain that way. Why did he act so strangely? Could business pressures cause such mercurial mood swings in this man? She had seen her father become slightly distant and unusually quiet when business pressures had become too great. But Clyde Hammond had always treated his family with loving respect. She remembered the few young men she had dated. They each had their own way of dealing with pressure, but thus far none of them had displayed this kind of behavior.

Another thought occurred to Courtney. Maybe it was her, just her own bruised ego that was causing her to question Antonio's actions. After all, what did he really do? Nothing, she told herself. He had many business related problems; of course he would be on edge. He was also Italian. She remembered the wonderful though overtly emotional people she had met in Italy. She was beginning to feel foolish for overreacting. Antonio was right, she was a woman now and she should start acting like one.

A hand on her leg caused her to turn her head.

"I have been driving too fast, no? I'm sorry if I have frightened you. Please, I am driving the safe speed now. Rest your eyes and sleep. I will calm myself and we will have a wonderful time at the wedding." Courtney smiled at him in the darkness. She noted that he had indeed slowed down. It was just the business pressures. Everything would be all right. She put her head back against the headrest and fell asleep, waking only once when they stopped at a small all-night gas station. Courtney felt the car slow, then come to a full stop. She felt the warmth of the morning sun on her face and a soft kiss on her cheek.

"Awaken, sleeping beauty," Antonio whispered near her ear.

She had heard her father talk about the Scolari vineyards and estate, but she was unprepared for the splendor that greeted her. In all directions for as far as the eye could see there were acres of grapevines. Antonio had already jumped out of the car and opened her door. He was chattering happily about the estate and pointing out the various buildings and their functions. It was very early in the morning and yet she could see people bustling to and fro unloading the oversized catering vans. There was more than one Rolls Royce parked nearby, three sports cars, and an assortment of Mercedes and BMWs.

They walked past marble fountains and beds of exotic plants. There were sculptures of the Madonna and saints throughout the lavish gardens. Covered walkways led to silent ponds filled with goldfish and each was equipped with quaint benches and bird feeders and small gurgling waterfalls.

Antonio was talking incessantly. She could hardly keep up with the flow of information. She really wanted a hot shower, some hot coffee, and something to eat in that order.

"Tonio!" A woman's voice called out from behind them. They turned and Antonio's face broke into a brilliant smile.

"Mama!" Antonio strode forward with open arms and embraced the short plump woman warmly. They stood conversing in Italian for a few minutes until the woman caught sight of Courtney. She had been reluctant to intrude on the familial reunion and had approached somewhat hesitantly.

"Antonio, who have you brought here?" the woman commanded.

The introductions were made and Antonio continued to talk unceasingly until Mrs. Scolari waved her hands in the air in exasperation.

"Stop! Stop! You are making me crazy with all of this talk. Besides your lady friend looks exhausted. Come with me, I will show you where to freshen up. Antonio go get her bags." The little woman waved her hand imperiously. Antonio smiled and meekly obeyed.

Courtney liked the woman immediately. She knew that those keen dark eyes missed very little as they stared directly into Courtney's.

A maid led Courtney to a comfortable guest room and showed her the call button which she was to use when she had finished her toilette. After her shower Courtney was delighted to find that someone had brought in a tray filled with fruit and dainty sweet breads as well as a pot of coffee.

Two hours later a refreshed and invigorated Courtney pushed the call button. The house was so large and sprawling that the maid had told her she would return to show her the way to where the family and guests would be gathering.

Antonio too looked refreshed and more relaxed as he greeted her in the courtyard. Courtney was astonished at the large number of people that had already arrived. There were tables loaded with food and uniformed waiters everywhere.

"It is a morning wedding and then a party for the next day or two," Antonio laughed. "Come, you must meet some people!" He took her by the hand and led her toward a small group of guests. It seemed that the introductions would never stop. Courtney's head swam with the names and faces of cousins, aunts, uncles, and friends. Just when she thought she couldn't listen to another new name a courtly young man walked through the crowd ringing a silver bell. The wedding was about to begin.

The crowd moved ponderously along a covered walkway. When at last they reached the clearing Courtney drew in her breath at the spectacle. She could only describe it as an outdoor cathedral. The altar had been erected complete with candles, statues, a robed priest, and altar boys. Rows of white folding chairs had been arranged in a semicircular fashion to accommodate the shape of the clearing and the large number of guests. Enormous bouquets of fresh cut flowers stood in tall white baskets. Sweating young men were ushering guests to their seats and a small orchestra played softly while everyone was seated.

Antonio and Courtney were ushered to the third row with the immediate family. No one questioned her presence there, but Courtney was mildly uneasy. She was not a family member and she hadn't even met the bride and groom. It wasn't long, however, before she was lulled by the soft music and gentle murmur of voices around her. She drank in the beauty of the day. A huge stand of trees encircled this portion of the gardens and she could see a gray stone wall just beyond. This place was obviously designed for private gatherings although there was nothing beyond the wall except the vineyards.

Courtney was distracted from her musings by Antonio's restless movements. Every few seconds he leaned forward to speak to a family member or he turned to someone seated behind them. He ran his hands through his jet black hair over and over. She watched him closely. She knew he must be tired. In fact, exhausted. He had driven all night and there had been no time for him to sleep this morning. She remembered that when they met at the rest area the previous night he had confessed that he had slept very little for three days. Suddenly she knew why he had been acting so strangely. He hadn't slept and he had been taking caffeine pills. She felt a rush of compassion and she leaned over to him.

"You must be exhausted. After the ceremony is over you should try to sleep for a couple of hours."

"No. I am just fine. I will rest later." His tone was tinged with impatience. But Courtney knew it was sleep deprivation that caused it. She had studied the effects it had on very polite people. After being deprived of sleep for an extended time they had all become more aggressive and their tolerance level for noise and other distractions dropped dramatically.

One of the young ushers appeared beside Courtney who sat at the end of the row. The dark-haired youth signaled for Antonio to come with him. Antonio jumped up and excused himself. He did not return until the bride had made her entrance.

The bride was heavily veiled and there were too many people for Courtney to see clearly, but she knew the girl's gown was exquisite. Antonio touched her shoulder when he returned and she smiled up into his eyes.

The ceremony was very long and except for the exchange of vows it was spoken mostly in Latin and Italian. Courtney had very little knowledge of Catholicism, but she rather enjoyed the elaborate service. The sun had grown very warm and she was hard pressed to keep her eyes open. She noted that more than one head nodded forward suspiciously. Antonio was the only one who seemed untouched by the serenity of the moment. He had contained his fidgety movements, but as Courtney turned to look at him she noticed that he had begun to blink his eyes furiously every few seconds. He is fighting sleep like a child she thought.

At last the veil was lifted and the groom kissed his bride. She gathered up her voluminous skirts and gingerly descended the steps from the altar. The orchestra played the recessional and the long line of flower girls, ring bearers, bridesmaids, and groomsmen filed grandly down the center aisle.

By the time Courtney and Antonio made their way back to the reception area the party was in full swing. Guests were filling their plates with food, a dance band played and wine flowed from champagne fountains. Courtney had never attended a wedding celebration of this magnitude. She was sure it would be a day she would never forget.

The chaos was beginning to wear on Courtney. Antonio kept disappearing. Once she had found him with a group of men in a heated discussion. They seemed strangely familiar though she couldn't imagine where she might have met them. When Antonio saw her approaching he quickly left the group and came toward her. Their conversation ended abruptly as they turned to look at her. "Just a little business, Cara Mia, we will be finished shortly. Go and enjoy yourself, I will join you soon." Antonio's grip on her shoulders was tight and his fingers dug into her flesh.

"You are hurting me!" she said indignantly.

"I'm sorry, I'm very tense. Please go back to the party."

"I think you need some rest. Why don't we..."

"I told you I am fine. Now go back to the party." Antonio was glaring at her. He spoke through gritted teeth. The cushion of rationale that she had chosen to rest upon had turned to cold hard marble. Fear once again opened the door to doubt. Without another word Antonio turned on his heel and followed the men who were walking down one of the covered walkways.

The late afternoon sun dipped lower on the Western horizon. Some of the children ran wildly amongst the guests and nannies were trying to capture them. Many of the guests were reeling from the effects of the abundant vino. A gray-haired man had fallen asleep at one of the tables. He sat with his chin on his chest and his hands were folded across his very round stomach. Several women chatted happily at the same table, one of whom was Antonio's mother. It was such an odd mixture of opulence and old world. Mrs. Scolari, though expensively dressed, looked for all the world like the average Italian woman who walked through the quaint open markets in Italy.

"Signorina!" Mrs. Scolari beckoned to Courtney, "Come meet my sister." Courtney smiled her way through more introductions.

"Mama come dance with me!" Antonio's father had waltzed his way over to the table."No, no, old man. This old woman has tired feet. Have you met Courtney Hammond?" Mr. Scolari had the rosy glow of vino in his cheeks but there was no mistaking the sharp wit in his dark eyes.

"I met you only once when you were a small girl. You have become a...a...belishima." He slurred his words slightly but he was still able to convey his admiration with a courtly bow.

"I have known your father for many years. I am sorry he and your mother could not attend our celebration. But is better you should come anyway." He weaved ever so slightly as he spoke.

"This is such a lovely place. It reminds me of one of the Spanish missions." Courtney liked the old man immediately.

"That is quite right. The Scolari family bought it many years ago!" Mama beamed.

"How intriguing. Well I'm certainly happy to see that this awful drought hasn't hurt your vineyards." Courtney knew instantly that she had said the wrong thing. The two Scolaris exchanged a glance that told her everything. A cloud had covered those two smiling faces. Mr. Scolari tilted his wine glass and drained its contents.

"Well uh, the wedding was very beautiful." Courtney felt compelled to fill the awkward silence.

"Grazie. My daughter is the baby. The last one to get married." Her eyes filled with tears. Courtney suspected that she had had her share of wine also.

"Courtney, there you are! Mama!" Antonio called out over the din. When he got to the table he and his father stared into each other's eyes. Their faces were unreadable masks. "Papa, it is good to see you." Antonio extended his hand to his father, who did not respond. The older Scolari's eyes then traveled to Courtney.

"You came here with *him*?" His heavy graying brows were knitted together in a dark scowl. Courtney nodded. He gave Antonio another angry look then turned his back and strode away.

"Ah! You stubborn old man, greet your son and his guest properly." That was as much of the Italian that Courtney could understand as Mrs. Scolari hurried after her husband.

"Come, let's leave this place." Antonio pulled

Courtney's arm so sharply that she spilled the red wine. Red drops stained the delicate chiffon skirt. She felt dizzy for a second. *Oh no, the vision of the chest wound.* She could feel the vision coming as Antonio pulled her by the hand. Her feet moved but she could see nothing except a blur of colors, people, streaks of light like fireworks and blood. Antonio was pulling her through the crowds of people and their forms seemed to interfere with her ability to see where the blood was.

"He will beg my forgiveness." Antonio had been muttering in Italian as he pulled the dazed Courtney toward the parking area. She had not heard anything except the last few words.

"What did you say?"

"Oh, I'm sorry I was speaking in Italian. I get around my family and I forget!" Antonio slowed his pace a little. "I said we are riding into the city with some friends of mine." Courtney was shocked. First because Antonio would lie about something so small and second he apparently didn't know that she understood some Italian. She thought she had told him that she did but he must have not remembered. She was always afraid that her accent wouldn't be right so she was reluctant to speak it, but she did understand it.

"My things are still in the ..."

"No. I had them brought to the car. We must hurry, we have a plane to catch." He spoke sharply and his pace quickened.

When they reached the parking area, Antonio led the way through a labyrinth of limousines and assorted exotic cars. Soon they approached a group of men who stood silently beside a long black limousine. Courtney recognized the men. She had seen them now three times. The man with the cold eyes was there too.

"Courtney, these are my friends. They have generously offered to give us a ride into the city. This is Angelo, Paolo..." She barely heard the rest of the names as a crop duster's engine droned loudly overhead. One of the men walked over to a white caterer's van parked nearby and got in. The motor rumbled and the van pulled away leaving a cloud of dust in its wake.

Suddenly everyone was moving. Courtney and Antonio sat with three men and the man with the cold eyes sat up front with the driver. The limousine spun its wheels in the gravel and then lurched forward. Antonio banged angrily on the tinted glass divider and yelled at the driver to slow down. The car moved more smoothly then.

"Why did you bring this woman with you? She will only get in the way and how do you know she can be trusted?" Angelo spoke in Italian but even if Courtney had not understood what he said the hatred in his voice was inescapable. Courtney was terrified.

"You imbecile, keep your voice civil. You see you have frightened her!" Antonio answered him in equally angry Italian. "She knows nothing and if things get difficult...she will be my safety insurance."

"If things get...difficult...you'd better put a bullet in her head." Antonio lunged at the man and grabbed him by the throat. Courtney shrieked.

"If you don't shut your flapping mouth I'll put a bullet in *your* head," Antonio threatened, still speaking Italian. Both men were sweating profusely. Antonio loosened his grip on Angelo's throat and sat back in the seat. He then turned and looked into Courtney's frightened face.

"Ah Cara Mia, I am so sorry. Don't be frightened. We are hot-blooded Italians, I forget you are not used to our ways. This oaf insists on talking business even when we are on holiday." Antonio touched her face and picked up one of her clammy slender hands. His touch was vile to her now and her flesh crawled with loathing. She knew now how foolish she had been. A wrong move and her life would end. She dropped her eyes and said nothing. She couldn't have uttered a word even if she wanted to. Her throat was swollen shut with the paralyzing fear that now consumed her.

"What is that plane doing?" Antonio spoke again in Italian to Paolo. He spoke with a smile and gestured as if he were merely exchanging pleasantries.

"It seems to be only dusting. I don't think it is anything." Paolo acted as if he was responding to Antonio in kind. His mouth smiled but the expression in his eyes said something entirely different.

Courtney swallowed the desire to give in to her rising panic. She didn't know what these men were involved in, but she knew it was illegal and dangerous. She realized instinctively that as long as they believed that she couldn't understand their language she would be safer. Perhaps she could even learn something important about their activities, something that might be useful to the police. She had to believe that she could escape. To consider any other possibility was unthinkable. If she allowed herself to dwell on the hopelessness...she would probably go quite mad with fear.

"The plane is gone," Paolo addressed Antonio.

"Good." Antonio smiled.

Courtney forced herself to lift her eyes to the men. She stretched her dry lips into what she hoped was a passable smile.

"I really enjoyed the wedding today." She knew her voice sounded nasal and high pitched so she coughed, pretending that she needed to clear it. "You know I loved that young lady's voice, the one that sang Ave Maria."

"Oh yes. Elena Bergati. A second cousin, the family's

pride and joy. Can you believe it, she is only nineteen years old. She will be attending Julliard in the fall." Antonio relaxed as he spoke about the day. Courtney was feeling better too. She continued to comment on the celebration and ask questions that would lead to long explanations. Even the other men seemed less tense though none of them spoke.

The sun had disappeared below the horizon. Lights twinkled across the landscape. Antonio was explaining how the Scolaris had come to acquire the old mission that was now their palatial estate. His story was interrupted as the tinted dividing glass suddenly lifted.

"Alec, what is it?" Antonio snapped at the man with cold eyes. Courtney could not grasp all of what Alec said between the hum of the motor and the man's rapid speech, but he said something about a white van. She wondered why that would make Antonio so angry. In fact all of the men looked shocked and angry. Then they all began to shout at one another in Italian. Courtney couldn't understand very much of what they said. She knew they were swearing profusely and she was able to guess that they were trying to make some sort of decision.

The shouting got louder and Courtney covered her ears. Antonio finally commanded them to silence. He spoke calmly but with an authority that none of them questioned. He seemed to be telling them that new action must be taken. He said something about different cars. She wondered if they were in the stolen car business.

Antonio barked an order to Alec in the front seat. Alec picked up the car phone, but the glass closed before she could hear any of the conversation. Courtney was frowning in honest puzzlement when Antonio turned to her.

"It must be frustrating to be left out of this conversation." Courtney nodded and smiled weakly. "My friends do not speak English very well and insist on speaking their own language. We don't mean to be rude." Antonio continued. He spoke calmly, but the nervous gestures and sweating had begun again.

"It's just that everyone sounds so angry. I hope nothing is wrong," Courtney said innocently.

"No. No. No. That is the way we always talk. It's just that uh, they want to go a different way, so I am arranging for another car for you and I."

They drove on for another thirty minutes and then the limousine turned off of the main road. She saw the neon lights of stores and gas stations. She knew they must be near San Francisco but she couldn't quite determine where they were. The driver turned into a residential area and they drove down quiet tree-lined streets for some time, then the glass divider lifted. This time Alec said nothing, but Courtney saw the almost imperceptible nod of his head and the glass came down once again.

The limousine turned back onto the main road. They were not going very fast and Courtney could see from the distant lights that they were indeed on the outskirts of San Francisco. They were passing a car dealership when the big limousine made a sharp left turn. They drove past the bright lights to a dark street just beyond the car lot and rolled to a stop. Paolo got out of the car and walked back toward the brightly lit car lot. No one said anything. Courtney sat tensely awaiting their next move.

With each passing moment Courtney's tension mounted. It took all of her self-control to keep from screaming. She was grateful for the darkness as it made her feel a little safer, at least they wouldn't be able to see the terror in her eyes and the trembling of her hands. She only hoped that no one could hear the hammering of her heart. The silence was deafening and her ears rang with it. She must speak or move or scream...then it was over. Car lights flashed behind them. The limo moved forward a few blocks going deeper into the shadows of the tree-lined street and then stopped again. They were in an old but respectable neighborhood filled with graceful aging homes perched on top of their hilltop properties.

Tires squealed and Paolo appeared next to the limo driving a light-colored Mercedes. The men all seemed to move with one accord. As Angelo moved to get out, his suit jacket opened. Courtney gave a little gasp as she saw the unmistakable outline of a gun. She had no time to think, however, as she was urged to move quickly. She was pushed into the new car with Antonio right behind her. Paolo returned to the limousine and another man slid behind the wheel of the Mercedes but Courtney could not yet see who it was. "What about my things?" she asked.

"I will send for them later." Antonio's tone was cold and commanding. Courtney said no more, nor could she think. Mercifully her mind had temporarily numbed. She sat in a dark void clutching the seat as the car lurched around corners. Just like her life she thought from somewhere far away, dark and lurching and going...who knows where?

CHAPTER TWELVE

Courtney was aroused from her stupor by the city lights. She didn't remember how they arrived or when. She had no idea what time it was or even what she had been thinking about. Antonio leaned forward and spoke to the driver. She could see now that it was Alec. She took that opportunity to glance at her watch; it was nine o'clock.

Antonio caught her movement.

"It is getting late, I'm afraid we will miss our plane. Are you hungry?" The question caught her by surprise, but her sluggish mind clicked into gear.

"Oh, well yes I am," she lied. She didn't know if she could swallow a morsel, but if they were in a public place she could...could what? She didn't know what she could do, but surely she would think of something!

The beige Mercedes pulled into a gas station and Alec got out.

"I would like to go to the ladies room." Courtney smiled and reached for her small handbag. It wasn't there. She must have dropped it in their hasty car exchange.

"I will escort you, this looks like a bad section of town." Courtney's heart sank. She had no way to write a message on the mirror, but then she remembered she didn't wear lipstick anyway.

When she stepped out of the restroom it was Alec who stood a few paces from the door, smoking a cigarette. Antonio was talking on the pay telephone a few yards away. She watched as Antonio banged the receiver down once and then several more times. He thrust his hand into his jacket pocket, and then he put his hand to his mouth and tossed his head back as though he were swallowing something.

Alec motioned her toward the car. Courtney's feet refused to move as she watched the raging Antonio hit the pay phone with his hand and then he began pacing furiously. Alec gestured again. When she still didn't move he deliberately pulled his jacket open revealing the gun that was tucked into his waist band.

Courtney felt faint. She knew something had gone wrong and that all gentlemanly pretenses had been abandoned. She would only be shot if she tried to run. Where would she run to in this section of town? She saw no passing police cars. The few ramshackle stores in sight were closed and only homeless people sat on the curbs drinking out of bottles covered with brown paper bags. She had no money. Her purse was gone. Alec strode over to her and grabbed her arm roughly. He half dragged, half pushed her to the car and shoved her into the back seat. Her teeth chattered as the chilly San Francisco wind bit through her flimsy dress. It was as though her fear had joined forces with the night air and at this moment there was no escape or protection from either.

The two men stood on the driver's side of the car arguing. All of the car doors were tightly shut so she couldn't understand their words, but she understood the sound of anger and desperation.

A thought flashed through her mind. If they had left the key in the ignition perhaps there was a chance she could crawl over the seat and drive off before they could catch her. She reasoned it would be better than trying to run on foot and it certainly seemed better than waiting for something that might be worse.

The whipping wind and Alec's rough shoving had caused her hair to fall from its pins. It hung loose partially covering her face. She peered stealthily through its protective veil. The angry men had moved a few paces from the car. Their backs were turned and they were still arguing. She straightened her body and looked at the steering wheel. She could just make out the key chain dangling from the ignition switch. She knew that once she made a move there would be no turning back. She used a few of the precious seconds to plan how to throw her body from the back seat to the front seat. She tried to imagine how she could grasp the wheel and the ignition key with no wasted motion. She only prayed that the motor would start with one try.

Courtney's slim agile body moved easily across the seat back. She clutched the steering wheel and turned the key in the switch, the motor turned over easily, but in the split second that would be needed for her to press the accelerator pedal to the floor, the car door was jerked open. She had not thought of locking the door.

Antonio's face was red and twisted with rage as he jerked her arm violently. She was sure that it was out of the socket as she screamed with pain. She could feel cold concrete with her left foot. A part of her wondered idly where her shoe was. She could not seem to focus on anything. She could see the red wine stains on her chiffon skirt. She really should stop drinking red wine.

Antonio shook the girl as he screamed obscenities. She was not the intelligent innocent he had expected. She was just like all of the others taking everything he gave and then running away when he needed her the most. How stupid she was! She could have gone to Europe with him. When things cooled off they could have come back and lived like royalty on the Scolari estate. The estate would belong to him. His father would soon be bankrupt or dead from a heart attack and he, Antonio would save the family by buying the vineyards. His father would respect him then and with a woman such as this by his side life would hold unlimited opportunities.

Didn't she understand that she had been carefully chosen to fulfill this important position in his life? Couldn't she understand that everything he had done, Lilia, the movies, the drugs the guns... he was about to have so many millions of dollars that he would be able to be free of the greedy old pig who thought he could boss everyone around. Didn't this stupid girl understand that she would be queen and he would be king of the greatest organization anyone had ever seen?

"Answer me! Answer me!" Antonio raged as he continued to shake the dazed girl.

Courtney was unable to speak. She could hear babbling sounds coming from her throat. She knew she was crying and grunting as the man shook her and air was forced out of her lungs with the violence of the movements. But everything was beginning to seem very far away.

"Paisan! Paisan! Presto! We must go now! You create a scene. I will kill her for you later. But we must leave now!" Alec grabbed Antonio's arm in a desperate attempt to get his attention. Antonio turned his crazed bloodshot eyes toward Alec. There was no doubt in Alec's mind that Antonio had gone completely mad. He had always known that this would one day happen. He had hoped, however, that it wouldn't happen until after the "big" money was in his possession. He had made a small fortune working as a hit man/bodyguard ever since Antonio had literally plucked him from the Italian gutters. He had felt an allegiance to the wealthy Scolari for so many years, but this kind of life had begun to sicken him. He wanted to go back to Italy and buy a house where he could live in peaceful solitude. He longed for an easy life of entertaining warm plump Italian girls and eating pasta. His dream had occupied more and more of his thoughts in recent months. He knew that this one last job would have done it. His share of the money from the contraband would have been enough for him to slip away into quiet obscurity.

"Antonio, please, we must go. The van has been taken. Angelo and Paolo do not answer, they may be dead. We must get away. It is over!" Alec stood facing Antonio. He tried to think of what to say to calm a man who had not slept in several days, a man who had taken large quantities of cocaine and most probably other drugs.

"You are an idiot! It is not over! It is not over!" Antonio dropped Courtney's arm and grabbed the front of Alec's shirt with his left hand. In the same moment he pulled the semiautomatic from Alec's waist band and jammed the barrel into his stomach. Without a moment's hesitation Antonio pulled the trigger. Alec slowly dropped to his knees then fell face forward on the asphalt. Courtney screamed.

"Shut up!" Antonio whirled around and swung the pistol striking her head.

####

Despite the chill wind, sweat rolled down Raeford's face. He shook off his weighty fatigue like a bothersome gnat. His pompous adversaries had made some grievous errors. They should have left their contraband under the altar at the Scolari estate instead of trying to transport it in the caterer's van. "Lucky for me they were greedy and cocky," he mused as he surveyed the grisly scene. Red lights flashed incessantly on wooden crates filled with movie film canisters that would later reveal pornography. There were hundreds of kilos of cocaine scattered across the floor after the violent impact and bound stacks of money that law enforcement would label as counterfeit after a thorough inspection.

Raeford walked around the van carefully stepping over one of the bodies. There had been three men armed with fully automatic weapons hidden in the back of the van. All of them were now dead. The driver had apparently lost control during the high-speed chase and the van had careened across the center divider crashing into the concrete bridge support. Both the driver and passenger had been killed instantly. The two young patrolmen who chased them were only concerned about the expired tag on the license plate. Now one was dead and the other seriously injured.

"Hey, your name Renfort? C'mere. Got something on the radio for you." A plain clothes detective beckoned. "This could be the limo that the duster spotted." Raeford frowned at the young man. How did he know about such classified surveillance?

As if reading his thoughts the young man answered his unspoken question. "My brother-in-law is a pilot. He's been working on some big case lately. I just figured this was the assignment he was working on. My name is Les Wiggans." He smiled reminding Raeford of a Saint Bernard puppy and he was in no mood for a puppy. Actually, he realized that there was probably only a few years difference in their ages, but he felt much older, especially right now.

"The name is Raeford. What have you got for me?" he said gruffly.

####

Violet Dreyson sat in her favorite recliner. She felt warm and comfortable. There were some things that truly made life worthwhile, she thought contentedly as she pushed a button on the remote control and the television clicked on. She could sit right there in her chair and change channels. She had never mollycoddled herself, no sir. She believed that it was important to stay active no matter how old you get. But when the arthritis in her feet became too painful there was nothing that could take the place of a reliable old recliner, a heating pad, and the T.V. remote control.

"Sage, what you barking at?" The woman turned her head and squinted through her thick bifocals at the excited dog. Sage was covered with a thick mop of tangled beige hair. The aging dog suffered with arthritis much like his owner and his limbs would not move like they once did, but there was nothing wrong with his senses.

Violet groaned as she released the lever on her recliner and put her aching feet on the floor. Sage was the best dog she had ever owned. She knew all of his habits just as he knew hers. He had never betrayed her...unlike some of the men in her life. She knew that Sage was barking for a good reason. She hoped that reason was not a prowler, but if it was she would be ready for him.

When the elderly woman turned her television set off, her house was dark and silent. She didn't like to have too many lights on at night. Electricity was very expensive, besides she could see out and no one could see in. She learned that from her frightening experience with a prowler the previous summer.

Violet shuffled along behind Sage until he came to a stop in front of the bay window. He had learned that his owner liked to stop there and peer out whenever he alerted her to something. Like many homes in San Francisco, hers sat high above the street. From this vantage point she could see the four flights of steps leading to her front door and she could also see most of her neighbors homes on both sides of her street.

She could just make out a long dark car parked at the base of the stairs that led up to her front door. She squinted hard. "Why, it's a limousine!" She exclaimed in a loud whisper. "I wonder if I've won the lottery! No, no," she told herself, "they would never come this late at night. Maybe it's a movie star or a famous politician!" She watched in fascination. Nothing more happened. The car did not move and no one got in or out. Her feet were aching. She really wanted to go back to her recliner. She turned and began to shuffle back the way she had come. She had only gone a few steps when Sage started barking furiously again.

"What! What!" Violet turned around, "Oh!" She saw the lights of another car flashing at the far end of the block. The smaller car drove up beside the limousine. Suddenly the doors all seemed to open at once. Darkly clad male figures swarmed back and forth between the two cars. She thought she saw the form of a woman in light colored clothing being shoved out of the limousine and into the back of the smaller car...but it was so dark she couldn't be sure. The smaller car was already moving even before the door was shut. Within seconds both cars were gone and the street was again empty.

Violet's feet throbbed and she sat down heavily on the window seat. Sage jumped up beside her and whimpered.

"Well, you ought to whimper. You haven't jumped that high for a year!" Violet patted her friend fondly. Sage was looking out of the window intently. He panted then yipped shrilly. "What? What do you see?" Violet leaned forward and stared through the glass. She could see something white lying on the street. "One of those crazy people dropped something, Sage." The old dog barked and wagged his bedraggled tail.

"You don't expect me to walk down those steps and get that thing, do you?" Violet asked her friend incredulously. Sage yipped and jumped from the window seat, this time without a whimper.

"So all of this excitement's got you going does it?" Violet stood up slowly and moved toward the front door. Sage waddled ahead of her and stood waiting. They had played this game many times. Violet had trained him to fetch the newspaper when her feet first got bad. It had become a useful activity. Sometimes she dropped things while she was on her morning walk. Sage always picked them up for her.

The woman stood watching as the dog waddled carefully down the many steps to the street. Without hesitation or command he picked up the object in his mouth and started back up the steps. When he stopped once to rest, Violet frowned with concern. "Now don't you overdo it, old man!" She cautioned. "You rest until you feel better. When you get back here, I'll have a little treat for you." She always carried small bits of dog yummies in her pocket. She had learned early on that Sage would do nearly anything she wanted him to do as long as he was rewarded with one of those."My, my!" Violet shook her head, "that certainly *was* a lady I saw and she dropped her purse!"

####

"Miz Dreyson?" Raeford raised his voice as he spoke into the telephone. He explained that he had just learned that she had found a purse belonging to a missing girl. He realized from her voice and manner of speaking that she was quite elderly, but he also sensed that she was in full control of all of her faculties.

"Miz Dreyson, I realize that it's late, but I wonder if I could come by your house for a few minutes."

"Tonight?" Violet was surprised.

"Yes ma'am, I have reason to believe that the girl is

being held against her will. Therefore it is essential that I speak with you right away. You may be able to remember something that could help us find her."

"Oh my, well yes if you think ..."

"I do, ma'am and I thank you."

Raeford glowered as he memorized the address and the cross streets.

"Wiggans!" Raeford barked.

"Yo!"

"You know this city real well?"

"I grew up here!" Raeford gritted his teeth. He hated the thought of dragging this puppy with him but there seemed to be no other choices. At least the kid was plain clothes and had an unmarked car. The fact that he knew the city would eliminate wasted wrong turns.

"Saddle up," Raeford said dryly. "We gotta be on the other side of San Francisco yesterday."

"Yahooo," Les yipped as he slapped a red light on top of his car.

"Whoa! What are you doing?" Raeford growled.

Les had picked up the microphone as he screeched out into traffic.

"Gotta call in. I only told 'em I was taking you to a pay phone!"

"You can't." Raeford reached over and yanked the cord loose. "Your radio is temporarily out of order." Raeford had seen the remains of the shattered police radio in the van. If the rest of those thugs were monitoring police calls let them think that everyone was occupied with the van.

Forty minutes later Violet was ready with hot tea and

homemade cookies when Les and Raeford arrived. The tiny woman blended perfectly with the delicate antiques in her home. In careful detail she repeated everything that had taken place. The two men were delighted with Violet's sharp mind and appalled with the fragile teacups. They were both large men and they obviously felt uncomfortable sitting on the ancient furniture.

"Won't you have more tea?" Violet asked hopefully. "You've been here barely twenty minutes."

"No ma'am Miz Dreyson. I wish I could stay, but the bad guys might get away. We thank you for your kindness and the information." Raeford stood up carefully trying to avoid bumping anything with his large boots and long limbs. "May I use your telephone?"

"Where the hell have you been?" Raeford rasped into the mouthpiece. He was calling the field command post which consisted of little more than a telephone and portable computer.

"I might ask the same question of you. I've been trying to do everything here. Jack got mugged by a wino and..."

"Holy Christ, just tell me what you got!" Raeford was on the outer fringes of his self control.

"I'm trying to if you'll just shut up!" snapped the exasperated man. "Just before Jack got hit he radioed that two men and a girl in a beige Mercedes had pulled into a gas station across the street. Jack was on a surveillance for..."

"I don't give a shit what he was doing there, tell me what happened," Raeford roared. Violet and Les jumped and Sage yipped at the unexpected outburst. Raeford listened quietly as the other field agent gave the address of the gas station and a brief description of the people and the car.

"This is it!" Raeford roared at Les. Violet had been

showing him pictures of her family. He jumped to his feet, relieved to finally be going.

"We better gallop those horses, kid."

"Right, cowboy."

Raeford hated the thought of another hair-raising ride but he had to admit, the kid could drive. By the time they arrived they could see the red flashing lights of two squad cars and an ambulance.

"Is he conscious?" Raeford asked the EMT who was working over the bleeding Alec.

"Sort of," the young man answered. "He's been mumbling but he's barely alive. We've got the IV in him and I think it's helping but he's lost a lot of blood. We've got to get him to the hospital so make it fast!"

Raeford hurried to the gurney before it was lifted into the ambulance and leaned so that his ear was close to the dying man's lips. He focused all of his attention on the barely audible last words of Alec. He couldn't hear all of what the man whispered but he did hear the name Antonio, and what he surmised to be an address where he might find him.

"We found this woman's shoe. Looks like this guy fell on top of it. Got any idea who it belongs to? It looks like an expensive shoe. It's pretty hard to imagine why a woman who could afford a shoe like this would be hanging out in this section of town." One of the police officers handed the shoe to Les as they all stood waiting to see if Raeford was able to learn anything from the mortally wounded man.

####

Courtney watched, as the room appeared to grow

larger then smaller until it became the merest pinpoint of light in her black sea of pain. *I wonder if I have fallen into the looking glass or down the rabbit hole.* Her mind seemed to roll like the deck of a ship. If she tried to hold onto a thought, pain would rip it to shreds. Rather than fight, she found that floating brought such complete relief that she gladly let go and gave herself completely to the peaceful darkness. The pain receded as she floated away from the body that was tied to the bed. "How odd," she mused as she looked down on the girl in the chiffon dress. "I don't care anymore, I don't really want that body anymore." She studied the girl's bloody head with complete objectivity. She thought of the visions that had been trying to warn her about this event. She had not heeded the warning, but she didn't mind, nothing really mattered as long as she could stay in this peaceful place.

    Something moved below her. Curious, she allowed herself to float down for a closer look. A man was sitting hunched over in a chair. What is he doing? She moved closer still. He was putting something up to his nose. Time after time he dipped a tiny spoon into a container of white powder and sniffed noisily. Finally he leaned against the back of the chair and tilted his head up. She could see directly into his face. His eyes were wide and staring. His pupils were dilated nearly covering the dark brown pools of each iris. She could clearly see the blood red spider web that covered the whites of his eyes. She studied the greasy tousled hair that she once ran her fingers through with such pleasure. She studied the pallor under his olive complexion, the dark circles under his eyes and the residue of white powder around his nostrils. How could she ever have been attracted to this man, she wondered. She could see a gray mist undulating around his head. Small black dots appeared and disappeared within it. She could almost smell the sulfurous odor of negative energy emanating from him. "Ugh!" Courtney's astral self drew back with revulsion. As she did so the man below her jumped out of his chair and stared at the ceiling.

"What? Who's there?" he screamed as he looked wildly around the room. He ran over to the bed and grabbed the inert girl by the shoulders and shook her violently. "You! Wake up!" He slapped the already badly bruised face. "Wake up! Stop pretending, you ugly whore. You wanted excitement, money? Well, I can't get the money now, not yet! You turned me in, didn't you! You did it, you fucking bitch!" The man continued to scream into the swollen face of the girl. In his maniacal rage he grabbed the blue topaz that sparkled on its gold chain around her neck. A look of shock came over his face and he dropped the stone with a curse. He stared in disbelief at his burned hand.

The violent shaking of her body had begun to disturb Courtney's peaceful astral rest. She felt an irresistible pull from the injured body. She was looking up through half-closed eyes and at the same time looking down from her comfortable perch on the ceiling. She fought to maintain her distance from the unwanted body, but it drew her relentlessly downward. Then as Antonio grabbed the blue topaz she was slammed into her body with a roar in her ears. For a few seconds she could feel nothing but a suffocating weight. Then the pain filled her like the sound of a thousand screams. She moaned as she fully realized the hopelessness of her circumstances. Antonio was staring at his burned hand. When Courtney moaned he looked up. He cursed in Italian and then ran to the bathroom to run cold water on his reddened skin.

Courtney watched him. She saw several images of him. He moved so quickly and all of his images followed him almost comically. His hair stood up like the top knot of a rooster. It was so funny. She wondered if he would crow. She remembered the farmer-in-the-dell song that she and Shane used to sing with Grandma Hattie. "With a cock-a-doodle here and a..." Courtney jabbered in delirium.

Antonio rushed out of the bathroom his face was flushed with anger. He was yelling again and he picked up an ashtray and threw it across the room. He picked up a wooden chair and threw it as if it were a toy. Courtney watched in fascination as the objects broke against the wall in slow motion.

"Cock, I'll show you a cock you won't forget!" Maybe Antonio was going to join her in the song. She smiled. Rage boiled all reason from Antonio's mind. The fragile threads that linked him to sanity were stretched to the limit, then one by one the threads began to break.

Courtney was unable to comprehend Antonio's demented state. Like so many victims of trauma, her mind went to another place; she was singing with her little brother in a happy memory of the past. Something warm and furry brushed her arm. It was the tail of a lion! "How remarkable," she thought, this is exactly what the vision had shown her. She would be tied to the bed and someone would be attacking her. She remembered though that the man in the vision hadn't looked anything like Antonio. "Let's see now," she told herself, "someone else was there too, who was it?"

"It was me," a female voice answered her thoughts, "Aeonkisha." Courtney looked up. She saw the cape swirling over her head. Aeonkisha seemed to be standing in the air just above her. It didn't seem strange at all to Courtney, in fact the presence of the tall muscular woman made her feel quite peaceful. The woman smiled down at her as she stroked the lion's mane.

The sound of breaking glass startled Courtney for a moment and she looked around the room. Antonio had drained the contents of a liquor bottle and then threw it against the wall. He was staggering backward as he fumbled with the fastenings of his trousers.

"All is in readiness." Aeonkisha lifted her arms. A cool

wind whipped her cape and ruffled her feathered headdress. The air was refreshing to Courtney's fevered skin. Aeonkisha's deep melodic voice began a chant. It was soothing and somehow familiar. Courtney wanted to join in the chanting but her throat was too parched to make any audible sound. She tried to move her bruised and swollen lips but they were too painful to try to form words.

Another familiar figure stepped through the bright light that glistened behind Aeonkisha and her lion. Courtney recognized the disheveled dream self clad only in a hospital gown. The dream self was identical to Courtney with the exception of an awkward movement of the left hand and leg. Courtney wondered if the vision was about to come true. She would spend the rest of her life in a hospital, crippled. The dream self frowned down at her and shouted, "Noooo!"

Antonio had finally succeeded in removing his trousers. He lurched toward Courtney muttering obscenities. He threw his body on top of hers and began tearing at the flimsy fabric of her dress.

Courtney couldn't hear anything that Antonio said. She could see his mouth moving, but the only sound she heard was Aeonkisha's chant. Other voices had joined her and there were drum beats, rattles, and bells. The drums throbbed louder, closer, lifting the fear and pain from Courtney's ravaged body. A deafening primal roar rose above it all as the lion proclaimed his power.

The mysterious dream self merged with Courtney and with the merging came an unexpected surge of hope and strength. She could feel a power gathering within her and suddenly the dream self shot forward out of Courtney's body and thrust itself against Antonio. The grunting sweating man was thrown across the room. The dream self floated up and pointed an accusing finger at him. Aeonkisha too pointed at him. The lion opened his jaws baring his fangs. With another deafening roar he leaped through the air straight toward Antonio who screamed in horror as he saw the lion flying toward him. Aeonkisha uttered a command and the animal landed just short of the screaming man, its open mouth dripping saliva. One swipe of its huge paw left the front of Antonio's shirt in shreds and bloody slices across his chest. Antonio screamed in pain.

Something else pounded through the sound of the drums and another voice began to come through the chants. Aeonkisha and the dream self turned toward Courtney with smiling faces. She watched in dismay as they became transparent. Only the lion remained solid as he stood over Antonio, who had curled into a fetal position and was swatting ineffectually at the growling lion.

"Don't leave me here!" Courtney cried after the fading figures.

"All is well now. Remember, you are never alone. When you are well you will begin a new life." Aeonkisha's face had materialized directly in front of Courtney's face, and then vanished.

"Police, open the door!" The pounding went on accompanied by yelling angry male voices. Courtney wished they would be quiet. The crushing pain had returned. Her vision was playing tricks on her again. The lion was fading. He turned his back on the sniveling Antonio. With one leap he disappeared into the ball of light that floated above her. The light flickered and was gone.

Courtney tried to focus her eyes. She could see that the door was giving way. Splinters flew from the furious pounding. Antonio was moving. She could see the gun. Streaks of light darted from the barrel as Antonio fired at the place where the lion had disappeared above her head. More streaks of light, loud noises...more gun shots...a face... familiar but not Aeonkisha. No this face was a man...Antonio... No...I don't like Antonio...

"Raeford, Miss Hammond, it's Raeford. Everything's okay now. Can you hear me? You're okay." Courtney couldn't quite remember why she wanted to trust this man, but she did. She wanted to say something to him, but she couldn't think what it was. She wanted to tell him about Antonio and the lion. She wanted to tell him about the visions about how the spilled red wine had looked like blood, but there was so much, where could she start and the pain made it so hard to think.

Raeford watched the girl's swollen bloody face. He knew her head wound was probably severe but she seemed to want to talk. He was sickened at the sight of the damage that had been done to the once beautiful young woman.

"No need to talk right now. You just lay back here. We got an ambulance coming. You just rest. Everything's okay now," he crooned in his deep low voice. Raeford cut the stockings that bound her to the bed. He got a cool wet cloth from the bathroom and put it on her head.

"Guess I should call you Cinderella from now on. First your purse, then your shoe led me right to you! Want a little drink?" Raeford held her shoulders and head up and cradled them on one of his muscular arms as she struggled to take in the water through her horribly swollen purple bloodied lips.

"No! No red wine!" Courtney rasped. "I'll never drink red wine again!" She could barely form the words but she managed to keep the slurring to a minimum and make herself understood. The significance of her statement was lost on Raeford. He knew she would be incapable of coherent thoughts or speech for a while. He smiled indulgently at her. Sirens wailed in the distance. Raeford lay Courtney's bleeding head back down on the pillow.

"This guy looks like he was mauled by a tiger!" Wiggans had handcuffed the writhing Antonio and jerked him to his feet. Two uniformed officers marched Antonio into the living room.

"Lion. It was a lion!" Courtney corrected from her prone position on the bed. Raeford studied the man on the floor. He had been shot in the left arm and left leg but blood also streamed from gashes on his face and chest. His shirt front was in shreds. He knew Courtney's hands had been tied so tightly that they were blue from lack of circulation. Maybe it happened before the bastard tied her up…well one thing was for sure, he would have to wait until later to question her since her mind was so confused from that head injury at the moment. He only hoped that she would be able to remember everything. He looked at the carnage that had occurred in the beautiful townhouse. Everywhere he looked there was broken glass and furniture. There was blood on some of the chairs and bloody handprints on the wall and door to the bathroom and all over the bed where Courtney lay. "If I didn't know better I'd say a war was fought in here," he muttered in disgust. He didn't realize that he wasn't far from the truth.

####

Raeford yawned and stretched his large frame. He glanced at his watch. First he wanted some food and then a bed. He felt as though he had not eaten or slept in a week. Now he could relax. The criminal he had long sought was at last in custody. Courtney was in the hospital, critical, but alive. Her family had been notified and would be arriving soon.

"How 'bout somethin' to eat? I'm starved!" Les nodded his head toward the door. Raeford would have preferred being alone, but he was at a disadvantage, he didn't have a car and he didn't know the city.

"Yeah."

The two men ate in silence for a time. Raeford was grateful that the "puppy's" voracious appetite kept his mouth too full for conversation. The events of the frantic night and the preceding days replayed slowly in his head. He felt satisfaction, a luxury not often experienced in his line of work. There were always so many near misses, loopholes, and frustrations. Criminals were too often out on bail before the fingerprint ink was even dry. They had discovered that the wooden crates had only been laced with a few kilos of real cocaine and most of the film canisters were empty. Antonio was either scamming his buyers or had been the victim of a scam by his own men or maybe his superior. But somehow none of it really mattered now. Antonio could be charged and held for any number of things including kidnapping and assault and the counterfeit money. Of course from the look of things the bastard might spend the rest of his life in a strait jacket.

"Listen," Les looked up from his plate, "you got a place to sleep?"

"I'll get a motel."

"You oughtta come home with me. Patsy wouldn't mind and we got an extra bedroom." Les spoke with enthusiasm as he washed down the last bite of his omelet with a large gulp of coffee. "C'mon. You'll probably have to stay in the city for a few days anyway. You said you're going to try to question the girl and you probably got reports to write, right?"

Raeford started to argue but suddenly he was just too tired. "If you're sure your wife won't mind."

The room was small but comfortable. Raeford was glad he'd come home with Wiggans. It felt good to be in a home with decent people. He had spent far too many nights in cheap motels and surveillance cars. There had to be more to life. He closed the blinds and stretched out on the bed. He looked at the family pictures that adorned the walls. He thought of Jim Caufield. Jim had a family and they would mourn his loss, but his life had meant something. He had died bravely fighting to rid the world of one more evil. Jim would live on in the hearts of those he left behind.

Raeford tossed restlessly on the bed. He hadn't slept in how long? Two, maybe three days he guessed and now he couldn't sleep. He sat up and lit a cigarette. He thought about the report he'd have to write. Latoia's dark brown eyes smiled up into his. "Damn," he said aloud, "that's one I can't figure out." He mashed the cigarette in the ashtray on the bedside table and flopped back on the bed. His body ached with fatigue and longing. His restless thoughts carried him to the ranch. He had used this mental exercise for years to help him sleep. In his mind he had constructed a house, barns, corrals, gardens, and wide open spaces beyond. It occurred to him that he had never put any people on his ranch. He could see himself getting on the back of a long-legged thoroughbred. He looked up and next to him was the slim figure of a woman with black hair and light brown skin. He wondered if Latoia liked horses. He pictured the two of them riding across the Texas plains. The tension began to leave as they rode farther away. At last, he slept.

CHAPTER THIRTEEN

"Phone call for you, Mr. Clyde. It some man says his name is Rayfert, calling about Miss Courtney." Hattie's eyes were wide and there was a slight tremble in her lower lip. Clyde scowled as he lay the newspaper down and rose to go to the telephone.

Hattie didn't wait to hear what had happened. She knew. She knew that Courtney had been in great danger. She had awakened in the middle of the night knowing that something was terribly wrong. She had gotten out of bed and lit an altar candle, and then she alternately prayed and chanted until dawn. When the sun's rays finally pierced the night gloom she knew the danger had passed.

"Miz Clarisa, would you come downstairs for a minute?" Hattie found her in Esther's room. She had just settled her mother into the cherry wood rocker when Hattie appeared at the door.

"Of course!" she said brightly, "Mother, would you like me to bring you some tea when I come back?"

"Yes, thank you." Mrs. Camden had mellowed more than Clarisa could possibly have imagined in the short time she'd been there. She knew that two weeks could not make up for a lifetime of misunderstandings and petty resentments, but she felt as though she and her mother had opened a channel of communication that had never before existed. She was sorry for the discomfort that her mother suffered, but she would be eternally grateful for the opportunity to spend this quality time together. She thought of Hattie's oft-repeated phrase, "the Lord works in mysterious ways." Even if there isn't a Lord there surely is a master plan of some sort and that was something that she was absolutely sure of.

"Hattie, you are acting a bit strange. What is wrong?" Clarisa inquired as they walked together down the staircase.

"A man named Rafert has just called about Courtney." She didn't need to say anything more. Clarisa quickened her step and hurried into the library where Clyde had been reading the paper earlier. She found him sitting at her father's old roll top desk. His face was ashen and she could see the whites of his knuckles as he fiercely gripped the telephone receiver.

"Clyde?" she breathed shakily. He was listening intently to the voice on the other end of the line, but he heard his wife's soft voice and extended his free arm to her. She hurried over to him, her wide frightened eyes never leaving her husband's face. Hattie stood in the doorway twisting the corner of her apron in her hands.

"I see, yes, we can be there tonight or first thing in the morning. We'll get the first possible flight. Thank you." Clyde slowly hung up the telephone. Clarisa could see the muscles of his jaw working as he clenched his teeth. She knew he was fighting desperately for self-control. She held her breath as she waited for him to regain enough composure to speak.

"It's Courtney. She was injured." Clarisa's knees buckled. Clyde grabbed the desk chair and rolled it into position for his wife to sit down. "She is in a hospital in San Francisco. Her condition is critical."

####

Courtney floated in and out of darkness and pain for

what seemed like an eternity. Strange multiple images asked her questions, stupid questions. Why wouldn't they just leave her alone and let her go to sleep? She thought it would be nice to curl up beside that nice warm lion and listen to Aeonkisha's haunting voice. She called out repeatedly for them and when they didn't return she felt a sense of loss and sadness. She hated the prodding and pricks of pain that disturbed her every time one of those strange women bent over her. She hated the insistent questions that the man seemed to be asking her. For the life of her she could not fully comprehend what was going on. Then she remembered how nice it was to float above everything. She willed herself up. The voices became shrill and loud so she floated higher until at last they were gone. It was so peaceful in the soft white light.

    A flickering light caught her attention and she moved forward. She was amazed to see Hattie. She waved her arms and called, but Hattie didn't notice her, she was sitting in front of a candle with her eyes closed as her body swayed from side to side. Courtney moved closer. She could hear Hattie humming. It was the same haunting sound that Aeonkisha had made. Courtney loved that sound, it seemed to draw her closer. She floated down near the flame of the candle and it flickered wildly. Hattie opened her eyes and began to speak.

    "Child of Light, hear me!" Courtney was startled. It was Hattie's voice and yet it wasn't Hattie. There was a regal foreign quality to the voice and the accent was certainly not Hattie's comfortable southern drawl. "You are bound by your agreement. Your destiny must be fulfilled. There are multitudes who await the message you will deliver." Courtney wondered who she was talking to and she looked around the room. To her mild surprise she saw her disheveled dream self floating just behind Hattie. The dream self looked sad and frightened. She wanted to hug the frail image, but it began to back away from her.

"You must answer now! Fulfill your destiny. Do not break your promise." Hattie's voice began to echo. The room rippled in its reverberation as though the walls were made of liquid. Courtney felt strange, and more than a little frightened.

"Do you hear me? You must remember your promise. Do you hear me?" The voice was booming in Courtney's head. She couldn't take much more and she was getting angry. Of course she could hear. What did Hattie think for goodness sakes? She was talking in a voice loud enough to wake the dead!

"Yes I hear you for goodness sakes!" Courtney screamed with all of the energy she could muster.

"Whew, close call! I thought we were losing her for a minute." Courtney opened her eyes at the sound of the unfamiliar male voice.

"Hello young lady! How are you doing?" Courtney could see two faces looking down at her. They both wore glasses. Two more faces looked at her from the other side.

"What have you done with Hattie?" All of the faces smiled and she heard laughter."You must have been dreaming. My name is Dr. Simms and this is my right-hand nurse, Susan. Do you know where you are?" The two masculine faces were talking simultaneously.

"Are all of you twins?" Courtney's tongue was thick and unruly. Her lips felt like great pieces of rubber. They seemed to flap against each other uncontrollably as she tried to speak.

The two men wearing glasses laughed. "Well that answers that question. Your vision will clear up soon. You're in the hospital. You were injured, but you are going to be just fine. You rest now and we'll talk later." None of it made much sense, but those men were right. She was very tired. It would be nice to sleep for a little while.

####

"Well, you look pretty good for someone who got hit by a Mack truck," Raeford drawled. Courtney stared at him blankly. "I reckon your memory is just a mite sketchy just now Cinderella."

"My name is Courtney." Her throat was dry and her voice sounded hoarse.

"Not in my book. Course you weren't wearing glass slippers, but the principle is the same. Sip of water?"

"Raeford?" She tried to take the straw in her mouth. Her lips hurt, but she managed to suck in a little of the cool liquid.

"Good girl, that's my name. The doc says you may not remember much for awhile. But it looks like you're startin' off real good."

"Was I hit by a truck?"

"No! I was just making a feeble attempt at humor. Listen, I got to make some phone calls. I'll be back to see you later. Maybe we can talk more then."

Once on the street Raeford hailed a cab. He gave the driver an address and then leaned back against the seat. He had slept most of the day and was feeling somewhat refreshed. Patsy was a wonderful cook and had unknowingly prepared his favorite meal of roast beef, mashed potatoes, fresh string beans, gravy, and hot rolls. Les was a lucky man.

Raeford climbed up the dark stairs in the ramshackle building where the field office had hastily been set up. He found the door he was looking for and rapped loudly.

"Cowboy?"

"Yo!"

A well built middle-aged man with graying hair and glasses greeted him.

"Congratulations! Quite a piece of work." The man extended his hand.

"Thanks, but I'm afraid it's not over. Too many loose ends."

"The chief wants to talk to you right away. Just use that phone." The man gestured toward a table cluttered with manila folders, papers, and a small computer. "Sorry about the mess. Things have been popping right and left. The phone is under here somewhere." The man moved a stack of paper that was coming from the printer and found the telephone. "Knew it was here somewhere. Here have a seat. By the way, the name is Franks."

Raeford sat in a straight back wooden chair and made his call while the printer continued to spew out stacks of folding paper. The grinding rasp was beginning to grate on his nerves. He glanced over at Franks. He was setting up another computer terminal. Raeford hated computers. Oh, he knew of their invaluable contribution to time-saving and space saving capabilities. Valuable information could be extracted at the touch of a button. He knew that his own investigative work was often made much easier because of the easy access of computers, but he hated them just the same.

Franks finished making his adjustments and plugged in the terminal. He pushed a button on the side and the screen lit up. Franks smiled with satisfaction as he pulled a chair in front of the keyboard and within seconds his hands were flying over the keys with light pecking noises accompanied by the rhythmic grating of the printer.

"Listen, I can't hear myself think in here with all of

these machines. I'll call you back after I question Scolari some more. He was stark raving mad last night...yeah, he was babbling about a lion coming after him...yeah, he must have been plumb full of drugs...hallucinating big time. Yeah, I'll see if I can get a line on his counterfeiting operation." Raeford hung up the phone. Franks was completely engrossed in his computer. Raeford turned and strode to the door.

"Leaving?" Franks called out in surprise.

"Yeah!" Raeford never looked back. There was something insidious about artificial intelligence and the people who controlled it. In the wrong hands or even just a short circuit and poof...he imagined nuclear bombs going off, billions of dollars going into the hands of the wrong people. He hailed a cab. As he leaned back against the seat it struck him that he had probably been looking in the wrong place for the money that had no doubt changed hands. He realized that it was not a suitcase full of bills that he would find, it would be a bank transaction probably done with computers. He remembered the laptop computer that the police had found in the wrecked van. It was the latest model called the convertible. It had been released on April 3 by IBM and weighed only 12 pounds. It operated on batteries and had a whopping 256k of RAM. "Damn those contraptions! Leave it to the criminals to have the latest and greatest!" Raeford leaped out of the cab just as it started to move, much to the chagrin of the driver. He bounded back up the stairs two at a time and burst through the door startling Franks who sat where Raeford had left him. Franks listened intently as the tall Texan explained what he needed and even before Raeford had finished speaking the computer expert knew what to do. "We got `em, I'll access..." Franks was grinning with an almost diabolical glee.

"I don't want any details, just get me some results. I'll call you later." Franks nodded absently. He was already absorbed in his task.

"Jesus! Computer people are damn scary," Raeford muttered as he closed the door.

####

Courtney opened her eyes and for a few blissful moments she thought she was at home. Then little by little she realized she was in a hospital room. She could see a gray sky through the window and from the light outside she surmised that it was day time, but she had no idea if it was morning or afternoon or for that matter what day of the week. The double vision that she had experienced was gone and now she only noticed a slight blur. She surveyed her room and caught sight of an arrangement of colorful flowers sitting on a portable night stand near her bed.

"Good morning! I'm glad to see you're awake. How do you feel?" A matronly nurse bustled in. She went straight to the IV apparatus and checked it.

"What happened?" Courtney attempted to rise up and lean on her elbow. Pain clamped around her ribcage immobilizing her with its force. She grimaced and moaned.

"No. No. I wouldn't move around much if I were you. Those broken ribs are going to be a little painful for a while. The doctor will be in to talk to you later." The nurse finished her inspection and bustled toward the door.

Courtney felt angry with the woman. Why wouldn't she at least tell her why she was in the hospital? Then she had a terrifying thought. She didn't know what city she was in or what state. Fear shot through her as she struggled to find herself in her thoughts. Tears rolled down her swollen bruised face and their salty trail burned her raw skin. She could put nothing together and panic threatened to overwhelm her.

A soft tapping on the door caught her attention. A woman's hand, a face, two faces. They looked so familiar.

"Oh, my Lord, Courtney!" the woman sobbed as she hurried over to the bed.

"Mom?" Then she knew. Fresh tears flowed from her eyes as she remembered with healing relief who she was and that these were the two dearest people in her life.

Clyde Hammond was unable to speak at the sight of his daughter's disfigured face. If the nurse had not told him that she was in this room, he would not have recognized her. He was sick with anguish and then almost immediately the anguish was replaced with rage. He wanted to hit something. He wanted to tear someone apart, especially the foul beast who had desecrated his angel's face. Even with clenched fists and gritted teeth emotion rose up and nearly overwhelmed his British self control. He had to leave the room to calm down before he could utter a word. Once outside he put his clenched fists to his face and wept.

"Where did Dad go?" Courtney was not yet cognizant of the impact of her altered appearance.

"I th-think he went to find the doctor. He has a little trouble maintaining his composure in hospitals." Clarisa too fought hard for self control. Instinctively she knew that her daughter was not fully aware of what had happened to her.

"I hope Dad finds him. I'd like to know what's going on. I...I just can't remember and I hurt so bad and I don't even know where we are." Courtney closed her eyes in exhaustion.

"You sleep a little, Darlin', and I promise I'll get some answers for you. I'll tell you everything I know when you wake up." Her voice grew softer as though she crooned to a very small child. "Everything is all right now, honey," she placed a feathery kiss on her daughter's cheek as Courtney drifted into a light sleep.

Raeford stood in the hall at a discreet distance. He watched sympathetically as the distraught father released his shock and anguish in great racking sobs. He waited patiently until the heaving shoulders quieted and he wiped the tears from his eyes before he spoke. "Mr. Hammond?"

"Yes?" Clyde turned quickly at the sound of his name.

"How's she doin' this afternoon?" Raeford knew that small talk was not what this grief-stricken man wanted, but he wanted to ease in to the conversation knowing that he had to tell this good man some very harsh facts about what happened to his daughter.

"It is Scolari that is responsible, for what happened to my daughter isn't it?" Clyde rasped through an emotion ravaged voice.

"Yes sir, he is. Let's go sit down and I'll tell you what happened." Raeford led him to a private waiting room at the end of the long hall.

"I hope you nail that bastard's bloody ass to a cross." Anger vibrated in every word as he hissed through clenched teeth.

"How 'bout if I draw and quarter him first." Raeford could only guess at what this devoted father must be feeling.

Raeford spoke at length to the ashen-faced man. He concisely described what had happened but left out any details that he knew would prove too much for a father to hear at this moment. He failed to mention that Clyde's beloved daughter had been tied to the bed and instead said only that, when he found them in the townhouse, Courtney had been badly beaten and had gone into shock. He explained that Antonio had been so high on drugs that he had gone over the edge. He was currently being held on a number of charges and there was no way in hell he was ever going to get out on the street again.

Clyde removed his glasses and rubbed his eyes. "By God he'd better stay in prison, because if he does get out I'll kill him myself." He sighed and put his glasses back on.

"Yes sir. But you'll have a hard time beatin' me to it." Clyde looked into Raeford's strong face. He knew his daughter had been rescued by the best and had no doubt that Raeford was as good as his word.

"I believe that's true." Clyde liked this young man's unwavering look. He managed a tight smile as he extended his hand.

"Thank you for what you did for my daughter."

"Yes sir. I've got some things to do but I'll be back to check on her later.

A lovely emerald green haze floated on the ceiling above Courtney's bed. It looked as cool and inviting as the sea she so loved. She longed to immerse her hot tired body in the cool refreshing depths of the ocean and just swim lazily in softly lapping waves. According to her wish the green mist floated down...down... Courtney sighed with relief as the feather soft energy caressed and cooled her swollen painful face. The terrible ever-present pain in her head eased and she watched with objective interest as an angry black undulating mass rose above her. Great spikes shot out from jagged gray edges as though attempting to pierce the shield that now surrounded her, but she felt no fear or pain, knowing that she was fully protected now by the power of the light that grew stronger with each breath. The dark mass above her grew fainter, finally disappearing altogether just as she knew it would. The dark memories that hovered on the edge of her consciousness backed further away and she was filled with a sense of well-being and contentment. At last she could rest and sleep.

Raeford walked into the hospital room. He stood beside Courtney's bed silently watching her peaceful repose. How could it be, he wondered, she looked so much better already. It was only Monday evening and yet the swelling was already decreasing and the bruises were beginning to fade! He smiled, she would recover completely, and he now had no doubt of that. Finding her asleep was a disappointment though since he had hoped that while the Hammond's were having their supper Courtney might remember some tidbit of information that would be useful in the investigation of Scolari's illegal activities.

He turned his back on the sleeping girl and walked over to the window. The sky had just begun to soften as the day faded to dusk. Clouds on the western horizon showed the first hints of pink promising a brilliant display of color as the sun began its descent into what would be dawn in faraway lands. Cars moved restlessly in and out of the hospital parking lot below him. People hurried from cars and surrounding buildings, each with their own private thoughts and lives filled with the gamut of experience. What makes one man decide to step outside the law of decency, he mused. Most people would live productive lives within the confines of right action toward one another and thanks be to whatever power that kept the majority of people in that line of thinking. He had no idea if there actually was a God, per se, but he knew there was *something*.... something good that kept everything in place. Just what was it that caused someone to step out of that place, he wondered; a question he had asked himself endlessly and as always received no definable answer.

Deep frown lines etched themselves into the weathered skin of his high forehead as his thoughts turned once again to Courtney and the Scolari case. There was no guarantee that she could remember anything yet, even if she did wake up. Mrs. Hammond had said her memory of the last three days was still blocked. For a moment Raeford fought the rising desire to smoke but gave in with an oath after a very short deliberation. He inhaled deeply as he mentally retraced his movements on Saturday night. Strange, he thought, how it had all come together.

Alec Parnesi had apparently dropped to his knees and eventually fell forward landing face down. Somewhere in between Courtney had lost one of her shoes. Alec's body had fallen forward on top of the shoe. That wouldn't have been odd in most circumstances, but in this one...Raeford took another deep drag on his cigarette. The street people had taken Alec's shoes and probably everything in his pants pockets that might be of value. The fact that his body lay face down and though he bled profusely he was still breathing, prevented the human scavengers from taking Courtney's shoe and his wallet, which he carried inside the front of his suit jacket. If he hadn't found the man's wallet it might have been hours or days before they had figured out who Alec Parnesi was and his ties to Antonio Scolari. That knowledge coupled with the discovery of the woman's shoe helped him to follow and locate the crazed Scolari and his victim before she became another statistic wearing a toe tag in a numbered drawer awaiting a grieving family's identification.

Raeford was jolted out of his intense reverie by a moan coming from the bed. He blinked rapidly and swiped a large long-fingered hand across his eyes at the sight of the green haze that momentarily hovered over Courtney's still form. He cautiously approached the bed and looked down at her bruised face. Must have been a trick of the light he decided and went back to the window. His restless thoughts tried to find a reason for the green glow. Failing, he abandoned that question and returned to something more tangible as he again replayed the events that had led him to this hospital room and solved *some* mysteries but created new ones.

He remembered the day he had gone to search Courtney's Santa Monica apartment. There were traces of cocaine in her bathroom but not anywhere else. He knew that Antonio had spent the whole day there that Sunday. Was Courtney using drugs or was it just Scolari using them? Raeford lit another cigarette and blew a long plume of smoke toward the ceiling. He didn't want to believe that the girl was a user, but how could anyone be that naive? Caufield seemed to think she was innocent, but, his mind argued, when the abandoned limo was searched they found Courtney's luggage. Scolari's cuff link that matched the one found in the dead girl's hand was in Courtney's makeup case. They also found a broken earring. He was sure it would match the piece they had found in Lilia's ear. There had been evidence of a scuffle and some defense bruises on her wrists and arms. If Miss Hammond was so innocent, what was she doing with those things in her suitcase? Suddenly the Texan slapped his head as if he had just thought of something. "The restaurant," he said aloud. "The money is being laundered through the restaurant!" He dropped the cigarette butt on the floor and crushed it out with his boot. Then swore viciously as he realized where he was. Feeling sheepish he bent quickly to pick up all of the crushed butts and tossed them into a small wastebasket near the bathroom door.

"Smells like somebody been smokin' in here!" A short squarely built nurse bustled through the door just as Raeford disposed of the evidence. "This is a nonsmoking room!" The nurse glared at Raeford.

"Yes ma'am, I was just leavin'."

"I'll thank you to obey the rules if you evah come round here again!"

"Yes ma'am." Raeford hurried out; he needed to call Franks.

Courtney opened her eyes just moments after Raeford had left the room. She smelled cigarette smoke. "Antonio?" she mumbled as she strained to focus her eyes.

"No. I ain't Antonio. My name's Mary. A young man just left, but I didn't catch his name.

The pain in her head had diminished substantially and she could feel a gnawing in her stomach. Mary smiled and chuckled as she heard a long rumbling growl coming from Courtney's stomach. "You wouldn't be hungry would you now?" The nurse asked.

"Well, yes I think I am." Courtney croaked through dry swollen lips.

"Well, awright. I'll see if I can get you some broth and maybe some Jell-O," the nurse promised.

"I'd rather have a chocolate milk shake."

Mary threw her head back and laughed. "I'll see what I can do!"

After the nurse left the room, Courtney gazed at the window. The sun was setting and the sky was growing dark. She knew it was evening. She remembered her mother telling her that she had been injured and that she was in a hospital in San Francisco. Beyond that, her mind was dark and unyielding. If the truth be known she didn't want to try to invite that terror which lurked at the edge of her memory. When she tried to remember anything, her heart would start to pound and cold dark tentacles of fear began to squeeze the breath from her lungs... no, much better not to go there...much better to stay safe.

"Hello, Darlin'. How are you feeling?"

"Much better. The nurse said she was going to try and find a chocolate milk shake for me," Courtney rasped.

Clarisa's eyes filled with tears of relief. She knew that hunger was a good sign that her daughter was beginning to recover.

"Hello, Princess."

"Hi Dad. You look awful. Have you been getting enough sleep?" Clyde and Clarisa both laughed in relieved hysteria. Their daughter was back.

"I'm not joking, you both look exhausted. You need to get some rest."

Clyde struggled for composure realizing that Courtney didn't understand the humor of the situation. "Well, Luv, I have a strong feeling that we will do just that tonight. I must say, in contrast to your mother and me, you look perfectly wonderful. You seem to be healing before our very eyes."

"I'd probably heal faster if I could have a chocolate milk shake."

"Never fear. I'll see that you get one immediately!" Clyde bent to kiss his daughter lightly on the cheek, then hurried off to fulfill his mission. He was glad to have something...anything to do.

"Mom."

"Yes, Darlin'."

"I know that something really bad must have happened to me or else I wouldn't have forgotten it, right?"

Clarisa would never have understood what her daughter was going through if she had not had her own experience with memory loss and, after many years, a memory recovery. Inwardly she cringed as she thought of the long forgotten horror of what had happened after the debutante ball.

"Darlin', you had a severe blow to the head. When the

brain..."

"Mom, I know all that. The doctor told me about concussions and why my eyes won't focus. But I know something...happened...something really awful. I feel like it's on the tip of my tongue like a name or a book title that I've forgotten." Courtney closed her eyes. It was disconcerting to see everything in a blur.

"I truly don't have all of the answers for you. But I promise that tomorrow, if you are still improving this rapidly I will tell you everything I know. I do understand how you feel. But I want you to get a little stronger before we have that discussion." Courtney felt calmer as she listened to her mother's soothing voice. Everything would be ok now.

Clyde strode triumphantly into the room carrying a large white covered cup that he had purchased from the restaurant across the street from the hospital. He felt like a conquering hero as he looked into his daughter's eyes. Clarisa had fluffed her pillows and helped her to move into a sitting position. Courtney eagerly drank the cold rich shake and made small contented sounds as she savored each swallow. She had nearly finished it by the time Mary returned carrying a tray with a bowl of broth, a plate of green Jell-O, and some hot tea.

"Well, you got your milkshake, didn't you?" The nurse smiled. "I'll just leave this tray here anyway just in case." The Hammonds exchanged pleasantries with the friendly woman, each remarking about the amazing progress Courtney was making in her recovery. Courtney didn't join the conversation, but she enjoyed the happy normal sound of people talking.

An announcement over the paging system alerted visitors that it was time to leave. The Hammonds took turns hugging their daughter and saying good-night. The hotel they were staying in was nearby so they promised to return early the next morning with a breakfast that they could all enjoy together.

Courtney lay quietly listening to the hospital sounds after her parents had gone. Nurses came and went going about their duties with manufactured cheer. She relaxed into the pleasant blankness of her mind. She had no desire for any mental stimulation. She could hear the muffled sounds of an abrasive television program coming from another room. She wished for the healing presence of the emerald green cloud. Again according to her wish, green sparks of light flashed and came together above her. The emerald sea floated down and submerged her just as it had before. She felt so peaceful her body tingled as though she was immersed in a cool carbonated soda. It tickled and she giggled softly.

"Well little lady, I'm glad to see you are feeling better!" Courtney jumped at the sound of Raeford's voice. She noticed, though, that her ribs didn't hurt when she moved.

"I am sorry I startled you."

"Oh, well, I just didn't hear you come in." She hoped the green sparkles wouldn't be frightened away by his intrusion.

"If you don't mind me saying so I've never seen anything like this in my life! I've never seen anyone look so bad one minute and then look so good the next!" Courtney didn't know how she looked and furthermore she didn't really care at the moment. She only knew that she felt better and her ribs didn't hurt. She had no idea how to respond so she kept silent and simply smiled. How nice it felt to smile without pain.

"This is, uh, a nice room."

Courtney was silent.

"So you are feeling real good now?" Raeford jammed his fists into his pockets and tensed his shoulders. He was reluctant to break the pervading atmosphere of peace. He knew that as her memories returned it would be a long time before she could feel peaceful again.

"Oh I almost forgot, thank you for the flowers! They were almost the first thing I saw when I woke up."

"Glad you liked 'em. Hospital rooms ought to be painted bright colors. How a person can get well in such a drab atmosphere I'll never know. The creator even gave the desert cactus bright flowers." Raeford paced to the window and back.

"It's okay. You can ask me anything you want to," Courtney broke the silence, "But I can't remember anything except...I was packing a suitcase."

"Well, let's start there. What were you packing?"

Courtney began to recall the articles of clothing that she had put in her suitcase.

"You are doing great. Now where were you going?"

"To the wedding...in the Napa Valley...with Antonio." Suddenly Courtney felt like crying but she didn't know why.

"That's good, now tell me what you know about Antonio." Courtney rambled disjointedly through their first meeting and subsequent dates.

"Did you ever do drugs together?" The question took Courtney by surprise. She had never considered doing drugs with anyone. She had known of people who were very involved with drugs, but she had always tried to distance herself from them.

Raeford watched the girl's face. Her expression said it all. He had questioned enough people to know that no matter what words they spoke, the truth was in their eyes and expressions. He knew now that Courtney was not a drug user.

"Did you know that Antonio used cocaine?" Courtney

shook her head. "Did you know he used it in your apartment?" Her eyes opened wider. She wondered if Raeford was just making this up.

"What about Antonio's business. Did he ever talk about it?"

"Not very much. He seemed to be having some trouble with some business associates and there were times he sounded very distraught but he never told me exactly what the problem was. Once he said he was at a meeting almost all night."

"Umm. Would that have been a Saturday night?" Courtney nodded.

"Did Antonio ever talk to you about Lilia March?" Raeford watched Courtney frown. Something definitely troubled her about Lilia.

"Antonio said she was always trying to impress movie people. She wanted to be an actress. He said that's why she created the scene in the restaurant that night." Courtney closed her eyes as she remembered the wine and the vision.

"But there's more to it," Raeford coaxed, yet fearing what she would say.

"Yes, you see...," she sighed deeply, "I saw blood when she spilled the wine."

"Huh?" Raeford had no idea what she was referring to. He wondered if her head injury was still affecting her thinking.

"I...," Courtney sobbed, "I saw the vision...the bleeding wound in her chest...I should have said something...I should have warned her...but I thought it was nothing...I was jealous! And then she was dead...I saw it in the paper." Her words stopped as she gave in to her tears.

Raeford was thunderstruck. He had not expected an

answer like that. He ran his hand through his hair. He felt the hair on the back of his neck standing up.

"You...uh, you're psychic?"

"Yes. No. I mean I just `see' things sometimes." Courtney rolled her head to one side. Something was happening in the dark void where her memories had disappeared. A flicker. A light, images. She squeezed her eyes shut in an attempt to block out the light and the fear that accompanied the sight of those images. She rolled her head from side to side and blinked her eyes rapidly.

"Hey, you okay? I'm sorry I upset you. It's just that there are some missing pieces...some things I need to know." Raeford watched her with great concern.

"I...I'm okay." Courtney reached for a tissue and dabbed at her eyes and nose. The flicker of light in her mind refused to be extinguished. The dark curtain was drawn aside and the memories rushed unbidden to take their place forever a part of her life.

Raeford watched the girl's struggle. He knew the memories were returning and he wondered if she would be able to cope with them or if she would need a tranquilizer. He went to the door and looked down the hallway at the nurse's station. No one was there and the halls were empty.

"Oh no!" Courtney moaned as painful memories scraped against her bruised mind.

He hurried back to the bed and picked up one of Courtney's clenched hands. He felt a responsibility for this girl that he couldn't explain. His feelings for Latoia were clear and definable, although how it could happen so quickly and with such a classy young woman, he couldn't explain. But these protective feelings for Courtney, this need to make sure she would be all right was something unusual. He had encountered many female victims in his years with the agency, but he had always maintained an objective detachment, he was just doing his job. Then he reminded himself, this case had been different from the beginning. He had never become so obsessed with the capture of a criminal. There was something about Antonio Scolari that automatically invoked his rage. He knew nothing would stop him from keeping Scolari away from society for good.

Courtney was crying silently. Tears ran in a steady stream from the corners of her closed eyes. She watched the images in her awakened memory as they replayed the events that had brought her to the hospital room.

"It was a bad time for you, Miss Hammond, but you're okay now," Raeford spoke softly. "I know the memory is hard, but Scolari is a criminal and we have got to see to it that he won't hurt anyone else. Please understand that you must talk to me. Tell me everything that happened, even the smallest detail might help me put that bas...er, uh, him away for keeps."

Courtney opened her eyes and looked up at the tall man with new respect. She had misjudged his easygoing manner when her father had introduced them. Her vision was no longer blurred as a result of her head injury and her judgment was no longer clouded by immature romantic fantasy. She looked into Raeford's clear blue eyes. She could see truth, integrity, and real concern. How could she have missed that before? But then how could she have mistakenly seen love in Antonio's eyes? She knew then that she had simply chosen to see only what she wanted to see. She had lived in a world of fairy tales. It was time to face life and herself in the light of reality and truth.

Raeford pulled a chair close to the bed and handed Courtney a glass of water and a tissue to wipe her eyes. Then he sat down and pulled out his pack of cigarettes. He started to light one but decided against it as he remembered the nurse who insisted that he obey the nonsmoking rules. He realized he didn't really want to smoke right now anyway. The act of pulling out a cigarette and lighting it was nothing but a habit. It was something familiar, an action that he used when he was in unfamiliar surroundings. Strange, he thought, he had never tried to analyze his use of tobacco before now. Maybe he would actually quit smoking some day.

Courtney began to speak. Her voice was soft and hesitant at first, but it grew steadier with each sentence. She began with the night she met Antonio at her parent's dinner party.

"How'd your parents happen to invite him?" Raeford frowned.

"They didn't. His father is one of my father's clients and I think he was unable to attend. Antonio took his place."

"Why? Did your father do any legal work for him?"

"I don't think so. I really don't know why Antonio was there." Courtney continued her story. Raeford stopped her occasionally to ask a question, but most of the time he sat quietly listening and watching her face.

She told him every detail of the day that Antonio had come to her apartment in Santa Monica, the torn pocket, the diamond cuff link, the broken earring, the lies he had told about where he had called from and the fact that even though he had said he read about Lilia's death in the newspaper she had not seen one in his car. She recounted that strange night before the wedding. She described the cold silent Alec who had picked her up and drove her to meet Antonio.

"Oh! I think Antonio shot Alec later." Courtney gasped at the memory.

"Yeah. I got to him just before he died. In fact it was

probably him that saved your life. Course he wasn't the only one who helped, but he gave me the last clue."

Courtney's eyebrows shot up. She couldn't imagine the man with cold eyes wanting to help her; after all he had wanted to kill her for Antonio.

"He told me where Antonio was taking you with his last breath. When I got to the address Alec gave me, I was still not sure if I had understood him right. So, I drove through the parking lot. Sure enough I saw your other shoe lying in front of the door of the townhouse. It must have come off when Scolari carried you inside." Courtney's skin crawled at his words. It could so easily have turned out worse. Courtney stifled a yawn. She had no idea what time it was but she was very tired. They had gone over every detail that she could remember of the terrible ordeal. She felt cleansed somehow as though by talking about it she had freed herself. She could see everything so clearly now and she understood where she had made her mistakes in judgment. Silently she vowed that nothing like that would ever happen to her again.

"I am sorry, I've kept you awake too long. It's past midnight. Guess I better be going before they throw me outta here. I can't believe they haven't already."

Right on cue a nurse opened the door. "What are you doing here? Now you need to leave and let this girl get some sleep!"

"I'm leaving! I am sorry! Miss Hammond..."

"Courtney."

"Okay Courtney. Get some sleep. I'll be back tomorrow."

The nurse bustled around the room, checking her blood pressure, making notes on the chart, and finally turning off the light.

Courtney lay awake for a few minutes. She knew that it would take a little time to heal emotionally from her trauma. She knew too that something had changed deep within herself. Nothing would ever be quite as simple as it used to be. Maybe nothing ever was simple; maybe it was her unfocused perception of life that made it seem so. It was probably good in some way for her to have received a bump on the head to make her wake up, she thought. Indeed her vision was no longer blurred; life's realities were coming in loud and clear.

CHAPTER FOURTEEN

"What!" Raeford was livid. He had gone directly to the precinct where Les Wiggans was working after he had finished talking with Courtney. He found the young detective laboriously filling out reports. As soon as Les saw him he blurted out the news. Antonio Scolari was missing. "What happened?" Raeford roared.

"Seems like some guys waving a court order and official IDs took him away. Feds I think, anyway the papers were bogus, no tellin' who those guys were or where they took Scolari."

"Why didn't somebody check 'em out? Why didn't you call me?" Raeford's face was flushed as red as his hair.

"Hey! I just found out myself and besides its one o'clock in the morning, how th' hell am I supposed to know where to find you?"

"Yeah. Well what have we got to go on, descriptions or anything?"

"We got the police artist workin' on some sketches."

For the next two hours the two men worked to put together small pieces of information in an attempt to decide their next course of action. Finally Les leaned back in his chair and yielded to a mighty yawn.

"I'm bushed and you look like you haven't slept since Sunday. How 'bout we go to my place for some rest. Patsy's expecting me to bring you home with me."

"I thank you and Patsy too. Guess I could use some rest." Raeford had made no attempt to find a motel room.

Generally he couldn't sleep well in them anyway. He took catnaps in desk chairs and rental cars to keep himself going. He usually preferred to be alone, but the allure of the Wiggans' homey atmosphere appealed to his long suppressed need for family warmth.

####

Courtney mumbled in her sleep. The dream she was having had taken an odd turn. She was a young girl of fourteen. Her long black hair was pulled back with combs and hung in ringlets down her back. The grass beneath her feet looked as though it had been trampled flat, most likely by horses. She could see their droppings on the ground all around her. She lifted her long ruffled hoop skirt to avoid soiling the delicate fabric as she daintily stepped over the offensive fly-riddled piles. She was in some sort of camp. Bearded men in filthy gray ragged uniforms milled about. Many wore blood soaked bandages on their heads and arms. She walked between the cooking fires and bedrolls but no one even looked up as she passed.

She saw a tent in front of her and she made her way toward it. She blinked her eyes in the bright sunlight and within that second the sunlight disappeared. It was a dark night and cooking fires burned low as the men slept. Leaves rustled as dark figures moved stealthily to a crouch behind a tent. Filled with curiosity she walked boldly closer until she could just make out several ragged soldiers creeping silently through the shadows. She could see the wild, desperate look in the sunken eyes but even though she stood only a few feet away they never once looked in her direction.

The front man gestured and the others followed his signal. She thought the leader seemed familiar and she moved in for a closer look. Moonlight illuminated his face.

She gasped with the realization that the dirt-covered face of the soldier was also the face of Antonio. What was he doing in the Civil War?

Someone was sobbing in the darkness. She walked out of the clearing and into the forest. She found a soldier sitting cross-legged with his back against a tree. He rocked back and forth mechanically as he sobbed. She knelt by the distraught man and placed her hand on his shoulder. He did not acknowledge her presence or her touch. His vacant eyes stared straight ahead. She was surprised to see how young he was. Soft hair grew unevenly on his cheeks and chin. She guessed him to be no more than sixteen. A great wave of compassion engulfed her as she realized that the boy's mind had been set adrift by the horrors of the war. She sat on the ground near him. She tried to wipe the tears from his cheeks with her hanky. The more she wiped away the dirt and tears the older the boy became. He was a man now with red hair and sky blue eyes. Raeford?

Shouts from the camp caught her attention. She stood up and gathered her skirts in her hands to keep from stumbling as she ran toward the camp. Men were running and shouting curses mixed with orders. Gunshots blasted through the forest.

"Theivin' murderin' cowards! Deserters! Kill 'em!" Though she stood in the midst of the angry men her presence remained unnoticed. With a start she saw that they ran through her, not around her. She was transparent. She was dead, a ghost!

The men she had seen sneaking into the camp stood in a dismal cluster at gunpoint. Only the leader held his head up defiantly.

"Is the Captain alive?" one man growled.

"Barely. This one tried to slit his throat. They was tryin' to steal from their own army. Scum like this doesn't

deserve no trial!"

"Found nothah one. He's done lost it I b'lieve." The young boy was shoved into the fire lit circle.

Before anyone knew what was happening the deserter that looked like Antonio threw himself forward grabbing a bayonet from one of the men and plunged the blade deep into the chest of the vacant-eyed boy.

"You blubberin' walleyed boy! You ain't no man! You wouldn't take that girl, you wouldn't do nothin' but cry and give us away!" The rest of his words were lost in the angry shouts that followed. She started backing away, she didn't want to see or hear any more and she covered her face with her hands.

A blast of cold air sent a shudder through her body and she dropped her hands from her eyes and hugged herself in an effort to ward off the chill. Through the foggy darkness she could see the lights of the city. Water lapped gently near her bare feet and a buoy bell clanged with the rhythm of the swells. She could just make out the outline of a bridge high above her, and below, dark figures stood side by side. Great mounds of fog were rolling toward shore effectively shutting out the streetlights from across the bay. Courtney realized she no longer wore her billowing hoop skirt. In fact she wore only her hospital gown. Voices rose in anger from the dark figures near the water so she moved closer to hear what they were saying. They spoke Italian but now she had no trouble understanding what they said.

"You deceived us, your own family. For this you will die." The voice was low and calm. Courtney could see two men holding another man between them. It was Antonio. His hair was in wild disarray and his eyes darted from one face to another in a silent plea for mercy from his captors.

"No. No. I didn't. It was all part of the plan to insure

safe delivery. We found the intruder and killed him. I didn't know how much he had found out. I was afraid our plans had been discovered. Everything is still there. It's in the cellars at the estate, I promise! I can prove it!" Antonio sobbed in anguish.

"You had tickets to Italy and my sources tell me you made no plans to deliver the merchandise. They also tell me you are using drugs."

"No! No! Only a little!"

"You are addicted! You are a junkie! You can no longer be trusted. It is such a pity. You might have taken my place one day."

Courtney recognized some of the men. She had seen them in the restaurant, and at the wedding. She felt sorry for the fallen man that she had loved. He was so pathetic and broken.

The voices stopped and the two men who held Antonio bound his hands behind him and forced him to his knees in the cold water then turned their backs and walked as briskly as the wet sand would allow, away from him. Antonio was sobbing with his head down. One of the men raised a handgun and took aim as he called Antonio's name. The condemned man looked up and a red spot appeared in his forehead. His eyes never blinked. He just fell slowly back until his head made a little splash when it hit the gently lapping water of the bay.

####

"Good mornin'," Clarisa and Clyde entered Courtney's room wearing wide smiles and carrying some covered dishes.

"Hi!" Courtney was sitting up in bed. The large bandage had been removed from her head and replaced with a smaller one. The IV tubes were gone from her arms and the swelling of the left side of her face was only visible under close scrutiny. The bruises around her eyes and mouth were reduced to a purple blush. "The doctor says I can go home tomorrow!" she said brightly.

"Oh, Darlin', that's wonderful! Now you know your father and I insist you will come home with us. We will not let you return to your apartment until you have completely recovered."

"Good grief, Mom, I can sure tell you've been in the south!" Courtney teased as she listened to the pronounced intensity of her mother's accent.

"Sounds like a real southern belle, doesn't she, Princess?" Clyde winked at his daughter.

"Well, now I really shouldn't have to suffer this abuse." Father and daughter laughed at Clarisa's feigned indignation.

The plates were uncovered and soon they all munched on fresh cold fruit, hot buttered blueberry muffins, and honey. Styrofoam cups filled with freshly brewed French roast coffee sat steaming on the table near her bed. Courtney felt good. In some ways she had never felt better in her whole life. She realized that her life meant more to her now than it ever had before.

"Have I ever told you how much I truly appreciate you both?"

Her parents exchanged a glance.

"I mean, I'm not sure that you know how truly grateful I...I mean how much I love you both." She couldn't find words to adequately convey the depth of her feelings.

"Darlin' daughter, we feel the same way. How we could have been so fortunate to have you as our child...well I do not know why, I only know I am grateful."

Clarisa stood up and leaned over the bed to kiss her daughter's cheek.

"One could rightly state that it was *you,* Princess, who found *us*." Clyde reached for his daughter's hand and then his wife's as she sat down again.

"I remembered everything last night." Her parents frowned and looked at her searchingly."Are you all right?" her mother asked softly, not knowing what else to say.

"The memories are shocking...unbearable." Courtney squeezed her eyes shut for a moment before she continued. "It may be awhile before I can truly confront them. But...I think the important thing right now is that I lived through it and I hope I've learned some very important lessons and last but not least, I hope to be a better person." Courtney's lip trembled slightly as she struggled to control her emotions. "Thank you both for standing by me through all of my immature foolishness."

"I see before me the wisest, most beautiful daughter anyone could ever ask for. Wisdom and maturity come with experience and experience takes time to acquire, Luv. In my opinion you've quite enough for one weekend!" Clyde finished with a cheery wink.

"Thank you both. There are some things that I must face about myself and the direction that I choose for my life. I want to do something useful...meaningful." Courtney rubbed her hand across the small gauze bandage near her left temple.

"I think that some of those decisions can be made at another time. Why don't you just lie back against these pillows and rest a bit. Why I think the stores should be open now. I'll just bet you don't have anything to wear for the trip home, do you?"

"Well, I really don't know where my clothes are. I had a suitcase, but I don't know what happened to it."

"I will take care of *that* and your father can see about getting us on a plane tomorrow!"

Courtney leaned back against her pillows and shut her eyes. She was anxious to leave the hospital. She hadn't slept well. The nurses woke her often as they came in to perform their duties. Then of course, the dreams and the memories haunted her thoughts the rest of the time. She wanted to go home to familiar surroundings and normal wonderful mundane activities and Shane, oh she wanted to see her brother's teasing smile. She drifted into a light sleep and happy thoughts of home.

"Mornin'." Courtney had opened her eyes only seconds before Raeford walked through the door. "Well if you aren't a sight for sore eyes I don't know what is." His tone was warm and friendly, but Courtney noted that his eyes did not mirror the smile on his lips.

"Something is wrong," Courtney said simply. She stared steadily into Raeford's troubled blue eyes.

"Scolari is missing. I've assigned a security detail outside your door." He watched her face carefully. He was acutely aware of how fragile Courtney's emotional state might be. He was very concerned about telling her that her life could once again be in danger. He had prepared himself to face tears, maybe anger, and some sort of emotional outburst. But he was not prepared for the stoic calm that he saw in her eyes. "We're not sure whether you are in any danger, but there's no tellin' what that crazy bast...uh, what he might do." Courtney sighed and looked down at her hands. Raeford sensed that there was an inner struggle going within her. He walked over to the bed and waited quietly. "You okay with this?"

"Antonio is dead," she said simply. Raeford was stunned. He couldn't imagine what she was talking about. "I...saw...him die." Raeford felt the hair on the back of his neck standing up again.

"Why don't you explain what you're talking about?" Raeford sat down. His mind was numb. He couldn't form any questions or thoughts, so he just waited.

"All of my life, or I should say my adult life, I have denied the things I see...my visions." Courtney touched the center of her forehead. "That woman Lilia is dead. I saw danger for her but I didn't try to warn her and now she is dead. I saw myself strapped to a bed, but I ignored the warning. If it hadn't been for you, *I* would be dead. Everything I have seen has come to pass. Last night after you left I saw them kill Antonio. Before they shot him Antonio told them about something hidden in the cellar at the Scolari estate. They seemed to be accusing him of cheating his family out of something. He fell on his knees and begged for another chance. But the older man refused and then they shot him in the head. He fell backward into the water. I didn't know how all of that could be possible until you came in here and told me that Antonio was missing. Then I knew. I knew that what I saw was not only just possible, but it actually happened in my presence. I was there. I saw it. I don't understand how it's possible or why it happened. I only know it *is* the truth," Courtney sighed as she finished speaking. It was the sound of her profound sadness as well as relief. It was over.

Raeford watched the young woman's face as she spoke. He noted her calm voice and serene expression. Her eyes never wavered from his. She absolutely believed what she was saying, he was certain of that. The one thing he was not sure of was whether her visions were simply a result of a blow on the head. He remembered the publicity about the man that nearly drowned. That publicity is what had made it possible for him to get hired as a bodyguard for Courtney and thus more openly observe Scolari.

"I can't truthfully say that I believe all this. I've never personally had any experience with a psychic. Due to the fact that the trail has come to an end and I can't figure out exactly what to do next anyway...I'd like to check out your uh...vision. Now, do you think you can tell me where this uh...event took place?"

"I can describe exactly what I saw," Courtney frowned.

"Good enough. Listen, I've got somebody waitin' for me down the hall. This fella was born an' raised in this fair city. He knows it like the back of his hand. Would you be willin' to give your description to him?"

"Yes."

"Good, now one more thing. I would appreciate it if you'd keep this under your hat until we get it checked out."

"I don't want my name or my family's name publicized at all," Courtney stated firmly.

"You got my word."

Within two hours Raeford and Les stood on the wet sand beneath the bridge that Courtney had described. They stood silently listening to the gulls and the sounds of the distant traffic. A buoy bell clanged it's incessant warning to boaters and the bay waters played gently with the refuse which littered the shoreline. The two men stepped over broken bottles, discarded tires, and rusting cans as they walked closer to the concrete pillars which supported the bridge. Neither man spoke, though they both saw the body at the same time. They splashed through the shallow water unmindful of shoes or clothes. Antonio lay face up in three inches of water. Small crabs had already begun their cleanup work in accordance with the irrefutable laws of nature, but there was no doubt in Raeford's mind as to the man's identity.

"This was an anonymous tip right?" Les turned to Raeford.

"Yeah." Raeford's jaw muscles flexed as he clenched his teeth.

"Better pull 'im to shore, then I'll call it in." Les stooped to take hold of the body. They carried it to the sand, and then Les went to the car to radio in.

Raeford felt tired as he stood looking at Antonio's body. He knew that the evil actions of this man had ended with his death, but fighting evil itself was like climbing a sand dune. A change of wind and you had to start all over again. He lit a cigarette and blew the smoke slowly through his pursed lips. It didn't taste good, so he flicked it into the water. He tried to ask himself what had just happened here. A woman who could not possibly have left her hospital bed had obviously *seen* a murder/execution take place miles away in the dead of night. He couldn't explain it. He thought of his dream ranch and Latoia. Maybe it's time for a vacation, he told himself.

Courtney stared at the tray of food that the nurse had placed in front of her. She decided that it didn't look too bad considering it was hospital food. She had asked for a vegetable salad and that's what they had served, but what she saw on her tray did not quite measure up to the picture she had in her mind.

"Don't touch that pitiful excuse for a salad, Darlin'! Look what your father and I have found!" Clarisa and Clyde hurried in laden with packages. The hospital tray was discarded and in its place Clarisa opened containers of clam chowder, spinach salad, and whole wheat rolls.

When the call came from Raeford, the family had just finished their lunch. Courtney answered the telephone and said nothing for a long moment as she listened to the information that he gave her.

"Thank you for calling me." Silent tears slid down her cheeks as she hung up. A sad relief washed through her along with the realization that a profound change was taking place in her life. She felt as though everything she had been doing up to this point was shallow and meaningless. Much of what had seemed exciting and important in a relationship no longer held her interest. She felt embarrassed to think that she had been taken in by all of the glamour and had forgotten to look for integrity, honesty and goodness. Only three days ago she had been in love with a man living in a fantasy, carefree and daydreaming of weddings and happily ever after endings. Today she was battered, her heart was broken and her foolish fantasy was dead.

"What has happened?" Clyde asked his daughter after a moment or two of silence.

"Antonio is dead," she murmured quietly, "He was shot by...some men...some criminals. I *saw* it happen in a vision. After you and Mom left this morning Raeford came in and told me that Antonio was missing. I told him about my vision so he and another man went to the place that I described. They found the...body. It happened just as I saw it in the vision."

Clarisa trembled as she listened to Courtney's voice. She suddenly felt like a child sitting at the feet of a wizened old woman. She sensed the change in her daughter and realized how much strength and courage she displayed, a courage that she herself could only admire as something far greater than her own.

"You appear very calm, Luv. Is that truly how you feel?" Inside Clyde wanted to shout for joy. He carefully refrained from any emotional display in deference to his daughter's feelings and the possibility that her emotions could be very fragile.

"I feel like I've changed. I...feel sad...angry, disappointed, embarrassed and maybe even a little lost. I'm only sure of one thing and that is I'll never be the same person again." She spoke in a flat monotone as she dropped her dark lashes down to watch the nervous play of her fingers on the hem of the sheet that covered her.

Clarisa's heart nearly broke for her daughter and for a moment she was utterly at a loss for words.

"Perhaps when we get back home you could talk to Dr. Epstein. I'm sure he could help you sort things out." Clyde stood up and planted a kiss on his daughter's forehead. "I've made our reservations. We'll be home for dinner tomorrow."

"That's great Dad. I'm really ready to go home."

The family passed the afternoon pleasantly. Clyde made a call to his office while Courtney tried on the clothes her mother had purchased for her. At three o'clock a nurse came in to take Courtney down for x-rays. She had told the doctor early that morning that her ribs were fine and she no longer needed the restrictive tape. He had laughingly promised to remove the tape if the x-rays showed that the bones had knitted. He thought it obvious that her head injury was clouding her reasoning. Certainly his patient would stop pestering him when he showed her the new pictures of her cracked ribs.

A smiling Courtney returned two hours later to find her parents were waiting for her with some fried ice cream, a San Francisco specialty they were all anxious to try. Everyone was trying very hard to be cheerful and not mention any of the unpleasantness but the forced smiles were putting a strain on everyone. Finally Courtney convinced her parents to leave and spend the rest of the evening relaxing or sightseeing. She was immensely relieved when they finally agreed. She was very grateful for the silence and the empty room. Before long she gave in to her sorrow and sobbed long and hard. Finally she had no more tears and lay back on her pillow and drifted into an exhausted sleep.

She had just awakened at ten o'clock when Raeford walked into her room.

"Evenin'. Sorry about comin' by so late. It was a busy

day."

"Hi. It's ok. I'm glad you came by. I'm going home tomorrow."

"I declare, that sure is good news," Raeford grinned. "You look almost as good as new."

"Thank you, thank you for my life."

"Like I said before, we got lucky. I, uh, spoke to a friend of yours, Latoia."

"How do you know Latoia?" Courtney's eyebrows shot up in surprise.

"It's a long story. Anyway I guess she can tell it better than I can. She said you are to call her as soon as you get back home." Courtney smiled and nodded. "You've been through a lot and I want you to consider callin' a doctor, a counselor. Someone who will help you sort through it all."

"Oh yes. My father has already suggested that I contact Dr. Epstein when we get home."

"Good." Raeford smiled then ducked his head and studied the toe of his left boot. He shifted his weight from one foot to the other and cleared his throat.

"Would you like to sit down?" Courtney could see that he was struggling with something.

"Thank ya. I really can't stay, but uh, here, I just wanted to give you this." He handed her his card. "If you ever have any problems or uh...*visions*," He dropped his voice to a whisper on the word 'visions', "just call this number and leave a message. Most likely, I can get back to you within a couple days."

"Thank you. I will."

"I've heard stories about people like you who work with the police but I never put too much stock in 'em. To tell you the truth, I still can't say how *much* I believe...but I will say that there is no doubt in my mind that you knew what you were talking about. Trackin' down criminals is gettin' harder. They got technology and creative minds. If you ever decide you want to do this again...well by God, when push comes to shove, I want you on *my* side." Courtney knew that it had been difficult for Raeford to accept what had happened. She understood completely. It had taken a life-threatening experience to awaken an acceptance of the truth of her gifts.

"I really don't know what I'm going to do yet. I don't know how I will use this ability, but if I ever *see*...anything that I think might be helpful to you I will call this number. Thank you again...for my life."

Raeford took Courtney's outstretched hand and squeezed it gently. He bent his tall lean body forward in a courtly bow, touched his hand to the brim of his hat and without another word he departed.

Courtney pushed the button to lower her bed. She knew she would sleep much more comfortably now that the tape had been removed from her ribs. She smiled at the memory of the perplexed Dr. Simms. He had been unable to comprehend the healing of the fractures. He simply knew that the first x-rays had been misread even though he remembered seeing those x-rays himself. The confused doctor left the room mumbling to himself and at the last moment dismissively waved a hand at her while giving orders for her to be released on the following morning. Well, she told herself, she couldn't explain it either, at least not yet. She knew that she had to find out more about her gifts and how she should use them. Maybe then she would know what to do with her life. Her eyes were heavy and she let them close. She wouldn't have to worry about those hospital dreams anymore, she thought as she drifted into dark dreamless sleep.

The actual flight from San Francisco to L.A.

International was very short in duration but Courtney was exhausted by the time the family stepped into the airport limousine, and her nerves were ragged. She had seen so many men that reminded her of Antonio. She jumped every time the airline employees made an announcement over the paging system. A businessman dropped his briefcase; it made a loud sharp sound and Courtney shrieked as she remembered the sound of gunshots.

The large elegant Palos Verdes house had never looked so inviting. Courtney went directly to her room and stretched out across her bed. At that moment she didn't care if she ever left that cozy safe room again. She felt a slight thump on the bed and her heart jumped. It was Pavlova, the white Persian. She walked across the soft comforter and stepped up onto Courtney's stomach. The aging cat purred loudly as she curled herself into a furry donut and prepared to take a little nap. Courtney smiled at her visitor and stroked the long white fur as she too drifted into a light doze.

The evening passed quickly as the family dined together with Maria hovering nearby to cater to Courtney's every need. Shane called just as the table was being cleared. He was studying for exams and promised to come home soon. The summer break was only a few days away. He was anxious to hear the details of Courtney's harrowing adventure. She agreed to tell *all* when he got home. The telephone rang constantly as friends and business associates discovered that the family had returned. When Latoia called, Courtney invited her to come for lunch the following day. Latoia piqued Courtney's curiosity even further by refusing to divulge any information about her encounter with Raeford. The girls agreed to share their experiences over lunch when Courtney was more rested from her trip.

By eleven o'clock that evening they were all exhausted and retired to their respective bedrooms. Courtney sat in front of her makeup mirror and brushed her long auburn hair. For the first time in several days she noticed the blue topaz sparkling on its gold chain. She watched her reflection as she put down her hair brush. She lifted her left hand and touched the blue stone.

"How amazing that you've managed to stay with me through all that insanity," she said aloud to the stone. "I wonder what other stories you could tell. I wish you could talk, I'm sure they would be fascinating. Well now you have one more story to add to your repertoire." Courtney's head ached slightly and the stitches pulled uncomfortably. She removed the loose bandage from her head and leaned toward the mirror for a closer inspection. The jagged cut had healed shut. A fine red line was all that remained. Anger momentarily flared as she recalled her conversation with the doctor. He had refused to remove the stitches before she left the hospital stating firmly that it was entirely too soon for such a deep wound to be healed enough to remove the stitches. Furthermore he was absolutely certain that if the stitches were not left in for a few more days there would be a large ugly scar on her head. The anger left as soon as it had begun as she realized he was just trying to do his job and protect her. She leaned closer to her reflection and considered for a moment then reached for her small fingernail scissors. She clipped the dark threads and then pulled them out one by one with her tweezers. She patted the area with a cotton ball soaked in hydrogen peroxide and then coated it with an antiseptic gel.

When she was finished, she leaned back and studied her image. The jagged red line was almost indiscernible near her hairline. The bruises were mere shadows and the swelling was completely gone. "I don't know what power saved me and then healed me so quickly," she solemnly told her reflection, "but I'm very grateful." She touched the blue topaz again. "I know that someone or something is responsible and I want to know more. If I truly have a *gift* then I want to know how to use it. Maybe I can help someone else sometime. I can't think of any other way to say thank you or to repay this debt that I now owe." A warm tingle flowed through her body and her eyes grew heavy. She had almost expected a vision to form but nothing happened. She waited for a few more minutes but fatigue, not a vision, called upon her. Finally she turned off the lights and got into bed. The aching in her head stopped immediately as her head sank into the down pillows. Her eyes closed and nearly in the same instant, she was asleep.

The next morning, Courtney awoke with a jolt. For a few seconds she had no idea where she was. Then the memories slapped at her bruised mind like angry bats who are awakened from their dark sleep.

Her chest heaved as she fought to breathe. She jumped from her bed thinking she needed to run away from something, then suddenly she halted as sweet relief quieted her panic. *She was safe at home with her parents.*

"Latoia is coming for lunch," she whispered breathlessly. A part of her wanted to laugh hysterically and dance around the room. She ran to the wall and flung her arms out as if to embrace it. "How utterly wonderful it will be to see her and talk to her. I'm safe. Life can be normal now." Tears poured down her face and her slim shoulders shook with the sobs of the most profound relief and joy she had ever felt.

Latoia and Courtney embraced in the foyer.

"Well girl, it's time we talk!" Latoia grinned as Courtney led the way to the patio. Maria had set up their luncheon near the pool. And talk they did through lunch and most of the afternoon. They hardly noticed when Maria cleared the dishes away and refilled their glasses with lemonade. They had begun cautiously, each sharing their adventure with cursory details. As time wore on Courtney found herself telling Latoia about some of her visions and finally how she saw Antonio's execution. Courtney watched her friend's face for any sign of disbelief or derision but she saw only someone who seemed interested in every word she had to say.

"You know what I think?" Latoia said when Courtney had finished her story, "I think it's karma. We all had some kind of karma together." Courtney frowned in consternation.

"Well just think about it. How could all these things be coincidence, blind chance? My grandmother used to talk about it all the time." Latoia sounded adamant and there was no doubting the sincerity of her voice and expression.

"You are really serious, aren't you?"

"You better believe it! You took the same classes I did, don't you remember reading about Edgar Cayce and all those things he said about reincarnation?"

"Latoia, of course I read that stuff and I thought it was very interesting but I didn't take it seriously at the time."

"Well, maybe you should now." Latoia smiled and opened her eyes wide. "After all, some of the greatest minds the world has ever known believed in reincarnation."

"So, uh, what animal do you think you were last time around?" Courtney joked.

"Ok, Miss Smarty Pants, head of the class, apparently you didn't do your homework on this one. According to what I know your soul doesn't jump around from animals to humans and back to animals. The soul progresses to better circumstances each time. Like me, for instance, I think I was a slave in the South during the Civil War."

Courtney blinked as Latoia's words caused something akin to an electric shock to jolt her body. She remembered flashes of her dream, starving soldiers ragged uniforms, her own long ruffled gown.

"Why did you mention the South, the Civil War?" Courtney was slightly breathless and she felt her heartbeat quicken.

"I do believe you felt something didn't you? See! I'll bet you anything you were there too!" Latoia squinted her eyes and leaned forward. She studied her friend's discomfort for a moment, then extended her hand and rested it gently on Courtney's forearm. "You were there, too. I know you were. I'll just bet you and I knew each other then and that's why we are friends now. Think about it. Remember when I came to Madame's class the first time?" Courtney *did r*emember. From the preliminary 'hello' they had been friends. Due to their busy schedules they had not spent large amounts of time together, but during their visits they had always talked nonstop. They always covered every subject imaginable and though each was distinctly unique in opinion and background they seemed to share some intangible bond.

"How many other people from Madame's or school are you friends with?" Latoia reminded Courtney of a satisfied cat licking cream from her whiskers.

"You are right on that score!" Courtney couldn't help laughing. It seems they always did a lot of that when they were together. "Well you could certainly be right. I do know that something is happening to me and I need to find out what it is. I don't disbelieve it. Heaven only knows I've seen and felt so many strange things in my life, especially these past few months. I think reincarnation might be something I will look into more closely," Courtney added seriously.

"I can't believe the time!" I have to go!" Latoia stood up. "I promised Mom I'd do some shopping for her."

"I'm glad you came over today. I hope we can get

together again real soon."

"Me too. The doctor told me to give this knee two more weeks before I do any serious exercise so it looks like I am going to have plenty of extra time. So why don't you give me a call when you are feeling up to it."

"Great! Well how about sometime this weekend?"

"Well, I, uh, might have a date."

"You didn't tell me you were seeing anyone!" Courtney sensed that there was something special about this date.

"I'm not. I mean I wasn't. I mean we just met," Latoia fumbled.

"Whoa, wait a minute. Just who is this guy? Where did you meet him?" Courtney blocked Latoia's limping progress toward the front door.

"Well he's really nice, uh, good looking. Tall. I met him last week." Latoia was clearly holding something back.

"Confess right now or you are not leaving this house." Courtney was enjoying the light-hearted moment.

"You may not like it. I mean I don't know how you are going to take this."

"What on earth are you talking about? Why would it bother me?" Courtney couldn't begin to think of any reason why she would be upset by Latoia's choice in men.

"Ok, honey child, you asked for it. I might be going to dinner with Raeford."

"Raeford?"

"See, I told you."

"Now wait a minute, you and Raeford? Is this the same Raeford that I know? Isn't he a little old for you?" Courtney frowned in concern.

"Old? That's all you have to say?" Latoia's voice

trailed off.

"Well yes. I always pictured you with some young rich producer or some young athlete from school."

"Now listen, I appreciate your tactfulness but let's get down to the facts. I'm black and he's white."

"Oh. To tell you the truth I never really thought of you in those terms. You are just...Latoia...my friend," Courtney shrugged.

The two girls stood looking at each other in silence. Finally, Latoia held her arms out to Courtney. "I'm so glad we're friends in this lifetime," Latoia winked, her eyes were filled with mischief and a hint of unshed tears.

"Thank you for being my friend, too in this life, the last life and maybe even the next one too!" Courtney laughed but then her expression became more serious.

"Whew, this is gettin' a bit too deep for my taste. Now are you going to let me out of this house? Let me remind you if you don't, my mama will personally skin both of us alive!"

Friday morning dawned bright and clear. Courtney awakened in high spirits. She had not left her parents' home since they had arrived from San Francisco. Today was different. Courtney felt strong and she wanted to go to her studio apartment to check on her plants and pick up a few personal items. Maybe she could go to the library or a book store. Her initial reluctance to begin searching for books about reincarnation and psychic phenomena had vanished overnight. In fact, she surprised herself with the realization that at the moment nothing else seemed important. She had no desire to go to ballet class or call the university about make up exams. The only thing she wanted to do was go to her apartment and then search for information that she hoped would help her make sense out of the strange things that had recently happened.

"Good morning, Mom!" Courtney chirped as she joined Clarisa at the breakfast table. "Oh Darlin', you look wonderful today!"

"Thanks, I really feel good. I was wondering if you would drive me to Santa Monica. I would like to pick up some things including my car."

"Well of course I will, if you really think you're ready. You have only been out of the hospital for a few days."

"I know Mom, but sooner or later I will have to face the world again and well, today seems like a good day to begin."

"Okay, good. We can go right after breakfast. I can hardly see where the stitches were on your head," she commented with some surprise. "By the way dear, have you called Dr. Epstein yet?"

"No. I think I'll wait until next week." Courtney didn't relish the idea of a session with the staid practical doctor. So much of what happened was intertwined with visions and then there was the lion. She hadn't told anyone about that, not even Latoia. She was afraid that if she told Dr. Epstein about it he would have her committed and then those visions of her dream-self wearing a strait jacket would be a reality.

"You have been through a severe trauma, Dear, and I just want to make sure that the memories don't harm you. Some people suffer delayed reactions years later. I just don't want that to happen to you too."

Courtney looked at her mother closely. Something about Clarisa's voice was disturbing. It was as if she was seeing the woman for the first time and she was shocked to realize that maybe she didn't know her as well as she thought.

"Thanks Mom. I know that you're worried because you love me. I love you too!" Courtney reached for her mother's hand. "I promise that I'm going to do everything I can to work through all of this. In fact as soon as I get my car I want to go to the library and do some research. I've got to know, to understand what has been happening to me. I don't think Dr. Epstein would be able to cope with my...visions!" Courtney finished with a roll of her eyes.

"I'm sure you are correct in that assumption," Clarisa smiled. "But please remember that your father and I are always here for you. We want to help. I, well, *both* of us think you need to speak with Hattie too."

The drive to Santa Monica was pleasant and the two women enjoyed the closeness of their unique mother-daughter relationship.

Courtney's heart beat a little faster as her mother's white Jaguar rounded the corner and pulled into the driveway of her apartment complex. She saw her little white VW sitting where she had left it. She remembered the night that the nightmare had begun. She had the odd sensation that it had happened to someone else a long time ago.

"You know we don't have to do this today if you don't want to," Clarisa spoke softly as she watched Courtney's face and her obvious hesitation.

"No Mom, it's okay. I was just thinking...I feel as though I've been gone for weeks." Courtney got out of the car and started toward the front door with her mother following a few steps behind.

Courtney braced herself for the painful memories that would almost certainly rise to the surface of her mind as she entered her apartment, but she was unprepared for the sight that met her eyes. She stood just inside the door unmoving, her mind seeking reason in the wake of chaos. Drawers hung open and clothes lay in haphazard heaps. The day bed had been torn apart and stuffing oozed from the ripped mattress. Lamps were overturned and pictures had been removed from their frames. The love seat and wing back chair had been slashed to pieces. The air reeked of rotting food and stale tobacco.

Clarisa stood behind her daughter in silent shock. She felt a movement and instinctively caught Courtney breaking her fall. She eased the slender girl to the floor as her knees buckled. She hadn't fainted, her eyes were open wide, but she was deathly pale.

"Courtney!" Clarisa spoke sharply and her daughter looked up at her with large frightened eyes. "You sit right there. I will call the police and when we are finished with them, I'm packin' you up. You are movin' home and there will be no argument from you young lady." Clarisa marched to the telephone and dialed 911.

When a patrol car finally rolled to a stop in front of the apartment building, Courtney had recovered from her initial shock, although she spoke very little during the questioning. Clarisa had taken command and Courtney was grateful. She looked around her demolished apartment. It was no longer hers. It had been violated. Never again would it be the peaceful safe haven it once was. She could never call this place home again. "Now what?" she asked herself. She wandered over to the scattered pages of her unfinished thesis and absently began to stack them neatly. She uncovered an envelope addressed to Madame Dubois. She couldn't think why she would have mail addressed to Madame. She pulled out the typewritten letter. Then she remembered it was the letter from the Charleston Ballet Company requesting Madame's assistance in finding someone to help them with their summer program. Maybe this was her answer. She scooped up all of her papers and research books and put them into her book bag but she had no idea when she would feel like working on her thesis again. She made sure to put the letter in her purse though and a tiny tingle of excitement began to wriggle in the pit of her stomach. It nearly winked out during the tedious questions from the policemen and the long wait while crime scene investigators checked for fingerprints and other evidence. But every time she thought about calling Madame about the position the excitement came back. The weekend dragged dismally as details were attended to and her once cozy little hideaway was tidied and all of her belongings were moved, sold or given away. When Courtney closed the door for the final time on Monday at noon, she felt a painful stab of grief. It was as though all ties to her youth had been severed. Oh she knew she was still young but now it was different. Antonio had taken her carefree youthfulness and shown her a part of life that she had only vaguely thought about when she listened to the news or read the paper. It made her feel vulnerable and lost.

The rent had been paid for the year but Courtney knew she never wanted to come back to her apartment so she gave the key to her landlord and got into her car. The front and back seats were crammed with her personal items from cosmetics to hair care products. Books were stacked on the floors and clothes that had not been damaged were in a suitcase and several large plastic bags. She sighed and started the motor. Her mother was already pulling away from the curb in her Jaguar. Courtney pulled in behind her and as she did tears flooded down her cheeks. Suddenly she was crying so hard she had to pull over. Her mother seeing her in the rearview mirror pulled over as well.

Clarisa held and soothed her daughter for a long time. Finally the sobs stopped and the young woman grew calmer. "I'm sorry mom. I just feel so lost and scared!"

"Oh, Baby, I understand. Everything will be all right. It's just going to take some time for you to put everything behind you. You have a wonderful life in front you. You are so talented and beautiful and intelligent! I feel like this is my fault for letting you come to your apartment too soon and then to find out it was vandalized was just too much on top of everything else you have gone through. Now, Honey, everything is going to be just fine. Do you think you can drive home or shall we just leave your car here and you can ride with me?" Courtney was exhausted from crying so long but she did feel calmer and decided to drive behind her mother. Clarisa suggested that they stop at a designated restaurant for some tea and cake at about half way home just to break up the long drive. The little known cafe was quiet with only a few patrons enjoying an afternoon snack. The tea was herbal and the dessert was a rich strawberry cheesecake. "I really think we needed this little treat to give us some energy, don't you?" Clarisa smiled mischievously at her daughter hoping to help her by keeping the mood light. Courtney managed a wan smile and nodded assent. They were quiet for most of the forty-five minutes that they sat there, but soft music played in the background and water trickled from a fountain so their silence was not really uncomfortable.

When they arrived in Palos Verdes Courtney went straight to her room. She needed to think and be alone for awhile. She had to try to decide what she was going to do. She loved her parents and knew that she could stay with them for as long as she wanted to but that was not going to work for the rest of her life. The thought of staying in Los Angeles made her uncomfortable. She didn't think she wanted to go back to school right now either, maybe later but not right now. It was impossible to concentrate on anything mundane so *school* was absolutely out of the question at this time. Once again she thought of the job with the Charleston Ballet and the summer workshop. Interesting, it made her feel good to think about going there and being part of something creative. She glanced at the clock and was surprised to see that it was three o'clock in the morning. The hours had drifted by without her noticing. At long last she began to relax. She thought of teaching dance, maybe creating a ballet, working with other dancers and teachers. The more she thought about it the more interesting it sounded. Suddenly she wanted more than anything to call Madame and see if the position had been filled. "What if they had hired someone else, what would she do then?" she worried. Well she would cross that bridge tomorrow. Tomorrow she would make the call, maybe if that position was full Madame might know of another one. But, she realized she didn't want another one, she wanted to go to Charleston. Sometime later she fell asleep as she thought about music and costume ideas. She slept more peacefully than she could remember in a long time.

"Madame? This is Courtney Hammond. Do you know if the Charleston Ballet has found anyone to fill the position you told me about?" Courtney gripped the telephone tightly.

"Cherie, eet is so good to hear from you! In fact I have just hung up the telephone from my conversation weeth the director. They are quite desperate for someone. Are you now interested cherie?"

"Yes Madame, I am very interested." Smiling and frowning at the same time Courtney wrote down the name and phone number of the person she was to call. Most of the time she was very amused by Madame's quaint if overdone French accent, but this time she only registered the information she was given. Breathlessly she punched in the area code for South Carolina and the number of the man she would speak to. Within thirty minutes she had been hired sight unseen. They trusted Madame Dubois' recommendation completely. She was to begin in two weeks. As she hung up the phone she shivered with nerves. Her hands were clasped so tightly that her knuckles were white. Then she let out a long slow breath and realized she felt a happy anticipation. She had no idea if this was the right place for her for the rest of her life but it would be the right thing for now, for this moment. She could stay with her grandmother in the old plantation house where she and Shane had played as children. She had fond memories of the enormous sweeping lawns and the vast gardens filled with flowers and shrubs. Suddenly she was very excited and hurried to find her parents to tell them the news.

"Mom, Dad I've just accepted a position with the Charleston Ballet Company for the summer. I'm to start there in two weeks." Her parents were sitting in the family room when Courtney made her announcement. They exchanged looks and then simply smiled. They had just been discussing the fact that their daughter needed to leave California for awhile. Neither of them was sure how to persuade her that this would be a positive move even if it were only temporary. It would seem that the matter had been taken out of their hands.

CHAPTER FIFTEEN

Charleston, South Carolina - 1986

Stephen Baylor tossed restlessly on the hard lumpy mattress. The neon motel sign blinked from red to blue as the light cleverly found its way through small spaces between the closed blinds. He had tried to pull the drapes together but they stuck after moving only a few inches.

The young man flopped over to his left side and forced his eyes shut. Within seconds they had popped open again. The blue tie, he was absolutely certain, the blue tie would be the right one. Dr. Leonard had assured him that people in the south dressed casually, but he would meet the staff first and then decide what to wear later. The blue tie would be fine for his first day.

Sirens screamed in the distance. The sleepless man turned on his back and stared up at the ceiling as the sirens grew louder. He sat up and then slumped forward as he dropped his face into his hands. He was certain that it must be almost dawn. He reached for his glasses and peered at the faintly glowing face of his wrist watch. It was only two thirty in the morning. He removed his glasses and fell back onto the flat pillows. The bed shuddered under his long wiry body. Something snapped and the right corner of the bed suddenly dipped. Stephen found himself slowly sliding head first toward the floor.

With an angry curse he scrambled off the torturous bed and picked up the telephone. He would call the office and demand a different room. The line was dead. Then he remembered that he had decided not to pay the fee to have the telephone connected. Who would he call anyway? He didn't know anyone in Charleston, South Carolina. He had said good-bye to his family and friends in Ohio. He slammed the telephone down and sank heavily into a nearby wooden chair. The chair wobbled and creaked dangerously. He wriggled in the chair daring it to collapse. The chair complied obediently as the right rear leg buckled and Stephen once again found himself headed toward the floor.

    He lay for a minute where the chair had dumped him. He was angry, tired, and nervous about his first day at the hospital, not to mention lonely. "What is this, a conspiracy?" he shouted at the furniture. The sound of his own voice startled him. What was he doing talking to furniture? It's a good thing Dr. Mann couldn't see him now. Instead of becoming part of the staff he'd be put in a straitjacket like one of the patients. He had to chuckle at the thought, but he was still feeling frustrated and angry.

    He decided it was time to get up from the floor and try to figure out how to fix the bed. The chair had other ideas. He pulled himself forward in an effort to move free of wooden arm rests, but the tenacious chair moved with him. He tried again and again, the chair moved with him. He twisted around to try to find out why he couldn't rid himself of the damnable thing and he heard something rip. His boxers were caught on a small nail protruding from the seat near the wooden back supports. The more he struggled the more the fabric ripped. With one mighty yank he finally succeeded in pulling himself free. He stood up and walked over to the mirror. In the blinking red and blue light he looked over his shoulder at his reflection. Even without his glasses he could see the gaping hole of the separated seam on the back of his shorts.

    The young man hung his head and put his fists on his hips. This was not good. He prayed that this was not an omen as to how his first day was going to be. He looked from the uneven mattress to the broken chair. His scowl began to fade and the beginnings of a smile twitched at the corners of his mouth. Actually the whole thing was very funny. He chuckled softly but the more he thought about it the funnier it became. The chuckle grew until he laughed uproariously and tears ran down his cheeks and into his closely trimmed brown beard. At last he wiped his eyes and gasped for breath as the laughter died away. He truly felt better and decided to seriously figure out a comfortable way to sleep.

"I'll beat you at your own game!" he huffed at the mattress. He pulled the unruly thing off of the damaged bed frame and dragged it to the floor. Then he flopped down on it. It seemed more comfortable and he realized that the blinking neon was no longer in his eyes. He took a deep breath and expelled it slowly, he was certainly feeling more relaxed. He even felt drowsy. Smiling sleepily into the semidarkness he felt congratulations were in order for his heroism. He had vanquished the attack of the killer furniture. He chuckled again just before he drifted off to sleep.

"Good morning, Dr. Mann?" Stephen stood just inside the office door. The older man continued to study a sheaf of papers that he held in his hands and he didn't respond to Stephen's greeting.

"Uh, Dr. Mann, I'm Stephen Baylor. I, uh, was to report to you this morning," Stephen tried again thinking that the white-haired doctor hadn't heard him.

"You, sir, were to report at 0900 hours." Dr. Mann finally looked up.

"Yes sir. It took me longer to get out here than I thought it would. I'm sorry, sir." Stephen made a mental note; Dr. Mann was a fanatic about promptness. After all it was only 9:05.

"You'll be stayin' out here from now on. Liz will show you where. I expect every member of this staff to be where they are supposed to be on time! Everyone here depends on everyone else. If someone is *late*...it could cause serious problems!" Dr. Mann had raised his voice. "Do you understand, Dr. Baylor?"

"Yes sir. Thank you. I'll remember that." The truth was that Stephen didn't understand exactly. But he was familiar with the idiosyncrasies of high ranking physicians. They were accustomed to having their rules followed without question.

"I don't like people who hide behind beards either!" Dr. Mann snapped as he rose slowly from his chair. "You can stow your gear later. Kevin Lowry will take you through our facility. You will familiarize yourself with our staff and procedures today, and tomorrow you will begin patient interaction. I will meet with you in the cafeteria at 1200 hours sharp at which time I will present you with some interesting reading material with regard to our procedures. We are understaffed and overworked. The only way to insure proper care for our patients and still get our work completed is to play by the rules." Dr. Mann walked out of his office with Stephen following closely. "Kevin here has been with us for five years. He understands the importance of discipline. Former military man, you serve in the military, Dr. Baylor?"

"Uh, no sir."

"Humph. I don't trust people who haven't performed their patriotic duty." Dr. Mann turned and stalked back into his office.

Stephen sighed. It was going to be a long day.

"Hey, don't let the old man get to you. He is ex-military too and he has a `thing' about rules, but underneath his bluster he's a good doctor and a fair man. But whatever you do, don't be late for anything!"

"Yeah, I noticed."

"C'mon, I'll show you around."

Kevin led Stephen down one corridor after another. He pointed out treatment rooms, therapy rooms, and recreation rooms. Most of the ambulatory patients gathered in the common rooms. Some watched a television set, others played cards. Some merely sat staring at nothing. He saw the usual percentage of those who talked to themselves and those who refused to talk at all. The sight of the mentally and often physically disabled was not a new one for Stephen. During the long years of study, prior to becoming a clinical psychologist, he had worked as an assistant to one of his professors. He had conducted tests and gathered data hundreds of times in a state institution in Ohio. He was well aware of the hopeless plight of most of the unfortunates housed in these facilities, but deep within his heart burned the fire of hope. He hoped that he could make a difference.

Stephen studied his friendly tour guide silently. Kevin was a few inches shorter than himself, about five feet eight inches he guessed and compared to Stephen's six feet two inches he really seemed short. Muscles bulged under the dark skin of his biceps and Stephen doubted there was an ounce of fat to be found anywhere on what was obviously a well-conditioned body. Kevin kept up a running patter about the hospital and its workings interspersed with bits of information about his own life. He had received his medical training in the military and along with his technical knowledge he had a real compassion for the suffering of others. Stephen liked him immediately.

"Mutt 'n Jeff. They've brought in the cartoons! Why not? This is all a joke anyway. See me laughing? Mutt 'n Jeff, Mutt 'n Jeff..." A diminutive woman blocked their path. Her straight gray hair was cropped short in the back. Greasy strands were held in place by bobby pins on each side of her face. Her right arm was drawn up tightly to her chest. It reminded Stephen of the newly hatched chicks he had raised on his family's farm in Ohio.

"Well it looks like Terry has already named you. I'm afraid you are going to be stuck with her nickname for the duration."

"Terry Toon has named the Mutt 'n Jeff," she sing-songed the refrain over and over.

"Then I will nickname you. From this day forward you shall be called Little Chick." Stephen had raised his voice to make himself heard over the little woman's piercing chant. She stopped her refrain to listen. She stared blankly at him for a few seconds.

"Little Chick, Little chick, oh lolly lolly lolly...Little Chick, Little Chick..." The expression on the woman's face had never changed, but the tune she sang and the happy lilt of her voice was unmistakable.

"Well Dr. Baylor, it looks as though you've made a conquest." Kevin smiled as the lady limped away. The two young men felt at ease with each other in spite of their diverse backgrounds. They found themselves discussing sports as they climbed the stairs leading to the ward housing the more heavily sedated patients. Stephen was extolling the virtues of cross-country bicycling when they reached the top of the stairs. He realized how loud his voice sounded as it echoed through the empty corridor and stopped speaking with a frown.

"Spooky isn't it? I never get used to it. In fact I don't come up here unless I absolutely have to." Kevin rolled his eyes.

The eerie quiet was broken by someone moaning. The two men stopped in front of each door and peered through its window while Kevin disclosed bits of information about each inhabitant.

"None of 'em are really violent to anyone except themselves. This here is C.C. She's autistic. Only been up here a couple of months. She used to talk a little but all of a sudden she took to havin' fits, throwin' things, bangin' her head against the walls. Sad case. Her family's all dead. She's been here all of her life as far as I know. Course which one here isn't a sad case." Kevin shook his head.

Stephen watched the girl as Kevin talked. She rolled her head from side to side with a typical incessant repetition. Her hair was an impossible tangle of matted auburn curls. He could see by the clear smooth skin of her face that she was young, maybe in her twenties and if circumstances were different, she could maybe be considered pretty.

"Hep ya with somethin'?"

"Hey Jubal, this is Dr. Baylor. I'm just showin' him around. This is his first day at The Oaks Country Club," he announced with obvious sarcasm.

Stephen turned and found himself staring into a clump of curly black hair which protruded from an open shirt collar. He lifted his eyes to a square jaw framed by heavy jowls and finally to heavily lidded eyes topped by enormous bushy black eyebrows. He was probably the largest most frightening looking man Stephen had ever seen.

"I uh, glad to meet you, Jubal." Stephen held out his hand though he wasn't sure whether this man was an employee or one of the patients. Jubal nodded and held out his hand but said nothing.

"Dr. Baylor, it's almost time for your meeting with Dr. Mann. We'd better be going." Kevin looked at his watch.

"Yes, thank you. I don't want to be late," Stephen was relieved that he had somewhere else to go. Jubal's large presence made the hair on the back of his neck stand at attention. He was sure that Kevin felt the same way. They walked to the end of the corridor and began to descend the stairs. Stephen glanced over his shoulder. He could see Jubal standing where they had left him, his expression unreadable and his dark eyes following their departure.

"I am assuming he is an employee?" Stephen asked carefully.

"Yeah, makes you wonder doesn't it?"

When Stephen arrived in the cafeteria Dr. Mann was already waiting for him. Kevin excused himself and went to sit at a table with some other hospital employees.

"Did Kevin give you a satisfactory tour?"

"Yes sir. He was very thorough."

"Good. Kevin is a good man. Never known him to be late!" Dr. Mann seemed to snap out his words. It was a habit from his military years but it seemed out of sync with the southern accent that likes to curl around the tongue and flow in lazy rolls through the air.

After they finished their lunch Dr. Mann instructed his secretary, Liz, to show Stephen to the room that would serve as his office.

"I've taken the liberty of stockin' your office with a few small items. As you decide what you'll be needin' you just let me know," Liz smiled up at Stephen.

"Thank you, Liz." He liked the matronly little southern woman immediately. Her official position was to serve as Dr. Mann's secretary, but Stephen was certain that it was she who kept things running in a smooth and orderly manner.

There was a window in his office overlooking green lawns dotted with giant live oaks, which he surmised, must be the very source of the name of that institution. He stood for a moment enjoying the view of the grounds then turned toward the desk. He opened drawers and found pencils, pens and note pads neatly arranged in one, empty file folders in another and a map of the facility in yet another. He noticed a paper in his IN box and discovered it was a handwritten note from Liz indicating which files Dr. Mann wanted him to review. After studying the list for a moment he looked around the room to find the file drawers. He noticed how clean everything was. In fact he had noticed that the entire facility was exceptionally clean. He took a deep breath and smiled, the office was small but he liked it. He had a good feeling about this place. He was sure that everything would work out. Finally he could do the work he wanted to do. The long years of study and internship were over. He was in the real world, in a real job and he was ready for the challenge. He walked to one of the filing cabinets and pulled on the metal handle. The drawer reluctantly rumbled open. The files were jammed tightly together and bits of paper stuck out haphazardly as though there simply wasn't room to stuff one more item into any of the folders, which wasn't too far from the truth. After searching for the files on his list he wrestled out a few and carried them back to his desk. The first thing he would ask for would be another filing cabinet he decided.

"Dr. Baylor?" Liz stood in the doorway, "I'm going home in thirty minutes. I thought I would show you where you will be stayin'."

Stephen looked at his watch. It was four thirty. His immersion in the material at hand was so complete that the passage of time was far from his awareness.

"I had no idea it was so late. Thank you. I would appreciate that." Stephen climbed into his old van and drove behind Liz in her Ford sedan. They traveled along a tree-lined drive for a short time going around what must have been the original structure. Walking paths and benches situated near well-tended flower beds gave the impression that he drove through the grounds of a stately old Southern home. Of course the bars on the windows were a dead giveaway as to the real use of the property. As they rounded the corner of the large rambling structure he was surprised to see a number of additions made up of four-story wings. It made him think of a giant peacock with its tail feathers fanned out. They wound around abandoned out buildings and others that might be used as storage. He was struck with the realization that he really would need to study the map that was in his desk drawer. Uniformed hospital personnel walked to and from buildings and a small construction crew put away their tools for the day. They drove by a painting crew who were folding up their ladders and gesturing as they called out to one another in anticipation of stopping their daily toil. A delivery truck drove by and a few cars followed on their way to the exit road, but all in all the entire hospital site was very quiet, he noted with interest.

    Liz's car angled away from the buildings and followed a narrow drive which took them under an arbor of enormous trees. Abruptly in the open again the Ford made a hard left turn and pulled up in front of a small cottage. It looked worn and weathered like much of the older portions of the hospital, but the front yard sported a neatly trimmed lawn and a small flowerbed on either side of the stairs that led to a small covered porch and front door. As he turned to admire the big tree in the front yard he was surprised to see several other cottages identical to this one further down the road. Although the lawns and shrubs were well cared for, none of the other buildings sported flower beds. There was an empty feeling to the other structures and that was confirmed as he squinted at the front window of cottage nearest his. One of the shutters hung at a lopsided angle and there were no blinds or drapes making it easy to see the vacant room inside. He wondered at that and why these places were vacant; well just another question he would add to his list, he mused. Liz had already climbed out of her car and was looking expectantly at him as she rested one foot on the bottom stair, effectively putting an end to his reverie.

"Here we are. I have arranged for some coffee and paper products to be put in for you. The kitchen is small, but I suppose you will be takin' most all your meals in the cafeteria anyway," she smiled knowingly, "there are a few dishes, pots 'n pans, and linens. It should be enough to get you started." She walked briskly through the rooms opening drawers and closets making comments and flicking light switches to check for burned out bulbs. She stopped now and then to peer into a shadowed space making little humming noises. When she arrived at the door to the kitchen she halted abruptly and tsk tsked as she shook her head and drew her brows together in an annoyed frown. Her friendly little tour was also an inspection of the premises worthy of any good commanding officer. Stephen suspected someone would get a good dressing down at having left a bag of debris in the kitchen and soiled cleaning rags in the sink.

"This is perfect, Liz. Thank you." Stephen was pleased. He didn't mind the small sparsely furnished accommodations. There were no neon lights or sirens and the bed, though old, looked sturdy enough for a giant.

"Supper is served at five thirty in the cafeteria. It would be my suggestion to go get yourself a hot meal then come on back here and get a little rest. All that work on your desk will still be there tomorrow and maybe even the next day," she winked and smiled.

"Yes ma'am. I think I might do that."

"See you in the mornin'."

Stephen walked Liz to the front door and listened to her instructions about the keys and garbage disposal. She rattled off a few regulations for resident employees and with a little wave climbed into her car and drove off.

He watched as the Ford turned to go back through the tree arbor and then walked toward his van. He unlocked the back door and hefted a large duffle stuffed to the brim. Next he pulled out an old hard suitcase with a strap around the middle. The latches on either side had long since been broken and bits of clothing stuck out at irregular intervals After several groaning sweat laden trips from his van to the cottage he had cleared a path to his beloved ten-speed bicycle. This was no ordinary two-wheeler. This was his baby, his winner-maker, and he treated it accordingly. He lifted the light frame easily with one hand and with the other he picked up the tire and carried everything inside. He knew he would have little time for training or participating in any long distance treks for pleasure or for racing, but he intended to keep his baby in top shape and when the time came he would once again feel the wind on his face and the muscles in his legs pumping away the miles. A rumble from his stomach informed him that it would be better to eat first and assemble his bicycle later. He placed the frame carefully in his living room and laid the tire and various other tools on the floor nearby. Everything was arranged quickly with the assurance and precision of one who had performed this very act many times. Once he was satisfied that everything was in order he locked the front door and hurried to his van in anxious anticipation of the meal ahead.

The next day arrived with a torrent of challenges overflowing into the first empty minute, which spilled into the hours that followed. He hardly noticed the passing weeks until one late afternoon, he glanced at his desk calendar and gasped. He had been working there for more than a month. He smiled to himself as he realized how comfortable he had become. He really liked his job!

Stephen's exuberant energy and fresh approach were a welcome addition to the routine of the staid old institution, at least for most of the cognizant patients and younger staff members. Some of the older employees liked their secure routine and the thought of changing something that they had always done unnerved them completely. Disgruntled exchanges took place during whispered meetings in supply closets or at the far end of a corridor. The new guy was a veritable machine driving everyone at an inhuman pace according to the mutterings of harried old-timers. New deadlines, new rules, faster, faster, someone better find the OFF button for this machine, the gossip mill ground out complaint after weary complaint.

"Doc Mutt. I think you and me better have a little chat." Kevin stood in the doorway of Stephen's office.

"Sure Kevin, come on in." Stephen took his glasses off and rubbed his bloodshot dark blue eyes.

"Listen. You and I have gotten to be pretty good friends in the few weeks you've been here, right?"

"Yes we have. Is there something you need?" Stephen raised his eyebrows.

"No, but you do! Let me ask you a question. Why did you decide to get into this profession?"

"So I could help people, of course." Stephen was tired and his voice had a sharp edge tinged with indignation.

"You think you're going to be able to help people when you have a nervous breakdown? You got to pace yourself. Just a few weeks an' you already got dark circles under your eyes. You got some of the staff whispering in corners and it's only a matter of time before they organize an all out rebellion."

"But look at the progress I've already made with `A' ward, and the line of communication is now so much faster from patient to doctor to staff and..."

"Hey! The patients love you, but some changes need to be made more slowly. Use some of that psychology training on the staff and for God sakes get some sleep."

Stephen blinked. Temper flared up briefly and he could feel his face redden. The truth would not be denied though, he knew Kevin was right. He had been pushing everyone at a furious pace in an effort to prove himself and to make his mark as soon as possible. Dr. Mann had been called away on a family emergency four days after Stephen arrived, giving the young doctor his blessing and permission to make a "few" changes in procedures. Stephen had decided to implement as many of his new ideas as possible during Dr. Mann's absence hoping to win the director's approval on some of his innovative ideas about art therapy and group activities. He was also interested in raising public consciousness about the mentally disabled.

"Too pushy, huh?" Stephen breathed sheepishly after his temper began to abate.

"Try a bulldozer."

"You might be right," now that he thought about it he realized he had been acting like a maniac. Just what had he been thinking? He rubbed his forehead as though he had a headache.

"Now listen. I think your ideas are great. But I think you'd better slow down. The ol' man will be back on Monday. He isn't too receptive to change when it disrupts the staff. But if he sees things working in an orderly manner he might be more cooperative."

"I see your point." Stephen leaned back in his chair and sighed. Already he felt the weighty restraints of bureaucracy tugging at his youthful idealism.

"Lighten up, Doc. In the immortal words of Terry Toon, `It's all a joke.' Life's just a cartoon! Today is Tuesday and if you just concentrate on organizing the new art therapy you could have it running nicely before Mann gets back next week. Why don't you plan to knock off early and get some rest? Talk to the staff tomorrow when you're fresh."

"Thanks Kevin. I appreciate your honesty. How do you think everyone would respond to a regular staff meeting?"

"Hey, now you're talkin'. Most of 'em would like it. I wouldn't count on Lurch to attend though." Both men laughed. Kevin was referring to the unresponsive Jubal. He was one of those who showed up on time, performed his duties and took home his pay check, but he was mostly unsocial toward other staff members. His size and imposing presence made him a perfect candidate for subduing patients who exhibited violent behavior, but at the same time other employees often expressed their uneasiness about him when he failed to respond to their friendly greetings or conversations.

It was a beautiful late April evening. Stephen rode his bicycle around the sprawling grounds of The Oaks Institution. He liked to think on his bicycle. The wind rushing through his hair and the rhythmic pumping of his feet on the pedals was a satisfying combination. He thought of Kevin lifting weights in a stuffy gym smelling of sweat and the noisy bedlam of loud rock music and people straining to make each other heard. No, he preferred to be outside in the fresh air with bird songs and muffled traffic sounds as his only disturbance. He peddled around the perimeter of the facility two times before coming to a stop in front of the large glass doors of the main building.

Trickles of sweat oozed down his temples as he looked up at the clear sky. The setting sun cast brilliant colors across the horizon, setting fire to the clouds on one side even as the eastern sky dimmed. Inspiration rushed through him as he dreamed of capturing the moment in watercolors or oils. Though, try as he might, he had never been able to quite duplicate the genius of the Creator's canvas when creating a sunset. His eyes wandered over the grounds, taking in the now darkening shapes of the gnarled Live Oaks. There was a mysterious air about them as their silhouettes became more pronounced in the deepening dusk. He imagined small lined faces looking out at him from twisted trunks and massive root systems that curved sharply into the ground and undulated beneath the earth. He shook his head as if to clear it. It had been some time since he had done any sketching, not that he was a great artist, but he loved to sit with a sketch pad and work on something detailed like those old trees.

Suddenly he had an idea, an art show...he would put together an art show. He was certain that his patients would like to participate. It would give everyone a goal and it would serve as a tool to begin his dialogue with the public. He couldn't do it until well after the yearly Spoleto Festival. It could maybe be midsummer, maybe the Fourth of July. By that time he would have been able to secure permission from the board and of course collect enough artwork from the patients to create a good showing. There might even be some real talent among them. This would be a perfect opportunity to launch his public awareness campaign. His mind fairly exploded with ideas and plans. "Yes!" He told himself enthusiastically. He picked up his bicycle and hurried into the building. He had gotten into the habit of riding his bicycle every day rather than driving the short distance from his cottage to the main building of the hospital. Everyone was accustomed to seeing him carry his bicycle through the halls to his office since he wouldn't dream of leaving it outside.

The squalls, moans, and babbles had become so common place to him that he hardly noticed them as he secured his bike and settled himself at his desk. He planned to write a memo informing the various departments of the meeting on the following day. Maybe he would call the cafeteria and see if they could whip up some extra sweet rolls for the occasion. When the memo was finished Stephen jotted down a few ideas that he wanted to communicate to the staff.

He glanced up at the window. The sun had now completely disappeared taking with it the breathtaking crimson that had so inspired him earlier. He yawned and stretched. He really didn't feel tired though so he decided to work on his outline for the new programs he wanted to start. Dr. Mann would probably respond to a well organized neatly typed outline. As Assistant Director, Stephen knew that he had the power to make some decisions on his own, but he knew that the intangible intricacies of the power structure in any institution could be tricky to overcome if not handled with delicate diplomacy. He vowed to try to do better in that category.

That, of course, wasn't the only problem. The budget cuts that had taken place a few years ago had created impossible problems. Many people who should be institutionalized were virtually cast out of the protective environment of public facilities. Very few had families and most were left to fend for themselves...on the streets. He thought again with overwhelming sadness about those unfortunates who now had no shelter or means of support. In some respects he mused, the severely mentally handicapped were the lucky ones. They at least had regular meals, medical care and shelter. The marginals were on the street eating from garbage cans and sleeping in alleys. Stephen gritted his teeth. He hated injustice. He hoped that in his lifetime something dramatic would occur with regard to health care for all of the mentally handicapped. Maybe for everyone in the United States...maybe the world! And he, Stephen Baylor, son of a farmer, would have had a hand in it all.

It was the silence that caused Stephen to look up from the mound of papers on his desk. He wondered why it had grown so quiet. He looked at his watch and was shocked to find that it was nearly midnight. His neck was stiff and he realized that his eyes burned. He removed his glasses and rubbed his eyes. He really had not intended to stay so late. His work and thoughts had so consumed his concentration that he was completely unaware of the passage of time. He sorted and stacked his completed work then carefully stood up stretching stiff muscles. He picked up the finished memo and walked down the now quiet hall. He would make some copies and then hand deliver the memos to each department before going back to his cottage.

    He relished the brisk walk as his soft-soled sneakers made only muffled sounds in the empty corridors. He had learned his way around the large facility and he proceeded to his destinations with comfortable confidence. He stopped to speak with various members of the night staff and joined some of the more friendly ones in a cup of coffee. They enjoyed the attention of the new young Assistant Director. By the time he reached the last wing it was nearly two in the morning.

    Stephen realized he was exhausted as he paused at the bottom of the stairs. An unexplainable pang of nerves churned in his stomach. This high security wing was eerie at this hour. Secretly he dreaded running into Jubal, there was something so unnerving about those cold expressionless eyes. Hopefully Jubal wasn't on night shift this month. Then he thought maybe he wouldn't need to take the memo up there right now. Tomorrow would be just fine. He shook his head trying to shake off his mounting apprehension. He knew that working late so many nights had taken a toll on his mental state. It was a proven fact that sleep deprivation could account for irritability and...

    A sound interrupted his thoughts. It reminded him of an animal's roar. Strange noises being the norm in that environment, he quickly dismissed the idea that anything could be wrong. In the few moments of silence that followed he shook off his fatigue and the accompanying foreboding as he resolutely trudged up the stairs to the secured ward.

A woman's voice, another roar and a man's agonized scream paralyzed the young doctor. He froze mid-step. There was no doubt in his mind now. These noises were not the normal ravings of those whose minds wandered through an altered reality. Someone was screaming and the terror in the screams was very real.

Stephen bounded up the remaining steps two at a time. His long muscular legs stretched into a dead run as he reached the top of the stairway then came to a screeching halt in front of the heavy doors which lead to the secured facility. His nervous fingers fumbled as he struggled to enter the security code. The doors swung open and he headed down the hall toward the screams. One of the doors flew open directly in front of him. He jerked himself hard to the left to avoid being injured by the door and instead collided with a large male figure. Both men fell to the floor as the heavy door banged shut with a loud crash in the silent corridor.

The breath was knocked from Stephen's lungs and he clamped his hand across his rib cage as he struggled to breathe.

"It was a lion! That bitch is a killer! She tried to kill me!" The man's shirt was in shreds and blood oozed from the scratches across his chest. His eyes were wide and he scrambled across the floor as he tried to pull his trousers up from his knees.

"Jubal! What the hell is going on?" Stephen managed to croak.

"She's got a goddamned lion in there! They got me surrounded! Those bitches tried to kill me!" Jubal was hysterical and incoherent as his wide eyes darted to the room and down the hall as if he expected someone or something to come after him. His breath came in hoarse gasps and he continued to cry and babble incoherently, clearly he was frightened out of his wits.

Stephen staggered to his feet. He was still breathless from the blow to his midsection. He managed to get hold of the door handle and with a mighty yank pulled the heavy door open. He didn't know what he expected to find when he entered the room but he was prepared to fight if necessary. He coughed and panted as he scanned the small space for the adversaries that Jubal had described. There were no windows in the little room and the only door was the one he had just come through. It was empty except for a bed and a nude young woman strapped to it. The girl's head was arched back and Stephen hurried over to her. Her eyes were wide open as she stared intently at the wall above her head. He squinted his eyes but nothing could be seen but the smooth white painted surfaces of the wall and ceiling. He tried to slip his arm under the girl's neck in order to restore her to a more comfortable position, but she rigidly resisted his efforts.

His breathing steadied and he looked around trying to understand what might have happened. The girl was securely restrained, she couldn't possibly have attacked Jubal but there had indeed been a struggle and he groaned inwardly as he saw the ugly bruises on the girl's arms, legs and pelvic area. He bent down and picked up the discarded hospital gown. The fabric was ripped. He was sickened at the knowledge of what had happened. He carefully pulled the sheet over the girl's body.

"C.C. I think I know what Jubal was doing in here. I'm sorry. I'm going to try to make sure that you are never hurt again." He didn't know if she understood him but she straightened out her neck and turned so that her blue eyes stared directly into his.

"C.C.," she said clearly.

"Can you tell me what happened?" Stephen asked hopefully as he tried to hide the shock of hearing her voice. But the girl's eyes had gone blank and she began to roll her head from side to side as she withdrew to some faraway place.

Voices rumbled in the hall and grew louder when the door banged open. Several members of the night staff had responded to Jubal's screams and had hurried to his aid.

"Take her to the infirmary and make sure she isn't injured, and she needs to be tested for a possible rape." Stephen motioned to the bed. "Where is Jubal?"

"He curled up on the floor cryin'. What happened up here?" A buxom black woman dressed in hospital whites spoke.

"I don't know what happened exactly. I need to talk to Jubal and I'll want to question all of you," Stephen said with authority as he strode through the open door into the hall where several more staff members had gathered. One man knelt beside the quivering Jubal.

"What were you doing in that room, Jubal?" Stephen too knelt beside the cowering man so that their eyes were nearly level. It was only then that he smelled the alcohol. His stomach rumbled dangerously as it threatened to give in to the rising nausea he had begun to feel while he was in C.C.'s room.

"I wasn't doin' nothin' but my job and look what they done to me." The big man whimpered as he toyed with the bloody shreds of his shirt continually trying to make them go back together.

"Who are *they* Jubal?" Stephen asked as he stood up in an effort to distance himself from the sour liquor smell.

"They?" Jubal shouted incredulously. "The big black

one with the feathers and that lion that came outta the wall...and then I was just leaning over her I was just gonna give her what she wanted and somethin' came up out of her...an' another one comes right up outta thin air...and the lion come at me...you gotta put the bitch away or somebody's gonna get killed!" Jubal's voice rose to a hysterical pitch as he crawled closer to Stephen, with his hands outstretched. Jubal's face was blood red and smeared with tears and blood from the scratches on his chest. Clearly the man was completely undone. He grabbed at the leg of Stephen's sweat pants and buried his face in the fleece alternately sobbing and cursing.

"Anybody see a lion around here?" Stephen asked flatly as he arched his eyebrow and glanced up and down the hallway.

Wednesday morning dawned crisp and cool. Stephen opened his eyes slowly. The sun seemed brighter than usual at this hour of the morning. He stretched and yawned. He felt surprisingly alert considering the small amount of sleep he had gotten. He sat up and squinted at the alarm clock which sat on the bedside table. Both hands were pointing straight up. It was twelve o'clock. He had slept until noon! Then a sick feeling crept into his stomach as he remembered all of the shocking events of the previous evening. Police had been called immediately. Investigators from the state board had arrived within two hours. Employees had been questioned, patients were upset and restless, the newspapers had gotten wind of the incident and shown up in force with cameras, microphones and obnoxious questions. The dignified old Oaks Mental Retreat had been thrown into chaos. Stephen had fallen into bed just after dawn. He had the vague feeling that he had forgotten something.

"Oh great! I missed my own staff meeting on top of everything else," he groaned. Stephen showered and dressed quickly as he wondered if anyone had shown up anyway since all of the excitement of the previous night. Of course the people who were just coming in to work for the morning shift would not have heard anything about what happened unless, of course, it was on the morning news...God forbid. Within thirty-five minutes he hurried through the front door of The Oaks facility and headed down the hall for Liz's office. He was happy to see that there were no visible signs of reporters or police this morning. He was sure though that there would be endless questions and more investigations about the hospital routine. He knew too that there would be some extensive research into their staff. He decided that he would take it upon himself to find a way to insure that there would be no possible way any employee would be able to drink on the job. He only wished that he could have somehow prevented that situation from happening.

Kevin stood talking to Liz with his back to the door as Stephen walked in.

"Good morning! I'm sorry I'm so late. I...guess I overslept," Stephen announced sheepishly.

"Guess you had the right to get a little extra shut-eye. Sounds like you had some excitement in here last night. Why can't something exciting happen when I'm on duty?" Kevin said with his usual dry humor. Then he caught the look of distress on his friend's face. "Look you did a great job last night from what I hear. There was no way you could have known what Jubal was doing.

"Stephen sighed and nodded. "Why me?" He moaned as he rolled his eyes to the ceiling. "I missed my own staff meeting too and officials are crawling around everywhere. The police don't seem to be around this morning but I know they'll be back. God I wanted to be able to talk to everyone and try to help the staff cope with the investigation procedures. I suppose they really hate me now," Stephen moaned miserably.

"Aux contraire, Mon Amie."

"Huh?"

"It seems you've become something of a hero around here," Kevin grinned.

"Huh?" Stephen grunted again.

"Yeah. It seems that Jubal has been a busy little bee. He has harassed other women patients as well as some of the staff. He gets liquored up on night duty and a lot of people were afraid of him but they were also afraid to complain. This morning as soon as everyone got wind of what happened last night they've been coming out of the woodwork with stories and complaints big time."

"Well what about the staff meeting?"

"Oh it went great! Everyone showed up. By the way, the sweet rolls and coffee cake was a big hit!"

"But who...?"

"I did. I found your notes and I went over them with everyone. They liked your ideas but they suggested that donuts would be nice next time," Kevin's eyes danced with mischief.

"It gave everyone a chance to express their thoughts, Dr. Baylor, and in so doing it eased some of the tense feelin's that these folks have been holding onto. Everyone wants to know when they can have another one," Liz smiled. "Things have a way of working out in the most unexpected fashion."

Later the two men sat at a table in the cafeteria and discussed the events of the previous evening. Staff members stopped by with pleasant greetings and favorable comments about the staff meeting. Stephen watched their faces and their body language. He had forgotten something very important in his fervor, the hospital staff was made up of people. People with feelings, fears, insecurities, and lives outside of The Oaks. They deserved to be treated appropriately with as much compassion as the residents. He vowed silently not to forget that again.

"So, what is C.C.'s condition this morn...er today?" Stephen inquired.

"She's bruised but no broken bones, and there is evidence of sexual assault and evidently last night was not the first time," Kevin sighed.

"Jesus! That sicko should have been locked up long ago."

"Yeah, well, it's ironic isn't it? After all is said and done he'll probably end up here on the other side of the doors. I gotta get back to work." Kevin rose.

"Listen, I'll come with you, I want to look in on the girl. You know she spoke last night?" Kevin turned to stare at him with a look of shock. He had never heard any sound from her that could be called speech. He thought that his friend might be mistaken, but given the difference in their position of authority, Kevin decided not to question Dr. Baylor any further.

Stephen tried not to have any expectations as he stood looking at the frail girl who sat on the edge of the bed. Her hair had been washed and brushed. The long curls bounced slightly as her body rocked back and forth.

"Hello C.C."

"C.C.," she echoed.

"How are you?" he asked, but the girl continued to rock in silence.

"I'm starting a new art therapy program. Would you like to come to one of the sessions?" The girl didn't respond.

"I thought we would do some painting. It might be fun."

"Painting might be fun," the girl said flatly.

Stephen heard the nurse gasp at the girl's words and he turned.

"What's wrong?" he asked the woman whose name he had not yet learned.

"Do you know how long it's been since she has spoken to anyone?"

"I hear that it has been quite awhile. Maybe nobody has taken the time to try to talk to her."

"Maybe so, but when she goes into one of her fits conversation takes a back seat."

"Yes, I think I can understand that. I think I also understand why she began having those violent episodes. It was a cry for help. It probably started when Jubal began to molest her. Of course I guess we'll never know the whole story unless a miracle happens and C.C. here finds a way to tell us what happened to her." The nurse nodded her head silently. He could see the concern on her face. He felt it too. An incident like this could cause problems for all of them. There would undoubtedly be a long thorough investigation. He thought of the probing and endless questions he had been faced with the previous night. The place was already crawling with various officials who were questioning everyone and of course the press had converged on the property like hungry hounds. Stephen sighed as he stood up; he had hoped for an exciting job, it looked as though he would have his wish. "Facing Dr. Mann with all of this could be exciting too," he mumbled sarcastically.

Stephen left the infirmary and stood in the hall just outside the door. He decided to go speak with Liz. He wanted to know if she had been able to contact Dr. Mann yet. He walked slowly in the direction of her office when he became aware of movement behind him. He stopped and turned around. C.C. stood a few paces away. He took a few steps and sure enough the young woman followed. She stopped when he stopped.

"Hey, are you following me?" The girl remained silent and stared straight ahead.

"Listen, I don't think you need to be out here wandering around. Come on let's go back to the infirmary. The nurse will look after you until we are sure you are feeling better." Stephen retraced his steps and the girl followed in silence. She dragged her left foot slightly and from the way she held her left arm he was sure that she had little use of it.

"Uh, nurse?"

"Madie is the name Doctor."

"Thank you, Madie. I'm sorry I haven't learned everyone's name yet. I'm afraid we've got a runaway on our hands." Stephen waved his hand toward the girl standing behind him.

"Oh! For goodness sakes!" Madie exclaimed, "What are you doing? Come on now, back to bed. I'm sorry Doctor. I don't know how she slipped away without me seeing her! But of course it's been a long time since I've seen her do anything except...well never mind, I'll watch her more closely."

Stephen watched the girl limp back to her bed. "Madie, would you see to it that she is brought to the art session tomorrow?"

"Yes, I'll be sure she's there," she responded dutifully, but inside she wondered what earthly good it would do for someone who had been so unresponsive to go to an art session of all things.

"Painting is certainly good therapy for me and it is being accepted more and more as a means to find out about the troubled psyche..."

"Painting might be fun," C.C. spoke again in her flat monotone voice repeating the phrase as she had done earlier.

Stephen realized suddenly that he didn't remember seeing a file on the girl. But of course he had not originally thought that she should be included in any of his new therapy programs. He had researched which patients might be responsive enough to participate and therefore benefit from the session. He thought of C.C as being too remote to comprehend what was going on. He chastised himself for having closed his mind to the possibility that she could be part of any form of communication. It was a humbling feeling.

"Madie, I don't suppose you would happen to know C.C.'s last name would you?"

"No sir I don't. Everyone just calls her C.C."

"Don't you have her file there?"

"Yes Doctor, I do but it's just the infirmary admit file. It does have her patient number on it but her name is just listed as C.C. I am afraid we get a little casual with our long time residents."

"Humh! Well that's okay, I'll look it up later, thanks." Stephen hurried out completely forgetting about his need to speak with Dr. Mann about everything that had happened. Of course if the truth be known he was happy to forget about it for the moment as he shifted his focus to more pleasant things.

"Oh, Dr. Baylor, I'm so glad you came in. I have Dr. Mann on the telephone. He would very much like to speak with you." Liz widened her eyes and gave him a sympathetic look.

"Yeah, I'll just bet he would," Stephen sighed. "I'll take it in his office, Liz." He walked resolutely into the Director's office and sat down at the desk. He noted how cold his hands felt as he picked up the telephone and punched the blinking extension button.

The conversation went more smoothly than Stephen had expected. Dr. Mann had actually said very little as he listened to Stephen's words. Was it fatigue that he had heard in the older man's voice?

"Liz, I want to look into the history of one of the patients here, but I can't seem to find her name written out anywhere. How would I go about finding it?"

"Go down to Records and ask for Judy, she'll help you. How'd it go with Dr. Mann?"

"Much better than I expected!" Liz smiled at the surprise on the young man's face.

"Dr. Mann is stern and demanding, but he is not unfair and he has a great capacity for compassion. He also thinks that you are doing a good job."

"Thanks Liz, I needed that." It was nearly five o'clock before Judy tapped softly on Stephen's open office door. "I'm real sorry Dr. Baylor. I couldn't get that information for you."

"You couldn't? What happened?" Stephen was unable to imagine any reason why a patient's history would be unavailable to him unless it had been lost, which was unthinkable, or maybe misfiled. If it had been misfiled then it would simply take time and perseverance to find it.

"It has been sealed." The girl stood with her hands clasped in front of her.

"Sealed? I don't understand."

"I don't either. I put the record number in the computer and it says `Records Sealed - Information Not Available.' So I go downstairs to the paper files and that number is in a section that is locked," Judy shrugged.

"Well, who can get access to the sealed files?"

"I dunno. Maybe Dr. Mann."

"Well did you at least find out her real name?"

"No sir. All it had was the patient number and the initials C.C."

"Thanks anyway Judy." Stephen frowned in consternation. He had found the records of C.C.'s medications and notes about her violent episodes and subsequent regression. The first records of her pica and echolalia behavior were made when she was five years old. The pica was noted when she was discovered eating crayons. Shortly thereafter the first violent episode was recorded. She had banged her head against a wall until the skin broke and blood streamed down her face. According to the records she had been quite verbal at that time exhibiting frequent echolalia, which is a common phenomena in persons with autism. This speech pattern was so named because of the curious habit of echoing a few words from a sentence spoken by someone else. He couldn't determine exactly when her speech disappeared, but he guessed that it had been from seven to ten years ago. No wonder the nurse was surprised to hear her speak.

"You aren't going to pull another all-nighter are you?" Kevin stood in the doorway.

"No. My how time flies..."

"When you're havin' fun?" Kevin finished for him. "I'm going to the gym, want to come along?"

"No thanks. Not tonight, but I might actually take you up on that offer this weekend if you promise me one thing."

"What's that?" Kevin frowned.

"You have to try bicycling with me." Stephen raised one eyebrow.

"What? That sissy kid stuff? Anybody can do that. Now pumpin' iron is a real man's workout!"

"Do we have an agreement?" Stephen persisted.

"You're on!" Kevin walked over to the desk and the two young men solemnly shook hands.

Stephen woke early Thursday morning. Despite the pressure of the officials who were still investigating the staff and procedures, the daily routine had returned to a normal pace. In general, hospital personnel were functioning well and an ease had returned to the overall attitude. Dr. Mann had told him that he would be returning earlier than he originally planned and would be in the office on the following Monday. Stephen looked at his closely trimmed bearded reflection on the mirrored medicine cabinet door. He had given serious consideration to Dr. Mann's disapproving remarks about facial hair. The Director had not ordered him to shave off his beard; he had merely voiced his displeasure. Stephen liked his beard and was going to keep it. Maybe.

Bird song filled the air as he rode his bicycle toward the main hospital building. The cool spring morning filled him with energy and expectation. Today would be his first group session. He had designed some new behavior assessment charts which would enable anyone to see at a glance how the patient was responding to treatment. He planned to keep accurate, detailed records. "Who knows," he told himself, he might write a book about all of this someday. Maybe he would make a truly significant contribution to the medical community with his innovative approach to therapy. He could see himself humbly accepting praise and applause from his peers.

Because of the disastrous budget cuts in funding for state facilities, Stephen had to create his art and music therapy program from almost nothing. He brought in his own portable tape player and a selection of tapes ranging from classical to rock. The art materials were sparing to say the least. He found crayons, chalk, and water paints in some of the recreation rooms and, with Liz's blessing, he confiscated some extra large copy paper from the supply room, it was almost never used anyway. He was sure that in time he would be able to collect more supplies for their creative work, especially if his project seemed to be having positive results.

Two developmental care technicians had been recruited to assist him during the session that day, but one of them had called in sick. Stephen was distraught. He felt certain that he would need an extra pair of helping hands. This would be the first session. It would take time to get the patients accustomed to him and the routine, and too, he didn't know the patients very well yet. Anything could happen. There was no doubt in his mind he had to have at least one more assistant to help out during the session. "Liz! Where can I find someone to..."

"I've already looked into it Dr. Baylor," Liz smiled reassuringly. "I found a college student who works here part time. She didn't have any classes today and she has agreed to come in for half a day. Her name is Theresa and she will be here at noon."

"Thanks, Liz. You are an angel!"

"And you are a very smart doctor." Liz smiled.

The morning passed agonizingly slow and yet suddenly it was gone. Stephen hurried down the hall with his list of names and clipboard clutched tightly in his hand.

Several patients were already assembled in the designated therapy room. Stephen checked his list and saw that three more were expected. He directed his assistants to help seat everyone at the table. Each person had been provided with paper and a small selection of crayons, chalk, and watercolor paints. The patients were excited and conversations grew louder. Stephen was trying to answer questions and maintain order. He barely noticed Madie who brought in the last three patients and seated them in the empty chairs. One of the assistants motioned in the direction of the new arrivals and Steven rushed to prevent one of them from removing her clothes. After some persuasion the woman was distracted from her desire to disrobe and she began to focus on drawing a picture of a nude person with no head.

Before he could catch his breath two women began to argue. One sat too close to the other and inevitably push came to shove before anyone could stop them. Barbara was a large person and she stood up suddenly knocking over her chair. Taz was much smaller but had a domineering spitfire personality. The two were constantly bickering but at the same time appeared to be inseparable. Barbara started to cry loudly as Taz gave her a hard push that nearly knocked the larger woman down. The assistants scrambled to stop the argument before it escalated.

"Quiet everyone! I'm Dr. Baylor..."

"Mutt 'n Jeff, Mutt 'n Jeff, what's up Doc Mutt!" Terry's shrill sing song cut Stephen short.

"Okay, Little Chick, you made your point. You can call me Doc Mutt if you want to, now let's get started." Terry Toon grimaced in what was meant to be a smile and she cocked her head to one side with what could only be described as a coy look. Dr. Baylor smiled back realizing that he had just been the object of her flirtation. It warmed his heart beyond anything he could have imagined.

At first the soft Chopin Nocturne went virtually unnoticed, but as time passed the noise level dropped. Everyone became absorbed in their artistic efforts. Occasionally Katie would torment Reva by scooting her chair too close. Reva would squeal and Katie would scoot even closer. Stephen made a mental note not to seat those two so close together next time. Barbara and Taz seemed to have settled down and were now chastising Reva and Katie for causing problems. He moved from one to another watching and commenting on their efforts. Some merely scribbled, others used only one color. A very interesting design was actually emerging on the restless Katie's paper. Next to her sat C.C. who rocked gently in perfect rhythm to the music. She dipped her brush in water, in the paint, and then on the paper. She made a few strokes and then repeated the process with an almost mechanical regularity.

"She was trying to eat the crayons and the chalk so I had to take them away from her."

"Thank you Theresa. And thank you too for coming in today." The slender black girl flashed him a brilliant smile.

"Dr. Baylor? Katie needs to use the bathroom. I'll just walk down the hall with her again okay?" Stephen nodded absently as the assistant left the room with Katie in tow. The Chopin tape ended and Stephen walked over to the machine wondering what kind of reaction he would get with his next selection.

"How about something a little more upbeat! Everyone use another piece of paper and see if you can draw or paint this music." Stephen was pleased with himself as he slid the soft rock tape in the chamber and pushed the PLAY button. He stood for a moment savoring the gentle drum beats of the introduction. Loud giggles interrupted his reverie.

"Hey! Hey! Ladies, we paint on the paper not on each other!" A dollop of paint hit him full in the face causing him to spew water color and swipe frantically at his mouth and eyes. Rule number one he thought, never turn your back on them when they are armed. No matter how hard he tried, the group was unable to settle down. Everyone ended up with paint and/or crayon on their clothes, faces, and hands. He was exasperated with the bedlam. They were all laughing and...wait a minute he thought, they are laughing and interacting! He looked around the room. Terry Toon, wielding her paint brush was painting the heavy set woman next to her. Both women were moving with the beat of the music. Both were laughing and taking turns as they danced little jigs. Stephen had never seen Terry really smile or touch another person until now. He felt his own surprised hearty laughter flow out into the room and join with the ongoing merriment. Gasping for breath he tried to quiet everyone as he wiped tears from his eyes. Several passing staff members peered in the door to see what was going on. It was time to change the music he decided and turned to go to the tape machine. Someone had spilled a puddle of blue paint water and Stephen's foot went out from under him. He grabbed for the end of the table and managed to drag his sleeve through someone's wet painting. Taz set up a wail at seeing the destruction of her work. It took some concentrated effort to calm her but she finally quieted down after being given a new paper.

The only person who didn't join in the revelry was C.C. She seemed to dislike the noise. She had put her hands over her ears and sat rocking back and forth with her eyes squeezed shut. .As soon as he could get his hands cleaned off he put a different tape in his machine and adjusted the volume. This one played soft music in conjunction with the sound of ocean waves and the call of sea gulls. The noise level dropped almost immediately but most of the patients had lost interest in their art work. The young doctor sighed knowing that the session had come to a close. His assistants began to take some of the participants back to their wards. He started to gather up crayons and papers. He was anxious to examine the drawings and record his findings.

Theresa returned after delivering her last two charges.

"Dr. Baylor, want me to escort her back?" she nodded

her head toward C.C. The girl was still quietly working with her paints and colors. She appeared to be completely absorbed in what she was doing and had not uttered a sound during the entire session.

"Well maybe that would be a good idea Theresa. I guess Madie got busy with something." Stephen was scribbling names on the back of each drawing so that there would be no confusion later.

"Oh my lord. I do b'lieve she's got the gift!" Stephen's head jerked up at the girl's exclamation.

"What? What's wrong?" Stephen frowned.

"Dr. Baylor. You've got to see this." Theresa's eyes were wide with wonder.

"My God!" Stephen's mouth dropped open as he looked down at C.C.'s paintings. She had completed two and was working on a third. The first painting was a black whirlpool. The leering face at the center was easy to recognize as Jubal. A lion stood above him with its mouth open displaying large vicious fangs. A woman wearing a cape and head adornment floated in the upper left corner. At the bottom was the unmistakable shape of C.C. in her hospital bed. A second figure of her seemed to rise in ghostly fashion toward the images above. Stephen swallowed hard and the hair on the back of his neck bristled.

The second picture was a close up of the face of the woman with the cape. The third picture was streaked with blue. C.C. had used only one color and yet it was clearly a sea gull in flight. The blue sky seemed to fly with the bird. The whole painting appeared to be in flight.

"My Grandma Hattie would say `she got the sight'," Theresa breathed.

"The what?"

"The sight. The gift. You know...she can see things...visions," the girl tried to explain.

"Well I don't know about that, but I know one thing, she sure can paint!"

Stephen had read about the phenomena of the autistic savant, but he had never witnessed it. His heart pounded as he studied the paintings. This would certainly be a welcome addition to his community outreach program. He looked at the lion and the hair on his arms prickled. *Jubal had insisted that he had been attacked by a lion...* The young doctor felt a little out of focus and he removed his glasses with one hand and rubbed his eyes with the other hand.

"Shall I take her back now? She seems to be finished with this one."

Stephen had forgotten that the girl was standing beside him and he jumped when she spoke."Oh, uh yes Theresa, thank you." Suddenly, Stephen was tired. He was glad that the men's session would be held the following day. For the next few hours he straightened up the art supplies and organized his notes. At long last he leaned back in the chair at his desk and simply stared at the remarkable watercolors. He would see to it that C.C. was provided with better paper and a more versatile collection of colors. He wondered just how much he would be able to learn about the amazing spirit being held captive in C.C.'s uncooperative body and mind. Absently, he nodded and smiled in anticipation.

CHAPTER SIXTEEN

Courtney was glad to be out of the crowded aircraft. As a child she had enjoyed air travel. It was an exciting adventure. As an adult it was a tiresome experience to be herded into the stifling interior of huge silver airplanes and sit in the cramped environment for hours even though, due to her family's financial status, she was able to travel in the first class section.

Her legs felt heavy as she walked through the busy terminal. Her heart felt heavy too and a lump was forming in her throat. Tears stung the back of her eyelids and she gritted her teeth as she fought for control. She felt old and used on the one hand, and on the other she felt as vulnerable and lost as a small child.

Clyde Hammond had made arrangements for Courtney to lease a car for the summer. She stood at the rental counter and signed yet another copy of the lease agreement. The young man behind the counter was trying to flirt with her, but Courtney hardly noticed, she just felt too tired. His hand brushed hers and he looked meaningfully into her eyes as he gave her a map and detailed instructions to the Ashley River Road. She had been very young the last time she had visited Willows. At last the papers were signed and she was directed through the numbered lot to her rental car. Her fingers fumbled with the keys and she was surprised to see that her hands were shaking. She shook off the nerves and with iron-willed determination got the trunk open and hefted her suitcases inside. She got the motor running and turned the AC lever to high. She was sweating as much from nerves as from the exertion of juggling her luggage into the trunk.

The psychologist had told her she might have these moments of anxiety; everyone did, after suffering a trauma. She breathed deeply and willed her heart to slow down to a normal rate and at last she was ready to make her way to her grandmother's estate.

Traffic was heavy as Courtney wound her way through Charleston. The June afternoon was laden with humidity. Courtney noticed that the air-conditioning in her rental car had stopped working. The fan was blowing hot air into her face. She angrily flipped the lever to the OFF position. In her haste she misjudged the distance and caught one of her long nails on the metal knob. The nail bent back causing her to cry out in pain.

Tears of frustration filled her eyes as she realized she had made another wrong turn. Finally she pulled over to the side of the road and stopped the car. She wriggled out of the cotton blazer that had felt so good in the air-conditioned plane and tossed it into the back seat. Then she found a tissue in her purse and dabbed her eyes. The breeze that blew in the open window was warm but not unpleasant. She heard birds chirping nearby. Her rental car had come to a stop under a huge old tree. She looked at the gnarled roots and thick trunk with admiration. A fat gray squirrel skittered up to a branch and peered down at her switching its tail nervously.

Courtney had to laugh at his antics and immediately felt calmer. She reached for the city map and studied it for a minute, and then she picked up the handwritten instructions. It occurred to her that maybe she hadn't taken a wrong turn after all; she just hadn't gone far enough. She looked up from her paper and squinted at the road ahead. Just to the right of the next intersection she saw the Route 61 and Ashley River Road sign.

The warm damp air whipped at her auburn curls, but the humidity only made them curl tighter. The road was familiar to her and even though there had been many changes in the years since her childhood she was sure that she would easily recognize the lane which led to her grandmother's plantation home. The lush green of the tree lined road soothed her raw nerves and the ugly flashbacks of Antonio's brutality were replaced by happy childhood memories at Willows. She did indeed remember the turnoff to her grandmother's home and she felt a surge of excitement as well as nerves as her tires crunched the loose gravel on the unpaved road.

Courtney was delighted to see that her grandmother had maintained old George's topiary designs in the shrubs and trees bordering the plantation. The house itself looked very much the same except perhaps not so imposing. In fact, everything seemed somehow smaller. She drove around to the kitchen entrance and stopped the car near the screen door.

"Lord have mercy!" Hattie's beaming face appeared as she pushed the door open. Courtney caught a whiff of the mouth watering aroma that came from something cooking in the kitchen. Hattie stepped outside and watched Courtney get out of the car.

"Child, you done growed up on me. My, my, my, you are beautiful!" Hattie flung open her arms and Courtney ran into her warm embrace. Tears of joy streamed from their eyes and their words were choked with sobs. Courtney felt as close to this woman as if she were of the same flesh and blood.

Josh, Hattie's grandson, was summoned to carry Courtney's luggage to her room. Hattie had momentarily regained her composure and was chattering nonstop as she poured three glasses of iced tea.

"Ah hem," came the polite interruption.

"Grandmother Camden! I'm so glad to see you." Courtney had stiffened at the sight of her grandmother, but she was careful not to change the expression on her face. She walked over to the older woman and bent slightly to kiss her on the cheek.

"I'm happy to see you too, Courtney. You have grown into a lovely young woman. I wish your grandfather could be here to see you." Esther stood ramrod straight with the help of a cane which she gripped so tightly that her knuckles were white. Her steady gaze seemed to appraise everything about Courtney. *She has the Camden eyes and the bone structure of the British nobility. She truly does look like my granddaughter.*

"You must be fatigued from your flight. Wouldn't you like to freshen up?"

"Now that I'm here I feel wonderful. I'll go upstairs after I've had some of Hattie's sweet sun tea."

"Shall I serve in the parlor, Miz Camden?" Hattie asked knowing her employer's fondness for formal traditions.

"Well, actually I see no reason why we can't sit right here in the kitchen," Esther nodded toward the stools near the butcher block kitchen island.

Hattie's eyes bulged in their sockets and the glasses on the tray that she held rattled with her startled movement. Never in all the years that she had worked for Mrs. Camden had she taken tea in the kitchen.

Courtney knew from Hattie's reaction that something extraordinary had happened, but it wouldn't be until later that night that Hattie would explain the full significance.

The three women sipped their tea under the whirring ceiling fan. Courtney talked about her parents, her brother, and her job with the Ballet Company in Charleston. Her grandmother nodded and smiled making appropriate comments, always the perfect hostess. Hattie said nothing. She continually jumped up to check the roast or chop vegetables or pour more tea.

"I've taken the liberty of inviting a few friends over for Sunday dinner. You may remember the Woesters and the Hamiltons, at any rate they are all looking forward to seeing you after all these years."

"I think that would be very nice, Grandmother. I would very much like to see everyone again." Courtney knew better than to refuse her grandmother's subtle invitation. The Sunday dinner drop-in was one of those Camden traditions that would remain intact much as the rising and setting sun. She remembered these gatherings with fondness.

"Miz Camden, it 'peers to me like you need to rest awhile now and take your medcin'. I'll have supper ready right after the evenin' news."

"Thank you, Hattie, I believe I will lay down for a short while. Courtney, will you accompany me upstairs?"

"Of course, Grandmother. I think I would like a shower now and some comfortable clothes."

The evening passed pleasantly. Courtney and her grandmother had their supper together in the formal dining room. It was so different to be sitting at that long dark table as an adult. She remembered feeling so small in the high-backed chairs and now they seemed just...normal. After their meal they went into the library. Esther pointed to several large picture albums on one of the shelves near the roll-top desk. Courtney lifted them down and the two women sat on the leather couch. As Esther pointed out the various family members that Courtney had never met, the young woman noticed a subtle sadness settle over her. She loved looking at the pictures of the Camdens and hearing about their noble British heritage. How wonderful it would be if these elegant people truly were her ancestors. The truth was that she didn't really belong here and she knew nothing about her own bloodlines.

"I hope I haven't tired you with all of this family history," Esther looked sharply at Courtney.

"Oh no, Grandmother, I think it's fascinating, it's just that...jet lag I guess," Courtney finished jokingly.

"I see that you are wearing the blue topaz."

"Yes. Mom gave it to me on my birthday. I know that it's a family heirloom. I hope that you don't mind..." Courtney's voice trailed off as she touched the glittering blue stone.

"I gave that stone to my daughter, Clarisa, with the understanding that she would someday give it to her daughter, which is exactly what she did. You are her daughter and my granddaughter. It is an heirloom and therefore it is rightly yours. Someday I expect you to pass it on in the same manner," Esther spoke quietly. She had never displayed very much warmth to Courtney, but now there was the unmistakable hint of affection in her voice. Courtney was filled with gratitude and she had an overwhelming desire to throw her arms around her adopted grandmother.

"Now if you will excuse me, I think I will retire." Esther used her cane for assistance as she stood up. "I would imagine Hattie has your plate of cookies waitin' for you in the kitchen." The glimmer of a smile played across her face. She raised one eyebrow and then turned to go upstairs.

Courtney was shocked. Her grandmother had known the secret that she and Hattie had shared. As a child she had been expected to go to bed very early when she stayed with her grandmother. She had often been restless and when the house was quiet she would tiptoe downstairs and slip into the kitchen. No one knew for awhile, but one night the heavy milk pitcher slipped from her small hands and smashed on the floor. The noise awakened Hattie and from that time forward Courtney always found a plate of cookies and a glass of milk waiting for her in the kitchen.

"You have a nice visit with your granmama?"

"Hattie, did you know that grandmother knew about the cookies?" Courtney whispered conspiratorially.

"Whooee, no I didn't but in a way I'm not too surprised, she's one smart lady awright! Hee, hee. Now sit down and eat; I have everything ready just like always."

Hattie watched the girl as she munched on the molasses cookies and sipped her glass of milk. The wise woman sensed that Courtney's surface demeanor of casual conversation was not a true reflection of her thoughts. She sensed the darkness held at bay by the girl's will and denial. She could see a sparkling light on the other side of the shifting cloud and she knew that the only way to get to the light was for Courtney to walk through her darkness.

"Now child, why don't you tell me what you're really thinkin' about," Hattie finally spoke after the two women had lapsed into a comfortable silence.

"I'm scared, Hattie," Courtney answered honestly. "I don't understand what is happening to me. I don't know what to do with my life and I feel so alone, so worthless, so...so...victimized." Suddenly great racking sobs shook her and cut off her words.

"It's awright baby, you just let those tears wash over your soul. This is the best way to start the healing. Everything's going to be awright now. Ol' Hattie is right here and she going to help you baby." Hattie had put her arms around the sobbing girl and held her as she rocked gently and crooned soothing words. At last the sobs subsided and Courtney was silent except for an occasional loud sniff.

"Now don't you feel better?"

"I guess I do." Courtney laughed.

"I expect that you been holdin' that flood back for too long." Hattie shook her finger at Courtney." It ain't good to do that baby. Didn't that big fancy school teach you better than that?" Hattie smiled.

"I guess the answers I need to find aren't in any of those text books." Courtney blew her nose and wiped her eyes with the tissue Hattie gave her.

"You are very right about that baby, but don't you worry none, you gonna find those answers and ol' Hattie gonna help you, but we are not gonna go lookin' tonight. You go on to bed now and we can talk tomorrow."

"Hattie, thank you...I..."

"Oh go on now, when you love someone you just naturally want to do good things for them...go on now...outta my kitchen." Hattie playfully shooed Courtney off to bed.

A sound at the screen door caught Hattie's attention.

"Well you finally decided to come home did you? I haven't seen your furry face all day. What you been doin'?" Hattie opened the door and Storm Cat sauntered in. "What? You're hungry? You want me to just up an fix you a meal anytime you ask for it?" Storm Cat walked over to the corner where his food dish usually sat and waited expectantly.

"Ha! Now you goin' to tell me that just because I cooked my famous roast beef today you think you gonna get some too?" Storm Cat meowed and licked his whiskers with his long pink tongue as he watched Hattie's every move. "I tell you what I'm gonna do." Hattie stood holding a small plate heaped with scraps of meat, "We are gonna make a bargain. You help me get that girl upstairs to feelin' better and you can have this plate of meat." Storm Cat meowed and the bargain was sealed. He carefully licked the dish clean and then trotted up the staircase to fulfill his obligation.

Courtney knelt on the floor in front of one of her open suitcases. She scooped up a handful of folded underwear and carried it over to the chest of drawers. She really wasn't in the mood to unpack. She opened the top drawer and put the stack of silky briefs in one corner and with a sigh absently shoved the drawer shut. Maybe she would just go to bed and try to go to sleep. She turned around to go toward the bed, but she stopped with a gasp at what she saw. A large gray cat sat in the middle of the bed staring at her through yellow gold eyes.

Courtney froze in fear. Were her eyes playing tricks? Was this one of those strange visions and those eyes...where had she seen those eyes before? The cat meowed a soft greeting and then nonchalantly began his evening grooming ritual. Her eyes darted around the room scanning for something stable or evidence that she was having a psychic episode. The bedroom door was standing ajar and she breathed a deep sigh of relief as she realized that this cat was very much flesh and blood.

"Oh, of course! I know who you are. Hattie told me about you. Your name is Storm Cat!" The gray cat blinked his startling gold eyes disdainfully and began cleaning his other paw. "You came to keep me company didn't you?" Courtney was thrilled that this special member of such an independent species would seek her out. She climbed up on the canopy bed and stretched out. The cat walked over to her and sniffed her outstretched hand. Then he moved closer and before long he was curled in a furry ball at her side. His presence was comforting and before she realized what was happening she drifted into sleep. Several times during the night the young woman awoke in a panic, not recognizing her surroundings, but each time a small sound or movement from Storm Cat would calm her and bring her back to the safe reality of her grandmother's home. Just before dawn Courtney awakened yet again. Storm Cat was gently touching her cheek with his paw. When her eyes opened he meowed softly and then trotted to the edge of the bed and leaped lightly to the floor. Courtney propped herself up on her elbow and watched his tail disappear through the partially open door. "Thanks," she whispered and she lay back on her pillows already asleep.

It was nearly ten o'clock the next morning before Courtney descended the winding staircase, fully dressed, to greet the day. Esther watched with admiration as her granddaughter gracefully negotiated the long curving flight of steps. The older woman was dressed in beige and violet and her white hair was swept back in a soft chignon.

"Good morning, Dear. I hope you slept well." Esther's greeting was cordial, but her formal manners always left Courtney with a distant lonely feeling.

"Good morning. Yes, thank you. I feel very well rested."

"I'm happy to hear that. I'm afraid that I must be leaving. My garden club is meeting this morning followed by a luncheon. I'm sure I will be out until late this afternoon. I hope you won't mind."

"Why, no not at all. I need to finish unpacking and then I thought I would wander around outside a bit."

"Good. Then I will see you this evening."

Courtney watched her grandmother drive away in the big Lincoln. Truly a remarkable woman, she thought. She is elegant, charming, impossibly determined, and utterly unfathomable.

Hattie sat at the kitchen island polishing a silver candlestick. Her rich voice filled the large kitchen as she sang happily.

Courtney stood quietly listening to the soothing sound

of the old hymn. The song spoke of walking in a garden with the comforting presence of Him. She remembered her own walks in the gardens of Willows. There had always been a special magic there. She remembered butterflies that landed on her small dimpled hands and birds that seemed to sing simply because she wished it. Many of the flowers grew as tall as she and she fancied herself in the land of enchantment.

"Child! How long you been standin' there? It's not nice to startle an old lady thataway," Hattie exclaimed breathlessly, as she chuckled.

"I'm sorry. I enjoyed your singing so much it reminded me of the times I used to play in the gardens here," Courtney answered apologetically.

"Un huh. There is a special magic in those gardens. How about some fresh hot coffee?" Hattie bustled over to the coffee maker and pushed the ON button. Within a short time Courtney was devouring Hattie's breakfast muffins dripping with honey butter and sipping her strong hot coffee.

"Miz Camden is going to be out most of the day and I got the day free. We got some serious talking to do. I think the best place to do it is in the magic garden," Hattie said with a grin and a raised eyebrow.

They rinsed the dishes and put away the gleaming silver. Hattie gave Courtney one of her grandmother's straw hats and the two women walked arm in arm toward the gardens.

"Oh Hattie, the gardens are just as beautiful as I remembered them. Did Grandmother take out some of the beds? I thought there used to be a lot more." Courtney squinted as she surveyed the expertly manicured lawns, walkways, and flower beds.

"Hee, hee, hee. Nothing has changed except you

honey child. You're just seein' things from a new perspective," Hattie chuckled. "Whooee, I do believe summer is blowing his hot dragon breath on us today." Hattie took off her straw hat and began to fan herself vigorously.

Courtney only half heard what Hattie said as the sunbathed flower beds of Willows momentarily disappeared and she saw instead the vine-covered walkways of the Scolari Estate. The young woman squeezed her eyes shut with a shudder as Antonio's face devoid of life, appeared in front of her. The face that had once been so beloved was twisted into the terrifying mask that chased her in her dreams and leered at her from the dark corners of her mind during every waking moment.

"Child, you can't turn it off and you can't run away. You got to face your fear and then move through it. The light is on the other side. C'mon baby, set yourself down here on this bench and tell ol' Hattie about that dragon you been trying to slay all by yourself. Start from the beginnin' and don't leave out even one detail!"

The two women sat on the shaded bench as Courtney began her story. She felt safe there with the singing birds and bobbing flowers. Insects hummed and buzzed and huge fleecy clouds floated silently in the sky overhead. The sun climbed to its midday position and then began its descent toward the horizon. At last Courtney was finished. She had told Hattie about her visions and every detail of her experience with Antonio including the foretelling of his violent demise. She leaned back against the bench exhausted.

Hattie had listened silently, sometimes nodding and making little clucking noises as she fanned herself with her hat. Occasionally she reached out to pat the girl's hand or give her another tissue to soak up the constant flow of tears, but she didn't attempt to interrupt Courtney.

"Now sugar, tell me how you feel," Hattie said softly.

"Sad. Empty. Tired. Hattie can you tell me what all of this means? Am I crazy?"

"No baby, you're anything but crazy. We are gonna talk about what is happening but first...ugh," Hattie groaned as she stood up, "We're gonna go inside and get some ice cold tea. I'm goin' to melt away for sure!" Courtney managed a smile and the two women strolled back to the house.

The big kitchen was dark and cool as they stepped out of the heat of the early June afternoon. The tall glasses of tea refreshed them both.

"C'mon sugar babe. Bring your tea and come to my sitting room. It will be a little cooler in there and I can put my poor old swollen feet up while we talk." Hattie shuffled down the hall toward her living area.

Courtney was right at home in Hattie's sitting room. She had been there many times as a child listening to Hattie's stories about her childhood on Daufuskie Island. Aside from the persistent feeling that everything had shrunk like something from Alice in Wonderland, the room looked very much the same. For the first time, Courtney read the titles of some of the books on the shelves of the crowded bookcase. Shakespeare, African History, Psychology; Courtney had never thought about Hattie reading books like these. She realized with surprise that there were probably many things that she didn't know about her beloved and somewhat mysterious Hattie.

"So you're surprised by my books?" Hattie asked with a sly smile.

"Well a little I guess. The thing I am most surprised about is that I really don't know who you are at all. I mean I've always known you as Grandma Hattie who is kind and a fabulous cook and chock full of smiles and earthy wisdom. I know that you have always been one of the most important people in my life and yet...there are so many aspects of your life that I know nothing about."

"Hee, hee, hee! Go on now," Hattie chuckled, "That's just a sign that you're grown up. I think we are gonna have lots of time this summer to find out all of our secrets. Now sit yourself down in that other recliner chair and drink your tea."

Courtney sat down and lifted the foot rest on the recliner. The ceiling fan created a little breeze that gently lifted the wispy curls that framed her face. She leaned back in the softness of the chair and sighed peacefully.

"That's right baby, you just lean back and old Hattie will tell you a story."

Courtney smiled, she loved Hattie's stories. She felt like a little girl again, safe and protected.

"Once upon a time...a long time ago, before the world was tainted with greed and the lust for power...a girl child was born in a mountain village. Her momma and daddy was older than most and she was their first child. They knew they would probably never have another child so they named her One Beloved. If we were to hear the name in that ancient language it would sound like Aeonkisha to us."

Courtney had briefly described her visions to Hattie, but she had not mentioned that name and her eyes flew open when Hattie said it.

"Aeonkisha grew strong and tall. She was good and kind too. Everyone in the village loved her. Both of her parents died by the time she saw her twelfth summer, but she was well cared for by the people of the village.

One day as she walked in the jungle she found an orphaned lion cub. The gods had brought them together each as gift to the other to fill the void created by the loss of their loved ones. From that day forward they were inseparable."

Courtney had relaxed again. She listened to Hattie's low soothing voice which seemed to invoke living images on the screen of her mind. She was completely engrossed in the unfolding story and was only vaguely aware of the subtle changes in Hattie's accent and the refinement of her voice.

"One day Aeonkisha and her young lion went to the village holy man. She had been frightened by a dream. She dreamed that she and her lion flew over the tops of the mountains. When she woke up she and her lion were several miles from the village.

"The holy man knew at once that she was destined to be a spiritual leader. He took her into his home as his apprentice and adopted daughter. Ten years later when the old man died, Aeonkisha became his successor as holy woman and healer for the village.

"During the season of rains in her twenty-fifth year she took a young man, the tribe's best hunter, as her husband. Shortly after the birth of their twin daughters the young man was bitten by a poisonous reptile while on a hunting expedition and died within a few hours."

At the mention of the twin girls Courtney gasped. She saw her own face briefly transposed over the face of one baby and Hattie's face on the other. Suddenly she understood the bond between them.

"Aeonkisha knew she would see her husband again in the afterlife and though she was saddened by their separation, death could not end their love.

"The twins reached their thirteenth season of rains and Aeonkisha took her daughters into the jungle to gather the roots and leaves that they used in their healing work. Protector, their enormous full grown lion, accompanied them. When they reached the reflecting pool at the base of the waterfall, they decided to bathe and rest in the shade. They first gave thanks to the Goddess of the Water and then to the Earth Mother for the bountiful gifts of nourishment that they and their village enjoyed. At the conclusion of the solemn rites, mother and daughters splashed each other playfully in the cool refreshing water. Protector preferred to roll on his back on the mossy bank.

"As the girls and their mother lay quietly listening to the sweet music of the jungle sounds, a cloud blotted out the light of the sun. Darkness settled over them as if it were midnight instead of midday causing the women to be fearful. Protector growled threateningly and circled his charges, uncertain as to which direction the danger might approach from.

"A bolt of lightning sliced through the gloom and in its wake an apparition appeared. Aeonkisha had heard the legends about the Ancient One and his prophecies, but she never dreamed she would stand in his venerable presence. The specter showed them pictures of the great shadow of evils that would plague the earth in the centuries to come. They saw war born of the lust for power and the birth and rebirth of layers of hatred. They saw strange birds bearing men who dropped fire bolts on villages. They shuddered as they saw forests disappear and precious water fouled.

"At last the terrible visions were gone but the cries of the sick and the suffering still rang through the darkness. The Ancient One raised his hand and there was silence. Then in a voice filled with infinite gentleness he spoke in a vibration that they heard not with their ears, but with their hearts.

'A terrible pestilence is coming and it is inevitable, but it will be followed by a time of wisdom when hearts and minds will be lifted up to finally allow a great peace to return to the earth. But, there is one danger, the power of hatred is like a spreading poison that withers the heart, blinds the eye, and turns the mind from the quiet reflecting pool to the erupting volcano. If hatred continues unchecked for too long, the heart of the Earth Mother too will be withered and she will collapse and with her all life in this dimension will disappear.

'We are bound by the promise of free will. We, the council of guardians, must not interfere with the destiny of earth and her people. But we have created a plan that might help. There are those who will be chosen to walk softly upon the earth. During the time of blindness, they will help others see. During the time of hatred they will live in love. During the time of darkness they will be the spark of light. This will not be an easy task and we ask that you ponder at length all that you have heard and seen on this day. We the council, call upon you to join with us in assisting mankind with their perilous journey through time. It is your decision to make. You may accept or reject this calling as you wish and you need not fear reprisals should you refuse. I will not visit you again. I will read your heart and I will know your answer.'

"The specter vanished and the light returned to the clearing."

Hattie had stopped speaking, but the story played on in Courtney's mind. She knew that they had all agreed to carry the seed of love and keep it alive in every generation. They along with thousands of others would try to keep the hatred from lasting too long and each in their own unique way would try to keep the Earth Mother alive.

Courtney sighed as she relaxed in the recliner. She couldn't hear any sound coming from Hattie. She tried to smile as she realized that Hattie must have drifted off to sleep, but her face felt thick and she couldn't move her lips nor open her eyes. She didn't mind really, since she didn't want to come back to reality just yet. She let her mind drift back to the waterfall and the beauty of the wild orchids.

"What a lovely fantasy," she told herself. Maybe she should write a book about it. "If only it were true," she mused, "what a lovely thought, that my life could actually have a noble purpose."

The ceiling fan hummed louder and Courtney had the sensation that the fan was in her head. The whirring, the spinning...she tried to grip the armrests of the chair, she was dizzy...falling...

Water swirled around her bare feet and she raised her long skirts even higher, not that it really mattered she thought ruefully. She had grown taller and her newly curvaceous body had strained the seams of her dress to their limits. Since the war there had been fewer dresses and people to make them, she pouted. But they had heard rumors that the end was near. She would surely be glad. She wanted things to be as they were...parties, beautiful new gowns, and lots of handsome attentive young men. How she longed to have all of the servants back. She hated working in the garden and getting her soft white hands dirty. She hated working in the hot kitchen house with Mammy Lou.

The girl jumped as twigs snapped nearby. She parted the thick bushes and looked across the rolling lawns at the white columned plantation house. She was afraid Mammy Lou would notice her absence and make her go back to the kitchen, but she saw no sign of the old Negro woman. She sat listening for a moment longer. She thought she heard a distant shout. Stupid old woman, she thought, she thinks I've gone into the woods on the other side of the gardens. The girl giggled, Mammy Lou was getting old and feeble minded, not that her mind had ever been right anyway. She was always talking to people who weren't there, the friendly spirits she called them.

The girl sighed and turned back to the river. Insects danced above the water in circling swarms. She hated gnats and mosquitoes. Too bad Lily had disappeared. It would be nice to have the girl here to fan away the pesky creatures. Better yet, she wished to be away from here. Her parents had gone into the city and left her and her younger brother at home. Her father said he had business to attend to and roads were unsafe. She had cried and pleaded to no avail, they had left without her and were not due back until tomorrow night. She was certain they would be attending parties, sipping iced punch and having a thoroughly wonderful time. Tears of self pity rolled down the white petal soft skin of her cheeks.

    The constant flow and gurgle of the river was soothing and before long the tears gave way to girlish daydreams of pretty dresses and lavish cotillions where handsome young men in uniform bowed over her dainty hand as they asked her to dance. She rested her back against the trunk of the willow tree and closed her eyes. She listened to the music in her fantasy party failing to take notice of whispers and rustlings that moved ominously closer. A distasteful odor caused her to wrinkle her small nose. Before she could react, a grimy hand clamped over her mouth and she was pushed roughly to the ground. A face appeared above her. Dark brown eyes crazed with hunger, lust and the atrocities of war leered at her from their sunken sockets. The bodice of her dress was ripped away and she could feel his hands bruising her tender flesh. Bile rose up in the girl's throat, the fear, the smell of filthy unwashed bodies...she gagged and choked as she tried to scream for help. She clawed desperately at her captor's face before her arms were ruthlessly pinned down. The man's howl of pain was a brief satisfaction but no matter how hard she kicked and struggled she was unable to do any more damage. The hand across her mouth began to infringe on her ability to breathe.

    "Leb, c'mon boy, you better get some of this! It's better when they's still alive." Maniacal laughter came from two others.

She continued to struggle but was rendered helpless. Even in their emaciated state the three men overpowered her easily.

"Hey boy! C'mon over here. Be a man for a change!" The hateful voice jeered and taunted someone who remained out of her line of vision.

Rough hands tore at her skirts and she felt the air on her bare skin. Grunting noises followed by pain and a horror she could not define were her deathly companions. Fists battered her face and body as she feebly struggled to free herself and gulp in air. She bit at the boney hand that covered her mouth. The man momentarily released his grip and she gasped for breath. Her attacker was further enraged by the painful bite and grabbed her throat bearing down with all of his strength. The horror and pain of being brutally choked drove away every shred of reason and the scream of terror that rose up was heard only in her mind as she slipped into unconsciousness. She was engulfed by a dark silence and a floating sensation. Suddenly she was aware that the hands were gone from her throat and, unexpectedly, she was free! She opened her eyes cautiously and laughed with relief as she looked into the blue sky. It must have been a horrible dream she told herself. Scuffing sounds and male voices made her jump in alarm. The men she thought had attacked her were bent over someone else. She started to try to help the poor girl but the body was lifeless so she backed away without making a sound. The men were so engrossed in what they were doing that they took no notice of her. Someone was crying a few yards away. She carefully picked her way along the riverbank until she could get a closer look. A man sat slumped forward in the tall grass near the water. On closer inspection, she saw that he was only a boy probably not much older than she. His thin shoulders shook under the ragged remains of a shirt, as he cried great wrenching sobs. His lips worked as if he was speaking, but she heard no words. Clearly he had been traumatized and she was overcome with feelings of sympathy for the forlorn figure. Quietly she drew closer and gently reached out her hand to touch his face and dry his tears.

"Miss Priscilla, you come on up to dis house right now. It be time fo' suppuh!"

"Mammy Lou!" Priscilla pushed her way through the bushes and ran effortlessly up the gently sloping bank near the river and across the wide expanse of lawn. Suddenly she stopped short and looked down at her dress. It was no longer torn. "Oh Mammy Lou, I had the most frightening dream! I'm so glad to see you!" The girl threw herself into the large woman's arms.

"I know baby. I know."

Something felt wrong. Priscilla pulled back and looked into the kind dark eyes of Mammy Lou. The turban was twisted neatly around her head as always. She wore her white apron over her long skirt...the scar was gone! As a young girl she had been burned as a punishment by a cruel slave owner. But now Mammy's brown skin was as smooth as her mama's bronze satin ball gown."Yes, chile, it be gone." Mammy Lou seemed to read her mind. Eveythin' be wipe away clean now."

"What in the name of goodness are you talking about?" Priscilla exclaimed using one of her mother's expressions.

"You got to remember baby then we can be leavin' this place for awhile." Instantly they were in the kitchen house. Mammy Lou's body lay slumped across the cutting table. Blood dripped from the wound in her head. The room was in complete disarray. Chairs were turned over and their precious provisions were strewn everywhere.

Priscilla gasped and clapped her hand over her mouth

in horror. As she did she found herself looking down on her own inert and ravished body lying in a puddle of blood near the river. She realized that the poor girl who had been attacked was her. The fear threatened to consume her again, but Mammy's comforting arm encircled her shoulders and she knew everything would be all right.

"You almost forgot why we came here, child. You best be careful when you down there on earth, you got to keep your promise. Don't you go lettin' your heart be dried up with greed!"

The girl stared open-mouthed, as she and Mammy walked higher and higher. The plantation was far below and still they walked in a meadow! The roar of a lion...a swirling cape...a bolt of lightning...the ancient one...the promise...monks, peasants, royalty, male, female from time in the distant past to the present, she remembered the lives she had lived and the lessons she learned, it was all made clear in the blink of an eye... she would not forget her purpose again.

Courtney's mouth was dry as she opened her eyes.

"Welcome back, baby." Hattie's smiling face bent over Courtney's. "You've been on some long journey. I don't want you talking right now, you just lay back and then sit yourself up right slow. I have fixed you my very special hot tea and I want you to drink every drop before you get out of that chair. I'll be in the kitchen. Miz Camden will be home any minute and she will be wanting her late afternoon tea and her newspaper."

Courtney sat up and dutifully sipped her tea. Gradually the heavy feeling in her head lifted and she felt more focused though her hands still trembled so violently she was compelled to hold the cup with two hands. "Could it be true?" she wondered, as tears slipped from her eyes and down her cheeks. Emotions still rioted within as she fought to make sense of it all. There was no doubt that she had recognized the war-crazed soldier as the present day Antonio. She gasped as she realized the crying boy from the past was the strong self-assured Raeford of today. Again she thought of the vision she had while recovering from her injuries in the hospital. It would seem that Antonio had been responsible for her death in a previous life, if such a thing is possible, she told herself. Her breath came in short gasps as she relived the feelings of panic. She tried to swallow the lump of fear in her throat as the realization swept through her that he had nearly killed her again in this life. She put down her teacup but it rattled in the saucer as her hand shook. Somehow this time Raeford was able to stop him before he committed the same vicious acts which included her murder. Slowly she shook her head back and forth as she replayed the memory of her vision of Antonio's death at the hands of his men. Her head jerked back as she remembered the sound of the gunshot and the splash as his body fell into the shallow water. Twice he betrayed his own men and twice he died in violence. She remembered the rancid smell of sweating filthy soldiers as they held her down and tore at her clothing. Her stomach heaved as she realized those memories were as vivid and real as the events that had occurred in this life! Goose flesh rose on her arms and she shivered as the possibilities dawned on her...*she had actually lived other lives.* Her heart pounded in her ears and she wondered momentarily if she was going to lose consciousness.

"I have to calm down. I have to breathe. I have to think!" she told herself. Could there be a way to verify those events? Maybe there was some sort of written record that would help to prove what she saw, what she thought she remembered. She realized that if she could prove that the people, events and places were actual fact then it would change the meaning of her whole life, *everyone's life*. It would surely redefine everything that had ever happened to her *and to everyone*. This concept would certainly explain so many behaviors, phobias and belief systems. Her mind was racing with new thoughts and possibilities. This was something she had to pursue and she was determined to uncover every bit of information available until she had her answers.

Mentally she began to review possible avenues for research. There had to be some written records of the family tree, maybe there would be some statistics on file in the county archives about the property owners and possibly death records during that time. As she busied her thoughts with plans for her investigation, her trembles ceased and her knees felt less like pudding. It was time to go find Hattie she decided as she eased herself out of the recliner. With each step her legs felt stronger as she made her way slowly to the kitchen.

"Miz Camden is waitin' on you in the parlor," Hattie smiled at her as a pale but calmer Courtney entered the room. She felt rattled to the core and had no idea how she was going to cope with all of the information she had just assimilated. Hattie's wise dark eyes bored into her for a moment before placing one of her strong capable hands on Courtney's upper back. Almost immediately she felt better as a warm comforting energy crept through her body.

Courtney found Mrs. Camden settled comfortably in her antique wing-back chair. Her feet were propped up on the matching ottoman and her eyes were closed.

"Grandmother?" Courtney said softly, not wishing to startle her.

"There you are, Dear! Come in and sit with me. I am just resting my eyes. Did you have a pleasant day?"

"Yes thank you, I really enjoyed seeing the gardens again. The flowers are every bit as beautiful as I remember...only smaller!" Courtney finished dryly. She was surprised to hear Esther's laugh.

"Oh yes, I believe that phenomenon occurs with all of us at some time or other. The world always looks larger than life through a child's eyes, but as we grow into adults it magically shrinks. Everyone has a whole new perspective on magnitude without the benefit of Alice's concoction in her wonderland. I do believe I truly like you Courtney. So few people are fresh and direct these days." Courtney flushed pink with her grandmother's unexpected praise.

"How was your day?" Courtney asked with real interest. "What does a garden club do?"

"Gossip mostly," Esther quipped sarcastically.

A joke...she couldn't believe it, the stately, stern Camden matriarch had made a joke! For the next hour Esther regaled her granddaughter with the adventures of the well meaning garden club members from their beautification projects to their unique personality quirks.

"Oh dear," Courtney gasped wiping the tears of mirth from her eyes, "You should really write all of this down. It would make quite an entertaining book or series of articles. I can't believe that sweet Mrs. Pearl carries a flask in her dainty little pocketbook."

"Why do you think she is so easy going?" They both laughed again. "Well perhaps I should write some of it down but wouldn't it just shock poor Daisy McDougal to see her name in print?" The two women laughed at the mention of the prim little spinster whose antics and "witherin" influence' was a constant source of entertainment for club gossips.

"Well now, it appears to me you ladies must of worked up an appetite with all that laughing." Hattie was delighted to see them both so happy.

The light mood continued as Esther and Courtney munched on the fresh green salad that Hattie had prepared with vegetables straight from the kitchen garden.

"Grandmother, I would love to know more about the Camden family tree and the history of Willows. Do you have a written record here?" Courtney asked as they nibbled on cookies and sherbet.

"I'm so happy you are interested. As a matter of fact I do have a very extensive history. There are ten volumes of very detailed accounts of our family dating back to the end of the fourteenth century. They are in the library and you may read them all, but beware of the curse," Esther said mysteriously.

"What curse?" she asked unwittingly swallowing the bait.

"Why, it is rumored," Esther dropped her voice and leaned forward for dramatic effect, "that anyone who attempts to read the entire Camden family history is in danger of falling into a deep sleep." Her eyes twinkled with mischief and Courtney noticed how beautiful the older woman looked when she smiled.

Later that evening Courtney bade goodnight to Esther and Hattie, then took her milk and cookies into the library. She would be exercising furiously with the Ballet Company as of Monday, she thought, so all of the extra calories wouldn't hurt too much she hoped.

After a brief search she found the leather bound volumes containing the family history. She randomly chose one of the books and settled herself in the large leather chair near the roll top desk. She became instantly absorbed in the colorful lives of the earliest known Camdens. There were advisors to the royal family, lords, and their ladies, barristers, and physicians, each endeavoring to maintain an honorable link in the chain of succession from the past to the present. This would be fascinating reading for another time, she thought as she yawned and looked at her watch. She was surprised to see that she had been reading for nearly two hours. She stretched her cramped legs and went back to the bookshelves. She took down one volume after another and flipped through the pages until at last she found the one she sought and took it back to the leather chair.

Louis Winston Camden II born August 20, 1828, she read further, married Elizabeth Emma 1848. A daughter was born 1852 and a son was born 1855. Louis Winston II served six months in the War against Northern Aggression; Courtney smiled to herself, Southerners rarely referred to that conflict as the Civil War, even today. As she read she learned that Louis had lost a leg and due to complications was sent home to Willows. He was not expected to live. When he arrived he found that many of their slaves had run away and the once prosperous and well-ordered plantation was slipping into ruin. His wife, Elizabeth Emma, was ill with a fever and his children were forced to work in the house and garden. Courtney read eagerly, she still had not found the names of his children. There were several pages detailing the family's holdings and their losses from 1861 to 1865. There was no record of the loyal housekeeper's name, although the account did mention that she and her husband and a handful of other elderly slaves had stayed on the plantation to help the family.

Louis had become quite active in local politics after he recovered from his injuries. He and other plantation owners took an active role in support of the Confederate war effort. When the news came that surrender was imminent, he and his wife went into the city of Charleston, leaving their two children at home, thinking them to be safer there. Upon their return on April 15, 1865 they found their remaining servants murdered and their home ransacked. The ravaged body of their thirteen year old daughter, Priscilla, was found near the river. Their ten year old son, Louis III, was nowhere to be found. They presumed him dead also. Three days later the boy crawled from his hiding place and stumbled up to the front door. The boy was mute for two years. When he finally spoke he was unable to recount anything that he had experienced from the day his parents left for Charleston to the autumn morning two years later when he just seemed to wake up.

Courtney's hands were shaking. There had been a Priscilla Camden and she had died on the river bank near Willows! The account had speculated that their deaths had occurred on April 14, 1865, the same day that the union flag was raised on Fort Sumter. The same day that President Lincoln had been shot and...April 14th was Courtney's birthday...in this lifetime. Esther Camden's husband, Courtney's adopted grandfather had also died on that day and years later her uncle...Grandmother Camden's son Charles had died in a tragic car wreck on that same date. Courtney shivered.

Her heart was pounding heavily in her chest as she closed the book with a sharp snap. Her rubbery knees barely held her up as she stood and walked to the shelf to replace the old volume. She could take in nothing more. She was utterly saturated. There was so much to consider. Should she trust what her visions had shown her or was it some crazy coincidence? Perhaps her mother had told her the story of Willows when she was a child and she had retained it subconsciously. Her head was pounding. A needle sharp pain pricked at the center point between her eyebrows. She had to put her thoughts aside; it was time to go to bed. She would call her mother tomorrow as planned and try to ask some discreet questions.

When Courtney entered her bedroom she wasn't surprised to see Storm Cat perched like the mysterious sphinx on her bed. She was glad to see him. She knew he was just a cat but his presence was comforting. She felt safe with him there. Of course, she chided herself, she didn't know how a mere cat could protect her; and anyway, protect her from what she wondered...her own thoughts? Storm Cat blinked his large gold eyes and Courtney was again reminded of the lion called Protector from her visions.

"Don't tell me you think you are a reincarnation of that lion?" Courtney said aloud to Storm Cat. He stared unblinking at the doubting Thomas before him and finally answered with a firm meow. He seemed to feel that the subject was closed as he stood up and glanced meaningfully toward the pillows. It was time for everyone to get some sleep.

CHAPTER SEVENTEEN

Courtney slept deeply that night and when she awoke at nine o'clock on Sunday morning she was refreshed and well rested. For the first time in weeks she actually felt joyous anticipation at the prospect of greeting another day.

After a quick shower Courtney sprinted downstairs. She paused on the last step as a thought struck her. Priscilla must have skipped down these steps much as she had just now, only she would have been wearing long skirts. Courtney shivered as she looked down at her feet. She imagined seeing a ruffled hoop skirt instead of sandals and bare legs.

Hattie's powerful voice rang through the house as she welcomed the day in song. After a brief search, Courtney found Esther sitting in her wingback chair. Her white hair, waved and curling, created a luminous halo around her face as she listened with her eyes closed to Hattie's a cappella "Amazing Grace." Courtney sat down quietly unwilling to break the spell of the music.

"She has the voice of a living breathing angel, doesn't she?" Esther murmured without opening her eyes.

"Yes. She's wonderful," Courtney said with surprise, noting that her grandmother must have realized she had entered the room.

"Hattie's choir is performing at my church today. Would you like to come along?"

"Oh, I'd love to," Courtney decided quickly.

"Run along and change and I'll have Hattie fix you a quick snack."

The Hammonds had not been regular church goers,

but they had attended many diverse religious services in their travels around the world. Courtney had seen everything from a Buddhist temple to the Church of England. Much like her parents she had acquired a healthy respect for all belief systems. They had often attended weddings and special ceremonies at the invitation of friends, but the family had never become a member of any one religion. Their busy lifestyle and extensive travels had always caused them to cherish their Sundays as a time to relax and be together as a family.

 Esther led her granddaughter to her usual pew and the two sat down together. Her heart warmed as she listened to her grandmother's voice introducing her to acquaintances with a genuine pride and affection. It had been so many years since they had spoken in person that Courtney wasn't sure exactly how her grandmother felt about her.

 Precisely at eleven o'clock, Reverend Fishkin appeared behind the pulpit and began the service.

 "Right on time as always. I sincerely wish the good Reverend would extend his promptness to the end of the service as well," Esther whispered near Courtney's ear.

 Courtney giggled at her grandmother's dry humor. Smiling broadly, the Reverend announced that the visiting choir would perform near the end of the service and he promised to shorten his sermon in order to accommodate them. Courtney heard a polite laugh ripple through the congregation and a sarcastic `humph' from Esther.

 As the service proceeded Courtney was lulled by its peaceful rhythm, the hymns, the prayers, and the sermon. Her eyes traveled around the old sanctuary. The structure was essentially the same as it had been well over one hundred years earlier. Her gaze lingered on the architecture and finally turned toward the window. She marveled at the swaying limbs of the giant Live Oaks just outside and imagined ladies in long dresses setting up tables laden with food for the Sunday potluck. She saw children chasing each other as they tried to pass the time before they were allowed to sample the feast being readied by the women. She was drawn to two children in particular as they chased each other shrieking with laughter.

Courtney glanced at her grandmother, but she sat quietly with her head bowed and her eyes closed. In fact no one seemed to notice the noisy children even though Courtney could hear them clearly. She looked out of the window again. She saw that one of the children was a little boy; in fact he looked very much like Shane did when he was that age. The girl seemed to be a few years older. Her heart leaped as she realized that they were Priscilla and Louis, young and happy before the war that would change all of their lives. She was jolted to realize that Shane had been her younger brother then too. Except of course, she corrected herself, in that life they were related by blood. Then she had an odd thought, in this life they were connected by something stronger than blood. Their souls had traveled the corridors of time and somehow were able to find each other again. Goose bumps rose on her arms and she felt lightheaded. She closed her eyes and breathed deeply trying to block out the sounds of those children laughing and women talking, the sounds that apparently no one else could hear.

A nudge from Esther brought Courtney back to the present. Ushers were passing the collection plates and Hattie's choir members were filing in quietly at the front of the church. For the next twenty minutes music filled the room and the hearts of everyone in the congregation. It was an experience that most of them would never forget.

They began with a medley of lively spirituals. Heads bobbed with the rhythm and Courtney watched serious expressions transformed until every face was wreathed with smiles. At times it seemed as if a moment from the past transposed itself over the people of the present. Women, who wore pants suits, were suddenly wearing long dresses as they did in the 1860s. Those fanning themselves with the Sunday program fanned with lacey summer fans popular in another time. The men too, sitting ramrod straight wearing modern silk ties and summer suits, wore instead stiff white collars and even a Confederate uniform or two appeared briefly. Had they all been here before, Courtney wondered?

    Finally it was time for Hattie to perform her solo. An expectant hush fell over the congregation. Hattie walked to the piano and smiled at the audience. The music began softly and then paused as she started to sing. Her powerful voice reached out to each person and then soared to the peaked roof. Courtney was tumbled about with emotions. She wanted to laugh but found that tears poured down her cheeks. Utterly spellbound, no one dared to breathe for fear of breaking the holy peace that had come upon them. Then as the last few bars of "His Eye is on the Sparrow" faded, the room was silent for a long moment. No one could move. Then Reverend Fishkin jumped to his feet applauding enthusiastically and the rest of the congregation followed his lead. Even the stoic southern gentlemen wiped their eyes with clean white handkerchiefs as their emotions spilled over. At last everyone quieted and the director announced they would close their performance with the choir's inspiring rendition of "The Lord's Prayer." The congregation was asked to stand and as their voices blended and rose, tears glistened from every eye. The good Reverend himself was so overcome with emotion that for once, to everyone's immense relief, he could say nothing more than a quiet "God bless you, Amen."

    Esther and Courtney left as quickly as possible after politely greeting the Reverend and members of the guest choir. Hattie too said her good-byes quickly and then the three women hurried to Esther's car. They wanted to get back to Willows in order to prepare for the *little* Sunday drop-in. Esther was expecting fifty people. As usual though, Hattie was as organized as any professional caterer so the only thing they had to do was set out the food, buffet-style on the long dining room table. Several ladies from the church arrived early with helping hands and a burning curiosity about the sudden appearance of Esther's granddaughter, the ballerina. Throughout the afternoon Courtney found herself surrounded by her grandmother's doting friends and Hattie's smiling choir members. She was plied with questions about her extensive travels and the lifestyle of a professional ballet dancer. The genteel manners of the ladies and gentlemen of Charleston made Courtney feel like a celebrity.

    Secretly Courtney was surprised and a little puzzled by the open adoration of the drop-in guests. She had never really thought of herself as a ballerina. She certainly loved dancing and considered ballet to be an important part of her life, but it had never been much more than a hobby in her own mind. In truth she could never quite picture herself in any career. She was embarrassed to admit that at twenty-five years old, even though she was well educated, well traveled, fluent in more than one language, and an accomplished dancer, she still had no idea what she really wanted to do with her life. She felt as though something was missing and if she could just find that illusive part of herself, she would miraculously discover the one thing that she could passionately pursue. But, she thought with a sigh, she could hardly begin to try to explain these feelings to anyone when she herself didn't fully understand them.

    "Right now I'm working with the Charleston Ballet Company, Ms. McDougal, and that will probably keep me very busy this summer. I think I will try to do a little sightseeing and maybe investigate my own family history."

Courtney was trying to answer Daisy's impertinent questions about her future as vaguely as possible.

Esther stood nearby; she admired the way her bright young granddaughter was responding to the many questions her friends asked of her. She had just swallowed some iced tea when Courtney remarked that she wanted to research her own background. The tea suddenly seemed to solidify in her throat and she choked. The violent coughing that followed stopped all conversation for several minutes. Her worst fear loomed large in her mind. She knew very well what Courtney intended to do and she must not let it happen. She was sure that none of her current friends knew for certain that Courtney was adopted. Esther had taken great care to make sure that all of the details were unavailable to nosy busy bodies. That had been relatively easy, but keeping this intelligent young woman from uncovering the dark secret that she had protected all these years would be no easy task.

Courtney rushed to her grandmother's aid. "Are you okay?" she asked with alarm.

"Oh, I'm fine," Esther rasped between coughs, "I've just swallowed wrong!" Esther waved the concerned guests away. "You all go on and visit now, I will just go into the kitchen for a glass of water." She was still coughing as she limped out of the room.

Courtney waved good-bye to the last of the guests at six o'clock that evening. The choir members had helped with the clean-up and the old house seemed to sigh with gratitude in the peaceful silence.

"Courtney dear, I'm rather tired, I hope you won't mind if I go up to my room now." Esther did look tired and Courtney thought she should get some rest. It had not been too long since she had been in the hospital. Courtney cursed herself for not being more watchful and perhaps even insisting on having her grandmother lay down even before the guests all left.

"Please don't concern yourself with any more tidying up. Hattie and I are getting old now so I've hired a cleaning service to come in every Monday to do the heavy work and they will take care of putting away the heavy serving dishes."

"It was a lovely day. Thank you for introducing me to all of your friends," Courtney said warmly.

"Well dear, the Sunday drop-in is a fairly regular occurrence here."

"Yes, I remember them when I was a little girl, but it is different to participate as an adult. It was a very special day and I love you for going to all of this trouble for me."

Esther was obviously flustered by Courtney's open use of the word she herself avoided. She was not accustomed to speaking of love. Family honor, respect, those things she could understand, but love more often than not brought pain instead of joy, no she didn't understand love at all and what she didn't understand she wanted no part of.

"I do declare, you are as charmin' as..." Esther stopped herself abruptly and then continued, "can be. I'm glad you enjoyed the day. I enjoyed it too." With that she turned and made her way to the staircase.

Courtney frowned as she watched Esther walk away, her cane tapping on the hardwood floor. She had the feeling that her grandmother had almost said something important. Who would Esther compare her to? The antique clock on the mantle chimed eight times and Courtney went into the library to call her parents.

Clyde answered on the first ring. Courtney could hear the love in his voice as he realized his daughter was on the telephone. After a few moments of light conversation Clarisa picked up the extension. Courtney kept them both laughing as she told them about the Sunday drop-in.

"Oh darling, it sounds as though you and your grandmother are going to get along just fine, that makes me very happy," Clarisa chuckled.

"We truly are, Mom. She seems different than I remember her. I think she actually likes me!"

"Well Luv, I'm sure she does. In fact, I'll wager that the old iceberg has a very warm heart," Clyde said dryly. He and the Camden matriarch had never seen eye to eye on most subjects. They had often argued hotly on political matters, but through it all he rather liked Esther.

"Now Clyde, you saw how much Mother has mellowed when we were there."

"She was mellow because she was helpless in that wheelchair. But I think she liked all of the attention it got her," Clyde finished with a laugh

"Mom, did you ever read any of the Camden family history?"

"No, I never did. I got so tired of hearing about it while I was growing up that I just didn't want to read about it."

"Did Grandmother ever tell you about any of the Camdens who lived at Willows during the Civil War?"

"Many times, I'm afraid I didn't listen very carefully though. Why do you ask?"

"Just, curious. Did you ever tell me about the girl who died here?"

"What girl is that?"

"You mean Grandmother never told you about the young girl who was killed by the soldiers near the river?"

"No, I'm sure if she had I would have listened more closely. Your grandmother always talked of those people as if they were saints. I don't recall anything about any young girl being killed."

"What has happened, Luv?" Clyde asked, sensing the tension in his daughter's voice.

"I'm still trying to sort it all out. I've been talking to Hattie...I've experienced some bizarre things...not dangerous of course," she put in quickly as she heard her mother's small gasp. "When I have more answers I promise I'll tell you both everything." Then Courtney's tone lightened and she rushed to change the subject. "But you two have to promise me something."

"Of course!" Both of her parents spoke at the same time.

"If I tell you everything...no matter how crazy it sounds, don't put me away in a mental institution." She finished with a chuckle, but as she said the words a little shiver quivered down her back and goose bumps rose on her arms.

"Perhaps we'd better give the matter some consideration before we make that promise," Clyde teased.

Courtney sat thinking long after she had ended her conversation. She was only partly joking about the institution. Her visions had taken her to a place like that many times. She had witnessed her own prone body tightly restrained on what appeared to be an institutional bed. It was obviously not an experience from a past life such as the time she might have lived as Priscilla, so she surmised, it must be something in her future. She recoiled at the thought. The idea that something like that could happen to her was utterly unacceptable. Maybe those dreams and visions were symbolic, she mused, instead of being literally prophetic. She leaned back in the big leather chair and closed her eyes. She had learned one thing; her mother knew nothing of Priscilla so it was unlikely that anything had been planted in her subconscious. If reincarnation does exist, then she had surely caught a glimpse of the path that her soul had traveled.

"You all right sugar?" Hattie stood in the doorway.

"Yes, I think so."

"Life can be one big picture puzzle," Hattie sighed sympathetically. Courtney nodded in agreement.

"Next weekend me and my choir are going to do some singing on Hilton Head Island and in Savannah."

"Oh, that sounds really nice."

"Miz Camden already give me the weekend off. I want you to go with me. There is a group of very special people I would like you to meet." Hattie paused.

"What people?" Courtney couldn't fathom her meaning.

"They are people just like you and me. They have ordinary jobs and troubles just like everybody, but they also got the gift. They got the sight. They are a circle of psychics." Hattie watched the girl's eyes widen with surprise and anticipation.

"Do you think they can help figure out what is happening to me?" Courtney asked with some suspicion.

"Honey, I believe these people are pure messengers bringing wise words from beyond the veil. They have been taught by loving spirits from the other side and they have been told to help people who are troubled with strange visions and troublesome dreams."

Vertigo overcame Courtney for a moment. The room spun and expanded while Hattie's voice multiplied and echoed. She shivered as a chill passed through her body. As quickly as it had come it was gone. Courtney took several deep breaths and after regaining her composure she slowly nodded her head.

"Good! They are looking forward to meeting you. They don't usually meet on a Saturday night but I explained that this a special need," Hattie winked.

"You crafty lady! How did you know I would agree to go?" Courtney laughed.

"A little bird told me." It was Hattie's turn to laugh a bit smugly.

The two women enjoyed another hour of happy chatter before Hattie declared she was just "all in" and needed to go sit in her recliner with her feet up.

Courtney climbed to the top of the stairs then stopped to listen. The house was quiet. She rose to her demi toes and executed a series of chaine' and pique turns that brought her to her bedroom door. She was to meet with members of the Charleston Ballet Company the next morning. Little butterfly nerves fluttered through her stomach. She realized that she was really excited about the prospect of being part of their organization. With one last grand move, she did a beautifully extended arabesque and ran into her room as though she were leaving the stage after a performance.

Steam rose in a slow spiral from the coffee in her Styrofoam cup as Courtney listened to the Ballet Company staff members discussing their plans for the midsummer art festival and Fourth of July celebration. Like most dance companies, financial difficulties plagued them constantly. They had welcomed her warmly at nine o'clock that morning. It was now ten thirty and already she had gained their confidence as they repeatedly asked for her opinions and ideas. By noon she felt as though she had known them all of her life. She suspected that the feeling was mutual.

"So, how would you feel about putting together a little number for the outreach festival?" Lexi inquired just before he bit into his cheeseburger. He was a tall slender man in his mid-thirties. He wore his long dark brown hair pulled back in a sleek ponytail.

"But, that's only a few weeks away!" Courtney's stomach jumped nervously as she tried to swallow a bite of spinach salad.

"That's why I suggested that you create a *little* number," he smiled coyly. "We are all tired from the Spoleto. Usually the company has a break this time of year, but we were asked to be a part of this new program that brings the community closer to the needs of the disabled. I think they're trying to start an art festival that will be a little bit like the Special Olympics only centered around various art modalities that have been created by all sorts of these people. The profits are supposed to help give scholarships to gifted people who might otherwise never be noticed because of their handicaps, either physical or mental. I personally believe in the cause, and anyway, our ballet company could use the exposure, not to mention the money."

The group had gone to lunch at a quaint little restaurant near the rehearsal studio. Courtney glanced around the table at the expectant faces.

"I think it sounds like a great idea!" Courtney responded thoughtfully. "Well, there is a piece that has been rattling around in my head for awhile. It would be about the ocean...sea gulls, and maybe a girl on the beach."

"Fabulous! I love it! That's perfect for the summer," Lexi gushed, "Why don't you conduct the two o'clock class and start picking your dancers." His fingers fluttered through the air as he spoke.

"I don't even know what music to use." Courtney hadn't expected this turn of events.

"No problem, Sugar. I just happen to know a musical genius who could probably whip up something in a few days. He can do anything and I mean anything!" Lexi rolled his eyes and fanned himself with his napkin.

"Lexi is right, Courtney. Kenny is a genius. He does things for us all the time. I've got some ideas for costumes. Why don't I make some sketches while you're teaching and then we can go over them when you're finished." Tia was close to Courtney's age with long straight black hair and glasses.

By the time they finished their lunch they had discussed publicity for their performance and possible themes for next season. Courtney was not accustomed to this unabashed enthusiasm. Dancers more often than not exhibit a practiced indifference, especially in the presence of a newcomer. She found their open warmth refreshing. One of the reasons she had rejected the idea of an exclusive career in ballet was because of the cold and sometimes ruthless people she had encountered in the past.

At five minutes to two, Courtney followed Lexi into studio A, the largest of the ballet classrooms. Most of the dancers had already arrived and were engrossed in various warm-up exercises. Some held on to the ballet barre and studied their posture and feet in the full length mirrors. Others sat or lay on the floor stretching their legs. The quiet murmur of voices ceased as the teachers entered the classroom. The dancers responded to Lexi's eloquent introduction with polite applause. Then, with a pounding heart, Courtney called for the dancers to go to the barre for plies. Two hours later the dancers were flushed, drenched with sweat and applauding furiously after the last combination. Many of them stopped to thank her for such an inspired class. Courtney was elated. She had never expected to enjoy teaching so much. A photographer from the newspaper had come in during the last thirty minutes of the class and had succeeded in taking pictures without being too intrusive. He now pressed Courtney for interesting tidbits from her background and wrote furiously as she told him about her former training and performing experiences. Tia hurried in a few moments into the interview waving her sketch pad. Courtney knew at that moment that the summer would indeed be busy, productive, and extraordinary. In future years she would look back on this Charleston summer and marvel endlessly on just how extraordinary it really *had* been. But for now she simply felt good, almost happy, and almost free of the painful memory of Antonio.

####

The Oaks grapevine had no lack of interesting gossip since Dr. Baylor's arrival in April. Though his innovative thinking often interfered with comfortable routines, most of the staff found their jobs infinitely more interesting. The scandalous actions wrought by Jubal Pusser and the uncomfortable publicity that followed had faded somewhat, but nurses and orderlies still teased each other with lion jokes. The sad news that Dr. Mann was undergoing cancer treatment had been the subject of choice for a while and C.C.'s artistic ability was another favorite topic, along with her amazing progress. She now spoke short sentences which asked questions and made thoughtful comments on a variety of subjects. She had not exhibited a single violent episode since Jubal was taken away.

Stephen flipped through the pages of his presentation. Satisfied that everything was in order he took a deep breath and stood up. He fervently hoped that Dr. Mann would be in an open-minded mood. Last week he had been almost jovial, at least considering his usual stern demeanor, a chuckle could be considered jovial...almost. But this was Monday, a new week and a new month. Maybe he should have shaved his beard off by now. Dr. Mann made pointed comments about his dislike of beards, but he had never actually asked Stephen to remove it.

"You look like a man with a mission!" Kevin had fallen into step with his friend. "Need I ask where you're headed?"

"Three guesses," Stephen muttered as he glanced at his watch.

"You up for a sumptuous lunch in the cafeteria later?" Kevin grinned.

"Sounds great! See you at noon. Uh, maybe you better bring a bottle of scotch just in case," Stephen joked.

"Relax, the old man actually likes you...I think."

"That's a relief...I guess! I'd hate to think of what it would be like if he didn't!"

"If he didn't like you, you'd-a-been outta here back in April. The last guy who worked here lasted two weeks!"

Kevin's attempt at reassurance did little to bolster Stephen's self-confidence, but he pushed forward with dogged determination.

"Good morning Dr. Baylor," Liz smiled warmly. "Is Dr. Mann expectin' you?"

"Well, not exactly, but I do want to speak with him, is he available?"

"Well, let's just see," Liz said brightly as she stood up. She walked to Dr. Mann's door, knocked and opened the door at the same time. Dr. Mann sat behind his desk frowning down at the open file that he held in his hands.

"Yes?" he said curtly as he looked past Liz and glared at Stephen standing directly behind her.

"May I speak with you for a moment, Dr. Mann?" Stephen noticed the older man's haste in closing the file.

"Uh yes, yes come in." He tucked the file in his desk drawer as he spoke.

Stephen sat down and handed his notes to Dr. Mann. He took a deep breath and plunged into his explanation. He described his ideas for a group home and how to gain community support. He then launched into a proposed plan to get some of the patients involved in the Fourth of July Open Air Market and artistic outreach program. He outlined possible trips to the Summer Symphony and maybe the Ballet and Community Theater Productions as a good way to bring the needs of the mentally handicapped into the awareness of the public as well as creating a better quality of life for those who could not care for themselves. He explained that he had spoken with the leaders of various organizations and that the Outreach program was a perfect way for The Oaks' patients to begin their contact with life outside of the institutional environment and who knows what good results might come out of this process.

"You have some good ideas here, Dr. Baylor."

"I do? I mean, thank you sir, I'm glad you think so."

"After our recent disastrous incident..." Dr. Mann paused and cleared his throat, "We could use some good publicity. The question is how will the board respond? Do you have a list of names of the patients you think can make these excursions?"

"It's in the file sir. I took the liberty of outlining activities as well as the logistics of departures, arrivals and those employees available to chaperone." Stephen spoke quickly feeling a little breathless when he had finished. He was about to continue when the older Doctor interrupted.

"Thorough. I like a man who is thorough." Dr. Mann made a flicking motion in the air with his hand. Stephen understood that he had been dismissed and got up.

"I'll present this to the board and let you know their decisions Monday week."

"Thank you, Dr. Mann." Stephen kept a solemn

expression on his face as he rose to leave, but as soon as he had softly closed the door he flashed a dazzling grin at Liz and gave her a thumbs up. She responded with an affirmative nod and a wide smile matching his.

Dr. Mann glanced at the names on the patient list, after a few moments he grimaced."Damn!" He slammed the notes down on his desk and ran his hands through his wavy white hair. The damned chemotherapy was causing his hair to fall out! He grunted in disgust as a shower of white hair fell to the surface of his desk. He felt tired and old and sick. He observed the quiver of his once firm powerful hands as he reached for the rolodex. He equated illness with weakness and that was something that he could not tolerate in himself. Little darts of fear pierced his stomach and chest making him feel almost short of breath. He clenched his shaking hands and virtually willed himself into a state of composure and then once again began to look for the card he wanted. After a brief search he found the phone number he was looking for and punched in the numbers.

"Good morning, I would like to speak with Miz Camden. Oh? When will she be back? No, no message. I'll call again later." He replaced the receiver with a sigh and leaned back in his chair. The day had only just begun and already he was exhausted.

####

The days passed quickly for Courtney. She rose with the sun and, after hours of classes, rehearsals, and brainstorming, fell asleep the moment her head touched the pillow each night. Lexi had been right about his friend Kenny, it had only taken the young man three days to create a twenty-minute piece. First he recorded the sound of ocean waves and sea gulls. Then he and another musician improvised a melody which was played on a flute. Next Kenny filled in some background on his keyboard synthesizer. Rolling arpeggios from a harp completed the hauntingly beautiful sound. As Courtney sat listening with the other dancers, her mind visualized a lone figure of a girl dancing on the beach. She wore a filmy sky blue sun dress and her feet were bare. Then as the music changed men dressed in white pants and shirts carried tiny muscular women who were poised as though in flight...the sea gulls. The dancers executed a series of flowing steps and difficult lifts. The girl watched, and was swept off her feet by two of the male gulls. Her legs extended into a full split. Her head was thrown back and her face was joyous as she experienced simulated flight. They all danced together and then a fog rose. The lighting changed as the sea turned gray. One at a time the gulls disappeared into the mist and the girl danced alone with the sound of the waves.

"Wow!" The soft exclamation brought Courtney back to the present. The girl who had spoken wiped a tear from her cheek. "I could see it all," she breathed, "A girl dancing on the beach, sea gulls..." her voice trailed off.

"Me too," Zack chimed in, "I saw the same thing."

"I think there should be some fog in there somewhere," another girl said dreamily.

"Yeah and you know what would be really cool?"

"What?" Courtney asked the exuberant young Michael.

"We should have a movie screen as the backdrop and show actual moving pictures of the ocean!"

Suddenly everyone was talking at once. With great effort Courtney managed to hold her emotions in check. She had not told any of the dancers ahead of time about her ideas for the ballet and yet without prior knowledge they saw and expressed the very pictures that had formed in her mind. This little ballet, her first creation was going to be something special!

"Lord have mercy child!" Hattie chuckled as Courtney wearily dragged through the kitchen door. It was nine o'clock on Friday evening. Courtney had spent the entire day working on the new ballet. The steps had veritably materialized out of thin air and wonder of wonders, the dancers were so in tune with her thinking that they very nearly anticipated the combinations before she even finished speaking. She smiled as she recalled Lexi's reaction when he and Tia were invited to see what they had done. Lexi had run from the room when the dancers finished their demonstration leaving everyone stunned and worried. He returned shortly bringing some other members of the staff and a camcorder. He demanded that everyone perform the ballet again so that he could record it. Quietly the dancers took their places and repeated the difficult piece. The music faded and the dancers stood breathless and sweating wondering if they were about to be chastised for not using enough energy or for some other detail that they might have missed. The silence of the room was as oppressive as the heat that steamed from their athletic bodies as they waited for Lexi to speak. He, the man who was rarely at a loss for words, made one short statement. "Many great sculptors think that their image already lives in the marble or wood and it is only his or her job to chip away the excess and make the image visible. I believe this ballet existed in that way." Then he turned to Courtney, "Thanks to our sculptor it has been manifested for all to see. Bravo," he said quietly and then he began to applaud.

"What an extraordinary week, Hattie! Can you believe it? Except for a couple of rough spots and some polishing, I finished my sea gull ballet today."

"Looks like the sea gull be finished all right. Looks like it come through a hurricane." Hattie closed one eyelid and squinted with the other making Courtney laugh. "You sit right down and I'll fix you a plate of my broiled chicken and vegetables." Hattie was already opening cupboard doors and rattling dishes.

"Oh Hattie, I'm so tired I don't know if I can eat anything." Courtney sighed as she sank wearily onto the kitchen stool.

"I thought you'd say something like that. You drink a cup of my special tea and you will eat just fine." Hattie plunked a cup of steaming pungent liquid in front of the bedraggled girl.

"Now, how did you know I would need some special tea?" Courtney asked playfully. Hattie turned to look at her with a sly smile and a raised eyebrow. "I know, I know, a little bird told you."

"You're getting smarter every day honey." Both women laughed.

Between huge bites of chicken and cornbread, Courtney recounted her experiences of earlier that day. Storm Cat lounged on an empty stool occasionally twitching his ears while she spoke. Hattie too listened with wide open eyes and soft murmurs of awe and pride.

"You are truly talented. But it sounds to me like your dance steps might have come from the great ballet dancer in the sky!" Courtney giggled at Hattie's expression. She was just too tired to try to make any comments or arguments.

"Now you listen baby, it is time for you to get some rest. Don't forget, we are leaving at ten o'clock in the morning."

Courtney was not feeling very enthusiastic about making the trip to Hilton Head the following day. She wondered how to tell Hattie that she wanted to stay home.

"I feel that it is very important for you to meet these

people that I told you about." Hattie continued, reading her thoughts, "They can teach you about your gifts and your work. It's going to help you find meaning and purpose to your life. You are going to teach *them* too and between all of us we are going to do our share to help this old world."

Courtney smiled. She resigned herself to the fact that she might as well agree to go. Hattie had made up her mind and there would be no changing it.

"I'll be ready, Hattie."

"Yes little lady, you *are* ready. The time is right," Hattie said firmly. Storm Cat stretched and yawned. He leaped from his perch on the stool and trotted toward the door with his tail straight up. He stopped and looked back at Courtney expectantly.

"Looks like his highness thinks you need to go to bed too!" Hattie chuckled.

"You know it really has been nice to have him with me at night, but don't you miss him?" Courtney asked with concern.

"He comes in and checks on me during the night too. Don't you worry none about it. He just loves to play the role of the great protector. Makes him feel macho!" Courtney burst out laughing. Storm Cat turned his back and made a dignified exit.

Later as she lay quietly in the darkened room she was aware that a peacefulness had settled over her. She loved watching the moonlight as it cast a pale glow across the foot of the old canopy bed. She listened as the old house sighed and creaked in its own language telling stories of days gone by. Storm Cat lay with his head on her arm purring contentedly. Her mind was filled with happy images from the recent week. A whole day had passed and until this moment she had not thought of Antonio. The nightmare she had lived was moving into the past and taking on a slightly blurry quality. The pain of the memories was no longer haunting her every waking moment. With a deep sigh she offered up a prayer of thanks for the peace and safety of her grandmother's home. As she drifted off to sleep she knew that tonight there would be no nightmare.

CHAPTER EIGHTEEN

Two large white and blue church vans pulled up near the kitchen door at exactly ten o'clock the next morning. Courtney and Hattie climbed in and as soon as the introductions were made, their voices joined with the happy chatter of the choir members.

Two hours later the vans pulled into the church yard on Hilton Head Island and they were greeted warmly by the pastor, his wife, and a group of women from the congregation. They were led to the social hall and treated to a home cooked banquet that would have earned the favor of royalty. After the feast the Reverend gave a little speech of welcome and then outlined the early evening service. Later Courtney sat in the back of the sanctuary and listened while the choir practiced. She propped her feet up and leaned her head against the back of the pew and closed her eyes. She was very glad to be alive and she truly loved being with these warm wonderful people. She fell into a comfortable doze until she felt a gentle touch on her shoulder.

"The evening service will be starting soon. I'm sorry to disturb you, but it wouldn't be good for my reputation if the congregation saw someone sleeping before the sermon even starts." The kindly Pastor Busby chuckled as he spoke. Courtney smiled up at him and tried to apologize, but the reverend assured her that it was unnecessary.

The service was over at eight o'clock and at eight thirty the church vans were turning down a dark street one block from the ocean. They rolled to a stop in front of a two-story house on the corner. Restless butterflies fluttered in Courtney's stomach.

"C'mon honey, I'll introduce you to everyone then we have to get down the road and over to Savannah before it gets too late. These here are good people. They promised me that they would take care of you. We're gonna be back to pick you up here at about two thirty tomorrow. We are lined up to sing at both morning services. They are going to serve a potluck lunch and then we will be on our way to pick you up!" Hattie talked quickly as she led the way to the steep wooden stairway which looked none too sturdy. Courtney followed somewhat reluctantly with her dance bag slung over her shoulder.

"Maybe you should wait for a few minutes and I'll call a motel. That way the driver will know where to pick me up."

Hattie was halfway up the stairs. "You are going to end up staying here or with one of the other folks!" she replied firmly.

It was too late to argue. The determined woman was already knocking on the door and, to Courtney's horror, she opened the door without waiting for the occupant to respond. Courtney would never dream of imposing herself on strangers. She was sure she would be impossibly uncomfortable in the presence of these people and she would much rather have the privacy of a hotel room, her thoughts fumed.

"Hey child, where you at? Come on in here!" Hattie's smiling face appeared out of the interior semi-darkness. Hattie reached behind Courtney with her ample arm and urged her firmly forward.

"Well, hey sugar, come on in. We're just regular folks here!" said a masculine voice in cheery greeting.

"This here's David." Hattie smiled and nodded toward the man who had just spoken. David was a tall handsome man with silver hair and glasses. He exuded a witty charm, genuine warmth and the manners of a fine Southern gentleman.

"Courtney's worrying about a place to stay the night."

"Well didn't you tell her we stay up all night doing our hoodoo voodoo stuff anyway?" David teased. "Now Hattie, you know we'll take care of her. She can sleep on my sofa or she can stay with one of the girls if she'd rather." David opened his arms and gathered Hattie up in a big bear hug.

"Hey, I'm not the one who is doin' the worryin'." Hattie gave a little shriek as David nearly lifted her off the floor.

Courtney was still tense. She looked around the large living room. Some people were sitting on the shag carpet; others were on the overstuffed sofa. Everyone seemed to be involved in intense conversations, but they did acknowledge her presence with smiles and nods before they went back to their various discussions. The room was comfortably ordinary and so were the casually dressed people. She felt herself exhale for the first time since she had entered. While Hattie and David were chatting amiably her eyes strayed to the pictures on the walls and then she saw something that made her gasp. It was a white plaster cast of a man's face mounted on a dark matt and surrounded by a heavy gold frame. Hollow deep set eyes stared at her and the wide full mouth twitched as if to smile. The face of the Ancient Wise One from the time of Aeonkisha was perfectly represented in the white sculpture. Who are these people, she wondered? Oh my God what is happening! Her heart started to pound furiously and her breath came in short gasps as she remembered the scene in the jungle clearing and the visitation of the specter that had elicited the promise from her and Hattie.

"Well, I see you've met Tobias," David was grinning like the Cheshire cat.

"I've seen him...I mean in a vision ...and he moved. I uh, he's the Ancient One...Wise One," Courtney stammered through dry lips and tight throat. She swallowed audibly and little beads of sweat formed on her upper lip.

"Old Tobias seems to have that effect on people. Why don't you come in the kitchen and get some herbal tea. It will help your mouth and tongue get rid of their knots, and then we'll talk." David raised one eyebrow and grinned. He was obviously amused but she sensed too that he understood her discomfort and he was sympathetic.

"Okay, thanks. Where did Hattie go? Did she leave already?"

"Well, yes. She left about fifteen minutes ago. She said goodbye to you but you didn't respond. That doesn't surprise me though. One time the group and I stood right here and watched Tobias change shapes for positively hours. None of us was aware of the passage of time at all." David rolled his eyes.

As she and her host prepared their tea from a selection of boxes on the counter in the small kitchen, other guests wandered in laughing and talking. David introduced each person but Courtney couldn't make her mind focus. The names and faces ran together, her head felt...detached. Dark hair, blond hair, red hair, tall, short, heavy, thin, most of them were women. They all smiled and exuded warmth and for that, Courtney was grateful.

Finally everyone had their tea or coffee and they decided to settle into the purpose of the gathering. David invited her to sit beside him on the sofa while the other guests seated themselves on the floor and in chairs forming a loose circle.

A blond lady with huge blue eyes was lighting the candles which were arranged on the coffee table. David introduced her as Sharon. Martha, a voluptuous redhead with a ready wit sat in a straight-backed chair in what David referred to as the *power spot*. He explained that the group had discovered a vortex of energy there that enhanced the channeling ability of anyone sitting in it.

"Martha, why don't you go get some coffee and get out of that chair? We want to talk a few minutes before you go into la la land." David grinned and everyone giggled. As Courtney turned to look at Martha she saw that her eyes had a sort of glazed expression and her lids were drooping to a half closed position.

"Martha slips into trance easier than I fall asleep." Laughter bubbled around the room again and Courtney relaxed a little more. These people talked of trances and visions so easily that it made her feel less like an outcast.

When Martha returned from the kitchen with her coffee, David told the story of Tobias. It seemed that for some time David had been visited by a spirit guide who gave him advice about the affairs of his life and hints about future events. He often imagined what Tobias looked like. One day David visited an artist friend of his named Joseph whom he had not seen in quite some time. The moment David entered the studio Joseph picked up the mounted sculpture and gave it to David. Joseph had no prior knowledge of David's experience with a spirit guide, but he knew that David must have this creation.

"Joseph said he just kind of watched his hands create Tobias, they just seemed to have a mind of their own. It was a bizarre experience." David finished his story and slowly shook his head from side to side. "Like I said before, all of us just sit and stare at Tobias in the candle light and watch his face change. It's better than TV!" Other members chimed in with stories about what they saw in the sculpture. Finally a lady they called Bonnie turned to the silent Courtney.

"We have all been talking about our experiences with Tobias. Why don't you tell us what you experienced when you saw him?" Bonnie had very pale skin and short black hair. Her beautiful round face lit up as she smiled and no one could resist her impish giggle. Courtney had overheard the stocky little woman earlier as she related an incident with such a comedic delivery that everyone laughed hysterically long after the story was finished.

With Bonnie's gentle encouragement Courtney took a deep breath and cleared her throat. The group looked at her expectantly, but no one was prepared for the depth of Courtney's tale. She told them about her vision detailing her past lifetime with Aeonkisha and her meeting with the Ancient Wise One which was, according to her memory, the perfect likeness of Tobias. As she spoke members of the group made no comment but she heard little gasps and sounds of awe as she described everything in great detail. The group remained silent when she finished her story and then everyone started talking at once. David's eyes had grown very round. Bonnie squealed and everyone talked of chills going through their bodies and their hair standing on end, but no one told Courtney that she was crazy. The varied faces smiled their acceptance and they actually looked at her with respect and admiration.

A quiet voice came from a dark corner to Courtney's left. "Welcome to the group," she said, "You are one of us. We have all had what most people would call strange experiences, but to us, visions, spirit guides and disembodied voices are normal everyday things." The group had quieted to listen to the blond woman's words. "Anything that you say within the group will remain confidential. If you have problems or questions we will be glad to try and help. We have been taught everything we know almost entirely by spirit. We share our experiences with each other and we learn. As far as we know there aren't any books on many of the subjects that we discuss here and finding someone to teach us about these subjects is virtually impossible...at least someone in the physical world." The woman smiled warmly.

"Well there goes Martha," Bonnie droned comically. All

eyes turned to the red-haired woman in the *power* chair. A man seated on the floor near her switched on a tape recorder.

Martha's left hand twitched rhythmically and her eyes were closed. "Welcome." The voice that spoke from the women's throat was considerably deeper than her normal speaking voice, Courtney noted.

"Who is speaking?" David asked the voice.

"Runs with the Wind," came the prompt reply.

"Do you have a message for our visitor?" David asked.

"I do. Before becoming a warrior a brave must pass many tests, so it is with you. The Great Spirit has something special in mind for you and that is why your test was severe." Courtney was shocked at these words. Hattie must have told these people about what Antonio did to her.

Martha continued in that strangely accented speech pattern. "You have seen death and felt violence. You have helped to make right a wrong from the past. But your test is not yet ended. You have one more task to complete. The Great Spirit will reward you when it is finished." Martha's eyes blinked open. "Guess that's it!" she said in her normal voice, "David, I'm freezing, can you do something with that air-conditioner?"

"I'm burnin' up sugar. Why don't you put this afghan around your shoulders?" David playfully tossed her the afghan that had been folded across the back of the sofa.

"Uh oh, there goes Colette." David nodded toward another woman who sat cross-legged on the floor near Bonnie. Courtney learned later that Bonnie and Colette are sisters.

Colette wore her shoulder length jet black hair pulled straight back in a pony tail at the nape of her neck. The white skin of her heart-shaped face appeared translucent in the flickering candlelight. Her head bobbed as if she had palsy. Courtney frowned as she watched in silence.

"It's the energy that makes her head shake." David whispered reading her thoughts. "Did you notice Martha's hand twitching?" Courtney nodded. "Bringing in the energy of a spirit guide seems to affect each of us in different ways."

"Is it safe?" Courtney asked with sincere concern.

"We've learned that if we ask for the protection of God and his angels it is perfectly safe. Some of us ask for the protection of the White Light or for the Highest Good to be in control. Each one does it in their own way, but essentially it means the same thing. I'd better shut up, Colette's going to speak now." David's voice dropped to a whisper.

"You are connected by blood and by soul to those who have created a web of lies. The web is thick and tangled, designed to hide the truth. Saint Michael offers his protection to those who seek truth. Call upon him and his blue sword to cut a clear path and set everyone free. You will find your answers in the light of that action." Her voice touched Courtney like velvet cloth. Each word was pronounced with measured precision. She could detect no particular accent as she did with Martha's guide. Courtney was trembling inwardly. She knew that these words carried an important message, but she had no idea what any of it meant.

"The stone will help you." The voice came from the blond woman in the corner.

"That's our madam guru," David rasped in a loud whisper.

"I am Matisima," the voice said firmly.

"I stand corrected," David quipped. Courtney could

hear giggles around the room, but she couldn't join in. She had not told anyone of her experience with the Blue Topaz and surely that is what the woman was referring to. Unconsciously her right hand sought the stone which hung around her neck hidden beneath her shirt.

"The stone was a gift. It has followed you through time waiting for the proper moment to remind you of the great gift that you possess. It acts as a key to unlock the Blue Vision." The soft voice paused and Courtney gulped. Tears she couldn't explain coursed down her cheeks. Wordlessly Sharon passed a box of tissues to David and David put it in Courtney's lap.

"The ancients called it the Blue Pearl. When you see the blue light just before the vision opens...know that what you see is truth. The blue vision carries with it a grave responsibility. It is up to you to use this power wisely. You must live according to the truth of your heart and walk in the Law of Love. Integrity and respect for all forms of life must guide your every action. This is not an easy path, but it is the destiny you have chosen. You have powerful forces from the Law of Good which are standing by to assist you in any way you require it. You are never...alone." The voice paused again and Courtney dabbed at the persistent tears with one of the tissues. The room was silent. She felt as if they had all been transported to some distant dimension where time and space did not exist. She was intensely aware of the light shining from the center of each person in the room and she noted with delighted surprise that her own light reached out to blend with theirs. She felt love and peace in the light as the woman continued to speak.

"In the beginning, there were sparks of life that issued forth from the Creator Source. Groups formed. Soul families. Each spark contained the completeness of its Source, the yin and yang, the masculine and feminine. The sparks divided in their desire to grow and experience more and, in the spirit of free will, they traveled their separate ways. They grew in wisdom through eons of time, but in their physicality, they forgot their Source and their Light Families. Truth, however will not allow itself to remain buried and lost. It rises up in each of us demanding to be known. It is so within the sparks of life that so long ago went their own way.....and now they seek out each other. The one that is called the twin soul...the other half. You...in this life...will find the lost one...the other half. You will also find life-long love."

"Well just how am I supposed to do all of this," Courtney sobbed. "I don't even understand what you and these other people...spirits...are saying!" She was surprised at the harshness and desperation in her own voice. She was surprised too by the depth of her emotions. Since the ordeal with Antonio she had been plagued by frightening memories and an undercurrent of sadness, but she was unprepared for the rise of violent trembling and dark rage that now threatened her self-control.

"The emotion you feel and express now is long overdue." The quiet voice continued, apparently unruffled by Courtney's outburst. "Don't be afraid of it. Face it. Feel it and once you *know* it...then you can let it go. That is an important step in your healing process. When you are calm, empty of the anger and fear which restricts the thinking, you will be receptive to your ever-present guidance. If you become unsure about something, call upon the group, someone will be able to help you. But ultimately you, like everyone, must walk your own path. As the days pass you will find the meaning of the words you have heard tonight. In less than one month you will know the answers. You will find your life-long love. You will be changed forever. We leave you now with blessings." The voice was finished.

The only sounds in the room were the hum of the air

conditioner and occasional snuffles. Several members of the group had been moved to tears so the box of tissues was passed around.

"Well, I don't know about the rest of you cry babies, but I'm ready for some dessert." It was Martha who broke the silence. She, who was probably the most sensitive of the entire group, was always the first one with a comically satirical remark. She wiped away her tears and pulled herself to her feet with a loud sniff.

"Martha is a chef," Bonnie said shakily, "She always brings one of her *channeled* recipes for us to sample." Visibly struggling for control she sniffed and giggled but despite her efforts huge glistening tears continued to stream down her already damp cheeks.

"I think we should have a closing circle first." It was Mark, a six-foot-three black-haired Adonis that spoke.

Amid nods of assent the group began to stretch and get to their feet. Courtney felt disoriented and dizzy as she rose from the deep cushions of the sofa.

"After we finish with the closing circle you'll feel better, I promise." David noticed her stagger and gripped her arm firmly preventing her from losing her balance.

"I hope so, I feel terrible." She was shaking and her hands were cold and clammy.

The coffee table was moved and everyone stood in a circle holding hands.

"Okay, now this is the hardest part of the circle," Sharon chuckled in her husky voice, "You are supposed to turn your left hand up to receive energy and then your right hand down to send energy," she instructed.

Courtney didn't care what her hands were doing; she wanted her head to stop spinning. She allowed a warmly smiling woman named Sarah to adjust her left hand. David stood to her right. "Everyone take a nice deep breath of light energy." It was the soft voice of the blond woman, "Relax and feel the energy of love fill this space. Doubts are dispelled and your entire being is re-energized."

    A flood of warmth seeped into Courtney's left hand and traveled up her arm. It filled her body and she could feel it travel down her right arm and continue on into David's hand. Immediately she felt better. The shaking stopped and her head was completely clear. She looked around the circle. Most of the people had their eyes closed and a peaceful expression languished on each face. They exuded love and acceptance. A soft green glow shimmered in the center of the circle. Courtney remembered, for the first time since her stay in the hospital, the green sparkling light that had floated down from the ceiling and made the pain go away. She remembered the sparkles that used to come from her hands when she was a little girl and how warm and good it felt when the sparkles made the butterflies come to life again. She saw the sparkles now coming from the clasped hands in the circle. These truly were her people. She was one of them. Fate had led her a merry chase from one coast to another to find them. Here she stood in a house filled with strangers on an island three thousand miles from the place she called home and yet these "strangers" knew about the visions, the violence in her recent past and most astounding of all they seemed to know her future, something she herself could not see.

    There were several voices that spoke while Courtney's thoughts wandered. They spoke of guardian angels and the protection of God's love. Mark suggested that they speak the names of people who needed healing. Voices murmured as names were spoken and Courtney watched in fascination as the names seemed to take on form and actually enter their circle. The sparkling green light surrounded each form and carried it high above their heads. Finally the voices ceased and silence fell. Courtney felt the group swaying a little and at once she knew she had to speak.

"I want to thank all of you for allowing me to be here tonight and for the information you've given me. I have a lot to think about, but I would like to come back again sometime."

"You are welcome here any time," David assured her. Others smiled and nodded in agreement.

"Let's eat. It's past my bedtime." Martha gently disengaged herself from the circle and headed for the kitchen.

"I'll make the coffee!" Sylvia chirped.

"No!" Several group members fairly screeched. It seems that Sylvia was in the habit of making coffee so strong that several people swore they couldn't sleep for two days after drinking it.

Courtney was embraced by nearly everyone. She learned that they came from a diversity of backgrounds. There were hairdressers, computer operators, retail clerks and real estate agents to name but a few. Some sported degrees in higher education, others did not. She discovered, however, that they all spoke intelligently on a variety of subjects including politics.

Courtney was ravenous by the time Martha's *cosmic* dessert was served. She ate it quickly and went back for more. The lights were bright and the conversation loud and happy. When several people prepared to leave she was shocked to learn that it was a little past two in the morning!

"David, may I use your telephone, I need to find a motel." Courtney asked.

"You are welcome to use my phone, but it's so late,

why don't you just stay here? You can sleep on that over stuffed sofa. I've slept there myself sometimes, it's really comfortable."

Courtney was grateful for the invitation. She was exhausted and the thought of trying to find a motel at that hour was distasteful. The last of the group said their good-byes by three o'clock.

"Whenever the group gets together we seem to get into a time warp." David grinned.

"How often do you get together?" she asked.

"At least twice a week, for official sessions, then, once for just regular group members and at least once more for people like yourself to come. Then of course there is a full moon every month and an occasional guest speaker. Some of us get together in smaller groups to practice channeling and/or healing. We get lots of healing requests." David talked as he prepared to wash a stack of cups and dessert plates.

Courtney picked up a kitchen towel and helped him with the dishes. She was fascinated with the stories about the group's adventures and David was clearly delighted to relate them to her.

"So, you have all known each other for years then?" Courtney said wistfully. She tried to imagine what it would be like to be around other people who like herself saw visions and lights, people who considered conversations with discarnate entities as normal as a phone call from a friend.

"Ha! Not in this life." David laughed. "We gradually found each other about a year or two ago I guess. Our guru was conducting a guided meditation group once a week at her house and eventually we all showed up there. There used to be as many as fifty people in her living room on Wednesday night.

"You mean that none of you knew each other until a year ago?" Courtney was astounded. "Like I said, sugar, not in this lifetime."

"So...you think that the reason you all feel so comfortable with one another is that you had past lives together?"

"I know so," David nodded.

"Is that the reason why I like some people instantly and dislike others just as quickly?"

"It certainly is part of the reason. When you meet someone and you immediately have strong feelings about that person it's because you have known him or her *before*. That person may have been an enemy or even a lover, which would account for the emotions. The conscious mind doesn't remember, but the soul's consciousness does. The conscious mind has a way of developing a protective amnesia, otherwise all of those memories would cause a sensory overload and your poor little human brain would short circuit." David wiped his hands dry and lit a cigarette as he leaned back against the kitchen sink.

"If a person just sits back and looks at his life, it's pretty easy to figure out where he has been." He inhaled thoughtfully. "For example, some people are just crazy about Chinese furniture. Chances are they had a happy life in China in the past."

"That would probably explain phobias wouldn't it?" Courtney asked.

"As far as I'm concerned it's probably the only thing that explains phobias." David drawled sardonically, "Why else would someone be born with a fear of water. If you drown in one life it makes sense that in the next life you would be afraid of drowning." David tried to stifle a huge yawn. "Listen sugar, I'm exhausted and I'm sure you are too. Let me get you a blanket and pillow for the sofa bed.

In a few moments David provided her with a stack of bed linens and a soft fat pillow. They said goodnight and David retired to his bedroom. Courtney slipped into an oversized T-shirt and flopped down on the cushions. She lay quietly for a moment, marveling at her extraordinary experience with these people. She had so many things to think about; how could she possibly fall asleep! That was her last thought before her eyes closed.

####

Esther watched the small cloud of dust kicked up by the wheels of Dr. Mann's car as he drove down the dirt and gravel road away from Willows. The air smelled of freshly cut grass. The car followed the curving road and was soon hidden by the dense trees and foliage. She could still hear the crunch of the tires as they rolled across the gravel. When the sound faded she knew he had reached the pavement of the main road.

With a tired sigh she turned to look at the river. It had been a long time since she had walked down to the wooden dock that jutted out into the Ashley River. She had often gone there as a young bride. She smiled to herself as she remembered how she used to fret about giving a perfect dinner party and impressing the important people that her husband wanted to entertain. The river had always calmed and inspired her in those days. "I was so young and full of energy then," she murmured wistfully. "Why does life have to become so complicated and full of anguish," she frowned and rubbed her head where the beginnings of a headache pounded over her right eye.

The fracture in her leg had healed remarkably well, at least that's what the doctor had said. There remained a slight weakness, however, and she was happy for the support of her cane as she stepped up on the weathered but solid planks of the dock. She walked slowly to the wooden bench and sat down.

Dr. Mann was dying of an incurable cancer. She remembered the pallor of his face as they sat conversing. He had lost weight and behind the still strong personality she had sensed a great fatigue. A man so dedicated and hard working, not unlike her own beloved late husband. It just didn't seem fair, Esther sighed as though her thoughts pressed against her lungs.

A snowy egret bobbed its head into the water nearby and a squirrel scolded from a branch of the willow tree to her left. What an interesting puzzle life is, she mused. It begins with a spin of the roulette wheel. If one is lucky enough to be born into a comfortable loving family, things can be pleasant, but it seems that no matter what the circumstances of birth are, suffering will catch up with you.

Who could have known that things would turn out this way? She sighed deeply as images flashed through her mind. *A new born infant with the umbilical cord around its tiny neck lying in a pool of blood. The angry face of her son Charles when they had quarreled, the last time she saw him alive.* Tears rolled down her cheeks as the scene replayed itself yet again. She could hear the door slam and then the powerful motor of the little sports car she had given him. Hundreds of times she remembered that day and tried over and over to think of what she could have done to change the outcome. Maybe she should have given him that money. Maybe she shouldn't have told him that she would write him out of the will if he ran off with that cheap empty-headed...Esther sighed as she stopped her angry thoughts. The girl was dead and so was Charles. It was pointless to continue to condemn herself or the girl. But the memories persisted. She saw the graphic newspaper photographs of the tangled metal of the demolished sports car and the body of her son and his blond companion at the morgue. She thought of Tessa, dead in childbirth on the same day. Tessa, orphaned, poor, forced to abandon her education and then pregnant. Esther knew the truth. She knew that Charles had forced himself on that girl. Perhaps force was too strong a word, she chided herself. She had been well aware of her son's flagrant but fickle charm. One moment he could make you believe that you were the most important person in his life and in the next moment his soft Camden blue eyes would turn to glittering ice.

Tessa had steadfastly refused to name the man responsible for her pregnancy. She conducted herself with a queenly grace which was quite remarkable for one so young. Esther had been deeply saddened by the girl's death, but the tragic death of her son on the same day had over-shadowed everything else. A tremor passed through her body as the old memories replayed their drama.

The Camden name simply could not be sullied by the public knowledge of the unfortunate details of Charles' questionable activities. Let them wonder and speculate. Let the rumors fly. She had known that with no facts made public, the unsubstantiated rumors would fade quickly and the voracious gossip-mongers would find other stories to satiate their appetites.

Drugs, alcohol, bullet holes, yes it would have made juicy headlines Esther thought as she frowned at the setting sun. It had taken all of her persuasive influence to keep the lurid details from the press. Fortunately the police were happy to keep things quiet. They had been investigating the possibility that a large local drug syndicate was involved. They felt that too much publicity could endanger the undercover officers assigned to the investigation. She knew though that Charles could never have been involved in anything so sordid. He was just a little over exuberant, trying to sample all of life and perhaps he made an error in judgment.

No, she thought resolutely. No one must ever know. I made the right decision. The Camden lineage must remain untainted by ugly gossip just because of a little error in judgment. An almost cool breeze lifted the silver wisps of hair near her face. How she loved this land by the river. She had forgotten how peaceful and almost healing it could be to sit by the water or to take a leisurely stroll through the gardens. She remembered the laughter of Clarisa and little Charles as they played on the rolling green lawns as children. In more recent times Courtney and Shane had played there too. It was hard to imagine that Courtney was already a grown woman. Esther must see to it that she marry well, the girl was obviously no more capable of good judgment than her...than Charles.

Esther reveled in the river fragrances and drew in another deep breath. An airplane droned far overhead and birds chirped in the trees. Courtney, with the right advice would become an elegant representative of the Camden name, though neither she nor Shane would actually use the name; no matter; they both carry the Camden bloodline. A little smile of proud satisfaction brightened her somber countenance. The smile faded as the image of the listless infant pushed its way to the front of her mind. The child really should have died, but it too obviously bore the Camden blood and with it the indomitable Camden will. The doctor thought it wouldn't live through the night. It would have been better if his errant prediction had come true, deformity and mental illness had never occurred in the Camden family nor in her own noble family. No, bearing such a stigma was unthinkable. No! Something must be done. Now that Dr. Mann was ill and would indeed die soon, she must make some decisions.

Esther frowned as she struggled with her thoughts. Could it be wrong to keep the knowledge of the child from the family? No, she told herself firmly. After all a mentally retarded physically deformed child was better off in a proper facility and sparing the family the agony, the embarrassment of such an unfortunate situation was the only right decision. She was certain of the moral justification for her actions. After all, hadn't she provided very generous donations to that facility all of these years? She had visited that place only once, and had never returned. The sight of those unfortunates was more than she could bear. She made her dutiful contribution every year, but she could never go back. Those people didn't know when visitors were there or not anyway, she thought righteously. If the child were sent away to another facility...the records would also be sent and perhaps would even be lost in the process of the transfer. Surely she could find a way to accomplish this without involving Dr. Mann. After all these years he was still so squeamish about over-stepping the boundaries of his out-dated sense of morality. She must contact Beckman, White and Randall, the law firm that had handled the Camden family affairs since well before the war of Southern Independence. Esther, like most old southern families never thought of the war between the North and South as the Civil War.

An annoying hum near her ear caused Esther to awaken from her reverie. She slapped at the pesky mosquito and glanced at the western sky. The orange red sun had dropped below the tree line. Noseeums, the tiny gnats so common to the south were already darting around her eyes. It was time to retreat to the safety of the house.

Rising was difficult. Her joints felt stiff from the dampness. She leaned heavily on her cane and at last she was standing. The effort left her momentarily breathless. She stood still with her free hand on her chest as she tried to breathe deeply and calm her wildly beating heart, but try as she might her breath came only in short painful gasps. She hadn't noticed the pain before. A dull ache pressed slowly against her chest. With each moment it grew worse making it increasingly difficult to take in even small amounts of air. Panic threatened to consume her as the ache suddenly became a blinding pain.

A man's maniacal laughter rang out jolting her even in her pain. "Charles! Is ...that...you?" she cried between gasps. The laughter came again but there was no mirth or joy in it. It was chillingly sinister and his handsome face was twisted into an ugly snarl and his narrowed eyes exuded hatred.

"Why are you so angry? I love you!" Esther whimpered, but the young man said nothing.

The pain was becoming worse and Esther knew that without help she could not walk the length of the dock and if she stayed where she was she was in danger of falling into the water. Suddenly Charles was close to her. He held out his hand. His expression had taken on that sweet cajoling look that had always managed to melt her heart. She reached out her hand. Charles would help her. She had been wrong. He wasn't angry after all. He had come to help her. With all of her waning strength she willed her feet to shuffle closer to the outstretched hand, closer to the edge of the dock. Charles would help her into the boat. But as she moved nearer to the edge she could see only the movement of the water. Charles was not standing in a boat; he hovered just over the water.

A strong warm hand clasped her own and for an instant Esther was filled with relief. She wasn't hallucinating, Charles was real and he had come to help her. She felt the strength of the hand as it drew her forward. The pain in her chest was now so severe she could no longer draw a breath and at that moment she knew she was dying. What a shame, she thought with only slight sadness, that I couldn't finish my work. She just let go and waited to feel herself fall. The sensation was pleasant, almost restful. She had quit struggling to breathe and simply allowed the floating sensation to relax her. She had so wanted to make that one last effort to protect the precious Camden family name, but...maybe it didn't matter that much anymore. Most of the Camdens were dead anyway, and in moments, she would be too. She gave herself completely to the darkness. The water had no temperature, no sound. It simply wrapped itself around her. Her limbs were paralyzed and she knew it was useless to try to struggle. The crushing pain in her chest eased as the water covered her head. There was really no need to struggle for air. She could feel her consciousness drifting, floating like her body. She realized how clearly she could suddenly see in the water, it wasn't dark and murky at all. She could see fish swimming by and the vegetation growing in the soft river mud. The water was actually very blue and sparkling. She saw the body of a woman floating near her. How interesting, she mused, there are two of us down here. She looked closer and was filled with wonder as she realized it was her own body. The eyes were wide and staring. The mouth was wide too as if it were silently screaming.

Esther drew back. Poor old thing, she thought, you really did some terrible things. Too bad there is no way to make things right now. Something moved in the water as a shape began to form near her lifeless body. When Esther moved closer she saw a familiar face though she couldn't quite remember who it was. A woman wearing a cape had put her arms around Esther's body. At that moment she saw a blinding light and she was sucked into a cold dark box and the crushing pain in her chest returned as water spewed from her mouth with each gasping choking breath. Strong gentle arms cradled her and finally she breathed without effort as a voice near her ear whispered, "You have been granted your time, now right your wrong."

Silence. Darkness.

CHAPTER NINETEEN

Courtney was silent during the ride home the next day. Her thoughts were filled with the people she had met the night before.

Hattie and the other choir members chattered noisily about their experience in Savannah. A man from a recording company in Tennessee had attended the church service on Sunday morning. He was so impressed with their singing that he suggested they record it. Everyone was very excited about the possibility of becoming famous.

Courtney smiled and nodded as her outer self responded to the joyous conversation around her, but inwardly her thoughts probed the strange words of the previous night. What lost one would she find, she wondered? Who could be trying to deceive her? Maybe it was her mother, the young girl that supposedly died when Courtney was born. Maybe that was it. Maybe her mother wasn't really dead!

"Child, you are frownin' with some mighty powerful thoughts." Hattie spoke near her ear to make herself heard above the happy din in the van. "Let it go for now and we'll have a big talk after we get home."

Courtney looked into Hattie's caring brown eyes. How she loved this woman. She had never felt closer to anyone in her life. Their bond transcended background differences and age. Their spirits had always touched and blended in perfect harmony. She could not remember a time when Hattie had not been in her life. Even during the years she had lived in California, Hattie's presence seemed to fill her thoughts. Often she could almost hear the woman's earthy wisdom in her head and sometimes when she had felt sad she could almost feel Hattie's gentle touch on her hair.

"Yes ma'am. I love you too," Hattie half whispered as she mouthed the words to Courtney. As usual Hattie had read her thoughts.

Courtney opened her eyes as the church van turned down the gravel road that led to Willows. She and several of the choir ladies had fallen asleep, others were quietly looking out of the window while some chatted in low tones. Hattie sat forward in her seat. She was frowning and her hands were locked together at her chest.

"Hattie, what's wrong? Are you okay?" Courtney could feel the tension in the older woman's body even though they sat more than a foot away.

"Don't know baby. But somethin' ain't right."

Courtney's senses were instantly alert and a sudden chill made her shiver.

The van pulled around to the kitchen door. Hattie, carrying her small overnight bag and summer pocketbook, had already unlocked the door and disappeared inside before Courtney's feet touched the flat stone walkway.

"Hattie, what is it? Where are you?" Courtney called.

"Here child...here'." Hattie's voice dropped to a whisper. She stood near the kitchen island. Her overnight bag and pocketbook slipped from her hand and landed on the floor with a soft thud. She held a piece of paper and her eyes traveled rapidly from left to right as she read the handwritten note.

Courtney held her breath as she slowly moved closer. She knew something had happened, but her mind was frozen with fear so she simply waited in silence for Hattie to tell her what the note said.

"It's from Theresa, my granddaughter. She came over

to check on Miz Camden this morning like I asked her to and she found her lying by the river. She had a heart attack. Theresa called the ambulance. They took her to the hospital unconscious and barely alive. Theresa stayed with her all day as long as she could but she has to go to work tonight at The Oaks so she called her mama...my daughter, Marybeth, to go stay with your grandmamma. Honey, this time she's gone and done it. I truly don't know if she is gonna come back to us." Hattie shook her head sadly as tears glistened on her cheeks.

Thirty minutes later the two women stood near Esther's bed. A sympathetic nurse had allowed them both to enter the closely monitored cardiac care unit. Machines buzzed and beeped as they recorded the slightest change in Esther's heart rate and respiratory pattern. Oxygen tubes trailed from her nostrils and IV needles were taped to her hands. Her skin was beyond pale and had taken on a gray blue color.

Courtney and Hattie exchanged a wordless glance. There was no need to speak. The lively spirit that had once inhabited that body was nowhere to be seen. It was now just an empty shell forcibly kept alive by machines. They stood in silence for several moments, then Courtney bent to place a soft kiss on her grandmother's brow. Hattie stood on the opposite side of the bed and caressed the white withered cheek with her firm brown hand. The two women spent their allotted time in silence and were so attuned to each other that both rose to leave the room in the same moment without the benefit of a verbal signal.

"You gonna call your mama, baby, or you want me to call?" Hattie said softly as she placed a strong arm around Courtney's small waist.

"I'll call her, Hattie, thank you anyway."

"Then I'll round us up some coffee and meet you back in the waiting room. I want to talk to Marybeth and maybe I can find the doctor too."

It was well past midnight before Courtney lay down in the old canopy bed. She and Hattie had decided to take turns staying with her grandmother at the hospital during the day until her mother's arrival on Monday or Tuesday. Salty tears quietly fell from Courtney's eyes as she whispered a prayer for the grandmother she was just getting to know once again.

####

Dr. Mann drove slowly down the gravel drive away from Willows. His shoulders slumped forward. He had known Esther and her family nearly all of his life. He understood Esther better than anyone, he supposed. He knew how important it was for the older members of the families such as the Camdens to keep their lives very private.

Esther had fought to keep their family name free of scandal and he had a great respect for that regal lady. Wealthy old families had been a favorite prey for sensational publicity seekers. With most of her family gone, what else did she have to hold on to except the dignity of her family name, he mused.

"Damnit all to hell!" Dr. Mann pounded the steering wheel with his fist. Life was impossibly unfair. If he didn't comply with the old woman's wishes his own family would be caught in the scandal, not to mention the hospital and all of the years of hard work that he put in there. But was it worth it? What about the life of that helpless child? Would it really make any difference to her where she lived?

Blaring horns startled him as he realized that the traffic light had turned green and he jammed his foot down on the accelerator. The big black Lincoln jerked forward. He rubbed his forehead in an unconscious effort to bring order to his disturbing thoughts. He was surprised to note that he was sweating profusely. He reached into his pocket for a handkerchief. Where had he put the fool thing? The handkerchief was not in the pocket he searched.

"Damn!" he swore aloud as his hand continued its search. For thirty years he had carried a white handkerchief in that pocket, where was it? Sweat ran from his forehead into his left eye and he swore again as he pounded his hand on the steering wheel.

It was bad enough that a man had to know in advance that the Grim Reaper would appear soon to collect his soul, but the slow undignified suffering...how he hated the short bleak future that awaited him. It wasn't that he was afraid of death or feared any fiery retribution in the afterlife. After all he didn't believe in an afterlife anyway. To him death meant a blessed peaceful eternal sleep. Why did he have to know it was coming? Why couldn't he have died with his best friend Miles in the explosion thirty years ago, or was it forty years ago? At least it would have been quick, clean...heroic even. People respect that, a hero's death. Instead he now would waste away in physical pain and mental anguish as he lay contemplating the irreparable mistakes that he had made in his long, mostly lonely, life.

He thought about Bea, his wife and the only woman he had ever loved. He knew he was an impossible bore to live with. She had left him when their sons Trent and David went away to college. He didn't blame her for that. He only regretted the fact that she had died in the plane crash before he had the chance to tell her how much she meant to him.

Maybe that was it. Maybe the great meaning of life was that life had no meaning except for isolated moments of heroism and the great love between a man and a woman. Truth and honor too held an important position in life. Maybe that was the afterlife. He was convinced that when the life of the physical body ended, the one thing that would live on was the memory held by the living. If the deceased had lived by a code of honor which included truth and impeccable morality...that was the part that would live on...that was the legacy...that was immortality.

What legacy would he be leaving his sons and grandchildren? If they knew what he had done would their memory honor him, condemn him, or was he fooling himself? Maybe they really didn't care one way or another. But he cared. Suddenly he cared very much. He didn't want to spend his last weeks, or if he was lucky, months regretting...so many of the mistakes he had made could never be altered. This one could. True, he should have done something about it a long time ago, but...no matter, it could still change lives and for the better. True, it would upset Esther, but how many more people might it help? He had no way of knowing exactly what would happen, but it didn't matter. What did matter was that he knew now what he had to do. He had to make it right. That child had a right to know her family and the family should be offered the opportunity to know her. He had to do this thing and then he could face the pain and death.

He had no idea how long he had been driving and his surroundings were unfamiliar. The pain in his head was increasing and he fumbled again for the illusive handkerchief. The traffic ahead slowed due to a lane shift for a road paving crew. A large tanker ahead of him flashed its brake lights. Dr. Mann didn't notice as he stiffened his back against the seat and fumbled in his trouser pocket for the handkerchief. Sweat dripped again into his eyes. His foot pressed against the accelerator as he lifted his hips and fished deeper in his pocket.

The huge truck had come to a full stop. The black Lincoln accelerated. Witnesses said later that the explosion occurred only seconds after the impact.

Liz placed the receiver in its cradle and sat in stunned silence. Her mind refused to accept what she had just heard. Dr. Mann was dead. It was a car accident. How ironic, she thought. Mechanically she looked at her watch. Time to start the coffee. She walked briskly to the coffee maker and automatically performed the morning ritual just as she had for twenty years. When her task was completed she walked into Dr. Mann's office. An empty cup sat on his desk. She picked up the stained cup with the intention of washing it. In that instant she realized that Dr. Mann would not be having his morning coffee. He would never come bustling through the door again. She would never hear his deep masculine voice call out for her to bring a certain file or get someone on the phone. She felt herself falling into the dark void of grief.

"Liz, Liz? Oh, there you are. Good morn...ing. Liz, what's wrong?" Stephen's voice trailed off as Liz slowly turned to face him. She gripped Dr. Mann's coffee cup with both hands and tears streamed down her cheeks. He helped her into a chair and then sat quietly until she was able to tell him about Dr. Mann's sudden demise.

Dr. Mann was respected by the vast majority of the hospital staff. When the news of his death swept from floor to floor nurses, caregivers, maintenance and housekeeping personnel reacted with shock and regret. His presence would be missed.

Out of necessity, institutional routine must not deviate. The needs of patients were attended to with dedicated regularity as staff members performed their duties. But everyone felt the change. Dr. Mann had been so much a part of the institution that they were almost synonymous.

By midweek a formal memorial service was planned and the board had no trouble deciding to dedicate the new addition to the hospital in Dr. Mann's memory.

"That will be a nice gesture providing the board can

ever reach a final decision on the building plans," Stephen growled as he read the memo. How would anything ever get done without Dr. Mann's determined persistence to spur the board into decisive action?

Stephen took his glasses off and laid them on his desk. He rubbed his tired eyes and then ran his fingers through his already tousled hair. He thought about all of his plans for the group outing to the ballet and the street festival on the Fourth of July. He wondered if Dr. Mann had been able to get the board's approval before...the accident. What about his proposed community outreach program and the ideas for the group home?

Stephen sighed and rubbed his bearded face, a part of him almost wished he had shaved his beard off. It really wasn't the right climate to wear a beard. He remembered the look of amused respect on Dr. Mann's face when Stephen took his silent stand by refusing to shave. The old man had respected him for it, he was certain of that.

After the memorial service the following week he would ask Liz if Dr. Mann had been able to find out anything about his requests. Maybe he had something on his calendar or maybe he had dictated instructions into his tape recorder. Liz would be feeling better next week and they could look through his desk together. God, how he hated waiting, especially when there was so much to do. At that moment he understood the old doctor. It was his adherence to rules and protocol that kept him from going mad with frustration. The rules had taken on an all powerful position in the older man's life. He simply obeyed the rules, followed the protocol, thereby relieving himself of any responsibility to take action on any idea that fell beyond that protective shield. He would miss Dr Mann.

The memorial had been well attended. Dr. Mann had touched so many lives. Stephen yawned as he leaned back in his chair. It had been a long week already and it was only half over. He was tired but he knew that some of what he felt was due to the emotional sense of loss that he, along with many others, was feeling.

"In the immortal words of Scarlet O'Hara, `tomorrow is another day,'" he mumbled to himself as he prepared to leave the office. Dr. Mann knew how to make the rules work for him. Stephen was going to do the same thing. He was going to make a difference in the lives of as many of these forgotten people as he possibly could. Some day he would write a book...two books...lots of books. He would be instrumental in awakening the public to the plight of all mentally and physically challenged people. He pictured himself standing behind a podium in front of a rapt audience of thousands.

He flicked the light switch off with a flourish and shut his office door. He knew those thoughts were nothing more than childish fantasies, but then everyone needs a dream. Dreams keep hope alive and hope keeps people alive.

It was Friday. Clarisa sat on one side of Esther's bed and Courtney stood at the foot. Esther had lain unconscious and immobile for nearly a week. Clyde was to fly in on Saturday afternoon.

Courtney had been at rehearsal all day. She had walked in to her grandmother's hospital room without making a sound. Her mother hadn't even looked up when she entered. Clarisa's head was bowed almost as if she were in prayer. Courtney didn't want to disturb her thoughts or startle her so she simply stood quietly at the foot of the bed watching Esther's still face.

Memories of her own hospital stay flashed into

Courtney's thoughts. She remembered the green light filled with golden sparks that had hovered over her near the ceiling. She remembered how it had gently descended until her body was engulfed by it. Courtney closed her eyes as she remembered the comfort and relief from pain it had given her. *I wish something like that could come to comfort Grandmother Camden* she thought fervently. But she didn't know how or why it had happened to her and she had no idea how to make it happen for anyone else.

After a few moments passed Courtney opened her eyes. She blinked in astonishment. A green glow filled with tiny glittering sparks covered Esther's prone form. She drew in her breath and held it for a long moment. *How had that happened?* All she had done was wish for it. Surely it could not be so simple and yet there it was.

Minutes passed as Courtney watched the undulating color around her grandmother. Finally it began to fade until all that was visible were the golden sparks. Within a short time those too disappeared. Courtney watched Esther's face for any sign of change. Perhaps there was a subtle difference in the slack muscles around the eyes and mouth. Her color was maybe just slightly more rosy, but though she watched intently almost holding her breath, there was no movement, not even the slightest flicker or twitch around the eyes. With a sigh she let out her breath, not really giving up hope but wondering if her mind had been playing tricks due to her own high level of stress. She felt the need to touch the pale figure in the bed. Her hands found Esther's covered feet and she stroked the small feet tenderly. Almost immediately her hands began to tingle and in a rush of dizzying energy her vision blurred. Within a few moments she refocused and was shocked to find herself looking inside her grandmother's body. Waves of energy coursed through her hands, and into the unconscious Esther.

Courtney could see the energy traveling along a large

artery that led to her head. The energy stopped near her neck. As gently as she could Courtney mentally pushed on the blockage, digging and scooping until a tiny opening appeared and a small trickle of blood encouraged by the sparkling energy began to flow through the opening. She watched the blood and the energy as it moved steadily toward the brain.

A small sound caused Courtney to open her eyes. She drew in a quick startled breath as she realized that she was looking into her grandmother's wide open eyes and alert expression.

"Grandmother?" Courtney whispered incredulously.

Clarisa's head jerked up at the sound of her daughter's voice.

"Mama?" Clarisa leaned closer...Esther's eyes moved in Clarisa's direction. The corners of her mouth twitched with the merest suggestion of a smile. Even such a small movement required great effort. Her eyes closed and she drifted into a natural sleep.

Tears gathered in the eyes of the two women as they looked at each other. Clarisa stood and together with their arms around one another's waist they left quietly.

As the days passed Esther stayed awake for longer periods of time, but it was clear she had extensive paralysis in her left arm and leg. She had made only a few attempts to speak resulting in unintelligible grunts. The doctor explained that this was common among stroke victims and that sometimes through therapy they could regain their speech and some use of the affected limbs. He also explained that it would be a laborious and slow process. Mrs. Camden had also suffered a massive coronary as well as a stroke so the fact that she was alive much less conscious was nothing short of a miracle.

Clarisa and Courtney exchanged glances while the

doctor spoke to them at the end of the second week. Courtney reached for her mother's hand and held it firmly.

"Part of the success of the recovery process in any patient is the patient's attitude. His or her will or desire to get better can help or hinder the healing efforts of the body. Now this can be especially difficult with stroke patients. Because the brain has been affected they have a tendency to be very despondent. This means, of course, that everyone around them has to work double time to keep them in an uplifted and hopeful state of mind. We have an exceptional program here that provides physical therapy, speech therapy, and encounter groups for both the patients and their families."

Courtney's thoughts drifted as the doctor continued his discourse. For the first time since her visit to Hilton Head she found herself thinking about the *group*. She had nearly forgotten them and their strange words entirely in the wake of her grandmother's illness and her parents' arrival. She had been working with the ballet company everyday in preparation for their performance, then each evening she went to the hospital for an hour or so. After supper she and her parents and Hattie would talk long into the night.

Clyde had only been able to stay for a few days, but was planning to return in time for the Fourth of July and the debut of Courtney's ballet.

The words of the psychics floated into her mind again, "Within one month, you will find the lost one. You will find lifelong love," she heard the voice in her mind. Then too, there was something about a web of lies...and being related by blood and soul.

"Darling, are you all right? I hope all of this is not upsetting you too badly. I believe that mother is going to recover beautifully, regardless of what that doctor says." Clarisa patted the top of Courtney's hand.

"I'm really fine, Mom, I was just thinking." Courtney

was surprised to see that the doctor had left the room.

"You must be exhausted dear. Why don't we go back to Willows and see what Hattie has fixed for supper."

####

"Dr. Baylor? You have been at it long enough don't you think?" Liz stood in the doorway with her fists resting on her hips. "You have been working in here all week. Why I believe you are looking positively pale, young man! Today is Friday and it is time for you to go home and get some rest. Tomorrow you get on that bicycle of yours and go for a nice long ride in the fresh air."

Stephen looked up and smiled. He really was tired. He felt as though he had aged ten years in the past week. Each day he had gone into Dr. Mann's office in order to take care of any loose ends that might require immediate attention. He found to his dismay that Dr. Mann had kept a more grueling schedule than he imagined. The double work load was not what had made him feel so exhausted, however. That came from what he had found in the locked files. The patient he knew as Terry Toon had been born to a wealthy family and was committed to institution life as a young child. He recognized the family name from prominent political circles. They made very large mostly anonymous contributions to The Oaks facility on a regular basis. He found also that Dr. Mann had been closely involved in over-seeing admittance and transfer procedures in all of the cases like Terry's. The true names of all such patients had been carefully concealed.

"Why do people think that a mental disorder is something to be ashamed of?" he asked himself over and over again. None of these people had had any visitors in the months since he had come to The Oaks. Of course, The Oaks was an excellent facility, in fact, one of the best of its kind. But could it be morally right to place a relative here or in any institution and virtually deny the existence of that person for their entire lifetime?

Stephen sighed heavily. He knew that he had no right to make moral judgments on any of those people including Dr. Mann. After all, Dr. Mann had only been doing his job and he was an excellent doctor.

The tired young man looked down at his feet in surprise. He found himself walking toward his cottage. He didn't remember saying good-bye to Liz or leaving the hospital! Yes, Liz was right, he needed to get on his bicycle tomorrow and ride and ride and ride.

The color drained from Courtney's face as she watched Renee hobble into the theater on crutches. This was dress rehearsal. The performance was scheduled for July third, the next evening. The choreographer's nightmare had manifested on the eve of her debut. Renee was to have danced the leading role, the girl on the beach. Madame Dubois had flown in for the performance as had Latoia and Raeford. Madame had hinted that a friend of hers from the New York Ballet Company would attend.

Courtney had no aspiration to become a choreographer for a large company but the perfectionist in her cried out in frustration at the thought of her first ballet being canceled or ruined by an inadequately rehearsed replacement.

Everyone listened with sympathy as Renee tearfully recounted the details of her mishap earlier that morning. Ordinarily an understudy could easily have taken Renee's place, but this was a small company and many of their dancers had accepted teaching positions at dance camps in other states, leaving the Charleston Company very short-handed.

"Well, as I see it, we have only one option," Lex looked directly at Courtney, "You need to dance the lead."

"I haven't performed in at least two years!" Courtney groaned, "I haven't done any serious training since then!"

"So? You are wonderful and I'm sure none of us are going to share your dark little secret with the audience." Everyone laughed nervously at Lex's dry humor. "Besides, there is simply no other choice! Just think how the audience will eat it up when we make the announcement that you will dance the leading role in a ballet that you created especially for the city of Charleston!" Lex's voice rose with enthusiasm, "Wait until I remind them that you performed with the Royal Ballet in England, they'll love it!" Lex had jumped to his feet and waved his arms expansively as if already addressing a vast audience. He stood silently in his grand pose hoping to convince Courtney with his dramatic antics. The other dancers turned to look at Courtney one by one, even the injured Renee. Having the choreographer dance the leading role in her place would not threaten her position in the company as a principle dancer and though she was deeply disappointed at having to give up the performance due to her injury, she was relieved to think that Courtney might dance the role this time and she might be given another chance at it in the future.

Courtney sighed, and then shrugged as she held her hands up in acquiescence, "Ok, ok, I give up. I'll do it." The dancers loudly cheered their approval.

"Thank you. Thank you." Courtney responded with an exaggerated bow. "That's enough, gang, now we'd better get to work or the audience will not follow your example. I'd rather be showered with flowers than tomatoes."

The dancers hurriedly positioned themselves on the

empty stage for a pre-rehearsal warm-up barre. Courtney's heart pounded with nervous excitement as she executed the slow plies with the other dancers. She had to admit that the thought of performing her own ballet was exhilarating.

The dress rehearsal progressed with the usual frustrations and triumphs, some costumes needed last minute adjustments, shoulder straps snapped, scenery wobbled, and one of the musical tapes broke. The opening piece had to be restaged due to the injured Renee, but thanks to a gifted understudy named Sonya, the piece came together quickly.

Courtney's ballet was to be the finale and was the last to be rehearsed. The dancers who were not performing in her piece were excused, but none of them left the theater. Instead they sat in the first two rows for a close look at Courtney's rehearsal.

The house lights dimmed and the curtain opened. Courtney was delighted with the supple strength she felt in her limbs. Her leg rose well over her head in a developpe' a la seconde. Her double pirouette was clean and effortless and she was surprised to feel the perfect balance of her arabesque on pointe as her leg rose high behind her.

The small troop of dancers sat spellbound as they watched their new choreographer perform. Even Renee found her moves completely captivating. They all agreed that the ballet and the dancer had become one. They leaped to their feet as the performers glided from the stage in the mist created by the fog machine.

Their enthusiastic applause meant more to Courtney than the standing ovation she had received as a performer with the Royal Ballet in London. The dancers practiced their final bows and then stood panting and sweating as Courtney and Lex made their remarks and gave final instructions for the performance the next evening.

"Hi Mom, hi Dad!" Courtney walked into the cool semidarkness of Willows relieved to be out of the late afternoon heat.

"How was dress rehearsal, Darlin'?" Clarisa smiled up at her beautiful daughter. She and Clyde were sitting in the library sipping Hattie's iced sun tea from tall glasses.

"Well, you know the old saying about a bad rehearsal means a good performance." Courtney sighed as she sank into a big leather chair near her parents.

"Uh oh, have a bad one, Luv?" Clyde looked over the top of his reading glasses, his brows furrowed with concern.

"Not exactly. We had the usual problems with the scenery and costumes and of course one of the tapes broke." Courtney rolled her eyes.

"Oh dear," Clarisa sympathized.

"Well, you haven't heard the big one yet. The girl who was supposed to dance the lead in my ballet came to dress rehearsal on crutches."

Clyde's eyebrows shot up in surprise. He and Clarisa had been very worried about Courtney. She had endured more emotional shocks in the last few months than at any other time in her life. They had hoped that things would go smoothly in her new job with the Ballet Company.

"Sooo...yours truly will be dancing the lead tomorrow night." Courtney grinned and her eyes sparkled with mischief.

"Oh Honey, that's wonderful! You know Hattie has never seen you dance and we haven't seen you perform in so long. Of course I am sorry for your dancer and the pressure you must be feeling, but...oh, I wish Mother could see you!" Clarisa was unable to restrain her feelings as she hurried to Courtney and bent to give her a kiss on the cheek.

"One of the guys taped the whole dress rehearsal so Grandmother can watch it when she's feeling better."

Storm Cat trotted into the library with his tail held high.

"You ol' cat trying to steal the show and get into my good graces so you can have some of that roast." Hattie hurried in behind Storm Cat and shook her finger at him. "Supper is going to be ready in just about an hour. Lord it's good to have lots of happy people...family people in this ol' house again." Hattie beamed.

"It's wonderful for us too!" Courtney responded quickly. She had seen the telltale glisten of unshed tears in her mother's eyes.

"Oh we are so grateful that everything has worked out so well." Clarisa cleared her throat and bravely pushed through the emotions that rose up in her chest. "Courtney has a pleasant surprise to tell you about."

"What you got to tell ol' Hattie about, Child? You bringing five more people to supper tonight?" Hattie narrowed her eyes playfully.

They all chuckled at Hattie's expression and then Courtney told her what had happened at the dress rehearsal earlier that day.

"Mercy! My prayer has been answered. I just been wishing I could see you dance! I just know you got a gift from God and anyone privileged enough to see you perform is one truly blessed being!"

A sharp bang came from the kitchen as though something had been knocked to the floor.

"What was that?" Clyde rose quickly from the old leather chair.

"Storm Cat, where is your furry body? You better not be sneakin' round my kitchen when my back is turned!" Hattie whirled around looking for the suspect. But Storm Cat sat serenely on the back of the chair where Courtney had been sitting.

"I think I heard the kitchen door. I think someone came in." Clarisa had lowered her voice. "Are you expecting anyone else, Hattie?"

"No ma'am," Hattie said with a frown. "Maybe your friends Latoia and Raeford has arrived early." Before any of the women could move toward the kitchen Clyde walked in front of them and strode out into the hall.

"What's this? I see two wandering waifs. Looking for a handout are you? I must say your timing is impeccable as usual!"

The women looked at each other as they heard Clyde's deep voice booming down the hall. They could hear other voices and then footsteps.

A suntanned face under sun streaked blond hair peered around the library door.

"Shane!" Clarisa and Courtney cried in unison.

As the happy babble of their reunion subsided, Clyde explained that he had been able to convince Shane and Michele to fly in for the July Fourth holiday. He had decided that his family needed to be together.

Latoia and Raeford arrived while Courtney hurried through her shower and by the time she came downstairs the table had been set and everyone was preparing to have supper.

Courtney was nearly overwhelmed with love for these people. She was happy and secure surrounded by her family and friends. She knew that everything in her life was going to work out just fine and in her heart she felt a sense of anticipation as though there was something good waiting for her. Maybe this was what the psychics had foreseen. It could very well be that the lost one that they had referred to was herself, her own sense of well being and her goals for the future. As far as finding lifelong love, she knew that she need not look beyond this room. At this moment in time she was complete. For the first time in many days she thought of Antonio and her heart skipped a beat. The anxiety had lessened so much that the moment passed as quickly as it had come. She wondered if the web of lies mentioned by the group had anything to do with Antonio. Her thoughts were interrupted by the telephone. Hattie had been invited to eat with the family and when the telephone rang she started to go answer it.

"No, you stay there, Hattie, I'll get it. Tell them the story about the time Storm Cat stole the chicken!" Courtney jumped up and went into the library to answer the telephone. She could hear Hattie's voice and the laughter of her audience.

Courtney was delighted to hear Madame Dubois' voice. She had flown in that day and was staying with some friends in town. She planned to attend the performance the next evening.

It was eleven o'clock before the old house was finally dark and quiet. Raeford and Latoia had left for their motel in town. The family had all gone to their rooms and Courtney stretched her tired body in the canopy bed. She hadn't felt so happy and so hopeful in a long time. She knew she could dance well in her new ballet and in the coming months she decided to see about finishing her master's degree. After the emotional roller coaster she had been riding in recent months, she knew that helping other people get through life's challenges was what she wanted to do. She felt strong in the knowledge that she could handle anything life might send her way.

The contented young woman closed her heavy lids and sighed peacefully. The aging house creaked as it settled around the sleeping inhabitants much like a mother hen protecting her brood for the night.

Storm Cat jumped lightly onto Courtney's bed. He walked up near her head and looked at her for a moment. Then he made three little circles and lay down near her shoulder. He closed his eyes and within a short time he joined the household in slumber.

####

Stephen looked around nervously at his charges. Few of them had been away from the institution more than a handful of times in their entire lives. So far so good, he congratulated himself, but of course the house lights had not even dimmed yet.

The young doctor had taken advantage of the confusion and unresolved issues that followed in the wake of Dr. Mann's death. He had cleverly pushed the board of directors into allowing a select group of patients to attend the ballet. Miraculously they had agreed to most of his ideas for the new community outreach program including the display of art and craft projects at the outdoor market on Market Street the following day.

The popular Spoleto Festival was another bargaining point that Stephen had used. The Spoleto Festival was already over and would have been a perfect opportunity to expose some of the patients to the many cultural events that were available during that time. Introducing certain patients to smaller events would be the perfect way to prepare them to attend Spoleto the following year. He argued further that the facility needed some positive publicity after the scandalous behavior of Jubal Pusser.

The lights dimmed. A hush fell over the audience and the curtain opened for the first work of the evening.

Courtney stood in the darkness of the wings watching the dancers. The hair on her arms felt as though it was standing straight up with static electricity and she was feeling edgy. Her rest had been interrupted repeatedly the night before by a hodgepodge of disturbing dreams. A bearded man peered at her through thick glasses. Aeonkisha's strangely immobile face stared unblinking at nothing almost as if it were a painting or a photograph. She saw her other self, limping, dragging her left foot. She hoped that it didn't mean that she would be injured and left permanently impaired. She breathed in deeply in an effort to shake off the disquieting thoughts that kept her from focusing on her performance. She knew she would feel better as soon as she began to warm up so she moved away from the wings and began a series of slow plies and tendus concentrating on the alignment of her body and the turn-out of her legs and feet. She breathed more easily as her body responded to the familiar movements and before long she felt much calmer.

"Hattie seems a little uncomfortable," Clyde whispered to Clarisa.

"She does a little, I think it could be excitement. I don't think she has been to very many social events outside of her church."

"Hattie, I can't help but notice that you keep lookin' in back of you. Do you see someone you know? Are you uncomfortable?"

"I just have the feeling something's back there or maybe someone is staring at me or something! The hair on my neck is standing straight up!" Hattie whispered hoarsely as she turned her head yet again to survey the crowd behind her.

"Well, Hattie, I expect there are a lot of someones

staring at you," Clarisa chuckled, "After all we are sitting in the front row. Oh there go the lights, it's going to start." She cautioned as the lights dimmed. She sat back in her seat with a sigh. Her heart was beating just a little too fast with the nerves she always felt before she watched her daughter perform.

####

Stephen had at last relaxed. Everything had gone smoothly and the last ballet of the evening was just beginning. He was mentally going over the glowing report he planned to submit to the board when he felt a tap on his shoulder. Avery, who was sitting directly behind him, loudly stated that he needed to go to the bathroom. Stephen tried to persuade him to wait for a few minutes until the Ballet was over. Avery would not be persuaded. Instead he began to hold his crotch and moan pathetically. After some shushing and scrambling he and Avery left the main auditorium in search of the men's room.

Theresa was sitting with the women. She had been looking forward to seeing the Ballet and in particular Courtney. She had been unable to go to Willows to meet her since she had come to Charleston. Her grandma Hattie had urged her to come to Willows on several occasions, but she had been working at The Oaks when she wasn't attending summer classes at the college. Her schedule was so busy that even though she had gone to see Mrs. Camden at the hospital it was usually at a time that none of the family was there. She had heard many stories about Courtney and her dancing ability and she was looking forward to the Ballet. Hattie had also mentioned Courtney's interest in psychology which was Theresa's favorite subject as well. She was hoping to meet her and share some ideas about it.

"Theresa! C.C.'s goin' down there to see the tutu by the sea sea!" Theresa lost no time in interpreting Terry Toon's communication. One glance told her what was happening. C.C. had made her way to the aisle and was headed for the stage! She jumped to her feet with a groan.

The ballet had begun. Courtney was on stage performing as the girl on the beach. Ocean waves crashed on the movie screen behind her and the music played in perfect harmony to the sound of the water.

Courtney's nerves were gone as the music started and she made her entrance. She felt wonderful as her slim supple body stretched and flowed from one pose to another and she became completely immersed in her role.

Theresa climbed and scrambled across several people, bumping knees and stepping on toes in her haste. She had to get to C.C. before the girl made it to the stage. She knew the kind of chaos that could be created if she became agitated and went into one of her episodes.

C.C. was making steady progress as she limped forward with her right arm straight out in front of her with her finger pointed. Her lips moved as if speaking, but she did not make a sound.

At nineteen, Theresa was average in height, sturdily built, and wise beyond her years. Her training had taught her that people who are suffering from autism do not respond favorably to human touch. She knew she would have to think of some way to get C.C. to turn around without physical contact. Theresa quickened her pace and darted around C.C.'s left shoulder and came to an abrupt stop in front of the determined girl.

Theresa's dark brown eyes twinkled and her full mouth stretched into a wide grin. She put one of her fingers to her lips in a shushing position as she whispered, "Terry Toon wants you to do Oil Can Harry!" Instantly C.C. forgot about the stage as she hunched her shoulders and followed Theresa to the back of the auditorium. They were mimicking the sneaky walk of one of Terry Toon's favorite cartoon characters.

Terry Toon saw them coming and delighted with the game jumped up from her seat to join in. The others, anxious to see what Terry was looking at followed suit.

Inwardly Theresa groaned, she could see all of them standing up near their seats at the back of the auditorium. She knew that there was only one way out. She was grateful that at the last minute she had decided not to bring her pocket book and instead had put her wallet and car keys in her pocket. She would not have to stop to retrieve her purse and risk losing the interest of the Oil Can Harry line as they hunched their shoulders and tip toed down the aisle. People were beginning to shush and ask that the group sit down. As she and C.C. neared the back rows Theresa beckoned to the standing group and continued to do the Oil Can Harry out of the door. The rest of the group followed doing exactly the same thing in single file.

Theresa prayed that everyone behind her would make it through the heavy doors and into the lobby without any difficulty or, God forbid, any noisy tantrums.

"Is the performance over?" Dr. Baylor was standing directly in front of Theresa and her Oil Can Harry line.

"Uh, in a manner of speaking, Dr. Baylor." Theresa opened her eyes very wide and raised her eyebrows.

"Milshays and fwench fwies now," the sweet natured Downs Syndrome boy lisped. He and C.C. had become inseparable friends. He turned and gestured to C.C. to take his hand. He hadn't forgotten Dr. Baylor's promise of a trip to a fast food burger stand.

To everyone's amazement, C.C. stepped closer to Avery and took his hand. Avery's smile was brilliant.

"Dr. Baylor, that might be a good idea," Theresa

agreed. "I'll explain it later."

CHAPTER TWENTY

Courtney's cheeks flushed pink under Madame Dubois' generous praise. They had all gathered in an elegant little restaurant a few blocks from the theater.

Clyde ordered the best champagne the restaurant had to offer and they drank a toast to Courtney's success.

Hattie exclaimed over and over to anyone who would listen how Courtney was a professional ballerina and was the star of the evening's performance and the waiters and nearby patrons smiled as they enjoyed her enthusiasm even though it had become decidedly repetitious.

Latoia, Courtney and Michelle made plans to go to Market Street the following day for some shopping and to see the street fair.

Clyde, Raeford and Shane were discussing the possibility of playing eighteen holes of golf early the next morning. Clarisa heard them and raised her eyebrow at Hattie.

"Sounds like maybe I better fry up a mess of my chicken for tomorrow. Goin' to be some tired hungry people coming home in the evening!" Hattie frowned though her eyes twinkled. There was nothing that she loved more than cooking for "her" family.

"Oh Hattie, that sounds wonderful, I'll be visiting Mother in the morning, but I'll be home right after lunch to help you," Clarisa smiled.

"Madame Dubois, won't you join us for some of Hattie's famous fried chicken tomorrow?"

"Merci Madame Hammond, but I must leave tomorrow afternoon. I am expecting a veree important call and I don't want to miss eet!" Madame's face dramatically changed to express her words. "But I so much appreciate your kind invitation."

The family and their friends devoured their delicious meal and chatted over coffee and dessert until the amiable maitre d' informed them, with profuse apologies, that his employees were in dire need of a good night's rest in preparation for the holiday crowd the next day.

Courtney smiled into the darkness as she finally closed her eyes that night. She felt so completely happy. She didn't want anything to change, except of course, her grandmother's health.

"Thank you for this day," she whispered. She didn't think about addressing any deity in particular, she just wanted to say the words. She felt that God had probably assigned helpers like Aeonkisha to assist in caring for his human children. Her *thank you* was meant for any of those beings who were responsible for bringing her such good fortune.

####

Stephen threw his head back and laughed until tears rolled down his cheeks as Theresa recounted the details of her great escape with C.C. and the others.

"Theresa, that was a stroke of genius. I don't know how you thought of Oil Can Harry, but I'm glad you did!" Theresa was giggling too.

"Did something upset C.C.?"

"I truly don't know Dr. Baylor." Theresa shook her head. "All I know is Terry Toon pointed at the aisle and there she was, headed straight for the stage. She didn't look upset, but Lord she was determined!" They both laughed again.

"Well Theresa, you are a real trooper. Are you sure you're up for another day with the troops?"

"Yes sir. They really aren't much trouble. They just haven't had that much experience with the outside world, that's all. And besides, we'll have some extra help tomorrow. I heard that Kevin was going and maybe Annie."

"Yes, they will be there too. I really don't expect any trouble either. I think you're right about their lack of experience."

"I agree. I think actually that C.C. just got excited when she saw the ocean on the movie screen. You know she's always painting seascapes even though I doubt that she has ever actually seen one in person!"

"Well, I'm sure that explains it. That's one thing we won't have to worry about tomorrow, we won't be near the ocean. Hmm, but maybe we should plan a trip to the beach before the end of the summer. You up for it, Theresa?"

"Give me a couple of weeks to recover from *these* field trips, then I'll be ready, Doctor," Theresa laughed.

Stephen walked with Theresa to her car and then turned to walk toward his cottage. He smiled with satisfaction as he looked up to the star sprinkled night sky. The outing had been a success and he looked forward to the following day.

#

The Fourth of July dawned with all of the ingredients of a typical midsummer day in the South. From the moment the sun peered over the eastern horizon its radiant blaze scorched Mother Earth, her creatures and her people.

The kitchen door creaked open as Raeford and Latoia drove up. Within a short time the men were off taking the noisy clatter of golf clubs and good natured boasting with them.

Latoia sank onto one of the high backed stools near the kitchen island with a wide yawn.

"Ain't it miraculous how they can get up so cheerful and full of energy when they don't have to be going to work?" Hattie put her fists on her hips and raised her eyebrow. "How bout some strong hot coffee?" She had already begun to pour it before Latoia answered.

"You are so right, Hattie. Raeford was knocking on my door before the sun was up!" She giggled, "I'd really love some of that fresh coffee."

Clarisa glided into the kitchen looking fresh and cool in her mauve cotton summer suit.

"Good morning!" She smiled brightly, "I'd just love some of that good coffee before I go see Mother. That hospital coffee is positively wretched," Clarisa wrinkled her nose in distaste. "Anyway the doctor doesn't want Mother to have coffee now and I feel uneasy drinking it in front of her."

"You best have some o' my cinnamon-raisin muffins and fruit too. You goin' to need your strength if you going to be with Miz Camden all day!" The old kitchen seemed to brighten as their effervescent laughter blended with the sunbeams, which had found their way through the windows.

Before long Michele emerged from her room and finally Courtney. At eight fifteen Clarisa left for the hospital and an hour later the girls climbed into Esther's big white Lincoln.

Hattie stood at the screen door waving and calling out instructions for them to have fun, but drive carefully and above all be home in time for supper.

Storm Cat licked every drop of cream from his bowl and sat cleaning his whiskers when Hattie turned away from the screen door.

"Well, you better clean yourself up good! This is a very special day and..." Hattie paused as a chill rippled through her body, "and you better be on your best behavior you ol' rapscallion!" Hattie shook her finger at Storm Cat who simply blinked in innocent disinterest and yawned.

Hattie went about her work in the kitchen. She didn't like that chill. When she felt that way, usually something very unexpected happened. She hoped it didn't mean that Esther was going to take a bad turn. That poor woman had already been through too much. Hattie sighed as her thoughts became heavy with worry. She pulled a kitchen stool closer to the sink and sat down. Some nice repetitive task would help to ease her mind.

She had a large mound of potatoes to peel, so she picked up the largest one and began to slowly, carefully cut off the brown skin. She thought hard about Esther and pictured the hospital room, the bed and the white sheets. Hattie had removed only half of the potato skin when the vision took shape on the delicate white surface of the peeled portion of the vegetable.

Esther's smiling face suddenly appeared. Her hair was freshly combed and she was sitting up in the hospital bed. Another face came through Esther's and Hattie found herself looking into the dark peaceful eyes of Aeonkisha.

"Set aside your fear," the echoing voice commanded gently, "The great plan unfolds. The secret is no more and the lost is found. Rejoice. Raise your voice in song. Praise the power of love which guides all good works, for the hand of the Master has touched your life."

Hattie blinked. The vision was gone. "Well, well, well Storm Cat. Looks like I was right. This gonna be a special day all right and here I sit staring at a potato. I guess I'll take a magic potato any day over some beanstalk that just grows to some ol' giant land, hee, hee!"

Storm Cat walked over to the screen door with his tail straight. The chuckling Hattie climbed down from her kitchen stool and let him outside. A large blue jay landed on a tree limb near the gravel drive. When Hattie saw him she burst into song and as she sang, she felt a great peace settle around her and the burden of her guilty secret was lifted. She knew that after today she would carry it no more.

By nine o'clock that morning Stephen, with the aid of several volunteers had the craft tables and paintings arranged in an attractive display. C.C. hovered near her watercolors and Terry Toon sat with her paper mache cartoon characters. Everyone was in a festive mood.

Sweat dripped from Kevin's face as he and Stephen finished setting up the last umbrella table and folding chairs.

"What a scorcher!" Stephen breathed as he wiped his suntanned face with a hand towel. He had taken Liz's advice and resumed his daily bicycle rides. The southern sunshine erased his former pallor and sun-streaked his light brown hair.

"Major understatement." Kevin rolled his eyes as he wiped his own face. "Well, old man, what do you predict for the day other than the heat?"

"I predict that if you are in the market for some excitement like we had last night, then you will be disappointed," Stephen replied good-naturedly.

"Well, in that case I think I'd better track down some lemonade for all of us so we can face this long boring day,"

Kevin grinned.

"Good idea. I could probably drink a gallon of it right now. But I think you're wrong about the boring part. Judging from the number of people around here I think it's going to be very busy."

Stephen was right. The horse drawn carriage tours had already begun their day loaded with camera-clicking adults and restless pink-cheeked children. Cars filled with excited tourists rolled slowly down Market Street as frustrated drivers looked for parking places in the center of all of the festivities.

The humidity and heat climbed ever higher but the girls were cool and comfortable in Mrs. Camden's air-conditioned Lincoln. Courtney acted as chauffeur and showed them some of the many points of interest around Charleston. The city was always stunningly beautiful, dressed in unique architecture and large old shade trees, but during any holiday there was always a special liveliness in even the oldest structures.

"It's eleven o'clock. Shall we go to Market Street now?" Courtney asked her passengers.

"Oh, I'd love to." Michele said enthusiastically.

"Sounds good to me," Latoia agreed, "Besides, I feel a junk food craving coming on!"

The girls laughed and chatted as Courtney carefully picked her way through traffic. She found an empty parking space under a large old oak tree. They were all happy to get out of the car and stretch their legs. Courtney led the way and the girls walked at a leisurely pace along the shaded sidewalks of the historic district. As the side street ended so did the peaceful atmosphere. In front of them Market Street was crowded with cars and red-faced tourists. Cooking smells filled the air as the restaurants and street venders prepared to feed the hungry hordes that would soon swarm en masse in their search for a place to enjoy the noon meal.

"C'mon, let's get something to eat in here." Courtney pointed to a quaint little restaurant on the corner. Most of the tables were already filled with the early lunch crowd but a line had not formed yet. Within a few minutes the girls were seated and hungrily studying the menu.

After lunch they felt refreshed and were eager to see all that old Charleston had to offer. They all agreed that a horse-drawn carriage tour would be a good start. They quickly found one that was about to begin and climbed into the carriage. For the next forty minutes an attractive young woman directed a lumbering horse through the crowded streets while she described the lineage of some of the old structures. Courtney's eyes felt heavy as she stared silently at the homes they passed. For long moments the cars disappeared and horse-drawn carriages took their place. Women in long flowered gowns strolled with their chaperones. Gaily colored parasols shaded their faces from the blistering sun. Uniformed soldiers occasionally appeared bowing sedately before blushing young women and kissing the hands of the matriarchs.

She saw servants carrying armloads of bundles and nannies walking with romping children. Courtney sighed audibly as she observed the gracious lifestyle of prewar Charleston.

"Are you okay, Courtney?" Michele's ice blue eyes squinted with concern.

"Oh yes. I'm fine. I was just imagining what these streets might have been like before exhaust fumes and blaring horns."

"Yes. I know what you mean. I was just thinking that maybe the city should ban all motor vehicles from the historic district and allow only horse-drawn carriages!"

Courtney smiled at the seriousness in Michele's voice. She resolved at that moment to spend more time with Michele now that she was an adult. She was not only beautiful but Courtney sensed a depth in her that she had not noticed before.

"Amen!" Latoia chimed in. "You know I just love this place, but somehow this traffic has gotta go!" The girls laughed as Latoia rolled her eyes comically.

The carriage rolled to a stop by the curb near their point of origin and the girls climbed from their perch to the hot sidewalk.

"I say we do some shopping over there!" Latoia pointed at the raised concrete walkway in the middle of Market Street where the venders displayed their merchandise.

The girls crossed the street and began to inspect the hundreds of handmade crafts that they found there. They sought out the shaded areas in an attempt to escape the increasing heat. Each bought a large glass of freshly squeezed lemonade and stood in the shade as they sipped.

"Oh, look at the beautiful handmade jewelry," Michele exclaimed as she headed off in that direction.

"I want to look at those baskets that lady is making," Latoia said with enthusiasm.

"Okay," Courtney answered, "I see an art display over there I want to look at."

The girls agreed to meet Courtney near the artwork in a short while. As she walked from the shade to the sunlight she was startled by a sharp stinging sensation on her chest. Her lemonade sloshed over the rim of the cup as she jerked her hand up thinking she might have been stung by a bee. There was no stinging insect, but she could feel a burning heat coming from the blue topaz which lay against her skin under her silk tank top. She lifted the gold chain and lowered the topaz to the outside of the soft fabric. The stinging sensation was gone and Courtney started forward dismissing the whole incident. She was curious about the art display that seemed to be attracting so many people. She had to squeeze through a cluster of onlookers in order to see the paintings that were mounted on folding display screens.

Courtney had enjoyed the few art classes that she had squeezed into her heavily loaded academic schedule. She didn't feel that she had any particular talent in that area, but she had enjoyed working with colors and she found it relaxing to create a picture or design.

At first glance she could see that the collection had probably all been painted by the same artist. Whoever it was he certainly liked the ocean. Then Courtney looked closer as something about one of the pictures caught her eye. A girl stood on the beach facing a pot-bellied older man and a plump sea gull stood on the sand nearby. A floppy hat hovered in the air a short distance from the man as if a gust of wind had lifted it from his head. Courtney gasped and she felt the hair on her arms stand up as she was reminded of Bernie and his brush with death that long ago day in April.

Another painting showed a slender girl rising on her toes with her arms outstretched as if she wanted to fly with the sea gulls who soared high above her, the wind whipped at her dress and her auburn hair billowed out behind her.

Courtney's heart beat accelerated slightly. What an odd coincidence she thought as she remembered all of the times that she had danced on the beach with only the sea gulls as her audience. Her eyes scanned the other pictures. Most of them featured the same girl in a variety of dance moves.

Courtney bent down to try to read the name of the artist, but all she found were the initials C.C. She had hoped to see a name which would at least reveal the gender of the artist. Then she noticed several other display screens filled with paintings and she moved through the crush of people to get a closer look. Her breath was coming in short gasps now as she gazed at the next series of watercolors, which were much darker. As she drew closer she could see that some of them were portraits, a large animal was featured in others. Finally after shouldering her way to the front of the tightly clustered group of onlookers she stood directly in front of the largest painting. She was shocked to see that it was the strong, but serene face she had seen so often in her visions and dreams. The artist had captured Aeonkisha's expression perfectly. Her dark flawless skin, high cheek bones, and long slender neck gave her the appearance of royalty, but her expression exuded only peace. Breathlessly Courtney glanced around at the other paintings. A lion roared into the terrified face of a man. The face was not distinct, but then it didn't matter. Courtney knew the man was Antonio! Beads of sweat glistened on her face and a ringing in her ears drowned out all of the street sounds. The blue topaz began to hum and then to vibrate...she couldn't seem to breathe! Her limbs shook and she knew she had to move...to walk...something, anything to break this spell or she would surely go mad. *What is happening?* Her mind screamed as she gasped for breath...the lion roared, stilling her thoughts for a split second and she heard Aeonkisha's deep soothing voice, "Turn around my child and meet your destiny."

    Courtney's rigid body turned haltingly. Her eyes were wide in wonderment, then disbelief, her mind refused to comprehend and interpret what she saw. Everything around her stopped, there were no thoughts, no distinctive sounds, no crowds of tourists, no family, no past, no future, only this airless vacuum and another pair of blue eyes identical to her own.

A voice finally spoke from beneath the blue eyes. "Beau-tee-ful," the girl said softly.

Memories hurtled through Courtney's mind...the visions of her *other self...the girl in the hospital gown...the night her mother had given her the blue topaz, the vision in the mirror, the voice that had spoken in her head that night was the same voice that she had just heard. It was her own voice...but no, it belonged to the girl that stood in front of her. But how could this girl be a different person? Was she looking into a mirror?* A thought fought its way to the forefront of her consciousness, *she knew. She understood the truth. She was looking into the eyes of her double, her twin, her identical twin sister. She didn't know how this could be true; she only knew that it was.* As each stared into the eyes of the other, images formed holographic shapes between them. The dream self in the institution was wearing the *jacket.* She watched her dream self being restrained in a hospital bed. She saw the limping dream self throwing the crayons. She watched again in horror as the helpless girl was attacked.

Courtney knew that the girl who stood in front of her had been molested by the man that she saw in the dream just as Courtney had been attacked by Antonio. She knew that in both cases Aeonkisha and the lion had been there to help, but even more astounding the two young women had helped each other.

Voices whispered in Courtney's ears. "The web of lies will be swept away." Another voice whispered, "The lost one is found," and still another said, "related by blood and by soul." The voices closed in and Courtney was falling. She covered her ears and screamed. The voices were silenced. Out of the silence came a soft entreaty, "I've been waiting for you to find me for such a long time. Please don't go away." The voice was only a quiet whisper in her mind and yet Courtney knew that it came from the girl in front of her. The girl's mouth had not moved. The words had been transmitted telepathically.

Street sounds began to push through the tangle of emotions that had gripped Courtney in those long moments of shocking realization. A suffocating heat bore down on her lungs as she became vaguely aware of the circle of faces above her. Something burned the skin of her bare arms and legs. She tried to tell the faces above her how hot she was, but her tongue was thick and her weak voice and poorly formed words were lost in the clamor of the worried people.

A cool wet cloth was placed over Courtney's face and another under her neck. It felt so good that she was able to ignore her burning skin. She knew she must be lying on the concrete, but she didn't quite know why or how this had come about and at that moment she didn't care. Her head was cool and a lovely gray darkness was shutting out everything. All she wanted to do was sink into that dark quiet place away from the heat and loud voices.

"Oh my God! Will you look at this?!" Kevin exclaimed. "Doc, you better get over here. Either I'm seeing double or something mighty strange is going on."

Stephen's heart leaped as he recognized the urgency in Kevin's voice. He frowned with concern and hurried to Kevin's side.

"C.C. was just sitting there eating her hot dog and all of a sudden she just dropped her plate and made a beeline over here. Now you just look at this and tell me what you see and for God's sake, please tell me I'm not losing my mind."

"Twins," Stephen muttered in a hoarse whisper. He knew it was true. He had known for sometime that C.C. had a twin sister, but he never imagined that the two could meet, at least not like this. Such a thing couldn't happen after all, the girl lived out west someplace. What was she doing in South Carolina on this day of all days? The enormity of this coincidence utterly baffled him.

He stared incredulously at the two girls. Remarkably they were dressed alike in aqua shorts and tank tops. Both wore sandals and their long auburn hair was pulled up in a ponytail.

"She's gonna faint!" Kevin leaped forward pushing tourists aside. Stephen was right behind him. Several display screens collapsed as Courtney's slim body swayed and sank to the concrete. Stephen couldn't begin to imagine what sort of repercussions this incident would initiate. He thought about Dr. Mann's locked files and the day he had gone through them. It had been the first time he had come face to face with the harsh fate of those patients with prominent families who had sequestered their mentally handicapped relatives in an institution to be conveniently forgotten forever.

Stephen and Kevin moved Courtney's limp body off of the hot concrete and lifted her to the webbed chaise lounge where tired volunteers had rested from time to time. Her pulse began to stabilize, but Stephen asked Kevin to call an ambulance in the event that the girl went into shock.

It was quite obvious that this girl came from wealth. He noticed the large blue stone that hung from the gold chain around her neck. Courtney groaned. "The ambulance will be here in just a few minutes. Can you hear me?" Stephen leaned closer to Courtney's face and her eyes fluttered open for an instant. She frowned and closed her eyes again.

The face that Courtney saw was familiar. Then she remembered where she had seen it before. There had been glimpses of this serious young man in other visions. This time, however, his skin was tanned and his hair sun streaked.

"Can you hear me? What is your name?" Stephen tried again to bring the girl to consciousness.

This vision was different, Courtney thought, as she began to drift back into the solitude of the darkness. The voices and the heat were annoying. She just wanted to be left alone to rest.

"C'mon over here C.C." Theresa didn't fully understand what had just happened. She knew someone had collapsed in the heat and that the girl looked very much like C.C. A crowd had formed around the fallen girl and she could see that Dr. Baylor and Kevin had their hands full. C.C. had begun to rock back and forth. Theresa recognized this as common behavior. It was C.C.'s whole demeanor that worried Theresa. Tears were rolling down the girl's cheeks, but her face remained expressionless. Her blue eyes had a glazed look and she was making small moaning noises as she rocked.

Theresa guided C.C. over to one of the webbed folding chairs and motioned for her to sit down. C.C. did not respond. She just continued moaning and rocking.

"C.C. honey, sit down in the chair and I'll get you some lemonade," Theresa coaxed.

Finally C.C. began to move, but her body responded more like a wooden puppet than living flesh.

Theresa's heart pounded nervously as she placed the cup of lemonade in C.C.'s hand. As she did so a brief but clear picture flashed in her mind. She saw two babies lying side by side in a crib. Next to them stood two little girls with long auburn curls dressed exactly alike and so it went until the girls appeared as adults.

"Two C.C.s?" Theresa mumbled frowning. She didn't have her Grandma Hattie's gift of clear vision, but occasionally under special circumstances Theresa experienced her own extraordinary psychic flashes. After a moment of contemplation her large brown eyes opened wide in amazed realization.

"C.C., I think I need a swig of that lemonade. Oh my God, wait until Grandma Hattie hears about this!" Theresa took a gulp of C.C.'s untouched lemonade and then sank into the chair near her. "No wonder you look like that C.C., that poor girl over there too. What a shock it must be to find your twin, especially like this. This has been one amazing summer," she mumbled shaking her head, "I always thought this kind of work would be interesting, but I had no idea it would be anything like this!"

"Anything like this!" C.C. echoed.

Michele and Latoia stood in the shade admiring each other's purchases when they heard the shrill warning of the approaching rescue vehicle. It pulled up to the curb and two uniformed people jumped out of the cab and pushed their way through the onlookers.

"Didn't Courtney go down that way to look at the art work?" Michele asked.

"She sure did. Let's go find her. Maybe she'll know what happened over there. What do you bet that someone collapsed in this insufferable heat?" Michele nodded in agreement as the two young women hurried toward the crowd.

Latoia and Michele split up as they searched through the crowd for Courtney. Michele caught sight of her sitting in a chair near a young black girl.

"Courtney, I'm so glad I found you. Latoia and I were starting to wonder what happened to you." Michele smiled, but the rocking girl didn't respond. "Courtney? Courtney. What is the matter with you? Are you all right?" Michele bent down to get a better look.

"Excuse me, but this is not Courtney," Theresa said softly.

"What?" Michele responded.

"This is C.C.," Theresa started to explain, but she was interrupted before she could continue.

"Michele! She's over here! Come here quick!" Latoia motioned excitedly for Michele to join her. The beautiful blond straightened and turned around at the sound of Latoia's voice.

"Uh oh," Michele muttered as she opened her eyes wider. "Latoia, you had better come over here first."

Latoia hurried over exclaiming about how she had found Courtney and that she had fainted in the heat, but she stopped midsentence as Michele stepped aside. Latoia's jaw dropped as she looked at the identical image of Courtney who merely sat rocking and moaning as tears continued to trickle from her eyes.

"Well ladies," Theresa took a deep breath as she stood up, "It looks like we have us one incredible situation on our hands. I need to stay here with C.C. Why don't you two see to your friend. Dr. Baylor and Kevin are taking care of her, but I'm sure she would like to have you both with her when she wakes up. When things calm down a bit maybe we can find out what has happened!"

Michele and Latoia looked at each other, then without a word they turned and hurried off to be with Courtney.

An hour later a pale silent Courtney sat at a small round table sipping sweet tea. Her equally silent friends regarded her anxiously.

"I really am all right." Courtney tried to sound strong, but her voice cracked ever so slightly and her lower lip trembled in spite of all of her efforts to present a strong appearance.

"Girl, you should have let them take you to the hospital. They could have given you something to calm you down. I mean, after a shock like this..."

"No. No, really, I don't want to be groggy, I want to try to understand everything," Courtney said firmly.

"Yeah. I can understand," Latoia patted Courtney's hand, "You know, I had a twin once too," she said softly. "I got to grow up with him, but then I lost him. You didn't get to grow up with yours, but you will get to know her now."

Courtney nodded wordlessly. Her mind was racing. She tried to remember every word that Dr. Baylor had said, but she could remember very little. In fact, she thought, he actually didn't say a great deal. He had answered her questions and had "unofficially" confirmed that C.C. was probably her twin. He had assured her that he would search through the records for further details, but there was the patient confidentiality that may prohibit the amount of information he could disclose. Suddenly Courtney was angry. "If you ask me there's been too much confidentiality," she said abruptly breaking the silence. Michele and Latoia looked at each other puzzled. "Come on girls, let's go back to the Willows. I need to find some answers for myself."

Hattie stood facing the door as Courtney banged it open. It was almost as if she had known the precise moment that Courtney would walk in.

"Hattie!"

"Yes, baby."

"Tell me what you know about...my sister." Courtney's voice dropped as she referred to her twin.

The three girls sat on the kitchen stools as Hattie told the story of the birth of the twins. In a calm low voice Hattie explained that when she walked into the kitchen that day she found young Tessa on the floor. She had given birth prematurely to twin girls. She had done her best to cover the babies with kitchen towels and then she had tried to pull herself to the telephone, but she had been unable to make it.

Hattie's voice quavered as she described the two babies. One was healthy and red faced as she cried loudly breaking through the "veil" that covered her face. The other one was silent and still with a bluish tinge to her skin. "Nobody thought that baby would live. I never knew for sure that she did until just a short time ago."

"But Hattie, why didn't someone tell me about her? Did mother know?"

"No child, your mama didn't know there was two babies. Only Miz Camden, me and my George knew anything about it."

"But why should it have been kept a secret? It just doesn't make any sense?" Courtney frowned and rubbed her head.

"Well, baby," Hattie paused as she tried to gather her courage, "You see, I had to make a promise to your grandmother. Miz Camden has some very definite ideas about honor and family pride and family name."

"You can't mean that Grandmother thought that the Camden name would be tarnished because the hired girl gave birth to her babies on the kitchen floor of their hallowed plantation house!" Courtney's voice rose in anger and her chest heaved as she spat out her words.

"Now let me finish honey," Hattie's voice was quiet, "When you hear it all you are going to understand." The ceiling fan hummed and the breeze from its blades lifted wisps of hair around her face.

"You see, young Mr. Charles took a fancy to Tessa. Of course he could be a sweet talker if he wanted to. Tessa was young and sweet, not to mention beautiful. One night, according to Tessa, Charles talked her into drinking with him. He got real drunk and wouldn't take no for an answer. She was pregnant after that.

"Tessa started out bein' in love with that boy. He was handsome and rich and older than her. At first she wanted him to marry her. That was when he showed her his mean side.

"You got to understand now, Tessa was alone in the world She had no family, no nothing, so she told Charles if he wouldn't marry her he better give her some money to help pay for the baby. Well course Charles wasn't of a mind to spend no money on no baby. Not when he could spend it on his liquor and what all. So Tessa threatened to tell Miz Camden about her fair-haired boy." Hattie paused and walked to the sink to pour a glass of water for herself.

Courtney watched in silence as Hattie walked back to her kitchen stool and sat down.

"Listen Courtney, Michele and I can leave the room if you would rather be alone." Latoia gently touched Courtney's arm.

"No, please stay," Courtney replied earnestly.

"Are you trying to tell me, Hattie, that Charles Camden is my father? I have Camden blood in my veins?" Courtney was incredulous. Echoing voices rose in her mind. *"Related by blood and by soul,"* they chanted, *"By blood and by soul."*

"Yes, child. I believe Tessa told me the truth. I don't know exactly what happened. Your grandmother never discussed it with me. But, anyhow, she found out that the babies...you and your sister had the Camden bloodline. Well Lord have mercy, she couldn't let the world know that her son had fathered illegitimate children. She didn't want them to leave the family either! Miss Clarisa was the perfect answer. She and her husband didn't seem like they could have any children of their own so Miz Camden got the lawyers to fix it up."

"But that still doesn't explain why my...sister wasn't

adopted or...or why no one was told about her." Courtney was much calmer now.

"Yes baby, I know. That is the hardest part for me too. Your sister was smaller than you and she had the cord wrapped around her neck. Even after they got you all to the hospital and got her breathing they didn't think she would live. I overheard Miz Camden on the phone the next day. The doctor told her the baby, your sister, probably wouldn't live and if she did she wouldn't never be in her right mind."

"Whooee, what a story," Latoia breathed, "When the dust settles you could write a book!" Courtney smiled weakly, but made no comment.

"I never knew for sure if the baby lived. I saw her in my visions as the years passed but I never knew if I was seeing her in a physical body or on the other side," Hattie continued." Miz Camden is a good woman. I've come to care for her like my own family, but just like family you got to realize they have faults. If you don't accept that fact then you got a whole lot of problems on your hands. I have found out that people are afraid of things they don't understand. Your grandmother is no exception. She just thought that if the child lived and she had a problem, in her mind she thought it would be disgraceful."

"That's ridiculous!" Courtney retorted.

"Today, in 1986, that's right sugar. People are finding new ways to think now, but when you are raised up with certain beliefs and fears and prejudice they pretty much going to stay that way for most of your life.

"Each generation is born with the instinct and drive to be different, to be better than the generation before. That's a good thing. The hard part is that overlapping time where new meets old and somethin's gotta give," Hattie sighed.

"People put so much time and energy into fighting for

their beliefs. That's not all bad either, don't get me wrong," Hattie raised her eyebrows and shook her finger in the air for emphasis, "But it just seems to me if people put that much time into thinking up ways to be kind to each other they might not have to fight so much." Hattie stood up and walked around to where Courtney sat.

"Honey, I'm sorry that this has had to be such a shock for you. Miz Camden was nearly out of her mind when all this happened and later the same day her son...Charles, your father, died in a terrible car accident. There was somethin' strange about that too I'm here to tell you. It was that same day ten years earlier that her husband, your grandfather, died of cancer. Lord have mercy I thought at times that poor woman would lose her sanity for sure! She made me promise to keep the secret. I tried to warn her that it was a bad mistake to create a deception like that. I told her that lies beget lies until a powerful web is formed and once that happens, lots of people run the risk of getting trapped in it including the one who began it.

"Well, your grandmother is a wee bit stubborn doncha know," Hattie smiled gently and Courtney nodded in agreement, "She was moaning and takin' on so...well, I guess I just finally gave in and made that terrible promise. I regretted it every day of my life for the past twenty-five years." A tear glistened on Hattie's cheek as she finished speaking.

Courtney sat watching her in silence. After a long moment, she rose slowly and walked over to Hattie and enfolded her in a warm hug. When they pulled away both of their faces were wet with tears. Michele fumbled through her bag for tissues and dabbed at her eyes. She passed the package to Latoia who snatched a tissue and blew her nose loudly.

"Lord, ain't we a mess a crybabies?" Hattie joked as she fished in the pocket of her apron for a hanky.

The sound of a car door slamming outside startled all of them. A few moments later Clarisa opened the kitchen door.

"Good afternoon ladies, I didn't really expect to see you all...quite so...early." Clarisa's voice trailed off as she saw the four tear-streaked faces before her. Then her own face paled as she realized something must have happened.

"It's all right Mom. I mean, no one has been hurt or anything like that," Courtney reassured her mother.

"Thank the good Lord for that! But, what in heaven's name is wrong? When I left you all in the kitchen this morning everyone was happy. Now I come in and everyone is in tears!"

"It has been a most amazing day, Mom. Something has happened and I want to tell you about it, but I want Dad to be here too."

More car doors slamming and male laughter alerted them that they wouldn't have long to wait. The men were soon loudly trooping through the kitchen door. Courtney drew in a deep breath as she gathered her strength and courage to tell her beloved family about the strange new twist in their life's path.

Hours later Courtney wearily climbed the stairs to her bedroom, her feet keeping time to the midnight chime of the grandfather clock. How can one day feel like a lifetime and then sometimes days fly by like minutes, but still the clock chimes in the same relentlessly ponderous rhythm? My life has changed more than once almost in the blink of an eye she thought, and yet time goes neither fast nor slow. It just patiently, relentlessly keeps the same pace while life dashes madly along creating illusions that keep us guessing.

After a short but relaxing bath, Courtney felt better and stretched out on the bed. She turned toward the window to watch the stars sparkling against the darkness of the sky. Her eyes drooped and her breathing deepened.

A slight movement on the bed told her that Storm Cat was there to watch over her as she slept. He walked up near her face and touched her cheek with his nose.

"I'm glad you are here," she whispered sleepily to him. Satisfied that all was well he curled up next her, purring loudly.

So much had happened in her life since April Courtney marveled with an ironic chuckle. Until today she had very smugly believed that nothing could happen that would make her stop thinking that the encounter with Antonio was the most dramatic moment in her life. That memory was now moving to the back of her mind. Suddenly she realized that if it had not been for that trauma she would never have come to Charleston. Perhaps she would then never have discovered her...sister.

"This is a most mysterious life I have chosen, Storm Cat," she whispered as she stroked his fur. "Just imagine, for twenty-five years I believed myself to be a solitary being and suddenly I find out that I am a twin...that there is someone just like me, my blood...my sister."

Her thoughts wandered into the limitless possibilities of the future. She didn't care what might be wrong with her sister she knew they could communicate. She pictured long walks with her on the vast lawns of Willows; maybe they would share secrets and dreams...with a jolt she realized that she didn't know her sister's name! Dr. Baylor had called her C.C. What could that stand for?

Courtney looked at the clock. It was of course too late to call, what was she thinking? She lay back on the pillows with a sigh.

Her heart sped up with excitement at the prospect and it took some effort to calm down again and realize it would just have to wait until morning. Finally fatigue could not be fought back and her eyes closed as she succumbed to her need for sleep.

"Good night, C.C.," she whispered into the darkness. "I wish I knew your real name."

A soft fuzzy light formed behind her eyelids and a voice whispered, "My name is Caitlin."

Courtney recognized the now familiar voice, "That's a wonderful name," she whispered in response as she sank instantly into a deep sleep.

The old house creaked and sighed in contentment as it stood ever vigilant, ever protective of its own. The wind whispered a song of celebration through the Willows, "The lost one is found," it whispered as a tall cloaked figure lifted long slim arms to the sky, "and the web of lies is gone. This family has been reunited and this karmic debt has been paid. I give my blessing and I share your joy! Live in the light of truth from this day forward."

A deep low growl rumbled across the lawns and gardens as the lion turned to follow his mistress. The dry whisper of leaves shivered in the darkness as a feathered cloak was flung back with the passing of a powerful presence. The darkness deepened and the night was quiet.

The End

About the Author

Jimelle Suzanne

Award winning ballet teacher and choreographer, Jimelle Suzanne began dancing at the age of seven and performed in her first ballet company at the age of twelve. At fourteen, she went on to join the Sacramento Ballet Company under the artistic direction of Dean and Barbara Crockett.

While in grammar school, she enjoyed story-telling and writing plays. She was the editor for the Roseville Union High School newspaper and wrote inspirational essays as librarian for Job's Daughters, a Masonic based organization for young women.

As a young adult, she performed for the Los Angeles Regional Opera Ballet Company. Jimelle formed her own dance studio in Roseville, California and later she created the Golden West Theater Ballet Company. There, she was responsible for the artistic content including music selection, costume design, choreography and production.

After becoming a homemaker and mother, she developed her own psychic abilities. Her psychic knowledge was increased through the study of Edgar Casey's work and books authored by Rudolph Steiner. During yoga meditations, Jimelle began having visions which led to the enhancement of her abilities.

In 1985, while living on Hilton Head Island, South Carolina, she facilitated group meditations and mediumship classes. In 1994, she created and published a meditation